Only In My Wildest Dreams

Only In My Wildest Dreams

One Connection Can Change Destiny

H. R. Brock

authorHOUSE®

AuthorHouse™
1663 Liberty Drive
Bloomington, IN 47403
www.authorhouse.com
Phone: 1-800-839-8640

Published by AuthorHouse 12/04/2014

ISBN: 978-1-4969-5764-1 (sc)
ISBN: 978-1-4969-5765-8 (e)

Library of Congress Control Number: 2014921622

In loving memory of Mamie, who inspired me to write.

CHAPTER 1

True Colors

I woke up in a daze and for a second forgot what day it was. Honestly, I didn't feel any different when I finally came to my senses, but I knew how special the day was. It was May 17, my sixteenth birthday. I was ready to be sixteen, but not because I was going to get my driver's license or because I was old enough to model my own mother's high-fashion designs if she would allow me to—she would probably object as she did with my sisters, because a couple of them were far more beautiful than I. Tonight, the Anticipation would be held to settle the long-awaited question—which one of my five sisters or me would be determined the heir of our family's several-billion-dollar fortune. Needless to say, it was no ordinary day; today was the first day of the rest of our lives.

My sisters and I were all so different that people would stop and wonder how we could possibly have come from the same two parents. Mary, at twenty-six, was the eldest. She was known as the gawky bookworm with an over-six-foot, 130-pound frame. She got accepted to Yale on scholarship, but Mother didn't really care. Mother thought that girls should be beauties and not brains. She called Mary a "disappointment" on a regular basis.

Tara, at twenty-three, was the second oldest. Tara was a cheer captain and straight-A student at Stanford. She managed to bag a bachelor's degree in cosmetology and a wealthy fiancé in the same year. I could already see wonderful images in my head of her in a beautiful white gown, shining with her large brown eyes and a dazzling smile that would make everyone else burn with envy.

Amelia had always been known as the funny one, and she made friends easily, even though she wasn't athletic or stuck-up like all her so-called friends in high school. Her features were simple—a straight nose and pale blue eyes, not to mention extremely thick, wavy hair as black as a raven's wing. She wasn't necessarily beautiful on the outside, but because of her beauty on the inside, everybody loved her. The only person I could think of who didn't was Mother, who still picked on her for what everybody else was trying to forget—her crazy high school days. Freshman year and on, Amelia's charm made her the life of the party. Our parents took extra steps to keep her in the house after she came home intoxicated for the first time, but she still somehow managed to sneak out in the middle of the night without any suspicion until the next morning when some disaster awaited us. Police cars, men with badges, and injuries from bar fights. Most of us tried to tell ourselves that it was nothing more than a bad dream.

Then there was Leah at twenty, who was gorgeous with silky blonde curls that bounced when she walked and eyes the same color as the sky in the summer. There was nothing else I could really say about her.

Angela was known as the quirky redheaded ball of energy. Nobody was quite sure where she got her hair color from, and it was so wild that no number of hair clips could tame it. Her small eyes were green with the slightest tint of yellow to them, and her cheekbones were the only thing that stuck outward. Not even her boobs stuck out, if you're nice enough to call them breasts; they were merely two darts.

And then there was me, plain-old Adrienne, also known as the girl that didn't possess anything that made her stick out for the better. I wasn't particularly gifted when it came to looks, with my big brown eyes and large, round lips that resembled Angelina Jolie's, which I often commented about as the only good quality about me. Yet people still went as far as to mistake me for beautiful. I was not beautiful, no matter how many boys stared at me in the hallway, because I wasn't like Leah, and I never cared to be.

❉ ❉ ❉

Everyone had been talking about the Anticipation for my whole life. Many people have asked my parents why they bothered rather than giving each kid an equal share of money like a normal rich family would do. The answer was simple; it was an old family tradition—kind of like how normal families celebrate Christmas on December 25, only so different. Christmas was a harmless tradition that usually brought good tidings and joy, but the Anticipation only brought loathing and heartache over what could've been.

Here's the story of how the Anticipation came to be. My great-grandmother married my great-grandfather Arnold Chase, whose family had a powerful and successful automobile business. A few years later, she gave birth to my grandpa and great-aunt, who were fraternal twins. Having two heirs was unheard of back then, and everyone was in a slump about what to do, so some genius came up with the Anticipation. Only one child would win, and only his or her children would be able to participate in the next event. My grandfather was crowned heir painlessly. He married Grandma Marie, the woman my great-grandparents set him up with in an arranged marriage. Grandma Marie was the one who founded our fashion company in 1984.

After my grandfather died from a stroke when Mother was twelve and they had to sell the automobile business, the fashion company was the only thing that brought food to the table. She shed many droplets of blood and sweat to build it up from the ground into a huge success. She then declared Mother the heir of the second cycle. She married my father, the man my grandparents matched up with her as a child.

My aunt Margaret, the loser of the contest, was an extra that nobody wanted in their lives. Nobody cares for the extras, even if they end up on the street someday, because they aren't important for my family's legacy to live on. Even though I wasn't supposed to, I learned about that dirty little family secret a long time ago; let's just say that Mary was really persistent about how Mother met Dad.

She always lied, but we didn't think anything about it because Mother was naturally charismatic and could make people like her. She could just as easily turn someone off, but that would be bad for her business, so one of her greatest precepts was to keep friends close and enemies closer.

One day when I was in first grade, I overheard her slip up and admit to Mary how they really met. I'm sure that everybody else had forgotten all about that day, but I would never belong in the category of everyone else. I had just gotten home from school and had gone to put my backpack on the plush red sofa in the living room. I stopped when I saw my mother and Mary in the living room, their faces a bright crimson. I stepped to the side so that I couldn't be seen and poked my head into the room to see what was happening. Up to that point, I couldn't picture Mother angry, because she was one of those people who acted as if they had a perfect life. It was so easy to forget that she was a human being with emotions that just happened to have a pretty face.

"You mean you were matched up, like online dating except that you couldn't choose whether you end up with him or not? I've never heard something so wrong in my life!" Mary said tensely.

"Mary, don't use that tone of voice with your betters! You know there are things in life that you're not going to be happy with, and this is one of them." Mother scolded firmly.

"But the question is, are you happy with it?" Even though Mary was awkward, she had a gift for speaking. "You must be miserable waking up next to a man you don't love every day for the rest of your life. I don't want to be the heir, considering how awful you turned out to be."

Mother's face grew as red as a fire truck. "Mary, why would you ask a question like that? You know I love your father very much! I can't believe a girl with a grade point average of 4.5 can be so stupid! You'd better hope you are the heir, because no man would want to spend the rest of his life with such a hideous girl as you!"

Mary's eyes started welling up with tears. "You are the cruelest, most egotistical woman that ever walked this planet!"

Mother's comeback wasn't words but a hard slap that darted right across Mary's red, sobbing face at the speed of lightning, which made a sound similar to roaring thunder. "You are the most pathetic, awkward creature I've ever seen. I am your mother, and you will do as you're told! Go up to the attic. I'm taking away your room and giving it to the maid. Go and take all your stupid little belongings up to the attic; that's where rats like you belong."

"No!" Mary screamed, stomping her foot down. She was slapped hard over and over until a steady stream of thick, dark blood gushed out of her nose. She fell back onto the carpet, and Mother's eyes emitted a look that I'd never seen before, the look of pure hatred. She threw herself on top of Mary and went on with the abuse. Mary didn't even fight back. Was she physically too weak, or was she afraid that she'd feel the wrath of Mother even more if she dared to move a muscle against her?

"Fine, then. If you don't go to the attic, I guess I'll just make you the maid. I'll give all of your pathetic science trophies and nasty blue ribbons to her too. I bet it'll make her day," Mother threatened as Mary took several blows to her abdomen and face until she was black and blue.

Mary pleaded for Mother to stop over and over again for what seemed like an eternity. When Mary agreed to the punishment, she was finally released from Mother's grasp and ran up to her room, slamming her door loud enough that I wouldn't have been shocked if somebody had called the cops on us. I wanted to escape from the madhouse that I called my home and run outside. I wanted to tell the world how two-faced and maniacal my mother really was. Yet I knew I couldn't, because even though I wasn't a whiz kid, I still had enough brains to figure out that I was on Mother's good side. I didn't want to spoil it and end up in the attic with a bloody nose like Mary.

That's when Mother spotted me, but instead of getting cross, she smiled widely and asked, "Hello, sweetie. How was school today?"

"Okay," I answered quietly. At an early age, I figured out to keep my trap shut, even before I knew how she truly was.

"I heard from Mrs. Huntley that you did well on your spelling test; you only missed one word."

"Yes, I did; I missed *difficulty*." I stepped back a little. Was she going to snap at me because I wasn't perfect? "Are you mad?"

She laughed, but it was a nice chuckle that wasn't anything close to a mocking manner. "Of course I'm not! I was an awful speller; I couldn't spell *difficulty* if my life depended on it when I was your age. Why are you so afraid of your own mother?"

I bit back tears. I couldn't cry, at least not right then. Tears weren't allowed in the Hudson household. "I ... saw something I wasn't supposed to see, and it was terrible," I confessed at a volume that could compete with a feather falling gracefully down to the floor.

"Sit down on the couch, and tell me what's up," she said, patting her hand on her lap as a gesture to come over to her.

I took it step by step, like I was walking across a rickety old bridge uniting two cliffs suspended a thousand feet in the air. I gingerly sat down next to my mother on the couch. She put her arm around my shoulders and stroked my hair with her other one. It occurred to me that my hair was being stroked by a witch with sleek blonde hair with long bangs that made a horizontal line across her forehead, bringing out her dark chocolate eyes the same color as mine. There were a couple of features from her that I was lucky enough to inherit, like her perky freckled nose and plump lips.

In another life, she would be a beautiful woman, but in this life, she would never even be considered pretty.

"Tell me what's the matter, Adrienne. I deserve to know," she pressed, her eyes shining with concern and even a bit of remorse.

I took a deep breath and told her everything I had seen. I started crying as I was speaking, asking her why she did something so terrible to her own daughter. She held me close the whole time I'd blabbered on and on. I got to a point where I stop rambling on and did nothing but sob.

"Adrienne, I never meant for you to hear that. Today, I had to teach Mary a lesson; she thinks she's above and better than me. But I will always be above and better than her, and I had to tell her that by punishing her. Take this as a lesson for the future when you have a daughter of your own." She kissed me on the cheek and stroked my hair some more, like her affection would erase all of the new data that would be forever stored in my memory.

Little girls should feel safe in their mothers' arms. I didn't, and I never would feel safe in her arms again, because I remembered my grandmother's golden rule: "When people show you their true colors, believe them."

And I believed.

Mary was told at her wedding reception in Mother's toast that she wouldn't be the heir, but it wasn't only because Mary wasn't gifted in looks. Whenever a possible heir marries someone that he or she was not set up with, that person is automatically eliminated. Mary married a man named Frank Watson, who was as tall and gangly as a lamppost. Everybody in the family, even Mother, had to admit that it was a match made in heaven, because apart, Frank and Mary looked like two ugly ducklings, but together, they complemented each other nicely.

Mary was now pregnant with a bouncing baby boy on the way, and since her belly was really starting to show and she already knew she wouldn't be the heir, she wouldn't be participating in the event.

"One out of five," I said to her over the phone one night.

"Not exactly. Somebody's got a much more likely chance of winning than everybody else," she said.

"Who is it? Tara or Leah, probably, right?"

"You see, it's not like your name has to be drawn out of a hat to win the competition. Somebody was born to be the heir. The meaning of the competition is to make everybody else feel bad." She yawned. "I have to get the baby to bed; his kicking has been wearing me out. I swear, this kid's going to be a soccer star or a tap dancer. Love you. Bye," she said as she hung up.

* * *

I took a long, hot shower, dried my hair, and then came back into my room. Angela wasn't in her bed, so I guessed that she was already downstairs for breakfast. I got dressed in my lace eyelet top and some jeans. I walked down the stairs into the dining room, where I saw Mother and every sister except Mary sitting at the table. My four present sisters murmured when I walked into the room, like they usually did.

Mother's body language wasn't nervous—not the least bit excited, even. She acted like she just wanted to get this thing over with. I could tell that my sisters wished that they could pick up a TV remote and fast-forward to the next day, when the rightful heir had been crowned and the losers escaped humiliation of any form. I was greeted by Dad sitting at the table reading a newspaper. Dad never ate breakfast with us; he was always working and was rarely seen around the house. But of course, tonight was the Anticipation. He wouldn't miss the Anticipation for the world.

I was surprised that Grandma Marie and Aunt Margaret weren't there; it seemed absurd that the only two direct family members we had weren't coming to see the biggest and rarest-occurring festivity.

I sat down in an empty seat next to Mother and asked her where they were.

"Grandma's flight got cancelled because of fog," Mother responded.

The sharpness in her voice said it all. This was not a subject to press upon her. But I could understand why Mother was in disbelief. Grandma was the biggest celebrator of the Anticipation. Every time she'd visited since I could remember, the first thing she'd say when she walked through the door was how many days remained until the Anticipation.

"What about Aunt Margaret?" I tried for a second time.

I knew that in the widespread vocabulary of the Chase family—*two-faced, charismatic,* and *superficial* being a few examples—*Aunt Margaret* was considered a dirty phrase that should be bleeped out at all times, like cuss words on TV.

She hadn't been in a single conversation for years. She hadn't been over to visit since I was about six when she'd gotten fed up with dealing with Mother's cruelness. Mother cut Aunt Margaret's face out of all our pictures and family portraits after their big blowout—including a photo of her family when Mother was twelve and Margaret was ten, often called the most valued family portrait because it was taken two months before my grandfather's major stroke that ended his life, making that the last known photograph taken of him. Yet I don't focus on my long-gone grandfather like everyone else does when they look at the photo. I focus on body language between my mother and aunt; the way they gripped on each other's hands said it all. They were two sisters that had once been united, but their bond was torn apart like a piece of paper by the Anticipation. And that draws my mind to conclusions that nobody else would dare to think—that she used to be a face in the family photograph, a valued member of the family. Now she was a sad, pathetic little figure without a face. Would I have the same fate as Aunt Margaret when I lost?

To my surprise, Mother let my foul language slip past. "I don't know. I guess she's still a sore loser from the last cycle."

To overcome my recent slipup, I decided to focus on the food. There was a basket of blueberry muffins that could feed a family for a week. There was a crystal bowl filled with five different kinds of fruit: a big red apple, plump violet grapes, fresh oranges, slices of pineapple, and a sour grapefruit.

I put a large blueberry muffin and a cluster of grapes on my plate and alternated between the two, tasting the sweetness of the muffin and tartness of the grapes. Angela, Leah, and Amelia were murmuring softly in the way that they always did when the topic of the Anticipation was brought up, probably saying something about how unfair it was.

Mother looked at Dad. "Anything special in the paper, John?"

He shrugged as he took a sip of his coffee. "The stock market hasn't been in this bad of a state since the Great Depression."

He lowered the paper, and I was reminded that I was my father's daughter. We had the same caramel-colored, wavy hair, heart-shaped face, and skin tone the same light brown as a Starbucks' latte. The little bits of his personality made me who I am. That is a big reason of why I was sure that I wouldn't win the Anticipation. The heir would be the child with the features of Mother; she was the heir of the previous Anticipation, after all.

Everyone was hushed into a wave of silence as soon as the kitchen phone rang. Nobody ever called the home phone. I didn't even know what the ring sounded like.

"Hello?" Mother asked with her eyebrow raised. "Wait, what? No ... Of course, I care about the baby, but it's only the second trimester ... Oh? You're a ways into the third trimester? ... Well, there are so many other things that I need to take note of that I get facts all jumbled up in my head ... I don't care; you aren't in labor right now ... *Shut up.* You are coming, and that's final ... Mary! Are you there?" She slammed the phone down, making a big bang. I heard her mumble, "I really hate that girl sometimes."

Mary came at about ten. She looked kind of like a snake with a big lump in the middle because it had just swallowed a mouse. She was wearing a purple sleeveless maternity dress that looked like a cover-up over a swimsuit at the beach.

"You could've worn something more formal," Mother criticized in disgust.

"Mother, what's the big deal? I'm not stepping foot on the runway."

Oh crap, don't remind me, I thought. I could barely walk in a straight line as it was.

Frank trailed behind Mary like an overgrown puppy. Since Frank wasn't good enough for Mother, she didn't bother to give him a passing glance.

"That kid's going to be so ugly," Mother whispered loudly to Dad.

I'd figured out a long time ago that Mother wouldn't like her grandchildren unless they met her expectations.

Mary looked at Mother as if she'd murdered somebody. "This is why I didn't want to come. I don't want to see my flesh and blood being discriminated against! Nobody cares that you're beautiful if you treat your own kin like garbage!"

My sisters all gasped in unison. Of course, each one of them agreed, but no one would ever have had the guts to tell her that.

To everyone's surprise, she clapped and smiled deviously. "Oh, Mary, what a gift you have for speaking. If you were prettier, I'm sure you would make an excellent politician."

With Mary standing there speechless, it was needless to say that Mother won once again.

CHAPTER 2

The Event

Mary left after the argument, because there was no time for her to bicker with Mother. Everyone had to hustle and get into their rightful positions for the contest to begin. We were ordered up to our rooms, and there they would get to take a first look at our dresses for the Anticipation. My sisters and I were nervous, because we weren't the ones who'd picked out the dresses; Mother did, because it was yet another way to show how much she controlled us. Mary told me that she would give the girls who were going to lose ugly dresses as a foreshadowing of their misfortune.

On my bed was a red, strapless, tight gown that looked like something an Oscar-winning actress would wear on the red carpet. I glanced at my dress, trying to decide if this was a foreshadowing or not. Even though I wasn't supposed to, I got dressed and realized that it was much tighter than I thought it would be. Because of my slight muffin top over my size 3 jeans, I decided that Mother was trying to show that the odds weren't in my favor. I swiftly took the dress off so that I wouldn't get caught disobeying traditions. I was escorted into a limo, and before I knew it, it pulled into the parking lot of the stadium.

My dressing room looked like a pink flamingo threw up all over it, to say the least; bright pink walls hurt my eyes when I looked directly at them, and there was a pale, springy pink vanity and countless cheap, generic knickknacks only useful for collecting dust. There were two stylists who would try their best to make me shine—a girl with curly red hair with a lip ring, who reminded me somewhat of Angela, and a dark-skinned man built like an ox.

The stylists pampered me half to death. They tweezed my eyebrows until it stung to raise them, waxed every single last hair on my legs, and bleached my teeth up to the point where they shone like the sun. I was glad when all of that was over, so I sat down and shut up as they did my hair and makeup. They turned the swivel chair away from the mirror so that I couldn't see what they were doing to me, but it felt like they were maiming me with all the pulling and tugging of my hair. Finally, they said that they were done, and they turned my chair around.

I barely recognized the girl in the mirror.

My long, fake-looking eyelashes had blown my eyes upscale. My eyes were already large, so it made me look more like cartoon character than a human being. I saw a familiar nose, but it was without the faint freckles, which had been concealed. My bright-red lips were brilliant, though, and my dress didn't accentuate my muffin top; it made me look like a celebrity.

I was still staring at myself in awe and wonder at this girl in the glass when there was a knock on the door. I jumped but then went to answer the door. At the door waited the only person I could be myself with—Richard Taylor, my best friend.

Sure, I had other people in my life that could possibly compete to be my best friend, but at the end of the day, he was the one who was there for me—not Tori or Veronica or Pamela or Katy or Lauren, the five girls with noses stuck up high in the air that some kids mistakenly accused of being my best friends. Supposedly they were, but they could never compete with the companionship that Richard had given me for as long as I could remember.

My mother met his mom, Molly, at some exercise place to try to shed their baby fat a few months after they'd had us. They hit it off and had playdates for us, putting us on a blanket while they complained about how tired and fat they were.

Molly and my mother had barely anything in common. Molly was the owner of a four-star restaurant and the wife of a CEO of an exercise equipment company. The only two things they had in common were that their youngest children were the same age. Despite all their differences, they became inseparable, and soon enough, Richard and I became the same way. We were enrolled in the same private school from pre-K to eighth grade, which is where I'd befriended Tori, Pamela, Katy, Veronica, and Lauren, my counterparts who could also qualify as my best friends. There, Richard and I ate glue together and took naps together. Now we were both enrolled in Wilson High School and had only two weeks of our sophomore year left to go.

"What are you doing here? I mean, I want you here, but how did you sneak past the lobbyist?" I asked, choking on my own words, as usual.

His dark hair had been slicked back with a bunch of hair gel, and he was wearing the same suit he'd worn to his grandpa's funeral in seventh grade—not that it looked bad on him, but the clothing looked a little stretched out. I wondered why he would wear it when his dad had a closetful of suits he could wear. Don't get me wrong; he still resembled a Dapper Dan. His brilliant, twinkling blue eyes were unarguably the best part about him.

"We just arrived here," Richard said. "I almost got stampeded by a bunch of fashion editors. I bet you the stadium will be full."

"What? They're allowing people in? How long will it be before the event starts?" I asked, distressed.

"Tara is being let off the runway in about five minutes. There is a big countdown clock in the lobby. People are acting like they're in Times Square on New Year's Eve. Are you nervous?"

I knew Richard well enough to know that he wasn't being sarcastic, but it set me off. "Yeah, I'm going to make a fool out of myself in a few minutes, in front of thousands of people!"

"I wish you could see yourself right now. You look so beautiful."

At least somebody thinks so, I thought, but instead, I retorted, "I don't feel beautiful."

A woman wearing a fancy ball gown came to the door. "One more minute, Miss Hudson," she warned. I felt like she had been eavesdropping on us.

He walked a couple of steps toward me until he was so close that it got my heart racing. "Mark my words; it's going to be you," he whispered in my ear.

He leaned over to kiss me, and I let him. After the kiss, we gazed into each other's eyes for a moment, me in too much shock by his previous action to say anything and him staring into my face blankly. No, he wasn't staring at my makeup-enhanced face; it looked more like he was staring out into space and my face just happened to be in the way. What thoughts were crossing through his mind?

"Thirty seconds, Miss Hudson!" the lady warned.

I impulsively pecked him on the cheek, and then the lady escorted me to backstage.

That was my second kiss. My first kiss was at a football game the beginning of my freshman year, but I won't go into detail about it. All I will say is that I didn't tell anybody about it. I pretended it never happened. I guessed that was how I was going to handle my most recent encounter with Richard, but I wasn't sure. I should've jumped for joy at the thought of a possible romance with the person I loved most. Yet still I felt about my encounter with Richard just as I felt with my first kiss. Empty. Dull. A small amount of shame that I let him kiss me even though sparks didn't fly like I always imagined it would, like in a fairy tale.

What about Richard? How did he feel? Did he find a spark in me that I failed to find in him? I was reminded that I had to set my mixed emotions aside, because I would present and possibly humiliate myself in a few moments.

The girls in front of me couldn't have been my sisters that I'd grown up with. Tara resembled Marilyn Monroe in her sparkling, white, flowing dress. Amelia had on a tight black dress that magnified her usually small muffin top and hair like she'd stuck her finger in an electric socket. Leah looked like a delicate violet in her sky-blue dress. Her ash-blonde hair was put up with not a single strand of it out of place. She looked like she could've done her makeup herself, because all she had on was a trace of eyeliner.

Angela's hair that flowed down to her midback before had been cut to shoulder length and also straightened, gelled, and molded to where it looked as stiff as a board—even flatter than her chest.

As soon as Tara's cue was called, she fearlessly stepped out. Fashion editors took hundreds of pictures of her, and critics looked for the flaws in her appearance. Mother stood at the end of the runway in a cherry-red dress with crimson lipstick to match. She was wearing the beloved heir's crown upon her head. The crown usually sat on a plush red pillow in the dining room high enough so that we couldn't reach up and get our grubby hands on it when we were little. It was simple—pure gold with no garnish on it. While looking at its simplicity, thoughts went into my head. Maybe I could actually win. Maybe I would wear the crown. Maybe I would be on the covers of famous magazines ...

I had reality check and told myself that it would never happen.

There were five plush seats with nameplates on them. Tara reached the end of the runway and sat down in her assigned seat. Before I knew it, Amelia reached the end of the runway, and then Leah was called out. After Leah came Angela.

I could feel my heart beating outside of my chest and into my throat. My mind kept telling me not to fall with every step I took. Since the multiple camera clicks had blinded me, I tried my best to maintain a straight line. I sat down in my chair, preparing to get rejected.

Immediately after Mother gave a brief speech, the floor under Amelia's chair opened, and the seat slowly lowered until she completely disappeared underneath the floor. Tara's chair followed after Amelia's, and it was followed by Leah's chair. Mother eyed the two of us just long enough for it to get on my nerves. It took about five seconds for me to realize that I was the only one still onstage.

CHAPTER 3

The Heir

It was all a daze what happened next—uproars from the crowd, more blinding flashes from cameras, standing ovations, and people chanting my name. Maybe this was all just a dream. More like a delusion, if anything. I pinched myself to see what state of consciousness I was in, but after feeling a small prick of my arm, I knew that it wasn't a delusion. Mother took my hand and helped me out of my chair like I was too weak to get up by myself. Then she took the crown off her head and put it on mine.

"The heir of the third cycle of the Anticipation is Adrienne Hudson!"

She smiled the first real grin I'd seen her wear in years. Was she just showcasing herself for the cameras, or did I actually live up to her unachievable expectations?

That's when I saw Richard on his feet cheering me on just as the other spectators were. I thought of the words he'd said to me before I got onstage. Did he just get lucky, or did he know something I didn't? And what triggered the kiss? I knew I had to hide my confusion behind a brave face and try to conceal them with a winning smile. A halfway decent picture wearing the sacred crown was a must so that I wouldn't look like a fool on the cover of *Vogue*.

As soon as other people saw me on the cover of that magazine, they too would wonder if Mother had made a mistake picking me as the heir, because I could never live up to the expectations of the legendary heir—the perfect child with flawless skin and a face that poets could use as their inspiration. For the ultimate heir, a perfect figure was a must. The heir couldn't be too doughy, yet she couldn't look like an Auschwitz survivor. The heir couldn't be big-boned or muscular, either; she had to be just right. The happy medium. I couldn't be the heir, but denying it was no use. Somehow, Mother had found a particular glimmer of potential in me that everybody else, including myself, had overlooked. I was still up there in front of the large crowd, blinding lights flashing and people cheering. Mother squeezed my hand and raised it up, our fingers locking together.

Mother went on speaking. "As we know, the heir needs a suitable mate, as fair as he or she is. Will the chosen candidate come on the stage, please?"

I held my breath. With my luck, I'd end up stuck with a brainless jock or some jerk who happened to have a pretty face for the rest of my life. But the boy who walked onstage wasn't brainless. I knew he wasn't a jerk or somebody that wanted to harm me in any way.

The chosen candidate was Richard.

As he walked up onstage to join my mother and me, he embraced me tightly, but unlike the kiss we'd shared only a handful of minutes earlier, I felt something worth savoring. Instead of feeling vacant like I had with the kiss, our embrace felt natural. Because our embracing was in friendship instead of love, like it always had been. Like how I wanted it to be. Out of the blue, one tear went down my right cheek, and then a second one down my left.

Three ... four ... five ... six ...

It was no use counting them. Tears went streaming down my face one after another, probably smearing my eye makeup. Crying up there on that huge stage in front of all those people was so childish, so imperfect, so ... me. As far as flawless goes, I am far from it, and that's why I should have never been handpicked for such an honor. The crowd all looked with astonishment, like they'd never seen someone cry onstage at an award ceremony before. I wondered how Mother would react, because I had ruined her show.

"Why are you crying?" she asked, looking as baffled as the crowd.

"I'm just so happy!" I lied through my sobs to save my own skin, and I buried my face into Richard's chest, inhaling the scent of his father's stinky cologne. Yet my tears weren't out of happiness. Honestly, I didn't even know what I was crying about. What was there to cry about, really? I had just been crowned heir to a powerful business, for God's sake! Wasn't this a time to be happy? This was supposed to be my perfect moment, but somehow, I had managed to screw that up too. I was the heir; wasn't it my duty to be perfect? Yes, but as we all knew, perfection and I didn't mix.

The Anticipation was held like a big wedding. The reception that followed was supposed to be almost as huge as the event, yet only about a quarter of the crowd stayed for it, and half of those in attendance were journalists and paparazzi. The reception was held in White Garden Plaza across the street. White Garden Plaza was usually the place where really rich people got married, and if you wanted to book a wedding in the Plaza, you had to book it a year ahead of time—except in Mother's case, where she'd offered so much money that they couldn't resist squeezing her in. Money was nothing to her, and we had so much of it that it was her job to find something mediocre to invest in. Big bushes full of white roses were what gave White Garden Plaza its name, but Mother tampered with everything else. Lace-embroidered nameplates, crystal bowls, fine china plates, silver forks and spoons, and a string quartet.

The reception was fairly boring. In most ways, it was like a birthday party for an average teenager except with overly expensive deco and camera crews. Mother had said that there would be activities, but the only things to do were eat dinner and visit. Visiting with people might've been fun for social butterflies like Richard, but it was something that I failed at—another reason why Mother shouldn't have chosen me as the heir. I tried to eat, but the paparazzi kept trying to snap a picture of me taking a bite of food. It got to the point where it was so unsettling that I just didn't eat for the rest of the night, even though my stomach persistently growled in an effort to receive food.

When the reception came to an end, I could tell that everyone was relieved to have it over with. I was anxious to get out of the Plaza and into my bed until I saw all the cameras flashing at the exit.

Exactly what I need, I thought as I rolled my eyes in exasperation.

"Adrienne, how does it feel to be picked out of all those other gorgeous girls?" one female reporter with prominent cheekbones asked as I tried to make my way through the crowd and to get home unscathed, which would be a difficult feat considering that everybody was lunging at me, pushing and shoving in an effort to get a close-up view and flashing multiple cameras in my face. If this was how I would be treated in public going forward, then was being the heir all it was made out to be? What would the point of living be other than to satisfy my mother?

"So, Adrienne, what do you think of that young man your parents set you up with?" A man with a bulbous zucchini for a nose asked, putting the microphone in his hand against my jaw. I spaced out, staring straight into the camera.

Great; now everybody else watching will ponder why Mother chose me as heir. "Um, yeah, he's okay," I managed.

"You sure?" he pressured, pressing the microphone right smack-dab on the lips like he wanted me to make out with it.

By some miracle, somebody heard my silent cries, took me by the hand, and led me out of the crowd. I turned around and saw Leah standing right there before me. "Do you want to ride home with me?"

I looked at her in disbelief. "You're being serious, right? Or is this some kind of trick?"

Why did I ask that? Because it wasn't a big secret that Leah and I didn't get along so well. When we were kids, she always had to have the most dolls or get the biggest slice of my own birthday cake, and she always glowered at me whenever I was the center of attention. Leah had the memory of an elephant when it came to screwups. She never really was able to tolerate me, so why was she talking to me?

"It's a genuine offer, Adrienne." She appeared completely solemn.

I had a million questions to ask, but I shrugged and said, "Okay."

Leah's car was a 2005 Chevy that she shared with Amelia. Leah and Amelia shared everything—a room, a car, lipstick. I wouldn't have been surprised if I'd found out that they'd shared panties. Though it was a little bit shabby with two dents on the fender, I still liked it better than Mother's overly shiny cherry-red Volvo.

Leah's car reeked of cigarettes. "I thought you quit," I said.

About three years earlier when Leah had first started smoking, Mother forced her to go cold turkey when she found out about her bad habit. What surprised me was that Mother encouraged smoking for her models—something about smoking tobacco destroyed taste buds—but Mother told me herself that Leah wasn't "model material." In what world was Leah not model material?

"What Mother doesn't know won't hurt her," Leah retorted. "You like Kelly Clarkson?"

I shrugged. "She's okay."

Leah popped the CD in and turned it on full blast. I had no interest in listening to the music and even less desire to talk to Leah, so I stared out the window and watched the scenery move past at astonishing speeds. After a while of doing nothing but that, I realized that the road was unfamiliar.

"I thought we were going home," I said.

"We are. I'm taking the long route."

I didn't know there was a long route. Was she going to take me out somewhere into the middle of the woods and strangle me ... or worse?

"Why?" I asked impulsively.

She cranked down the volume of the CD about one hundred notches. "We need to talk about a few things."

"What do we need to talk about?" I asked.

Right then, Leah ran through a stop sign, and we almost collided with a green sport-utility vehicle, its driver slamming on his brakes just in the nick of time. He honked his horn and flipped her off in rage. That is when I took notice that Leah wasn't paying the slightest attention to driving. She was usually an okay driver; the dents in the car were an intoxicated Amelia's fault, and she was a road hazard even when she was sober.

Leah looked directly at me. Her light and vibrant eyes usually shone, but they were dim. "I'm sorry ... for everything."

"For what?" I asked stupidly. Of course, I knew what she was apologizing for, but over the past sixteen years of my life, I'd never heard Leah utter those two words once.

"For what?" she repeated mockingly. "All the crap I've done to you over the years. All the fights I've started. Never forgiving and forgetting. That's what!"

"If you're so sorry, why did you do all of those things in the first place?" I asked in a raised voice equally as loud as hers.

Now I had started another fight for her to remember, and like always, it would be all my fault. But it *was* partly my fault, because I'd predicted that being in the same car as Leah would've started another one of our infamous arguments.

She rolled her eyes. "Isn't it obvious?" When I didn't answer, she continued, "Uh, hello! You're the heir! You're the only one who actually means anything to Mother. It makes me so jealous! Whenever we were kids and Mother would have you play show pony, it drove me crazy!"

I scoffed, "Since when are you jealous of me? I was never the show pony—*you* were! You always were the center of attention, not me."

Leah opened the glove compartment and got out a cigarette and a lighter. I watched as the flame flickered in the night and wrinkled my nose when I smelled the odor of burning tobacco. She went on talking even with the cigarette in her mouth.

"I might've craved the attention, but I never received it. Growing up, everyone just watched you. There is a reason why you're the youngest child. I'm not the only one who's jealous of you. You intimidate Tara, Amelia, and me so much that we can't stand to be around you. Mary was forced to stay home 24-7 and take care of you, and Angela had to be your roommate, so they learned to tolerate you. You have a reason for living, Adrienne. The rest of us don't."

She rolled the car window down and threw the burned-up cigarette out into the street, but the smell lingered in the car.

"That's not true. Just because you aren't the heir doesn't mean that you aren't important."

"To Mother, I'm nothing, and she made sure that she beat me more than once in a while to remind me of that. She does it to all of us, and she almost got in trouble once. Mother used to hit Mary every time she could think of a reason to punish her, and during gym class, a girl saw all her bruises while she was changing. The girl told the gym teacher, and he took it to court. You've got Mother's favor. The rest of us don't."

I didn't really pay attention to her after she spoke of Mary. It reminded me of that day all those years ago when I'd caught Mother in the act. I almost told her about it, but Leah already knew about Mary's abuse and didn't need any convincing, so instead, I asked the next thing on my mind. "If you can't stand to be around me, then why did you invite me to ride home with you?"

She took a deep breath. "I knew you were going to ask something stupid like that. You have no idea what you've got."

"What?" I interrupted hotly.

She slammed her hand hard on the steering wheel with frustration. "I don't understand why I even bother telling you all this! You remind me of what I was like when I was your age. When I was your age, I was the queen bee of conceitedness. When I turned sixteen, I asked Mother if I could start modeling her clothes, and after she wouldn't let me, I threw a giant temper tantrum, and I locked myself in my room for days. Soon enough, I figured out that it was no use fighting with her about it. For a long time after that, I let all of Mother's lies seep into my head, but there was one thing that was the truth: I wasn't as beautiful as I thought I was. You were only ten when all of that was going on. Then, as you grew, you transformed into this creature that became more beautiful each day. Soon enough, you surpassed my beauty. It made me so jealous that I tried to sabotage everything you did as an attempt to be ahead of you again, but all I created was a whole lot of friction."

Leah pulled into our neighborhood. "It's not like I'm going to become a model, either." She shook her head. "You didn't know that along with being the heir comes a million-dollar contract with her fashion company?"

"Me, a model? Maybe when pigs fly," I said on impulse.

Leah didn't say anything back, and the peace gave me time to think crazy things. Would Mother make me smoke? Starve myself? Wear ridiculously high platform heels?

"You know you have your first photo shoot tomorrow?" Leah asked as she pulled into the driveway.

"I do now," I said sourly.

"Good luck with the photo shoot." She got out of the car, forgetting her car keys in the ignition.

I placed the keys on the table and reflected on the events of the day. How could all of that happen in one day? Because it was the day of the Anticipation. The day that everyone had been waiting for was over. Soon, everybody would forget that the day had ever existed, but not me. The Anticipation was over, but my journey had yet to begin.

CHAPTER 4

Model 101

"Wake up, Adrienne! You don't want to be late on your first day of work," Mother said harshly.

She was definitely not anything that resembled a morning person, yet what puzzled me was why she got a job where she got up at five thirty each morning.

I glanced over at the digital clock on my cluttered nightstand, and after I saw that it was only five forty-five, I moaned, "I thought I didn't have to be at the shoot until six thirty."

"Step number one to becoming a great model: knowing how to keep your body looking its best. Now get dressed in some workout clothes. We're going for a run," she instructed.

As soon as she enunciated those words, I knew that it was going to be a lousy day. I halfheartedly changed into some workout clothes.

When Mother put her headphones in her ears, I realized that I'd forgotten my iPod and groaned.

"Since this is your first time running, we're only going to run three miles," she informed me.

She was ten times more cheerful than she had been a mere five minutes earlier when she'd woken me up. Sometimes I thought that she had little people—an angel and a devil—on her shoulders arguing back and forth. If that was the case, the devil won the argument 99 percent of the time.

Long distance was a good thing. I was one of the slowest sprinters in my gym class, because I shared third period with all the medal-winning track stars. I only beat Madison Huffington in the sprints, who was made fun of by everybody—particularly my group of friends—because she was a doughy tub of lard that smiled at everyone, even when Tori, Veronica, and Pamela poked at her weight.

Just the thought of her name sent a chill through my whole body and drew the blood away from my usually brown face. But I felt an even stronger emotion than anxiety.

Guilt.

I can't think of a time when I didn't notice her. Was it really only a year and four months ago? Yes, it had been early January of the previous year when Tori had decided that she was our next target.

It was Health, Fun, and Fitness Week at our school, so it was the time of the year where our nurse, Mrs. Windelkins, weighed all of the kids to update their medical files. In previous years during this forsaken time, we would simply find the fattest girl in the cafeteria and gambled on how much she weighed, but Tori said that we were going the extra mile, it being our first year in high school. We were going to find out how much the fattest girl since first grade—Madison—weighed and tell the school that magic number.

It wouldn't be an easy feat, considering that Mrs. Windelkins had a big thing about privacy and always said something about weight being just a number that was none of other people's business, and she made sure that the medical files were locked and secure to keep kids' deepest, darkest secrets safe another day.

Of course, Tori's natural talent was sticking her nose into other people's personal privacy and finding out their deepest secrets to humiliate them by revealing them to the entire school. After school one day, Katy and I went with her to Geek Charming, a store that sold expensive but geeky techno gadgets across the street. We didn't know that it existed until a couple of weeks before New Year's when Katy's new geeky boyfriend, Gavin, said it was one of the best stores out there.

We all chipped in to buy the most expensive lock-picking kit they had. It looked cheap; it had several different picks like bobby pins and silvery keys with worn teeth similar to the ones we'd used once to break into Angela's diary when we were little.

We hid the kit in Lauren's locker and talked about our plan during lunch. By the time the other kids were dumping their trays, we had come up with a game plan. We would take a few lock picks out of the kit and hang out at the Hardee's near school until after the office closed at four thirty. Then we would go through the back way, because it was never locked. We would then get into the office and then the bright-yellow filing cabinets where they keep the health records and read Madison's weight. We made a guessing game at how much her weight would be. The one who was the closest would get to keep the lock-picking kit.

It was kind of like when I was little and the candy store had a gigantic jar of jelly beans, except instead of guessing the number of jelly beans, we gambled on how much a fat kid weighed, which wasn't as innocent as we'd made it out to be.

I had to admit, though, that sometimes it was really fun making someone's life harder. Probably because Mother taught me that I was better than everybody else, and walking over people was what kept you on top of the heap, but I shouldn't blame Mother. It wasn't entirely her fault that we were so corrupt.

Anyway, we successfully broke into the office and got into the cabinet that had the letter *H* on it. Veronica got out the file that said *Huffington, Madison* and paused shortly for dramatic effect.

"Holy crap!" I yelled in horror as soon as my eyes met the medical file. Madison weighed 247 pounds, but that wasn't the most shocking thing on the medical records. Madison Huffington, the buxom girl who smiled at everyone, was HIV positive.

Tori put the file back in its original place after making sure that everything was in the same order that it had been when we'd arrived so that nobody could possibly suspect anything suspicious. "Good thing we don't sit with her at lunch."

"Yeah, she probably has cooties in her airflow. She'd breathe all over us, and then we'd get it," Pamela said, chuckling.

"I just want to know what lowlife gave her HIV. I mean, his standards must be pretty pitiful," Veronica commented, sneering, and then she shuddered. "The thought of a human being actually wanting to have sex with that thing makes me sick."

That thing is a human being, I wanted to say, but I held my tongue, for saying such things wasn't allowed in the gang. Anyone who was lower on the social ladder was to be looked down on. Shame on me for thinking otherwise.

"Maybe he didn't want to. Maybe it was a triple-dog dare, or she slipped something in his drink, like those drugs Mrs. Windelkins talked about in health class," Lauren proposed.

Tori and Pamela started laughing, so I did too, because I didn't want to be left out of all the fun. Since my guess of 250 was only three pounds off, Katy handed me the lock-picking kit. To this very day, I have it cleverly hidden in the back of my closet. Of course, Tori told everyone about Madison's HIV the next day. Madison lost the few friends she had and was no longer known as the big tub of lard that smiled at everyone but was then known as the girl with HIV.

In gym class, when Tori, Pamela, Veronica, and a large handful of all the other girls in our gym class would shriek, "Cooties! Cooties! Cooties!" at the top of their lungs, I would join in the action.

Tori's new goal in life was to make Madison's a living hell. We once filled her locker with hundreds of cans of Lysol disinfectant spray by breaking into her locker with my lock-picking kit.

The lock-picking kit became an important part of our infamous pranks, but of all the evasive, devious, and sometimes dim-witted schemes we pulled, Madison Huffington would always be the best joke we ever played—only I don't think I should have called it the best joke ever. I should have called it the best game plan we ever had to ruin someone's life. That's why I didn't like to remind myself about Madison Huffington. But it seemed like the more I tried to forget, the more I remembered, because it was a different kind of guilt. It was not the kind of guilt you get when you eat ice cream with a shovel when you're supposed to be dieting. It was an immense guilt.

Then, without a warning, I tripped over a twig and face-planted on the hard ground. What made it even worse was that I tripped on a gravel road going up a hill.

I looked around confused for a few seconds. Thank God the gritty pebbles had narrowly missed my eyes. I didn't think I'd make it as a model if I went blind. I sputtered and spit up a tooth. I gasped and frantically looked to see what tooth it was. If I'd lost one of my front teeth, I would have made more progress in my career blind. Luckily, it was just one of my wisdom teeth.

Then I realized that I was alone on an empty, unfamiliar road all by myself. Mother must have been too distracted by her iPod to recognize that her daughter was no longer with her. I'd hit my head pretty hard. When I stood up, everything was a shaky mess, and I saw things dancing around. I fell back down, and everything went black.

I heard a familiar voice speaking, but I couldn't figure out what it said. I saw Mother in front of me.

"Huh?" I responded after looking around. I was on the ground.

"You took quite a tumble there," Mother said, her nose wrinkling a bit in disgust that could only mean one thing.

My heart sank. "My face is hideous, isn't it?"

"It's fine," she reassured me.

I tried to hide the sickening feeling that I'd always felt when I was in her arms. "Let me see myself in the mirror."

"We'll get to that soon enough," she promised.

I hadn't thought of my injured appearance until Mother pulled up to her workplace. Mother hadn't threat, so neither had I. I pulled the visor mirror down, but Mother stopped me.

"We'll have plenty of time to do your makeup inside."

"I want to see what I look like," I demanded.

I thought she would fight back, but she let me go ahead. There was a bright purple bruise under the left side of my lip, and my left cheek—the side I fell on—was dented with grooves like a golf ball from where the gravel had left its mark. If I was supposed to look perfect, I would be a disappointment with puffy lips and hamburger meat for a cheek.

"I can't do my first photo shoot looking like this!"

"Do you know how many models come in each day with huge pimples on their foreheads or dark circles under their eyes? That is why we photoshop pictures before they are put in magazines. Professional photoshopping could make a burn victim look gorgeous."

I knew arguing was against the rules, so I held my tongue. And as much as I hated to say so, Mother was right. The makeup alone concealed my raw-looking left cheek, and some red lipstick made my lip good as new.

I looked at myself in the mirror, and for the first time in my life, I began to see what everyone was talking about. It was like I'd been blind my whole life, and suddenly I could see my beauty, a beauty the world already noticed.

I wasn't nervous for a runway show or any of the following photo shoots, because I had finally found my niche, my beauty ... or at least that's what I'd thought.

CHAPTER 5

One Wild Night

There were a few things that were a blur to me on June 29; I forget what day of the week it was, what outfit I wore that day, or what I ate for breakfast. But there was one thing I knew: it would be the day my life would change forever. I spent another long day on the catwalk modeling strange fashions and stumbling in six-inch high heels. That evening at about nine o'clock, I got four texts about the same thing, but the only one I bothered to read was Richard's text.

Pool party on Tori's yacht 2night! Can't wait 2 c u in that cute little bikini of yours, babe! ;)

Richard <3 Adrienne

A couple of weeks earlier, I had shot for the *Sports Illustrated* swimsuit edition, and Mother pulled some strings to give me the black, lacy, and revealing bikini after she'd heard me say that it was pretty. Even though I usually didn't like the feel of skimpy clothing and stood clear of anything that looked like it belonged in a strip club, I loved the feel of the open air rushing against my bare skin.

"Thanks, Mother. I owe you one!" I acknowledged.

"No, I am the one who is in debt." She then kissed the top of my head, turned around, and walked the other direction without saying another word. But why? Strange behavior like that was what made me wonder what was yet to come. Was this some kind of manipulation or the deterioration of Mother?

I put on my bikini and even thought for a second about putting oil on my stomach to show off my abs. All of Mother's rigorous exercise routines and meal planners had paid off. In five weeks, I had lost fifteen pounds, and I could feel my newly prominent ribs sticking out.

Lauren's car horn honked so loudly that the ground rumbled like a thunderstorm.

"Get in the car, or else we're going without you!" Tori screamed almost as loudly as the horn.

Might as well tell the whole world that I'm sneaking out, I mumbled to myself. I threw on a cotton dress over my swimsuit and ran down the stairs and out to her car with a towel on my shoulder.

"Nice cover-up, slut!" Pamela snickered as I got in the car.

What I'd thought was a plain white cotton dress was made out of a material that was somewhat transparent, showing the black of my swimsuit. I knew that they weren't going to let me live it down anytime soon.

"Just because you model swimsuits doesn't mean you should dress like one of those hookers who hangs out by the dock," Veronica bantered.

"You're just jealous because you don't look good in anything that doesn't resemble a tent," they snickered, and Lauren switched the gearshift to drive and took off.

Tori's yacht was huge; it spanned across the length of four football fields. The place was packed, to my surprise. The yacht was given to her as a gift from her parents for her thirteenth birthday, and when Tori had a party, it was usually just us and her family.

"Why are there so many people here?" Katy asked.

"'Cause everyone knew how great this party was going to be!" Tori responded.

It was a great party, indeed. Her yacht had a rock-climbing wall, two indoor pools, a Jacuzzi, and arcade complete with an Xbox 360 and Kinect, a bar that Tori had opened with my lock kit, and a live band that called themselves the Amazing Crazies. The best part about it was that everyone who was halfway decent looking or had parents with a net worth of at least $5 million was invited. That was most of the school.

Wilson was a smaller high school with somewhere between eight hundred and one thousand people attending each year, but everyone who went there was rich or in the scholarship program. There were only thirty-nine kids on scholarship.

Tuition was $3,500 dollars per month, so the rest of the kids belonged to families of high-ranking social status. I was the third richest that attended my school, only behind Patrick Lexington and William Calvert, who both were colossal football players who, instead of human beings, resembled a form of *Homo sapiens* that hadn't gone through the full evolution process.

Now I was the only supermodel, which automatically made me the life of the party. People laughed at my jokes when they fell flat, peers gave me long looks in the hallway, and I was now considered the hottest girl in school. Before that, I came in a close second—the first place being Tori, of course. I was sure that it didn't make Tori happy that I'd stolen the title away from her. In fact, I wondered why we were still friends. She should've at least tried to fight for her previous title back, but she couldn't have cared less. She treated me like I was plain-old Adrienne, who would always be considered lower than she was, even if I was a supermodel and crowned heir of a world-famous fashion company.

It made me skeptical, but at least someone saw me the same way after I became heir. I still hadn't fully gotten used to everything, but who could? Back before I was heir, I was just another typical kid with a few more stuffed animals and a nicer house, and now my face was on the cover of magazines that were read by everyone everywhere. Now I was told all the time how I was beyond better than everybody else, and I believed it too.

I raised my glass full of champagne. "To us, the best dang gang there ever was!"

"To us!" The gang cheered as we clanked our wine glasses together with a little too much force, spilling the reddish-purple contents of the glasses all over the poker table.

I had only had champagne once when I was around ten or eleven. Whenever I asked for a sip, Mother would say that I wouldn't like it, but after all my persistence, she caved in and let me have no more than a sip when nobody else was looking. I remembered it tasting too tart and dry for my palate, and as far as my knowledge went, the taste hadn't improved over the years, but I kept drinking it because so many other kids—particularly Veronica and Pamela—were inhaling the stuff.

"I was wondering why you wanted to borrow the lock-picking kit. Now I understand. This is delicious!" Pamela said to Tori.

"Of course you think it's delicious—you're a drunk. Do us all a favor and join one of those alcoholics' anonymous groups," Tori snapped. Apparently, she was even meaner when she had alcohol coursing through her veins.

"Yeah, you need to stop hanging out with us; we could become alcoholics too," I taunted.

Pamela glared at me with her coal-black eyes that were filled with hatred. "At least I'm not a *Playboy* model."

"I'm not a *Playboy* model, stupid! I shot for *Sports Illustrated*," I retorted.

"Yeah, the swimsuit edition! You were showing as much skin as in a *Playboy* magazine, and you still are under that launderette you call a cover-up," Pamela growled.

We were loud enough that the jocks started listening to us.

"At least she looks good in it, unlike Katy!" William butted in to the conversation.

The other jocks laughed cruelly. I was confused at first, but I saw what they were talking about. Katy's cover-up was also a little bit see-through, showing her pink polka-dot bikini.

"You need to hit the gym yourself!" I said hotly, because Katy was the nicest in the gang, and I hated it when guys poked at her stocky figure.

"No, I'd rather hit on you."

"That's my girlfriend you're talking about!" Richard said in a threatening tone, but there was still a hint of a smile in his eyes.

"Oh, you are? Then why are you too scared to touch her? If I were her man, I'd touch her to my little heart's content," said a gorilla-faced jock whose name I can't remember.

After a few triple-dog dares and several ice-cold spirits, Richard and I found ourselves making out on a pool table with everyone cheering us on. We had some more wine, but I stopped after a while, because I didn't like the foggy, light-headed feeling the wine gave me.

I wondered how Pamela and Veronica hadn't collapsed on the floor by the time they stopped drinking, considering that they finished up a whole bottle of champagne. After making a wreck of the bar, we hit the pool.

Without thinking, Pamela jumped in the pool, and as drunk as she was, she still could swim. The jocks jumped with their shorts on, and I think a couple forgot to take their smartphones out of their pockets.

The jocks and a few guys that weren't a part of our advanced social ladder whistled as I took off my cover-up, and Richard looked like he was about to punch the next guy that hit on me. I couldn't help but smile at the fact that guys could possibly be fighting over me, but it made me nervous as well to keep up with my "hot" status.

After we were done trashing the pool, the gang split up. Veronica was drunk enough to stagger away with a seedy guy who wanted nothing more than to get in her pants. Pamela had thrown up and passed out on the floor. Tori, Katy, and Lauren went into the bathroom together and never came out, so Richard, the jocks, and I sat around wasting time considering what happened to them.

Then we hit the dance floor. I didn't mind not having my cover-up on, though the old me would've felt insecure and exposed. I couldn't dance to save my life, and everybody who went to homecoming knew it when I sprained my ankle. Still, I danced with the guys like there was no tomorrow. Since we'd all been drinking, we were all uncoordinated, and they tripped over their own feet, so I had no shame with my dance moves. The upbeat, catchy tune faded, and some love ballad started playing.

"May I have this dance?" Richard asked, extending his hand.

I took it with some hesitation. "Of course."

"You know that I've got some real competition," Richard said to me, putting his hands on my hips, which were bony and prominent.

"What do you mean?" I asked. I placed my arms around his neck and leaned into his embrace, and despite the foggy feeling in my head, I felt more comfortable with Richard than I had felt in a long time, because nobody was forcing us to kiss or forcing us into marriage. It felt natural, just as it had before I'd won the Anticipation.

He smiled a little, and the stars were reflected in his eyes. "You know what I'm talking about. It's like a pit bull sanctuary, and you're a big, juicy T-bone steak."

I laughed, thinking that it was still the good old days. "You'd better not be calling me fat."

He pecked me on the lips quickly. "Nope. Never looked better."

I said nothing, because I just then remembered that we were in a forced relationship that would ruin our previous bonding over the past years.

"So we need to start planning," he said with a smug half smile.

"Plan what?" I asked, raising my eyebrows.

"Our wedding. Your mother expects us to get married, doesn't she? I was the chosen candidate, after all."

The thought of saying *I do* when I was forced to made me feel so nauseated—or maybe that was the wine's fault. Maybe it was the wine talking, not him. There was an unpleasant stench of alcohol lingering on his breath, or maybe it was just the aroma of the yacht in general. I heard a retching noise and saw a girl with dark skin throwing her wine and cookies up all over the deck. Yep, that could have been the smell, as well.

Please, somebody tell me that he doesn't mean the words he's speaking, I thought. "I don't want to talk about it right now."

He looked at me like I had a big booger hanging outside of my nose.

"Richard, we're sixteen. Let's enjoy life while we're young and put this conversation on hold for another ten years, okay?"

He sighed. "But, Adrienne, I love you, and I just don't want to lose you. What some of the guys say about you and what they want to do to you ... it makes my stomach churn thinking about it—even more to talk about it."

Oh crap, I thought as my heart sank to my toes.

It was the first time that Richard—or any boy, for that matter—had said that he loved me. Sure, he'd said it in front of a camera one time or another, but this was the first time he'd told me face-to-face without any pressure from others.

It was official. He was in love with me.

I felt a strange sickening feeling in my chest when I thought about him being the only boy ever to love me for anything other than my looks. Then again, who else would? Then I was mad at myself, because I should've felt a rush, a tsunami of excitement like most girls do with their significant others, if that's what I was supposed to call him. Mother expected us to be. Yet I couldn't swallow the thought of being with Richard for the rest of my life, the thought that Mother was trying to shove down my throat so vigorously. Maybe we would have a relationship similar to my parents, after all. Maybe we would ignore each other when nobody was looking, and then, when the cameras were pointed directly at us, I'd have to pretend that he was the love of my life.

No, Richard and I were too close to ever be distant in any type of way, shape, or form. Or at least we had been before our every interaction was forced by others. After that, our relationship took a tumble down a slope at one thousand miles per hour. Yet I guessed that if I had to be married off to someone, I would have chosen Richard—but only because there were no other right candidates for the job.

Nobody else besides Richard would enjoy spending the rest of his life with me, anyway. We were compatible and complemented each other nicely. Mother had kept that in mind when she was choosing the candidate, or at least I hoped that she'd considered it.

I heard whispers on the streets that Grandma Marie saw a picture of my dad and fell in love with the handsome young man with the smile as white and dazzling as hundreds of little diamonds. It was just a rumor, but seeing how much my parents' personalities clashed, I couldn't help but accuse my grandmother of not thinking Mother's partner for life through.

My first instinct was to run, but instead, I replied, "You're not going to lose me, okay? I'm not going anywhere." I'd meant it in a warm friendship sort of way and not in the hopeless romantic way that I was so uncomfortable with—because at the end of the day, he would still be my best friend. He would always be there for me, unlike any of my other "friends."

Then somebody bellowed, "*Cops!*"

Panic immediately struck every cell of my body. Gravity itself could not hold me still, because every instinct of my body told me to run. So I did, not caring one bit that I left Richard, the boy who'd made the mistake of loving me. But the thought of him never crossed my mind, because I was too busy thinking about not getting caught. Not bringing shame to my family. Not making Mother sorry that she'd chosen me as heir.

A bunch of people had started running away in all different directions. Some people who were drunk enough were jumping overboard. Some surrendered. I was sober enough to get into one of the lifeboats. When I first got in it, the boat wobbled some, and I stumbled. Thank God I hadn't had any more wine, or I could've gone overboard into the roaring waters of the ocean. I covered myself with a rubbery tarp I found in the lifeboat and dozed off even though the little boat was hard enough to cause serious back pain.

The next thing I saw was a blinding white light.

"Put your hands up, you hooligan!" a man in the shadows shouted harshly as he shone his flashlight directly into my face.

I winced and turn away from the light. You'd think I would have been used to bright lights after getting my picture taken so many times.

"Is that Adrienne Hudson?" another silhouette of a man asked.

I didn't think a police officer could put names to the faces of fashion models.

"Who cares? Just because she's a celebrity doesn't mean she gets any special treatment. Come with us," the guy with the flashlight said.

Tears formed at the corners of my eyes as the man put handcuffs on my wrists.

I'd never ridden in a police car before, and I'd never thought about it much, either. When a police siren was heard or I saw flashing of white-and-blue lights, I never gave enough thought to ask myself what it would be like to be a crook sitting in the backseat of that car.

But now I knew.

I imagined that getting jack slapped in the face over and over again until all my teeth fell out would feel better than the stabbing pain of shame I felt in the backseat of a police car. In the next forty-five minutes, I was forced to change from my pretty bikini into a hideous orange jumpsuit and got pictures of me taken, but this time for a mug shot. I knew who I was going to call for the single phone call I was allowed, but Mother didn't answer the phone. Of course, it was four thirty in the morning, so I didn't really expect her to answer.

I left a voice mail. "Hey, Mother, it's Adrienne. I went to a party with alcohol last night, and it got busted. I'm at Stonebrook Juvenile Detention Center on 1349 Michigan Street in Brooklyn." I paused briefly. "I love you," I added. And only then did I hang up.

CHAPTER 6

Punishment

Mother bailed me out of the detention center the next morning. During the car ride home, there was no communication between us, but I could tell by the look of infuriation in her eyes that I wouldn't get off the hook easily. It wasn't something that everyone was going to forgive and forget. If Mary got her room taken away from her just by talking back to Mother all those years ago, then what sort of torturous maltreatment had Mother prepared for me?

I was on Mother's good side, but had I lost her favor? I must have. If I would've run a little bit faster—not hidden in that lifeboat—I wouldn't be in this situation. I wouldn't have spent the night in jail with all the other impoverished scum that were once good enough to be called the future of America. Maybe now I belonged in that category too.

Was Mother mad at herself that she had chosen me as heir just a few weeks earlier? Would everybody be as ashamed as I thought they would be? Could I ever make up for all the shame and disgrace I caused Mother? I had an infinite number of questions waiting anxiously to be answered. Infinite possibilities of what form of purgatory awaited me.

"Mother ..." I began.

She put her index finger over my lips. "Silence, child. There is something awaiting you at home."

Since when did she call me *child*? I thought about her strange behavior with the bikini. Maybe this was just another chapter in the deterioration of Mother. No, if anybody in the family was deteriorating, it was me. I was the one who had just gotten arrested, after all.

All I wanted to do was cry, but there was something that wouldn't let me—not in front of Mother, at least. Crying was weakness in her eyes, and I was a pitiful little puppy, even without any tears. It would also be better for me not to speak anymore. I thought I drank little enough to escape a hangover, but I was wrong. This was my first hangover, but it wasn't something I should've been proud of. Whenever Amelia came home drunk from partying on the weekends, Mother made sure that we all took our turns laughing at the sight of her, intoxicated and vulnerable. Once, in sixth grade, the gang was sleeping over at our house, when Mother got a distressed call from Amelia at the police station and brought her home sadly drunk. Mother went on to tell me that Amelia had gotten in a bar fight.

Needless to say, Amelia had a bruise a nice shade of purple under her eye and walked like Bambi did as he took his first steps. Tori thought it was hilarious, and we each took turns trying to trip Amelia with our feet, and I'm afraid to admit that we had fun doing such things. The next morning when she was taking a bucketful of Ibuprofen trying to live with herself for what she had done, Mother encouraged the whole family to torment her like we'd never made a mistake.

I wondered if Mother would do the exact same thing to me. Torment me in my moment of weakness—the moment I needed her support the most—like she'd never made a mistake. Then again, Mother had never gone as far as to get arrested. I had, and the sharp, aching pain in my head reminded me about my error even more. But when I got home, nobody pointed fingers at me. Nobody even said a word to me, like I had been up in bed all night like I should've been. I wished that I had been in bed the night before, that I had abstained from the hard partying. If I had been, I could've saved everyone a whole lot of trouble and heartache.

In the parlor sat Richard and his parents. Mrs. Taylor's eyes, which usually smiled, were vacant. Her sandy-brown hair that was usually up in a tight bun was down and askew. She was wearing a large, fuzzy, white bathrobe and matching slippers that made her look like a giant body pillow.

Mr. Taylor had far more wrinkles than he'd had the last time I'd seen him, which was just a couple of days earlier, but the last couple of days had felt like an eternity for me, and he probably thought of it as an eternity also. He was wearing beige dress pants and an awful red-and-green Christmas sweater. Who wore Christmas sweaters in June? I was going to tease him about it but remembered that they were probably awoken in the middle of the night by their son calling from a detention center, and he'd put on the first shirt and pair of pants he'd gotten hold of.

Both of them looked incredibly disappointed and shocked at what their son had done. They were probably disappointed in me too. Mrs. Taylor wanted a daughter, but it seemed like she wasn't capable of making anything more than frogs, snails, and puppy-dog tails. Mother, on the other hand, had wanted a son but only produced sugar, spice, and anything nice. In a way, Mother adopted Richard, and Mrs. Taylor adopted me. After school, when I went over to Richard's house almost every day, she would make us whatever my little heart desired. Richard and I would go outside and make mud pies for the remainder of the afternoon, and then I would usually have dinner at their house. We always ate that orangey Kraft macaroni and cheese that you can get at Walmart three for a dollar, my favorite meal.

The Taylors eating lunch at our house every Sunday had been a tradition since Richard and I were three. They always came over to our house after they went to church. Whenever Richard spilled ketchup on his Sunday best, which was a majority of the time, Mother would always be the one to put Tide on his tie, not his own mother. I was sure that Mother wasn't only disappointed at me but that she held some anger against Richard too.

Richard was a sorry sight, just as I was, so I could tell that he'd spent the night in jail too by the noticeable bright purple circles underneath eyes that were almost identical to mine. Richard's eyes were downcast and inflicted with shame in what had happened. I wondered if he'd had a night almost as bad as mine had been. Maybe he'd even had it worse. Looking at him made me feel even guiltier for leaving him right after he'd told me that he loved me. I wondered if he still did love me. I hoped he did, yet I hoped that he didn't at the same time, because—besides my guilt—I didn't feel any different about him. He would always be good old Richard, my best friend and nothing more. That was how it was until Mother forced our two independent hearts to beat as a dysfunctional, ailing one. He looked up at me for a second; there were so many things that I wanted to say, but instead, I stood there like a complete simpleton with my mouth open.

"Sorry," I finally whispered under my breath, tears coming to my eyes.

He kissed me on the top of my head and whispered back, "I will always love you, no matter what," and I immediately knew that everything was going to be all right between us. We were going to pretend that the night before had never happened. He loved me, and I loved him, as the naked eye would say. Yet it shouldn't matter what category of love it was; we loved each other. That was supposed to be the important thing. Yet it wasn't, because our love would be forced in the wrong direction no matter what attempts I made to amend it. I hadn't figured it out yet, but our friendship would become just as helpless as a train pushed off its tracks. Just another thing the Anticipation would take away from me.

I plopped down on my bed and did nothing but cry until I forgot what I was crying about. What was I really crying about? There were all too many things that had happened. Crying because I was such an idiot for going to that party, because of how I'd betrayed Richard when he was always so good to me. I didn't care if he accepted my apology, because I still had done him a wrong that could never be righted. That was another reason to cry, wasn't it? I longed for human companionship during this hell of a roller-coaster ride; this sudden turn in my own series of fortunate and unfortunate events. Of course, Mother was probably downstairs.

I could hear the words she'd say in my head. *"She is such an irresponsible piece of garbage, just like all the others! I never should have made that beast of a girl the heir, and after what she's done, I'll be lucky if I can afford a tombstone to mark my grave!"*

She'd wail to Dad and Mr. and Mrs. Taylor or whoever was listening, whoever was paying attention or even cared. I knew a lot of people who would care; thousands of people came to see me being crowned heir. As soon as word got out, her reputation would go down just as rapidly as mine. Crowning an heir that gets arrested just a few weeks later wasn't something to be proud of.

After what seemed like forever—even though it was only somewhere around twelve o'clock—someone knocked on the door.

"Come in," I mumbled through my pillow.

Mother walked into the room. "I hope you've had some time to think about what a reckless thing you did last night. Can you at least apologize for it? It's something I haven't heard out of you all day."

Her request got me flared up a little, because she'd told me to shut up in the car, and now she was trying to hold it against me! Now I could clearly see why my sisters tried their best to avoid doing anything that would cause any type of ridicule. I could also see why Aunt Margaret never came around anymore; she was exhausted being told over and over again about all the errors she had made. Then again, I guess I could see why Aunt

Margaret avoided Mother even before I'd gotten arrested or my talk with Leah.

I wanted to say, "I tried to apologize to you in the car, but you wouldn't listen to me!" but I knew that I had to keep my big fat mouth shut once more.

"Sorry," I muttered halfheartedly. "Will you forgive me?"

She sighed. "I guess, over time. You know how in the car I said I had something to show you?"

I nodded, and she went over to my desk and instructed me to log in to my laptop and get on to the Internet. When I obeyed, she leaned over my shoulder, and she logged on to my Twitter account. I thought Twitter was stupid, but after I became heir, Mother made me get an account to become more "of the modern era." Yet Mother didn't monitor it like she did every other detail of my life, so I never got on it once and had forgotten what my password was.

"Behold the digital scandal!" Mother said like she was hosting a cheesy talk show.

I looked in horror at all the pictures that I was tagged in. Pictures of me drinking wine with the gang. A nasty video of Richard and me making out on the bar in front of all those mindless jocks. Pictures of me on the dance floor wearing my skimpy bikini, a lot of them in which I danced with guys I'd never seen before. I started crying again, but that time, I didn't care if I was in front of Mother or not, and I didn't care how childish and weak she probably thought I was.

"Don't cry," she said in an unpleasant tone. "There is no point in it. Crying won't make all those pictures magically disappear from the Internet."

"It will make the hurt go away," I argued.

"No, it won't, trust me. I have lived a lot longer than you have, Adrienne. Hurt doesn't disappear with tears but with time. I've done some things I regret, but I didn't cry over them, because it was no use. You're wasting your valuable time as we speak." She sighed. "Your father and I will discuss what your punishment is.

It may take a while, so don't get some delusion that you're off the hook."

It was hard to swallow Mother's harsh words, but somewhere down inside, I knew that she was right about me wasting my time. Of all the things I was so unsure of in this darkness, there was one thing that was crystal clear: my life would never be the same again.

* * *

A couple of weeks later in the checkout line at Walmart, I found a picture of me making out with Richard on the cover of *OK!* magazine. It only reminded me that no one was going to forgive and forget my mistake.

Mother, who was at my side—she had been everywhere I'd gone for a couple of weeks—sighed deeply and murmured, "It's like Amelia all over again," like I wasn't standing right there beside her. Of course, all of Amelia's errors went without any recognition from tabloids, but she wasn't the heir. I was. Now my victory in the Anticipation had stolen yet another thing from me. It was bad enough that it robbed me of my best friend, but it had also taken my dignity, as well.

Getting arrested helped me develop a newfound hatred of being famous. I got so upset knowing that there was nothing I could do to get all the cameras and tabloids off my case. Even if I did something good like donate to a charity or read to the blind, they still wouldn't let me forget that I'd been arrested. It was bad enough that my mother had turned on me, but the world had also. I prayed that one of my fellow supermodels wasted away from starvation to get the press off my back, but even after Lindsay Lohan stole the spotlight by getting intoxicated in public, the cameras and my parents were still on my case. I guess all the unwanted tender loving care from the press meant that my punishment would be more severe than previously thought.

What was this punishment Mother spoke of? And why hadn't they delivered it yet?

I remembered Mother's words: *It may take a while, so don't get some delusion that you're off the hook.*

Maybe the waiting itself was my punishment. Of course, it was punishment enough for me. I had already been through hell for a couple of weeks, so why did I have to be punished? Maybe as I was kept up at night fearing my punishment, Mother and Dad were downstairs in the parlor laughing at how my fear was eating me alive. Many nights I stayed awake considering all the possibilities. Maybe I was to be uncrowned heir, if that were possible. Maybe my parents would disown me, and I would become one of those prostitutes that hung out in the dark alleys of Manhattan. Maybe, just maybe … but probably not.

One morning in the middle of July, Mother didn't wake me up, which was now a part of our routines. I saw how late it was by the amount of sun coming through my window. Mother and Dad were sitting side by side on the couch in the parlor. Why weren't Dad and Mother at work? There was nothing out of the ordinary about that day, so I had a reason to be concerned.

"Why aren't you two at work?" I asked.

"Take a seat, Adrienne," Dad ordered.

I obeyed his command and took a seat. "Why aren't you at work?"

"We heard you the first time!" Mother snapped.

"Maybe you should answer me, then," I argued.

"We both called in sick today," Dad, who was Mother's softer side, explained.

I was about to ask why again, but as usual, Mother spoke with her big fat mouth before anyone else could by saying, "We called in sick, because some things are more important than working."

"Like what? My punishment?"

"Yes. We've been thinking about what to do to you for the past couple of weeks, and since you've never gotten into any trouble of this magnitude …" Mother began.

"I'm off the hook?" I asked stupidly, yet beaming with hope.

Mother rolled her eyes with true annoyance. "How many times do I have to spell it out for you? No! You are not off the hook; just as I said before. I'm sick of it, Adrienne! When I try to give you a lesson about life, my advice always goes through one ear and right out the other! News flash: I've lived longer than you, and I know more about life than you do. Maybe you should get that thought through those ears of yours and into your head for once!"

Dad ordered for her to calm down, but no matter how golden his words were, they just went through one of her ears and right out the other.

"Go up to your room!" she barked, hammering her foot on the ground so that it made a big *thump*.

Without any hesitation, I ran straight up the stairs, tears welling in my eyes. I knew that if Mother saw my tears, she would accuse me of ignoring her advice even more so.

"Diana, that was very unnecessary! You should stop letting your temper get in the way of things. You knew how important this conversation was," Dad scolded.

Dad always ignored Mother's errs, much less brought attention to them, so I knew that my punishment must've been larger than what I'd hoped for. What was so important about my punishment, anyway? I had been humiliated enough without an additional punishment to add on to my torture. So I stood there right in the middle of the stairway, exposing myself to Mother's eyes. I didn't care about the punishment Mother would give me for staying in her line of vision. I was already getting punished, anyway, so I decided to stick around.

"We have the rest of the summer to break the news to her," she retorted, not paying the slightest bit of attention to my presence, like I was invisible. It was a feeling I'd had on a daily basis before Mother put a crown on my head and gave me a $1 million contract with her fashion company. Since I lived by routines, I felt right at home standing there, even if I wasn't welcome.

"That's not much time. It's already the middle of July, and the Tampa Bay orientation is in early August. She'll have to start packing by the end of next week if she wants to make the tour on time," Dad reasoned.

His words knocked all the wind out of me as I stood in the middle of the stairway looking like a complete and utter fool with my jaw dropped down to my feet.

"Tampa Bay? That's in Florida!" I butted in, screaming loudly enough that the people who lived at the end of the street could hear me. I was full-out bawling by then, looking as vulnerable as I had the day after I'd gotten arrested. I darted up my stairs to my room. The sooner I got myself out of Mother's sight, the better.

Out of the corner of my eye, I saw Dad walking after me, but Mother grabbed his hand before he could take a step toward me.

"There is no need to comfort her right now," she said. "Let her blow off some steam before we try to talk to her again."

I thought it was a mother's nature to comfort her daughter, but not mine. Why was I the one who had to deal with this corrupt matron? Nonsense—my sisters each had their fair share of stories about how Mother had wronged them. I could see why everyone had abandoned Mother's corrupt circle of allies that I was trapped inside. Maybe sending me off to Florida was her way of kicking me out. Should I be grateful? Aunt Margaret, Mary, and Leah would've been. Then again, they never could say that they were ever Mother's ally. I could.

Hours passed by as swiftly as straw in an open fire, and still no one was there to comfort me. Where had my parents gone? Had they abandoned me? Had they packed up all their worldly possessions and made a run for it? No, I thought I heard some faint murmuring from downstairs. I kept promising myself that they were coming back with every part of my body crossed. Yet as minutes turned into hours, there was still no one there to comfort me. I was wasting my time hoping for some miracle that was my parents to be there for me, but on a second thought, they never had really been there to comfort me in my time of need. So why should I have expected that by some miracle my parents would help me out? Silence again, and for what seemed like ages, that was all there was.

The next day, when my parents were finally brave enough to show their faces to me again, I had questions that needed to be answered, and Dad answered them, no matter how harsh the reality was. My parents were shipping me off to Tampa Bay Academy, one of the most renowned boarding schools in Florida.

Of all the crazy punishments I let my imagination create, the only thing I didn't think of was being shipped out thousands miles away from home. Of course, my punishment had to be just that.

Tampa Bay had an extended list of limitations that seemed to be endless. At nine thirty, all lights had to be turned out, and all noises had to be turned off; a rogue alarm that went off in the middle of the night equaled detention. I could get suspended for something as minor as chewing gum. I was only allowed to see my parents twice during the school year—Christmas and spring break. My parents might as well have sent me to boot camp instead of boarding school.

Mother was going to suspend my contract for the school year. Why did that bug me so much? It wasn't like I would get crow's feet in the next year. Then I realized why it bugged me: it was because modeling was the only thing I could do right, and Mother was taking it away for one year!

That made so mad that I punched a picture of Mother and me in a macaroni frame hanging on the wall that I'd made for her when I was seven for Mother's Day. My punch had enough force to obliterate the picture, leaving a large hole about the size of a hubcap in the wall. I yelped at the pain in my left hand and realized that I couldn't wiggle my fingers. Dad drove me to the nearest emergency room, and that was where x-rays showed that I had broken my wrist. It was a mere crack in the bone, but my pediatrician still said that I had to wear a cast for three weeks and a splint for another two weeks.

I was nervous enough as it was, and now I had to put up with wearing a bulky cast that would eventually stink up the place. Great. Now I would go into Tampa Bay wearing that wretched thing and become known as the smelly kid. Then the gang of Tampa Bay would break into my locker and put rotting fish in it just as my group of friends did to Stella Burking. Karma isn't one that forgives and forgets.

I came home with my lower arm in a cast the same shade of pink as a Sharpie highlighter and then ordered the maid to clean up the large, gaping hole in the wall in the rudest way I possibly could.

CHAPTER 7

Tampa Bay

The remaining two short, almost nonexistent weeks that were the rest of the summer were a blur of sunscreen and melted vanilla ice cream cones.

I do remember all of my farewells, though. When Richard kissed me good-bye, I gave him a friendly embrace instead of kissing him back. I had prepared a big speech about how I only liked him as a friend and that I wanted more than anything for us to remain as close as we were, but I didn't end up using it. Instead, I kept my mouth shut, which I'd gotten pretty good at doing. I promised him that I would e-mail him with regular updates on how I was doing, but besides that, I was basically a free woman. When I said my farewells to the gang, there wasn't much talking considering that being sincere wasn't really our forte. I don't mind admitting that I was kind of glad when it came to that, because attending Tampa Bay was a pretty good excuse to ditch them once and for all.

Angela offered to help me pack up my bags, and I allowed her to. Who was I to ignore help? Besides, that would be the last time I'd see her for months, so it would be our good-bye. I took some strange things most teenagers wouldn't even think about. I filled a small, portable suitcase with pictures of all the people I loved. Without thinking, I put the macaroni frame with Mother's punched-in picture in the suitcase, as well. I had that picture frame and my problematic pink cast—which smelled about as lovely as a big chunk of rotting meat—to remind me of my impulsive action.

"We both know it isn't as bad as you think. I guarantee you'll have fun. Look at it as an opportunity to make new friends," Angela cheered.

"We both know I'm not good at making friends," I retorted.

"I don't think that at all. You don't give yourself enough credit."

"Okay, let me rephrase that; I don't *want* to make any new friends! All I want is to get this year over with!" I snapped. At least that shut her up.

She looked at me with her mouth wide open and stared at me blankly.

"I can pack the rest up by myself," I said after a brief but awkward moment of silence.

She walked out of the room without saying a word. I knew that it would be the last time I would speak to her for months, but I didn't really care. I was sick of saying farewells. I finished packing my things, and soon enough, I found myself about to board the plane that would take me to my home sweet home for the next year.

At the airport, Mother kissed me on the forehead and said, "This is just as much of a punishment for me as it is for you."

We hugged for what seemed forever and ever. Even though I didn't feel the least bit safe and secure, I'd rather have been in her arms than boarding a plane heading thousands of miles away from home. When I finally released my grasp from her body, I saw that she was the one with a tear in her eye for once. Did that make me the strong one for once? She thought of me as a lesser person when I showed my weakness, so didn't that mean I should do the same to her?

No. I could never stoop to her level. Then again, I would one day be in her shoes, so I had to get used to the ways of the cruel world.

Dad was crying too. I'd only seen him cry a handful of times, but that was still far more times than Mother. That didn't mean it didn't come as a shock to me. With everyone else shedding tears, I wanted to cry with them, but my tear glands wouldn't function properly. Why? I bawled like a baby when I was expected to keep my cool, and when I wanted to cry, I couldn't shed a single tear.

Then it dawned on me: some things were too much of an emotional toll for tears. This was one of them. I kissed my dad's cheek the same time as he kissed mine.

"Last call for passengers to board the flight to Tampa Bay," the flight attendant warned.

On the plane, I dozed off. I could still taste the stale peanuts that I'd bought at the convenience store—ten packs for a dollar—and the room-temperature Sprite that had lost all its fizzy and sugary goodness.

All I knew was that I had a pretty awesome dream—a dream so awesome that if I were given one wish, all I'd wish for was for it to become a reality. Strangely enough, I couldn't remember what happened in it. All I knew was that it rocked so much that I could cry at the fact that it would most likely never be reality. The only memory I had of my dream was a single face. The most beautiful face I'd ever seen. It was the face of a boy who I'd never seen before, a boy who was as foreign to me as an immigrant is to American politics. I sat for hours staring at the back of the leather seat in front of me trying to jog my memory.

I knew this much. His skin was a bone-chilling ivory I'd only seen before in a vampire movie. The curves of his lips were subtle and gentle, adding a sense of security in me that I'd not felt ever before, not even in my father's arms. His nose was delicate, as well, almost like a woman's, but it only made him look even more incredibly handsome and masculine in his own way.

His large, round eyes were without a doubt the best feature of his face; they were a vivid emerald green that looked as if they could penetrate a heart of stone. They penetrated my heart with ease.

He had one imperfection on his face that would make some people consider him out of the ordinary for the worse—ugly, even. No. Most people would categorize him as ugly because of his imperfection, which was a large scar on his left cheek going from the corner of his piercing eye all the way down to his neck. All the affected skin on his cheek was jagged and uneven with no symmetry, and it was the same fleshy pink color as hamburger meat.

It looked sort of like my face had looked when I'd fallen right before my first photo shoot, only mine wasn't nearly as protruding, and the damage to it had faded rapidly. Still, I had been so insecure about it before Mother told me about the wonders of Photoshop.

Was he insecure like I was?

I found myself thinking back to my eighth-grade English class when we'd read an article about a veteran named Jeremiah Rodman who'd driven his tank over a land mine. The explosion killed the other man with him inside the tank instantly, while Rodman was left with facial burns so severe that he couldn't bite into a hamburger. The article talked about how he became a recluse after he was sent home from the hospital and about how he hid himself under scarves, hoods, and sunglasses whenever he went out in public. At first, I'd wondered why he was so afraid, but after thinking about it, I knew that I would've done the same thing if I looked as he did. Was this boy a recluse too? Of course not; he was a mere figment of my imagination. Besides, the look in his dazzling green eyes wasn't that of insecurity, it was of confidence. He didn't look like somebody who'd hide his face from the rest of the world, no matter how horrid it was.

I wanted to figure how he'd gotten that scar, even if he wasn't a living, breathing person on the face of the earth. But why was I so interested? I didn't find Rodman interesting. In fact, I wouldn't have remembered a thing about him if his face wasn't so painfully unforgettable.

But I saw the boy differently from how I saw Rodman. Rodman's was a face I couldn't bear to look at. I didn't care that he was a veteran or that he'd made a sacrifice for his country, because if I saw him on the street, I would have to gag.

I saw the boy in my dream as an angel with a broken wing. His scar should've revolted me, but instead, it allured me even more. I didn't care if my angel was just a figment of my imagination. He was real to me. I went back to sleep and dreamed more about my angel, my angel with a broken wing.

* * *

"Hello. My name is Mrs. Kelli, and I'm the girls' dorm room advisor," said a buxom woman with two bowling balls for breasts and skin the color of a dead, dried-out oak leaf.

I was in a crowded auditorium surrounded by hundreds of people I didn't care to get acquainted with, but I would learn to care, because these would be my classmates. Two of them would become my roommates. It made my stomach churn to think about having to share a room with somebody that I barely knew.

The school board of Tampa Bay should have had some kind of background check on the students before they entered the campus, but sadly, there wasn't anything of that sort, to my knowledge. And with my luck, I'd end up bunking with some man-lady with more hair on her chin than her head. I glanced at my phone anxiously, but it was only 6:12 p.m. The orientation wouldn't be over until six thirty. At that moment, there was nothing I wanted more than for the dumb orientation to be over. I was sick of being told all the things I couldn't do, and for what seemed like fifty years, she talked about guidelines for all the females attending Tampa Bay.

Most topics were plain common sense, like why I shouldn't share a toothbrush with my roommate and the importance of cleaning up messes, so I almost fell asleep a couple of times.

"Now it's time to assign your dorms, ladies!" Mrs. Kelli announced cheerfully.

Sure enough, Mrs. Kelli assigned me dorm room A-25 with two girls I'd never heard of in my life: Rosemary Parker and Elaine Fitzgerald. After the orientation, we were dismissed for dinner. On the way out of the auditorium, I grabbed my schedule and a map of the campus, while the palm trees and increased rays of sunshine only reminded me even more that I was so far away from home.

I didn't really need a map of campus to find the cafeteria, because I followed the big crowd of people who could walk the campus blindfolded. But I still took mental notes so I could figure my way around the place too.

I was walking into the cafeteria when somebody called my name. I turned around and saw two girls who looked like they could have been sisters. They were both a lot shorter than my five feet and six inches, but they were a tad bit more compact than my 110-pound frame. The girl on the left had skin of soft, smooth caramel, while the girl on the right had a skin tone the color of a bronze medallion. They both had long, wavy locks as black as oil slicks.

"Hey, you're Adrienne, right?" the girl on the right asked.

I nodded and tried to figure out if they were girls that I'd come to love like sisters or hate with a fiery passion.

"We're your new roommates," the girl on the left explained.

"From A-25," the girl on the right finished.

"Oh, yeah, Rosemary and Elaine, right?"

"You're right, but everybody calls me Laine," the girl on the right corrected.

"It's Rosie," the girl on the left introduced as she gave me a friendly handshake, like the kind you'd give at a job interview.

Laine did the same, but her hand was all shaky and trembling as it met mine. I guessed she must've been nervous or something, like most people were when they met me. Then again, I was kind of nervous too, because I wanted to make a good impression on these people considering that I was going to have to live with them for the rest of the year, so I had no reason to ridicule Laine for her nervousness.

"Come on. You're sitting with us," Rosie said.

Before I had any time to object, she grabbed my arm, led me to a table, and sat me down in a seat next to her.

The group at the table consisted of five girls, including Rosie, Laine, and me. I learned that the girl with bronze skin and super-straight, stringy hair the color of a peeled banana name was Emily. I learned she was a serious athlete—which wasn't hard to guess observing the rippled muscles of her forearm—and that she had science class with me during first period. Danielle had wildly curly brown hair that made up a lot of her treetop-tall height, and she leaned on a boy whose name was Jacob, so I got the vibe that they were a couple. Besides Jacob, there were three other guys at the table. Mark and Kody were brothers, which didn't surprise me because of their same deep brown eyes.

Connor was a cute, baby-faced boy with blue eyes and curly hair. He was a redhead, but not the color of orangey flames or carrots. His hair was the color of rich, creamy red velvet cake.

"Whoa, you're Adrienne Hudson, right?" Connor asked.

"Yeah, that's me," I said with a unenthusiastic nod.

"You're even more beautiful in person than you are in magazines or on cameras. I mean, most people look better when they're presented on the media because they have so much crud on their face, but not you."

"Thanks. You're pretty cute too," I allowed with a fake grin.

"Aren't you already dating somebody?" Jacob asked with his eyebrow arched.

I panicked a little bit at this question, because I didn't want to come off as slutty in front of these kids who didn't know what to think about me yet. It was bad enough that I was already at risk for the stuck-up, egotistical heiress judgment some acquaintances automatically labeled me with as soon as they found out what I did for a living.

Yeah, sort of, I wanted to say, but I took the safe route and said, "Yes, I am, but I just like telling the truth. Just because I'm beautiful doesn't make him any less handsome."

"Well, whoever he is, he's a lucky guy," Connor said, ignoring my compliment.

"I saw Adrienne and her boyfriend kissing on the cover of a magazine. He is h-o-t," Rosie implied.

"I'm lucky to have him," I agreed quietly, and the conversation carried on.

After all the guys got over a supermodel sitting at their table, things died down, and I was somewhat treated like one of them. I learned that like Emily, Kody, Mark, and Danielle were all trophy-winning soccer players, and Mark went on and on about how he was the only reason why Tampa Bay won the Florida Championship trophy the year before. While everybody else applauded, I found his boasting to be annoying, mainly because I was looking forward to bragging about being a *Sports Illustrated* bikini model. But then again, exposing so much skin for millions of dirty-minded men wasn't something to brag much about.

Emily, Laine, Rosie, and I went through the line to get dinner. I got the spaghetti, only because that's what everyone else was getting. As everybody sat back down with their dinners, I asked a question that was pretty innocent and would cause no first impressions in any way in my part.

"So what did everybody do over the summer?"

For a while, everything was fine. I listened as they told me tales about their summers from various locations—church camp, soccer camp, and Disney World. As I let my guard down, I went as far as to talk about my modeling, and everybody was truly interested in my work, not judgmental like I feared they'd be.

I noticed that Laine was the only one who seemed to remain silent. I asked Emily why.

"This is Laine's first year, like you. She was a little bit nervous, and her being Rosie's roommate and all, we invited her to sit with us. She's a little bit clingy and annoying, but I'm guessing she'll get over it eventually."

My head felt like it was spinning around. I thought I had finally escaped my nonexistent friendship with the gang. Now I realized that I was going to be trapped in that relationship yet again, only with a different group of equally cruel kids.

Emily may have thought she kept it an A-B conversation, but the whole table pretty much heard, but nobody cared about Emily saying such a thing, except for Laine.

"You know, if you guys don't want me here, don't beat around the bush and just tell me. Don't be all two-faced about it! I'm going to leave, and I won't look back," said Laine.

Emily scoffed, "Fine, go ahead and leave. You're a whiny little piece of garbage with no friends, anyway. Nobody will miss you sitting here. In fact, I'll be laughing as you're eating your lunch in a bathroom stall."

All the girls—including me—high-fived Emily, but inside, I was screaming, because I was once again trapped in the cliquey crap of high school I thought I'd escaped. I figured that I might as well get used to it exactly as I had for all those years with my former friends.

Laine, of course, was not laughing or high-fiving anybody. As soon as tears started falling, she made a beeline for the bathroom, and I considered going in the bathroom to help her out.

But what would I say? I stunk at pep talks, and, of course, it would tick off my new clique. I didn't want to end up in the bathroom with Laine crying all over the toilet seat. Yet it would be my ticket out of the cruel clique, so I got up and started walking to the girls' bathroom.

But I didn't, because when I only strayed a couple yards away from the table, I caught a glimpse of him for the first time and could no longer focus on anything else.

CHAPTER 8

First Glances

For a couple of seconds, I told myself that I was looking for things that weren't there, but I couldn't deny what I saw. All I saw was the back end of a boy who sported a head of shaggy, unkempt hair that fell in golden waves. Yet I could tell there was something different about him, even though I knew nothing about him.

All the other guys were wearing expensive sneakers they claimed to be worn by professional basketball players. All the other guys sported hundred-dollar name-brand jackets from Hollister or Aéropostale. But he obviously wasn't in the category of all the other preppy, immature, sometimes plain, dim-witted guys I had met, because I could tell just by the look of his worn-out jeans and scraggly hairdo that he was an original.

His hair and clothes weren't the only thing out of the ordinary. His skin was as pale as a sheet of blank paper that I could buy at Walmart—one hundred pages for $1.50. This skin tone was abnormal for a place like Alaska, much more somewhere like Florida; where I was considered an albino with my light, creamy cappuccino-colored skin. His skin was as pale as an angel; it was as pale as *my* angel.

I knew it had to be him.

You're looking for things that aren't there, I told myself. *You can't tell much about a person just by looking at the back of his head.*

He turned around, and the face of the boy knocked the wind out of me. He had the same soft curve to his lips. He had the same delicate but masculine nose. But most importantly, he had the same asymmetrical, eerie pink scar that went from the corner of his left eye down to his neck.

My angel was in flesh, standing in the same room I was standing in. It comforted me to know that he was something more than a figment of my imagination, even if he was a complete stranger to me in real life. He glanced in my direction, and I realized that I was staring at him. Since I noticed some people that were passing by looking at him in disgust, I expected him to look offended or even embarrassed.

Instead, he looked at me with disgust, like I was the one with the face people couldn't bear to look at. Even though I couldn't see the whites of his eyes, they still penetrated my heart in a way that I couldn't explain. Then again, I couldn't explain my feelings toward him, either.

A boy with a short and compact build and dark hair went up and talked to him. I watched as they gestured to each other, beaming in fascination at the two. I tried to guess what their conversation was about, putting words into the mouths of people whose names I didn't know, not caring that it was none of my business.

"Adrienne, what are you staring at?" Emily asked as she gave me a dirty look.

I had forgotten that I was standing in the middle of the cafeteria for no logical reason that I could explain to my peers.

I regained my seat and asked, "Who is that boy with the scar?"

"You mean Scarface?" Mark asked, giving me a quizzical look with his left brow arched.

"Who else would she be talking about? You don't see that many kids walking around with disfigured faces," Connor sneered.

I had so many questions to ask, but for some reason, I could only get out, "Huh?"

"None of us know his actual name, so everybody calls him Scarface. He's a new kid, like you," Kody explained.

"You know that dark-haired kid that's talking to him? That's his brother, Anthony. I bumped into him at the tour a couple of weeks ago. The kid's such a dope that he can't even talk; I don't know how anybody could carry on a conversation with him," Rosie bad-mouthed.

"I can understand why you were staring at Scarface; I've heard he's even worse looking up close," Danielle said with an almost microscopic glimmer of pity in her eyes.

"Yeah, we'll have to cross our fingers that he's not in our science class. He'll ugly up the place," Emily said with a snicker that only reminded me even more of Tori and her devious ways.

"Hopefully, ugliness isn't contagious, or else Adrienne's in trouble. She'll lose her job as a model," Connor taunted.

Everybody laughed at the table except for me. It made me angry to know that they treated me like I was some kind of a goddess and talked bad about a kid whose name they didn't bother to remember just because of our appearances. I was determined to at least figure out his name and maybe even go as far as to get acquainted with him. No, the question I wanted to find the answer to more than anything else wasn't his name but why I was so intrigued by him.

The dream I'd had about him was the only logical answer I could think of, because I knew that were it not for that dream, I wouldn't have given him the time of day. I would've snubbed him like everybody else did. I would've gagged when he wasn't around. I might have even complained about how revolting he looked at the lunch table along with the rest of them. But yet because of a dream, I felt like I was drawn to him instead of the companionship I had known whole life—the gang, my sisters, Mother, maybe even Richard.

For a mere split second, I thought I wanted him instead of Richard, but I took it all back as soon as I realized how unethical the thought was. Of course, I shouldn't think about, much less consider such nonsense.

I had a wonderful boyfriend who loved me enough to marry me someday. Richard had put up with me for so many years. I was foolish enough to abandon him as soon as he said the three most important words that he should've never said again, and yet he did. I had already made enough mistakes, and not even Richard would forgive me if I left him for a boy whose name I didn't know. Much less Mother, because I knew her well enough to know that she would be gagging along with my new friends if she could see the boy for herself. I wish I could see it, too, so I could be a normal person and gag along with them.

That evening as the sun set over the horizon, all the girls walked to the dormitory, which looked more like a prison than a place teenage girls would take residence in. As Rosie and I entered room A-25, I saw that Laine was sprawled out on the sole single bed. I wanted to say something to her about what happened at the dinner table, but I had no idea what to say.

Rosie swiftly jumped on the bed, right on top of Laine, and proclaimed, "Dibs!" before I could say something, anyway.

Laine, whose face was still streaked with tears, chuckled, "I don't think so!"

She maneuvered on top of Rosie, and Rosie made a crunching sound as if she'd broken something. The two of them broke out laughing, but I didn't laugh, of course. Did my eyes deceive me? How did Laine learn to forgive so quickly? And why was Rosie not guilty or awkward or anything of that sort? Had they both gotten hit on the head with a boulder and forgot the tension at the dinner table?

"Adrienne, join the love!" Rosie invited, motioning me to come toward her.

Sure, I'd only known them for a couple of hours. Sure, Rosie was in cahoots with making Laine cry, but if Laine could forgive Rosie in such a short amount of time, then I certainly could. Besides, I was going to share a bunk with these girls for the next school year, so it was time to get used to their company. I jumped on the heap, and we moved around, giggling with every movement each of us made. But it was kind of hard to enjoy myself like Laine and Rosie were, because I could feel by the dampness of the bed that it had been drenched in a waterfall of tears, and the dampness only made me feel guiltier about not doing anything remotely selfless.

All because I was busy staring at Scarface.

Mrs. Kelli walked in and jumped at the sight of us huddled up. "Ladies! I'm glad that you're comfortable with each other, but please keep the volume down! Girls at the end of the hall have complained about all the noise you're making."

The three of us glanced at each other, and I knew from then on that this would be a member of faculty to hate.

"'Kay, will do!" Laine chirped as she and I got off the bed to give Rosie some elbow room.

Mrs. Kelli motioned toward the large, askew pile of our suitcases, every single one of which had been overfilled to the point where they looked like the seams were about to burst. "Maybe you should clean that pigsty up; just a thought."

We began unpacking our things and getting everything in the right drawers and closets. As we were helping each other unpack our bags, I noticed that one of my bags was missing. To make matters worse, I was missing the small, red portable suitcase with wheels that contained all of the photographs that I mindlessly taken over something I could actually put to use, including the macaroni frame that still contained the punched-in picture of Mother. Yet I still wanted it back, because that suitcase and the things inside of it might've been crap, but it was *my* crap. In a strange way, it was a piece of me, and if I lost that piece of me, I could never gain it back.

"I think I'm missing a bag," I told my roommates.

"Did you leave it somewhere? Maybe you left it at the airport or something," Rosie reasoned, not out of true concern but out of her effort to please me, the supermodel.

"No, I remember taking it with me on the cab ride over here," I recalled as I tried to remember the previous few hours.

What had happened on the plane was all a daze. The only thing I could think of that had occurred during those three hours was my dream. Even after I got off the plane, memories were still all a hazy blur, like frost on a windshield during the late winter. I thought I could recall carrying the bag out of the airport, but I wouldn't have put all my eggs in that basket. Plenty of other things could've happened to that bag. For all I knew, my missing suitcase could be on a Greyhound bus on its way to Guatemala.

"You should ask Mrs. Kelli about it. Somebody may have found it and given it to her," Laine informed me as she took a blue blouse out of her bulging handbag and placed it in the drawer of her dresser.

"Okay, I guess I'll go ask Mrs. Kelli about my bag now," I said as I went toward the door.

"Have fun," Rosie grunted as she flopped on her bed that she'd just put the sheets on, even though it wasn't properly made.

"Why are you going now? The lights are going to be off in a few minutes, and it isn't like your bag is going to grow legs and run out of the lost-and-found section overnight. Besides, I heard that Mrs. Kelli is a Nazi when it comes to being out of your bed when the lights go off," Laine reasoned.

"Oh, well. I guess I'll go to lost and found first thing in the morning and see if I can find it. Thanks."

I'm not sure, but I think Laine mumbled "You're welcome" back at me.

Needless to say, I put all my stuff that was currently in my own care where it belonged. I made my bed. It turned out that I had taken Angela's solid purple comforter instead of mine. It looked like I had done yet another scatterbrained thing in the past forty-eight hours. By the way things had been going so far, I guessed that retracing my steps wouldn't be as easy as I'd thought.

One of my roommates flicked off the light a few seconds before Mrs. Kelli hollered for everybody to turn their lights off. Even though Mrs. Kelli was chewing out one of the girls for turning the light back on to find her way into the bathroom loudly enough to be heard across the hallway, I still fell asleep pretty briefly after my head hit the pillow. Before thinking about Richard and my mother and all the people who mattered in my life, I found my thoughts drifting over to the boy whose name I didn't know—the boy with the scar on his face that everybody who had eyes thought was ugly. Everybody but me, that was. And of course, instead of dreaming about the things that mattered, I dreamed about the boy.

In my dream, I was wearing an elegant ball gown that looked like something a Disney princess would wear. No, the dress had almost no back; Disney princesses were never that scandalous. But the dress was a light, pretty shade of purple and was made out of a soft material like silk. There was a flower of some sort in my hair, but all I could tell was that a lavender flower pulled my hair back in an elegant but firm bun, and the only hair around my face was a couple of soft ringlets that failed to be secured in place. I could hear a faint tune coming from a string quartet in the corner and realized that I was in an old-fashioned ballroom. That is when I saw the boy with the scar on his face wearing a worn but still dashing tuxedo, and as he walked down a flight of stairs, I waited anxiously at the bottom of the staircase. As soon as he reached me at the bottom, he ever so softly grazed his lips on the top of my forehead, and I took him by the arm. I think I could even feel his warmth.

He said something to me in a gentle and euphonious tone as if he were singing to me. But what did he say? His words became slurred over the increasing volume of the music.

Then I was all of a sudden transported to a different room, a room more crowded than the other one and not in the least way fancy. There was a band playing an upbeat, energetic pop song in the background. The boy wasn't in a suit any longer but wearing a worn gray T-shirt and blue jeans with more than one rip in them, but I was still in the same purple dress I had worn in at the ballroom even though everyone else was in casual attire. He asked me a question, and even though I couldn't understand him like I had earlier, I nodded. He took my hair down for me and reattached the flower in it.

The upbeat song faded into a slow, romantic love song of some sort. He asked me if I wanted to dance, and I didn't object; I was actually really eager to dance with him. I could see people around us giving looks at such an odd couple, but he didn't seem to care. To show I didn't care, either, I kissed him on his left cheek. Right on his scar.

I had to meet this boy.

CHAPTER 9

Lost and Found

When I woke up the next morning, I panicked at first because I was so used to waking up at the sight of the ceiling in my own room, lying down in my own bed. Then it came to mind why I wasn't in my own room where I belonged—I'd been shipped out more than a thousand miles away from home, and this was only the beginning of my punishment. There were 180 days left to go until home sweet home, but who was keeping count besides me?

"Morning, ladies!" Rosie said as she came into the room sporting a smile and a towel wrapped around her head to cover her damp hair.

"Not a morning person, are you?" Laine asked as she threw a pink sweatshirt over her head.

"What do you think?" I groaned as I got up out of bed and made my way over to the vanity to brush my hair. It was my goal on the first day to make it obvious to my roommates that I hated nothing more than getting up in the morning.

"You'd better suck up the pity party right now, or else it's going to be a pretty long year for all of us!" Rosie said as she tossed the towel on her head at Laine.

"What was that for?" Laine asked, but Rosie said nothing back.

Rosie and I walked to breakfast together, and instead of sitting at our table, Laine sat at Scarface's table instead. Apparently, I wasn't the only one who noticed, because Connor asked, "So, what's up with Laine's table situation over there?"

"She probably had nowhere else to sit," Danielle proposed.

"I wouldn't want to sit with her, either," Jacob mocked.

"I can't believe we even let her sit with us in the first place," Emily groaned. Then she chortled, "It is pretty funny, though, because everybody has figured out how annoying she is already. And this is only the first day of school!"

"At least you don't have to bunk with her, like Adrienne and I have to," Rosie griped.

Rosie was getting on my nerves about twenty times more than Laine was, so if I had my way, I'd send Rosie to the bathroom crying instead.

"You two are going to have fun this year," Connor said.

"She snores so loud, I couldn't get any sleep at all," Rosie complained again.

Okay, that was just a bald lie; I knew that much from last night.

"I don't think she snored," I said without a filter, and when everybody looked at me like I had a booger hanging out of my nose, I added, "I thought the snoring came from Mrs. Kelli. We do have a room right across from hers."

When all the girls at the table chuckled, it reassured me that I was still part of the group. My comment about Mrs. Kelli changed the topic of the table over to how horrible she was, which was safer ground, because it was something that I agreed with.

But instead of talking, I couldn't help but wonder why the table was so against Laine. I'd known her for fewer than twenty-four hours, but she had yet to make a bad impression on me in any way. And what was up with Laine and Rosie? How could two girls be fighting one moment and make up without any type of amender? And what was Rosie's problem with Laine? I thought of how she'd thrown the towel at Laine earlier that morning, and I could see what was going on. Rosie was a two-faced backstabber who was horrible at faking friendships and didn't deserve my friendship, much less Laine's. Or at least that was the only good reason I could come up with, because I was a horrible guesser.

I wanted to ask them what Laine had done to turn them against her, but I reminded myself that if I asked such questions, they'd kick me out of the table just as they had Laine … although maybe that was my free ticket out. I really didn't want to be in that group, but as far as I knew, they wanted me there. And what if they were the only ones that wanted me? So I decided to keep my trap shut and please everybody, which wouldn't be so hard considering I'd been doing it the past sixteen years of my life.

After that day, there would be 179 school days of this left to go. Joy.

* * *

When I found out that Connor and Kody had science with Emily and me, we all walked together to class. It was eighty degrees outside that day, even though it was only eight o'clock in the morning, so even though the walk from the cafeteria to biology was brief, I was still sweating in my capri pants that I'd foolishly worn thinking that it would be a mild day outside.

I made a mental note that I was in Florida now, not New York, and to make matters even worse, it was the middle of August, so less was more. I should've known that rule very well, anyway, being a bikini model.

"Great, just who we wanted to see," Emily said sarcastically as we walked into the classroom.

Sitting at one of the lab stations was the boy with the scar on his face and his brother, Anthony—or at least I'd thought that's what Rosie had said his name was. Observing Anthony from a distance, I thought he was short and compact, but up closer, I could now see that he was lanky, as well, but he still looked like he weighed somewhere around fifteen pounds more than his brother.

"Get some disinfectant out, Adrienne!" Connor taunted, spraying an invisible can of Lysol directly into my face.

"Spray some on me!" Emily and Kody said in unison.

"Sorry, guys, but I don't think you two can get much uglier than you already are." After they glared at him for a moment, he said, "Kody, you're my lab partner. Let's sit in back of the room so we won't have to look at *him* in the face, okay?"

"Sure, people who sit in the back are always the cool kids, anyway—so Emily, you'll have to stay here in the front."

Emily rolled her eyes at their idiocy and turned to me. "Be my lab partner."

I sat down at the nearest lab table, even though it was right in front of Scarface and Anthony. I told Emily that I had bad vision and that we had to sit in the front or I wouldn't be able to see the board, but the truth was that I wanted to see if he was as awful looking as everybody said he was or like how he was in my dreams.

The bell rang, and everybody else scurried down to their tables, except for Emily, who was still standing. "Please, anywhere else would be okay with me, just not by *those* freaks."

"Do you need your hearing checked? You heard the bell, Emily. Plop that humongous butt of yours down, or else I'll get a hot glue gun and glue it to the chair for you," Kody taunted as he and Connor sat down at a lab table in the back of the room. His taunting must've hit a soft spot in her rock-hard heart, because right afterward, she reluctantly sat down next to me.

A couple of moments after the bell rang, a woman with staggering orange curly fries for hair and thick-framed sapphire-blue glasses that magnified her already large eyes walked into the room.

"Good morning. I am Ms. Gredrickson, and I will be your chemistry teacher over the course of the year. I've been teaching chemistry for twenty-seven years at five different high schools, and Tampa Bay is the most outstanding school I've taught at so far."

After only a couple of minutes, I already found myself annoyed by her upbeat attitude. "This is going to be a long year," I whispered in exasperation to Emily.

She widened her chocolate-brown eyes and nodded in agreement as if to say, *I know, right!*

After being utterly annoyed by the new chemistry teacher for what seemed like an everlasting and excruciating fifty-five minutes, I was ready to get out of that classroom. Then I went to second period US history with Rosie and Danielle. Next came Algebra II, where I sat next to Connor and another guy named Lenny, who was supposedly Connor's friend and just as interested in me as he was—or at least that was the memento I received from the two. After that, I went through my two electives, ceramics and French III, with Rosie by my side every step of the way. I thought about asking Rosie why she and Laine had such a strange relationship, but I never seemed to find a right time to bring it up.

By the time lunch rolled along, I tried to forget all about Laine and Scarface and tried to enjoy a conversation with the people that I actually knew. This was nonsense, because I'd known them for merely a day. Yet I could sense that these were the people who I would be associating with throughout the year until I served my sentence at Tampa Bay. I couldn't risk my relationship with them by going out of my way to talk to this boy who I knew nothing about except that he had a large scar on his face and that he sat with Laine at lunch.

Besides, I couldn't let the fatal flaw known as my curiosity get in the way of things, as it usually did, but I still couldn't help but wonder about the boy. While other people saw something revolting upon his face, I saw an unread story with a big padlock on it. I was determined to read it, even though it was none of my business and could cause consequences. I would give an arm and a leg if it meant that I got to exchange my big, fat question marks and blanks for answers.

After lunch came the last two academic classes of the day, PE and AP English, and I got to sit out PE because of my wrist. I guess that's the silver lining of having a broken wrist.

AP English was the only class I didn't share with any of my friends, but that didn't mean that it was going to be the class I would dread taking for the rest of the year like I thought it would be, the sole reason being that I sat next to *him*. What made it even better is that I sat on his left, so I would get to see the scar for myself for the first time in real life instead of my dreams.

The English teacher, Mr. Fields, passed out textbooks and walked through classroom procedures most of the period. Since most of us had followed classroom procedures since nursery school, everybody pretty much tuned him out after thirty seconds of the lecture. While he was going on and on about the evils of talking during class, I decided to partake in the thing I had been anticipating the most in the past forty-eight hours.

I was taken in by all his features in one powerful punch. His emerald-green eyes were the very first thing on his face that I noticed. They were filled with all the things I wish I possessed—intellect, courage, and intense determination.

The scar protruded a bit more than it had in my dreams, and from a distance, and it should've repelled me. I tried to take note of the scar and to see the ugly in him, but I couldn't. I was too taken in by his stunning eyes that just seemed to pop out at me like fireworks.

In an instant, his eyes flashed up from the book he was reading and over at me.

"What?" he asked crudely, his voice exactly as pleasing to the ear as it was in my dreams.

My heart started racing as I locked my eyes with his. How could such a simple connection give me such a thrill? I blinked really fast over and over again as his eyes filled with more hatred every passing second that I stared at him.

"Um, nothing," I said, trying to focus my attention on Mr. Fields so that I wouldn't get caught in the act of staring at him again.

"Never seen a scar before, have you?" He continued with the same harsh, ridiculing tone. "Now that you've gotten a good look at one, turn your eyes to the front and don't look back again, or else I'll—"

Mr. Field stopped his lecture and turned toward us. "You'd think that kids wouldn't talk during a lecture about class procedures, but I guess that's the irony of it all. Do you find it ironic, Mr. Spears?"

"Nope, don't find it the least bit ironic," he said with the same annoyance and sarcasm in his tone that he'd used on me. Who talked to a teacher like that? While I thought it was disrespectful, a few of the kids thought it was amusing, and they giggled, which only further displeased Mr. Fields.

"That's the same tone of voice that'll send you to the office." Mr. Fields stood there with his arms crossed, and the class became as quiet as mice rummaging through the fields.

He rolled his eyes and halfheartedly exited the classroom. While most kids were staring at his scar as he walked out, I was assessing his tall, lean, yet muscular frame that I'd mistaken as lanky from afar. As soon as he left, Mr. Fields went on with his lecture about class procedures, and everybody went back to tuning him out.

I, of course, went back to thinking about *him*. What was his story? More importantly, why was I so interested? I thought it was because of my dreams and the scar, but I saw even more things that stood out. In fact, the only trait I could think that didn't stand out like a sore thumb was his rather common last name. A normal last name for an abnormal guy, I figured.

Right before the bell rang for eighth period—study hall—Mr. Fields received a phone call.

"Mr. Fields's room. Hello?" he said cheerfully. "Okay, I'll send her over." He hung up and motioned for me to come up to his desk. *Why me?*

"Is there any trouble?" I asked as innocently as I could.

"None at all. A suitcase just arrived at the office with your name on it. Would you mind going to retrieve it?"

"Not at all, thanks," I said, relieved but feeling dumb for forgetting all about my missing suitcase that I said I'd pick up first thing that morning. I'd forgotten all about it because I was too busy getting caught up in Scarface and Laine's business.

As soon as I entered the office, the first thing I heard was his melodious voice over the ringing of phones and printers coming from the headmaster's office, and I couldn't help but peek inside. He sat in a chair facing the desk, and the only thing I saw was the gold of his hair.

"I'm telling the truth. Some girl kept staring at me, and—" he began in an exasperated tone.

"Yeah, but that's beside the point. Mr. Fields sent you here because you talked back to him," stated Mr. Blake, the portly, balding man who I assumed to be the headmaster.

"More like outsmarted," he argued slyly.

Mr. Blake took a deep, annoyed sigh. "I should've never taken you and that imbecile brother of yours on a scholarship. I heard you were trouble, but I never thought you'd earn a spot in the office on the first day! You are a complete and total nightmare, Jeydon; you have absolutely no respect for your betters."

I winced at the sound of the word *betters,* because it made me think about how Mother used to give Mary the exact same lecture over and over again for all those years. I felt exactly as helpless as I had back then all those years ago when I witnessed all of those awful things that Mother did to Mary. But Mary was my sister; seeing her abused by our own mother as a six-year-old gave me a right to cry, while I'd just found out this boy's first name! Why should I care? Because of the dream? It was a dream, not reality. I had to have boundaries on things like this.

"Well, *maybe* if you showed me some respect, I'd respect you back. What goes around comes around," Jeydon growled.

"Okay, looks like I'll just have to force your respect. As of now, instead of a regular scholarship, you'll be on work scholarship. Have fun with four hours of cafeteria duty a week, and I'll expel your simpleton of a brother once and for all. And if you object, I'll kick your smart behind out, as well."

The snarl of his voice changed to a protective one. "Why would you kick Anthony out? Just because I've done wrong doesn't mean you have to punish my brother."

Mr. Blake laughed the nastiest, most nasal laugh I'd ever heard and said, "You just don't get it, do you? Jeydon, you have a brain like no other, and you still can't figure out that people like you and Dummy don't belong in such a fine institution. You two are tainting this fine facility as we speak. You might as well have been born with half a brain like your brother if you can't figure that out."

Jeydon's raging comeback wasn't words but a mouthful of saliva in Mr. Blake's face, and in one spastic move, Mr. Blake obliterated his coffee mug. A sharp fragment of the mug sliced through his flesh with ease and protruded out of his skin. Mr. Blake's face turned as red as the blood bleeding from his hand.

"Spears! You might as well count yourself expelled, because no amount of cafeteria duty will clean your slate now!"

Without thinking, I walked into the office just as scared as I had been when I'd had to face Mother for the demon she really was.

"What!" Mr. Blake barked when he saw me. "Can't you see I'm in the middle of a discussion?"

"I didn't only see it, I heard it all the way down the hallway."

Jeydon's face became immediately ten shades paler, which I thought wasn't possible.

"Why are you here?" Mr. Blake asked, still aggravated.

"I lost a suitcase, and Mr. Fields sent me down here to get it back."

"The small red one?" he asked, his face lighting up a little.

I nodded, but my eyes stayed on Jeydon. I could tell that he was trying to figure out who I was, and I hoped he wouldn't. But after a matter of seconds, he did.

"Oh yeah, you're the girl in my English class who was staring at me!"

I wore my bravest smile and said, "Yes, I was. Sorry."

"Don't be," Mr. Blake mumbled as he grabbed my suitcase from a shelf of lost items and handed it to me. "In fact, you did me a favor, Miss Hudson. Correct me if I'm wrong." I nodded, and he went on, "Because of you, this boy will be kicked back out on the filthy street where he belongs."

"There must be something he can do to prevent that," I said in a low whisper.

Jeydon looked at me as if I'd insulted him, and I could tell that he would have been more than happy to slap me in the face.

"Why do you care?" Mr. Blake asked, and by the look in Jeydon's eyes, I could tell he was thinking the same thing.

"Because I'm a good person," I reasoned, and at this, Jeydon rolled his eyes and scoffed. *Remind me why I'm helping him again?*

Mr. Blake ignored him. "For him to stay in the school, he'll have to pay two hundred dollars for my medical bill. Of course, he doesn't have that kind of money, but I know for a fact that you do. Honestly, I wouldn't waste good money on him, but I guess you can invest in him to your little heart's content."

I took the two items I'd put in my suitcase that actually had value—the crisp one-hundred-dollar bill that Mother had given me for an emergency right before I left the airport for Tampa Bay and the $175 I had in my savings, and I forked it over to him. I felt bad because that wasn't really my life savings but the remnants of it after I'd gone on a spending splurge with the gang.

After Mr. Blake counted the money, he smiled maniacally. "I believe you are short twenty-five dollars, Miss Hudson."

"He can work it off," I retorted.

Mr. Blake sighed. "Well, what do I have to say? I am a man of my word, but Mr. Spears, you'll have to work cafeteria duty as well until your debt is paid to society. As your first task for Miss Hudson, take her bag up to her room."

"I'm not a bellhop, and I refuse to be, especially to her," Jeydon objected as he put emphasis on the word *her*.

I wanted to pretend like I didn't care that he disrespected me—maybe even loathed me—and tried to tell myself that he would be this way to everyone who helped him out, but who would I fool? I desired nothing more than for this boy to be crazy about me like every other boy was. Why should I care? It's not like we'd end up becoming star-crossed lovers if he did, and I knew very well that if that ever happened, I'd lose favor of my mother, peers, and friends both at Tampa Bay and back at home. Yet his rejection of me was as sharp as a punch to the gut.

And while with any other person I would've let my temper get the best of me, I said, "It's okay; I can get it myself," as mildly as I could.

"You hired him to work for you, let him work. But if you can't stand a sarcastic pain in the rear end, I guess you're out of luck. Now scram, you two. I've got other people I need to see, and daylight's a-wasting."

We walked out of the room, and Jeydon slammed Mr. Blake's own office door in his face.

CHAPTER 10

Pet Peeves

Jeydon and I didn't say anything until we went outside into the Tampa Bay Plaza, which was vacant because school was still in session.

"Is it okay if we sit down here and sort this out?" I asked.

Jeydon scoffed bitterly and replied, "It's not like there's anything to sort out. I'm not going to work for you—end of discussion."

I tried to ignore what he'd said, but it was no use. I made us sit on park bench far enough away so that nobody could see us together if they bothered to pass by, knowing that it would be an end to my social status. Jeydon didn't object, but he made it obvious to me that he didn't care what people thought about him and couldn't care less about how talking to me would affect his social status. I began to think that there was a possibility that he didn't care about anything, and if he did care about something, it definitely wasn't me or my feelings.

"Sorry about staring at you in class," I said as an attempt to break the ice.

"Is that the reason why you saved my butt? Because if it is, don't be. There's nothing to be sorry about. I'm used to it."

With this reply, I foolishly put my guard down a little, thinking that he might want to talk, not realizing that there was still fiery rage in his eyes that would not be extinguished with any number of kind words or deeds.

"It must be hard," I agreed as I tried my best to give him a reassuring smile, but it was hard, because even though it was ninety degrees outside, I was shivering; the very sound of his voice gave me little round goose bumps that seemed to fade with every passing second he was silent. I had never felt this sensation before, not even with Richard. And I wanted more of it. I wanted more of him, even though Mr. Blake was right about him being a pain in the rear end.

He looked at me with anger and disbelief. "Don't pity me. I'd rather you hate me than pity me. We've talked now, so I hope you're satisfied. I'm still not working for you, and I still don't give a crap about what you're going to do about it. Good talk." And at that instant, he got up and walked away.

For a few seconds, I did nothing but stare at his filthy, ratty old Converse sneakers that looked like they were going to fall apart at the seams, counting every step that he took. *Step one, step two, step three, step four, step five, step six, step seven ...*

That was when my senses came to me, and I realized that he was leaving. "Wait!" I yelled a little bit too desperately.

A couple of kids walking past stood there for a few seconds staring at us but then shrugged their shoulders and walked away.

"You've got my attention now, so what more do you want from me?" he asked, letting out a growl just like the one in the office when he'd been arguing intensely with Mr. Blake.

"Jeydon," I began. Just the sound of his name in my mind gave me chills, much more enunciating it. Listening to the sound of his name out loud also gave me goose bumps.

He squinted at me, which made his scar more prominent. That was when I realized that his brilliant eyes were what distracted me from the scar, so the less I saw of his eyes the more I paid attention to the scar, just as any normal person would do.

"How do you know my name?"

"I heard Mr. Blake yell it," I explained, my voice wavering with the nervousness and fear of him not wanting me to know his first name. My obvious fear seemed to only make him angrier.

His already large eyes immediately blew way upscale, and his face grew even paler than it had been in the office. "How much of the conversation did you hear?"

For a second, I was mesmerized at his gems for eyes and wished I had a necklace half as cunning, but then I remembered that staring was rude, and Jeydon probably wouldn't forgive me if he caught me staring at him again.

"More than I should have," I admitted as I looked away from him and down at the brick path of the Plaza. More kids were passing by and looking, but Jeydon was totally oblivious to them. *If only I could be like him and not care what other people think … a lot of the troubles with my reputation as a model or as a person would be solved instantly.*

His face grew a little red, and I could tell that he wanted to punch me in the face. I thought he was going to for a moment, so I flinched and waited for the pain to occur. But all he did is mumble, "This conversation is over." He started walking in the other direction again.

"No, it isn't," I persisted. I tried to grab hold of his arm as he walked away, but he was so much stronger than I was that I didn't have much choice other than to yell louder than I should have. "I command you as my servant to get your butt over here right now, or you can kiss your scholarship good-bye!"

To my surprise, he actually came back to my command like a stubborn mule that had just learned a new trick. "How may I serve you, Miss Hudson?"

"The first thing you can do for me is stop calling me Miss Hudson, because it's my ultimate pet peeve. Call me by my first name, Adrienne. Understood?"

"Understood, Miss Hudson." He emphasized on the words *Miss Hudson* just enough for it to get on my nerves.

I rolled my eyes with agitation. Now I'd found a kid that was even more annoying than Rosie. "I just told you calling me that was my biggest pet peeve!"

"And my biggest pet peeve is you, but from what Mr. Blake says, I guess I'm going to cater to your every need and whim. Life sucks, and your daddy's money can't always buy you what you want. Get over it," he said in the rudest way anybody possibly could.

I stood there in a trance for a moment. Nobody, not even my friends back home, had ever said anything that hurtful to me and meant it, probably because anyone outside the gang would've been eaten alive if they pointed out a flaw in my appearance. But Jeydon was different. He was the first person I'd met who absolutely, positively didn't care what people thought of him. And I envied him because of that, but I had too much pride to admit it just yet.

Those words were like a slap in the face that brought me to what I thought was the bitter reality. Jeydon wasn't like he was in my dreams. In reality, he was the corrupt, broken-faced servant boy from my nightmares.

"Do you have any idea who I am?" I asked through gritted teeth.

"Don't know, don't care. And who do you think you are to think you're so much better than everyone else?"

"You'd better care, or you can kiss that scholarship good-bye!" I threatened loudly, not caring that the eyes of several students who had just been dismissed from class were upon us. "I can't believe I gave up all my savings to save your butt, and you haven't given me a simple thank-you!"

"You don't deserve my gratitude! I don't care what you or Mr. Blake do; I refuse to serve a narcissistic, spoiled little daddy's girl such as you!" he said as he started to walk away again.

"Wait! You have to help me with my bag, remember?" I yelled, but this time when he walked away, he didn't turn back, and there was nothing I could say to make him turn around.

I should've felt a small sense of joy that he, the horrifyingly ugly servant boy from my nightmares, had walked away and was probably out of my life once and for all. But instead, all I felt was even more desolate and empty, because the goose bumps on my forearms had faded along with the sound of his voice. And so when I got to my dormitory, I threw the suitcase that I'd gone through so much trouble to get on the floor, not even bothering to unpack it.

That was Jeydon's job, not mine, and I refused to unpack it, because as long as I was empty, I wanted nothing less than my suitcase to be empty too.

CHAPTER 11

Third Options

During the first two weeks of school, various rumors began circling around at Tampa Bay about Jeydon and me. The main rumor claimed that he'd asked me out and I let him down as easily as I could. That was what I'd told my friends what happened when they asked about the rumors. There were a couple of others that were even more ridiculous, like one that proclaimed that he'd paid me money to have sex with him.

No matter how ridiculous these rumors were, it made both of our lives even harder than they already were.

"What did you expect from Adrienne? She's a porn star, isn't she?" Lenny whispered loudly to Connor during algebra.

"I can hear you," I said as I felt my cheeks grow red from embarrassment and rage.

"And besides, Lenny, that's not what happened. He asked her out, and she said no," Connor explained as he gave me a reassuring wink.

I didn't know what else to do but grin and wink back at him.

Soon after that, a senior named Stacy Silverstein got in a car wreck and suffered minor injuries, so the spotlight turned over to her.

For the first week after our encounter, Jeydon and I were both too flustered about the rumors to give each other a passing glance, and even though I was seeing red from Jeydon's lack of gratitude and the rumors, I still longed for him to say something to me, because I realized that him calling me something as annoying as Miss Hudson was better than him not speaking to me at all.

During the second week, we began talking in seventh period, but our conversations were on the level of "Hello, Miss Hudson" and "How's it going, Scarface?" Yet it still became the highlight of my day, because whenever I got goose bumps from hearing his voice, I forgot how miserable and trapped I was at Tampa Bay with my lousy group of friends and bizarre roommate situation.

During the third week, I finally had my next dream about Jeydon Spears that was significant enough for me to remember. All the others had been a mere blur of our laughter.

We were standing out on a balcony perched above a swimming pool below. I could tell that it was at least ten o'clock at night, because the only light came from the lamps. I could feel the heat radiating from them too, and it was the perfect antidote against the cool breeze. Everything felt so real and natural, like it was reality instead of the illusion that it was.

Jeydon was so close to me that I could feel him breathing warm, steady air on my neck. My hands joined his, and I did what I was too scared to do in reality.

"What's your story?" I asked.

No answer.

He released his grip on my hands and backed up a few feet, so the only connection we made was that his eyes were locking with mine.

"How did you get that scar?" I asked a little bit louder.

He did nothing but stare at me blankly as he did before, like he didn't understand the words coming out of my mouth.

"Why won't you answer me?" I asked in a voice raised up a few decibels.

Still nothing.

He stopped making eye contact with me and stared straight ahead at something. The little color he had in his cheeks vanished, and his spectacular eyes were inflicted with an emotion I didn't think he was capable of feeling. Fear.

"Adrienne! There's a man with a gun behind you!"

I turned around and saw Richard standing there with a gun clenched in his hands. His expression was devious, so unlike the Richard I had come to know. He looked like he was on the edge of borderline insanity, like in an R-rated movie that would traumatize my subconscious mind into where I'd have nightmares for weeks. He pointed the gun directly at me and pulled the trigger.

My eyelids flipped open as fast as lightning, and I was taken into a place no less frightening and cruel than my dream— reality. I expected something extraordinary to happen the day that followed my dream, as I had experienced with my other dreams about Jeydon.

Yet nothing happened. Rosie and Laine had the same bipolar relationship that they'd had the day before. Lunchtime conversations were as cruel as always.

When language arts crept around the corner, I was less than enthusiastic, because although I was still crossing my fingers for something to happen, I knew very well how slim the chances for a miracle were. Jeydon hadn't looked at me, much less spoken a word to me. With the spotlight that was once beaming on us dimmed down about a thousand watts, I figured that we'd both pretend that our brief encounter on the first day of school never happened. We were strangers before, so why couldn't we be strangers now? Because now he was a name I could identify with a face, that's why. All I wanted to do was meet him, and I'd succeeded. So why did I feel like I failed so miserably?

Then it dawned on me. It was because I wanted to know him. No, I *needed* to know him. Call me crazy, but there was something about him that I needed, and I could tell that it wouldn't be the worst thing in the world if he received some assistance from me also.

As soon as I sat down in my seat next to him, I spent a moment sitting there trying to think of the words, trying to arrange them in a perfect order so that he wouldn't think of me as an even bigger brat than he thought I already was.

Yet what was I to say? *Hey, Jeydon, sorry I saved you from getting expelled* or *Sorry you were such a royal pain in the butt*?

What had I done wrong? Jeydon was the one at fault, not me! Then I replayed our conversation in my head and found all the little flaws I failed to recognize before.

The way I'd spoken with arrogance and cockiness when I'd asked, "Do you have any idea who I am?"

The way I'd harshly threatened to report to Mr. Blake more than once.

The way his eyes were inflicted with pain when he said that he'd rather be hated than pitied.

With that thought, it seemed like everything clicked together like the pieces of a puzzle merging as one. He'd rather be hated than pitied! He thought I pitied him because of my kindness and interest toward him, so he did his best to repel me as far away from him as he could. And man, he was good at it! It seemed like he'd done this more than once, possibly with any person who found him fascinating or tried to help him in any way.

Yet there was another large possibility that I was wrong. Maybe he did loathe me as much as he said he did. He did seem like he meant it, or maybe that could be his superb acting. If only the boy were easier to figure out.

With all of these thoughts jumbled up in my noggin, the puzzle that I'd mistaken as complete and perfect crumbled all up into pieces that were even smaller than before.

"Hey, Jeydon," I said like I was on the verge of a nervous breakdown.

He looked up from the book he was reading, and to my surprise, he wasn't suspicious or cranky or sarcastic as I'd thought he'd be—like he always was around me—giving me a little ghost of a smile instead. *Did he really smile at me?* Yes, the corners of his mouth went up just enough to classify it as a smile.

"Hey, Adrienne."

And with that response, I had hope.

* * *

After class ended and Jeydon and I walked out of the classroom separately as we always did, I tried to tell myself that it wasn't a big deal like I was making it out to be. Yet even though I didn't know Jeydon at all, I knew that it had to be a big deal, and there was no use trying to convince the opposite of an instinct my brain and heart both agreed on.

The next day during language arts, I tried not to expect much, but I was still crossing my fingers for yet another miracle.

And it happened.

"Adrienne," he began.

At first, I thought it was me dreaming again. I turned around, startled to see him there talking to me in flesh instead of my mind.

"I'm sorry for all of that stuff I said a few weeks back. I was a little fired up, and I guess I took it out on you."

A little bit? I wanted to say with disbelief, but I didn't because he was talking to me, and that was the important thing. "No, *I'm* sorry. You were right; I was being a spoiled little brat."

"But you *are* a spoiled little brat."

I would've been angry or insulted if any normal person said this to me, but I knew very well this was just Jeydon being Jeydon, so instead I replied, "Yeah, that too."

He seemed a little shocked that I'd kept my cool. "I know you're probably going to say no, but can I please work for you again?"

I nodded a little bit more than enthusiastically. "Of course, but I'd think in three weeks of cafeteria duty, you'd make more than enough money to pay off Mr. Blake."

He scoffed, but not in the mean way that he had a few weeks earlier. "You don't know a thing about working, do you?"

"Guess not. How much have you made, then?"

"Five bucks," he answered.

I studied his face trying to find a hint of sarcasm here and there, but since it was so hard to figure out what he was really thinking, I asked, "You're being serious?"

He nodded. "Mr. Blake isn't exactly what you'd call the most generous guy in the world."

I nodded as if I understood, but he was right. I didn't understand a single thing about the working class.

"I'll try to be, even though I have trouble with being stingy myself," I admitted as I noticed some of the kids around me eavesdropping on us. Didn't they have anything better to do than listen to a conversation that wasn't theirs to hear?

He shook his head. "You've done enough already. I'm not going to sit around and be one of your little charity donations, okay?"

"I don't do charity donations!" I denied hotly.

I guess my sassy denial gave him permission to sass me back.

"Then why did you save my butt? Why did you give up all your savings?"

"Because—" I began.

"You pity me? You felt bad for staring at me even though I said I didn't care and forgave you? Pick one," he interrupted. Obviously, patience wasn't his best quality.

"I'd rather choose the third option."

The bell rang, but Mr. Fields wasn't in the room—probably using his best small talk on the pretty ninth-grade astronomy teacher a little way down the hall again—so I was determined to carry on the conversation despite the shushing of other students.

Jeydon skeptically raised one brow and wordlessly studied me for a moment, probably trying to decide what to think of me. Was he going to shift back to hating me again? Or was he going to try his best to repel me?

"What do you mean?" he asked.

I had no idea what to say to this, even though I'd expected him to ask that. I paused for a few seconds.

"Please just work for me," I ended up pleading, because I didn't know what else to say.

"Fine. I'll work for you on one condition. You tell me what exactly you mean by the third option. Agreed?"

"Agreed," I said immediately, even though I hadn't listened to half of what he'd said. All I paid attention to were the words *condition* and *third option*. That was enough to know what he wanted.

"Miss Hudson and Mr. Spears," Mr. Fields said as he walked into the room. The sound of his booming voice made me jump. "Is there anything you two want to add to the class discussion?"

"Nothing!" I replied as the soft murmuring of disapproving kids plagued my ears.

"I know it wasn't nothing; I could hear you two talking in the hallway."

"Maybe you shouldn't be out of the classroom after the bell rings, or else students have a tendency to talk," Jeydon argued as other students' mouths that were formerly talking trash about his appearance formed a perfect little circle and figured out this wasn't a kid to mess with—if they hadn't figured that out already from a few weeks back.

Everybody expected Mr. Fields to be outraged, and he had a right to be, but instead, he said, "Very well, then," more timidly than I'd ever heard him speak.

For the rest of the period, all we did was go down to the library to read, and nobody, not even Mr. Fields, spoke a single word. I, for one, enjoyed the peace and quiet, because it was a place where I could think.

I found myself sitting on the thick, scratchy carpet with my back against the wooden bookshelf, trying to focus on the book I'd checked out instead of Jeydon. I tried to think about anything other than him. I tried to think about my friends at home, my friends here at Tampa Bay, Richard, Mother, Dad, or anybody else that affected my life. Yet I couldn't, not when Jeydon was in the same room I was. I stood up, peered over the bookshelf, and found Jeydon sitting in a corner with a book in his lap. I couldn't focus on anything else, so why was I wasting time when the one thing I could pay attention to was in the same room as I was? I found myself studying his eyes from afar, which moved back and forth so swiftly that I wondered how they didn't grow fatigued. His eyes shone as he absorbed all the new information from the book, just as they had on the first day of school when I first saw him up close. I recalled how he was reading back then too.

Come to think of it, during the few times our paths had crossed, he'd always had a book of some sort with him. Even when we were bickering out by the Plaza on the first day of school, I recalled him having a novel at hand.

Suddenly, Mr. Blake's voice popped into my head. *You have a mind like no other,* it said. I could be wrong, but I got the vibe that Mr. Blake wasn't one to pass out free compliments—and even if he did, he wouldn't pass a single one out to Jeydon. So that meant only one thing: Jeydon was a lot smarter than what everybody gave him credit for. The radiance of intellect in his eyes said it all, so even without Mr. Blake's words, I was very aware of one thing; Jeydon's IQ was higher than mine would ever be, even if I lived to be a million.

It was just another thing out of the ordinary about him. Yet strangely enough, the more things I found that were out of the ordinary about him, the more I found him alluring.

I had an urge to get up from where I was sitting and go over to join him, but I knew it would be too risky, because I had no clue as to how he was going to react. Still, there was an urge inside me that seemed to never cease, and I finally let it get the better of me. So I stood up, walked over to where Jeydon was sitting, and sat down next to him—but still far enough away so that we weren't touching in any way.

He didn't even notice that I was sitting beside him until the bell rang for eighth period. When he got up and realized that

I was there, I asked, "Can't you go through one week without wising off to a member of faculty?"

"Wise-mouthing is what I'm here for, isn't it?" he said, and I saw a flicker of a smile light up his face for a split second.

I laughed easily for the first time since I don't know when. "No wonder you almost got expelled on the first day of school."

Another ghost of a smile. "It's a good thing I had you to bail me out." He paused, and I could tell that the wheels were turning in his head, trying to figure out what to say next. His voice went down a couple pitches. "Thanks, Adrienne. I really mean it. But you don't have to go through any more trouble to help me out."

"It isn't any trouble, Jeydon. I enjoy it."

"Why? Is helping me out going to earn you a new badge for your Girl Scout sash?"

"No, and I told you why I'm trying to help you out already."

"You didn't even bother to specify what the third option was!" he said with fire in his eyes.

"Fine, I'll tell you," I said with a weary sigh.

All the kids in my study hall were entering the library and eyeing the two of us, but why should I care? If I was going to figure out the mystery that was Jeydon Spears, I had to get used to people eyeing us a bit longer than I wanted. I took a deep breath and began what was going to be difficult, mainly because I didn't know how he was going to react. Was he going to laugh out loud? Get all fired up and spit in my face just as he did to Mr. Blake? Or would he look at me like I was incapable of saying such a thing? I knew I had to put all my childish fears aside and tell him what he so desperately desired to hear.

I took a deep breath and began with a single syllable. "I ..." But then I stood there in silence for a couple of moments, having no idea what to say next. Where were the words? Why couldn't they just perfectly fall into place like they did for Richard and Mother? Because I was to be seen and not heard. It had been that way since I was little, and that wasn't going to magically change now.

I took another deep breath and knew that there was no turning back. Yet to my surprise, the words came in order to me naturally for the first time in my life. "You've completely fascinated me since the first time I saw you, and not because of the scar. It's because of how fearless and daring you are. I think I'll never get to know a person like you again, so why waste the opportunity?"

Jeydon's eyes widened, and I could tell by the look on his face that he was just as shocked as I was that those words had come from somebody like me. "Trust me when I say that you don't want to know me. If you do, it'll be something you'll look back on and regret."

"I already know you well enough, and it isn't something I regret," I said, trying to see if I could fool him in any way.

He scoffed, and I knew that he wasn't the least bit gullible. "You think you know me, but you believe the lie."

"I disagree, but that isn't the biggest concern right now. I've told you what you wanted to hear, so I believe you owe me what I asked for in return."

"You drive a hard bargain," he interrupted comically.

I giggled, which sounded more like a hyena's laugh than that of a sixteen-year-old girl. "Your bargains aren't exactly what they call an easy A, either."

He had no reply except for the traces of a soft yet enchanting laugh that I wanted to hear more of at a much higher volume. He then looked at the clock and was startled at how little time he had to get to his next class. "Meet me out in the Plaza like we did a few weeks ago after class is out, and we'll talk some more."

I nodded and replied, "Sounds great to me. See you there."

CHAPTER 12

Labeling

Even though I would never admit it, the truth was that I couldn't wait, even if I was going to see him again in fifty-five minutes. I stared at him as he walked away, trying not to count the number of steps that he took. I went to my locker, which was relatively close to the library and in the opposite direction that Jeydon was walking, and got everything I needed for study hall.

As I closed the locker door, I was ambushed by the very person I didn't want to talk to. Laine.

"Why are you talking to Jeydon Spears?" she asked, not in the mean, ridiculing way in which everybody else had asked this question but with curiosity and maybe even a bit of concern.

Totally startled, I had no idea what to say. If only the words would've come to me as they had a few minutes earlier, but it was obvious that *that* wouldn't happen, because I replied, "I have no idea what you're talking about."

"Then answer this: why did I hear you say his name the other night in your sleep?" she asked again, obviously not buying into my denial.

If only I were born a better liar, the wheels of my world would have turned so much easier.

My face grew hot, and I felt like I couldn't breathe. Yeah, I was that afraid of my subconscious mind being exposed.

"I need to get to class," I dismissed as I shut my locker door and started to head toward the library.

Before I could run away from her, she grabbed on to my arm with force and pulled me back so where I would have to make eye contact with her again. "I'm going with you, then."

"You aren't even in my study hall!" I exclaimed with irritation as I still failed to get away from her.

She shrugged. "So? I could use a little bit of studying time. I have home economics eighth period, so it's not like I'm missing anything important."

The way she said that hit my nerves in the completely wrong way. Who was she to think she could follow a girl she barely knew to a class she didn't belong in? What made her think she could grab on to my arm and drag me around like I was a pack mule? And of all the people at Tampa Bay, why was I the one she chose to drag around like a rag doll? I was the future of one of the most powerful businesses in the industry! She needed to show me some respect and kiss my butt like everyone else in the school did—with the exception of Jeydon, that is.

I jerked my arm away from her grasp. "Do I have to spell it out for you? I don't want you to go to study hall with me! Maybe if you wouldn't follow people around and grab on to them like they were animals, people wouldn't find you so annoying!"

I expected her to go off to the ladies' restroom with tears in her eyes as she did when Emily went off on her—and I wanted her to—but instead, she rolled her eyes. "You think you're so much better than everybody else, don't you? You know, I didn't want to believe what Jeydon said about you, because I wanted to grasp on to the illusion that you were a good person. I have to share a room with you, after all. Guess it serves me right; ten out of ten times, when Jeydon says something like that about a person, it turns out to be true."

"What did he say about me? And when did you two become best buds?" I asked, trying to keep my cool, but honestly, I wanted to do nothing more than smack her in the face and show her who was the dominant person. However, that would do nothing but prove to the world that I was every bit as awful as she'd said I was.

What Jeydon had said I was.

"You really are clueless about the world, aren't you?" she asked as if I had an IQ of sixty-two.

Of course, I knew that I was supposedly a dunce compared to Jeydon, and I also knew that I was a little bit on the naive side, but I knew everything about how the economy works and how babies are made and all the other things that counted. Who was she to say that I was dumb when she wasn't an Albert Einstein herself? Those had better be Jeydon's words instead of her paraphrasing, or else she would end up headfirst in the nearest garbage can.

"Oh, so he said that about me too, did he?" I bellowed a bit too loudly. "What else did he say? That I'm a mass murderer?"

She narrowed her eyes and said, "Do you want Jeydon's exact words about you? He said, and I quote, 'She's the classic case of a narcissistic little daddy's girl who's as rotten as a three-month-old jug of milk baking out in the sun.' I may be a tad bit over the top, but we both know you're far more despised than I am."

I had no idea what to say to this, so I turned around and hurried to the library, trying to hold back my anger and sting of being rejected again. I didn't care what Laine thought, or at least I told myself that, but there was no way around the fact that I cared deeply about Jeydon's opinion. The realization that he might still loathe me was too sharp and scratchy to be forced down my throat, which was still healing from the idea of Richard and me as a couple.

On the other hand, if Jeydon still loathed me, he would've treated me as he had a few weeks earlier—sarcastic, rude, and just plain mean. I contemplated whether he was pretending to please me, but I knew him well enough to know that if he disliked me, he would treat me as badly as he treated all his other foes, so I was 90 percent sure he liked me now. It was nothing but impossible to find out what was going through his head; even if I dug and dug for the rest of my life, I could never reach the bottom of his mind. So why was I wasting so much time going over the possibilities?

Because I was letting my curiosity get the best of me again, that's why. I found that my curiosity was too potent to fight, and I couldn't concentrate on anything other than Jeydon, but I was used to it, because every single passing day since he entered my life, I couldn't spend five minutes without the thought of him coming to mind.

After class was dismissed, I made a direct line to the Plaza, not even bothering to stop by my locker, even though my bag and all my other necessary things for school were in there. I wasn't thinking about that, however, because I was too busy trying to line the words up in my head half as perfectly as I had earlier in the day.

Although there was a chance that he loathed me, I couldn't help but think that everything Laine had said was nothing but bull crap and that she was trying to get revenge because I was in cahoots with making her cry. Then again, somehow, I knew that couldn't be. Laine and Jeydon sat together at lunch, and I recalled seeing them in the hallway talking more than few times.

When I got to the Plaza and saw Jeydon sitting on the same park bench on which we'd sat during our previous conversation, I saw that Laine was sitting beside him. As soon as he saw me, I put on my most dazzling smile and waved largely in an attempt to annoy her. Mother told me once that the Bible says eye for an eye and tooth for a tooth was the right way to live, after all. As I made my way over to Jeydon, Laine got up and gave me the death stare as we walked past each other.

"So Laine told me that you guys got into a catfight today during last period," Jeydon stated as I sat down next to him.

"You two keep no secrets, do you?" I mumbled, agitated and in a little bit of a panic. I'd just met Jeydon, and if he was friends with Laine, I knew he would choose her side in every argument we'd face.

"We are friends, if you haven't noticed; however, that's beside the point. I'm really intrigued about this fight. So what happened? Did those well-manicured fingernails of yours retract and razor-sharp claws pop out?"

"Ha-ha, so funny." *Heavy sarcasm.* "She asked me why I was talking to you, and the conversation went downhill from there. Why? Is that what she told you?"

He shook his head, and I had a bad feeling about what he was going to say next. "That's not exactly what she said, so no." He broke eye contact with me and looked straight ahead. What was he thinking about? More importantly, what did she tell him?

"What exactly did she tell you, then?" I asked.

He turned his attention back over to me and said, "What she said about you doesn't matter. What matters is that you know this. What she said is nothing against you. Laine likes to test people. It's just her nature and the way she deals with a lot of things, meeting new people being one of them."

A sigh of relief escaped my mouth. "Sounds like somebody else I know," I teased with a smile.

He chuckled a quiet, musical laughter that I'd already fallen in love with. "So what do I have to do first? And just so you know, there are going to be boundaries. I'm not going to paint your bathtub pink or give your hamster a deep-tissue massage. I may be your worker, but I refuse to be your slave. Understood?"

I laughed and nodded. "Yeah, because that was definitely what I was going to ask you to do for me."

He shrugged. "Hey, you never know." The casual expression in his eyes changed to a playful one. "So tell me, Miss Hudson, what will your first wish be?"

My first wish was for him to stop calling me Miss Hudson. I could tell that he was amused at my choice. "Done. Next request?"

I thought about what I was going to have him do, and after a couple of moments, it became clear what my first request would be. "You know how when I first met you in the office, I was sent to retrieve a bag?"

He contemplated this for a second and then nodded. "Yeah, I think I remember Mr. Blake handing you a bag. Why?"

"Because I haven't unpacked it yet and was wondering if you could unpack it."

He stared at me blankly. "Do you hate unpacking with a passion, or are you a gold medalist when it comes to procrastination?"

I shook my head. "No, I don't really mind it that much—unpacking, I mean. And I'm not that much of a procrastinator, believe it or not. I was just waiting for you to unpack it for me," I confessed.

"I guess unpacking your bag is better than giving you a piggyback ride—which, by the way, is also off limits," he said with an unexcited sigh but a hint of smile in his eyes.

"It's official. You're the worst servant in the history of mankind."

"That's bad news for you, because now you're stuck with me."

I shook my head. "It's even worse news for you, because *you're* stuck with *me.* I'm the narcissistic, spoiled-rotten daddy's girl, remember?"

He rolled his eyes. "Laine told you I said that, didn't she?"

I nodded, and he continued to talk. "I said that a few weeks ago, after we had that argument, and like I said before, I was really fired up. However, don't get me wrong. I'm not really guilty that I said those things about you."

"Why?"

"Because it was true; it still is true. You are a narcissist, a spoiled little brat, even. Yet while most people only see that side of you, I've learned to see past the simple, one-sided judgment and see who the person really is, the whole picture. And with a little bit of work—well, I'm not going to lie ... a *lot* of work—the overall picture will be beautiful. I was just too enraged to see that little glimpse of beauty within you until yesterday."

"What are you talking about? I already am beautiful," I retorted, trying to tell myself over and over again that what he'd just said was wrong. But he was never wrong.

He sighed as if to say, *I knew you wouldn't understand,* and it made me blush a little, because I sounded so stupid saying that. "You know what kind of beauty I'm talking about." He paused as if he'd lost his train of thought. "Whatever. You can disregard what I just said if you want, but all I ask you to do is to think about it."

"I will," I promised as I turned around and eyed the ladies' dorm. "Come on; let's go unpack that bag."

The walk to my dorm room was rather short and sweet, even though eyes were still among us. However, if Jeydon was oblivious, then I could learn to not care, either. Also, people weren't staring just because we were a swan and an ugly duckling walking side by side, conversing like two people on the same step of the social ladder would; Tampa Bay had strict rules about everything that involved males and females interacting, and even though boys weren't prohibited from the girls' dorm rooms until seven o'clock, boys were seldom seen around. A sole Y chromosome floating among all those X chromosomes wasn't something to ignore.

"I told you they were a thing, but nobody listens to me, do they?" I heard a girl with dot-to-dot freckles named Christy say a little bit too loudly to her friend whose name I can't remember.

"Well, what can I say? It's not like too many supermodels go out with guys who have gigantic, hideous scars on their faces," her friend said.

All I could remember about her was that she had one of the largest noses I'd ever seen, and to make it even uglier, it was twisted upright like a hog's. Compared to her snout, his scar was a minor imperfection at most.

I turned around and gave her my most fiendish you're-dead-to-me look, and when she didn't return my gaze, I wanted to go up and give her an extensive speech about how she needed to shut her mouth and then use the force of my fist on her deformed proboscis if my words didn't work. Getting into a fight wouldn't be the worst thing on my permanent record, considering that

I had already gotten arrested, and from what Lenny said, everybody already thought of me as a stuck-up ho, so I had no reputation to ruin.

Luckily, before I had the chance to ambush her, Jeydon tapped me lightly on the shoulder. "What's the holdup? Thinking about starting another catfight?"

"It's nothing you should be concerned about," I mumbled as I looked down at his feet.

While my shoes were name-brand sky-high stilettos that probably were worth more than Jeydon's entire wardrobe, his shoes were about as ragtag as the rest of him was. No wonder all the other kids were pointing, staring, dry-heaving, and possibly laughing behind closed doors. Even things as pointless as my shoes were better looking than his. Everything about me was better, so what did I see in him?

"It's okay; sometimes I want to jack slap them too. I hate nosy, ignorant, judgmental people; they're my largest pet peeve besides cafeteria duty," I heard him say. I didn't know if he was talking to me or not, but who else would he be talking to?

As soon as I looked into his eyes, I had an instant reality check that he was my equal. No, I knew for a fact he was a much better person than I was. "I thought your biggest pet peeve was me."

He shrugged. "Things change."

At this response, I couldn't do anything but smile ear to ear until my cheeks started to sting. I didn't care what people thought for a moment, because I was happy. Because of him. And no amount of ridicule or judgment could take that away from me.

CHAPTER 13

Hope

"Welcome to Casa de Hudson!" I announced cheerfully as we walked into my room.

The room was cluttered, just as it had been when I'd left for breakfast that morning. My two bipolar roommates were nowhere in sight, and at that recognition, I felt a wave of relief trail down my spine. I didn't want to deal with Laine at that moment—or ever—and if Rosie knew he was in our room, she would have cowered as if she'd seen a ghost.

He laughed in a know-it-all sort of way. "I think your Spanish is a bit off. I recommend doing some extra credit work, or you could buy some flash cards that are meant for preschoolers."

"I don't have to do, either, because I don't take Spanish. I'm taking French," I informed him.

"Why? Does taking French class give you an excuse for not knowing the proper Spanish vocabulary?" he asked.

"No," I objected as I tried to muffle a laugh. "I took it my freshman year because I liked french fries and french toast. Then I took it the following year, but only because I'm a creature of habit and couldn't find anything else better to invest my time in. And here I am, the only hot junior alive taking French."

He crinkled his nose as soon as I said the word *hot*, and I realized that I'd said something wrong once again without noticing it until the damage was done. "Sorry, I'm being narcissistic again."

"It's okay, but from now on, I'm going to have to attach an electric collar to your neck and shock you every time you say something like that about yourself." He smirked fiendishly at the thought.

I laughed at the thought of me wearing a tacky spiked collar and sporting a frizz head. "It would be a great plan as long as I get to shock you once in a while for calling my bluff and pointing out the wrongs of others. Mr. Perfect isn't so perfect once you get to know him, if you know what I mean."

Instead of laughing and joking around some more, he became completely solemn. "People have been calling my bluff my whole life, even before they get to know me as a person instead of an unforgettable face. If people can make assumptions about who I am, then I can make assumptions about them. The difference is that I'm almost always correct about how awful they are, while everybody who accuses me of a wrong isn't even close to finding the truth about me."

I stood there speechless for a moment, replaying his most recent words through my head. In a way, I knew exactly how sharp the pain of being misunderstood felt. In another way, I was completely foreign to the feeling, but only because I'd never noticed it was there even though it always had been.

Young, cute waiters checking on my table a tad bit too often ... boys staring at me as I passed them in the hallway ... girls—including my sisters—murmuring in low whispers when I'd walk into the room ... I had completely ignored the feeling all my life, because I was just so used to it. Jeydon's words finally helped me to understand what Leah had said to me that night after I'd won the Anticipation. While I'd thought I was being ignored, I was the shiny new toy that every kid wanted.

I was blind in that matter, and until Jeydon cleared my foggy vision like some miracle worker, I always had been.

Then I felt an enormous wave of sympathy for Jeydon. I wanted to call it empathy, but I never would be able to call it that and be correct, because while everybody approved of or was in envy of my beauty, everybody looked down on Jeydon and thought of him as a lesser person as a result of his appearance. I couldn't imagine walking in his shoes, having to hear your flaws pointed out every day as if you didn't already see them, people constantly talking about how disgusting you were when they didn't even know your first name.

As upset as I'd been when all the lowlifes at my table were gagging and carrying on about how awful looking Jeydon was before I'd met him, now that I had begun to see his inner beauty, all I wanted to do was to scream and yell and kick people in the face hard enough so that they could see how bad it feels to be made fun of for something you can't help. I'd kick them on the left cheek, too, so Jeydon and the unfortunate victim would match perfectly.

Yet if Jeydon could let the unceasing mocking be, then why couldn't I? He was the one being badgered, after all, and I was nothing but the bystander who didn't want to stay silent. That was only one of the many missing pieces of the puzzle that was Jeydon. Did he not care what people thought of him, or did he simply not show his hurt feelings? Why would I even think a question like that? I felt like slapping myself. He obviously didn't care. He even said it himself. I didn't know what to say. I didn't want to say anything that would make me sound like I had any sort of sympathy, because I remembered one of the first things he'd said to me was that he'd rather be hated than pitied.

"How do you see me now?" I asked intuitively. "Everybody's always seen me as a goddess instead of a human being. I've not noticed it until you pointed it out, and now that I'm noticing how people look at me, I want a different opinion for once. I want to know your full opinion about who you think I am. You say that you can see the whole picture, so what do you see?"

He looked at me with an expression I could only read as mixed emotions. "You really want to know?"

I nodded eagerly, sat on my bed, and gestured him to sit down beside me. I made sure that we were far enough apart for his comfort, not just because of an illusion my subconscious mind created but because I already cared about him more than anyone else in my life.

He looked straight ahead and appeared to be focusing on the wall. "You know how I said my first assumptions are almost always right? There's only one label I've put on a person that hasn't lived up to its standards, and that's yours."

He turned his head toward me, and I felt chills all over. "I completely wrote you off as this horrible person not only because of how you handled yourself in the office and the situation with Laine but because of all the times you stared at me. I don't know why, but for some reason, your gaze stood out among all the others. I guess it was because it was one of fascination—admiration, almost. I tried to make it out as a bad thing, because I'd never seen any look of that sort before and didn't know how to take it."

I waited a few seconds to make sure that he didn't have anything more to add and then replied, "When I was staring at you, I wasn't staring at your scar. In fact, I wonder why so many people fuss about it. I was staring at your eyes. They're so beautiful, unlike anything I'd ever seen. I may have a treasure chest when it comes to jewelry, but I would kill to have a pair of earrings half as dazzling." It felt as if a fifty-pound weight had been lifted off my chest after sharing that with him.

His eyes widened, and he sighed, but I couldn't tell if it was out of relief or exasperation. "I don't know whether to believe you or not. I still don't know if you're just trying to make me feel better about myself. If you are, I have no problems with insecurity or self-esteem. I'm perfectly fine with the way I look."

"You didn't need to tell me that; I could already figure out on my own that you had no issues of that sort. And I admire you for that." I paused and took a deep breath. "Just so you know, you can believe anything I say, especially when I say that your scar doesn't bother me at all. I'm a genuine person, or at least I try to be. Most of the time, it's too hard, though."

I noticed how Jeydon's eyes seemed to twinkle a bit after I'd said that, and I felt a sensation in my stomach I'd only occasionally felt before. Compassion. I began to love the feeling as I loved all the other feelings Jeydon had given me, like the goose bumps on the arms and the shivers that went up my spinal cord and throughout my body.

It was all so unlike anything I felt with Richard, which was nothing but vacancy and a large void ... a desolate depression that only Jeydon could fill up. Maybe I was right to want his companionship instead of Richard's. I knew without a doubt that I was right to want his companionship over that of my so-called friends'.

He nodded slowly. "You're being genuine now, so apparently it's not as hard as you think it is."

"You have no idea," I whispered.

He shook his head. "I think I have a pretty good idea of who you are as a person."

"You just met me!" *More sassy talk,* I felt like adding after that, but all that would have done was make me sound like a giant dork.

This time he didn't sass back but used logical reasoning. "Yeah, but like I said before, my assumptions are almost always 100 percent accurate."

I attempted his approach, as well. "*Almost* being the keyword. The first label you put on me was invalid, so how do you know that your current assumption isn't every bit as wrong as the first one was?"

"My first label was only partially wrong, because we both know you are what I thought you were, and the only area where I was at fault was that I thought you had no hope. And you do have a little bit of hope buried somewhere deep inside."

"I think I feel the same way about you in that aspect," I reasoned, thinking about how much trouble he could be if he put his mind to it. "I can't help but wonder if there's a little bit of hope in everybody."

He scowled. "Not everybody has hope. In fact, there are very few people that do, because most are stupid enough to waste their hope."

I looked down at the dingy gray carpet of the dorm room. "I thought I'd burned up all my hope when I went to a party with alcohol and got busted, but apparently not."

He looked at me with fascination.

"That's how I got here," I continued, asking myself over and over again why I was sharing this information with him. "My mother made me come here as a punishment after finding out that this hellhole was basically a boot camp."

He shook his head. "It's actually not that bad if you stay out of Mr. Blake's line of vision. Way better than some of the other places I've been."

"Where exactly have you been?" I asked dumbly.

"A little bit of everywhere. Since we're on the subject, where have *you* been?" he asked, clearly trying to push the topic on my dreary life instead of his.

I decided to go ahead and give him more information about my life, only because I didn't have enough energy to argue with him.

"I've lived in Brooklyn my whole life," I said just a decibel above a whisper. "I'd only been outside the city limits a handful of times until I started modeling. This is kind of a new experience for me. Being away from home so long, you know?"

He crinkled his nose. "Why did your mom pick a boarding school so far away from home? Were all the boot camps in New York occupied? Or did she stick you in a place far away so she couldn't hear you crying?"

I considered his logic. I had never thought of my punishment like that. I thought back to when she'd cried as we said our farewells at the airport and for a second felt as if the mother who beat her own daughter right in front of her other one actually gave a crap. I had a reality check and went back to when I was crying over my degrading encounter with the law and harsh punishment. She was oblivious to my crying when I was under the same roof as she was, so why would she care about me now when I was thousands of miles away?

Then I lingered on what I'd said about Brooklyn being all that I knew, and I realized what Jeydon was talking about. She'd wanted nothing more than to get rid of me because I was such a disgrace to her. I'd lost the stamp of approval I had desperately strived for, just as I feared. She wasn't crying because she was being parted from her daughter but because I was a shame to her.

No. Mother never cried, and she wasn't going to because of me, even if I was her daughter that would continue our dynasty. She was probably laughing as I shrieked my silent screams and cried my invisible tears.

Maybe she didn't even notice, because these were things only Jeydon seemed to notice. I thought I'd cleverly disguised my pain, but it was clear that he could see right through the concealing smile I'd managed to fool everyone else with. But it was obvious that he didn't belong in the same category that everybody else fell under.

Assuming that he knew what an awful person my mother was by the little information I gave away, I wanted to tell him so badly about all of the horrible things she had done to my sisters and me over the years. But I knew that I shouldn't, because I'd only just met him. I shouldn't tell him about my life story just yet, even if he already had the pieces to the puzzle that was me well figured out.

If only it were as easy for me to figure him out. I looked down at the floor, thinking about what to say to him without revealing my mother for the corrupt being she was.

Jeydon looked at my wrist, which was still recovering and wrapped in a layer of gauze thicker than the ozone layer. "She did that to your wrist, didn't she?"

The sound of his voice scared the living daylights out of me, but his words scared me even more. "What? No! She'd never do that to me."

He shook his head. "Denying it like that just proves that I'm right."

I started to get defensive. "I'm serious; my mother would never touch me, and I can prove it. Hand me my bag."

He gave me a weird look. "How does your bag have anything to do with your wrist?"

"You'll see."

He rolled his eyes but then went to retrieve my bag for me without a single complaint. When he handed me my bag, I opened it and dug around until I found the evidence I needed to prove that my mother was innocent.

I held up the macaroni frame that cost me a broken hand in the air and showed it off. "See? I told you Mother isn't abusive!"

He must've thought that I'd gone insane. "Adrienne, that's nothing more than a picture frame, if you haven't noticed. It isn't evidence against the fact that your mother abuses the human beings that she created in the first place."

"Look closer." I handed him the frame, and he studied it with one eyebrow slightly arched. After letting him analyze it for a few seconds, I said, "Now do you see what I'm talking about?"

His uneasy expression still didn't change. "Punching through a photograph as thin as a piece of paper doesn't break your hand unless you've been soaking all your bones in vinegar for the past sixteen years."

"Not when you manage to punch a hole through the wall behind it too." When he asked why I'd done such a brainless thing, I replied, "I punched the wall after my mother told me that I was going to be shipped out to Tampa Bay. I was so mad at her, and that picture frame contained a photo of her, so I obliterated both the picture and the wall ... not to mention the bones in my hand."

While I was saying that to him, I noticed that he was rummaging through my bag, "What's up with all the random photographs? Do you have a problem with hoarding?"

I blushed a little, knowing he'd caught me red-handed. "They aren't random photographs. They're pictures of everybody back at home. I just couldn't leave without a little bit of remembrance of them, you know?"

He shook his head as he went back to sorting through the pictures. "No, I *don't* know. I don't have a family, much less anything to remember them by."

I squinted at him. "Don't you have a brother?" I asked as I grabbed a stack of photographs and helped him sort them out.

He nodded as he continued sorting photos out. "Yeah, but he's in the same grade that we are, so I have a tendency to think of him as a friend instead of a relative."

"I wish I had a relationship like that with one of my sisters. I guess I kind of do with my sister Angela, but only because we shared a room back at home." I paused and said something that I knew I'd regret. "My older sisters hate me. They can't stand to be around me and talk crap about me whenever I walk out of the room."

Why was I telling this boy I knew nothing about things I'd never had the nerve to tell Richard? I wanted to say that it was because of my dreams about him, but if I did, it would be an obvious lie.

There was just something about him that made it impossible to lie to him. I couldn't, anyway, because I was a horrible liar and could never fool anyone, much less someone as perceptive as Jeydon. I expected him to say something—possibly one of his witty, sarcastic remarks—but he didn't for a couple of minutes. Instead, he looked through the photographs and studied all the unfamiliar faces of girls who were a whole other world away.

"Exactly how many sisters do you have?" he finally asked, still looking down at the photos instead of making eye contact.

"Five. Do you want me to show you who's who?"

He nodded without looking up, and I pointed out which face belonged to which girl and even found myself going into detail about who they were, chattering away about how Leah's eyes shone in the sunlight, Amelia's tendency to make me crack up even when I was on the verge of an emotional breakdown, and Angela's energy that never seemed to die. I expected Jeydon to tell me that he didn't care, like all of my other "friends" would have, but he listened thoughtfully and didn't speak a single word. That only proved to me even more how unpredictable he was and that he had a much better heart than everybody gave him credit for.

He remained silent until I presented him what I thought was a picture of my mother and I standing on a pier in Myrtle Beach when I was in first grade, but instead, I gave him a picture of Mary taken when she was in sixth grade, about the same time Mother went to court after being rightly accused of abusing her children. I didn't tell him about what was up with all her bruises—for that would only bring attention to me—but I held my breath as he held the picture up to his face, crossing my fingers that he wouldn't notice the obvious bruises all over her body.

Then again, in a fair share of family photographs, my sisters were covered head to toe with bruises, and he didn't say anything, so he couldn't be as perceptive as I'd thought he was. Or maybe he'd already figured out about the deep, dark secret my mother failed to hide but nobody brought attention to just by looking at a couple of photographs.

But he could tell who I was just because I gave him a couple of meaningless clues here and there. He could tell how corrupt people were by giving them a passing glance. He had to be holding his tongue on my behalf.

He took one last look at the picture and then looked up at me, his eyes full of sympathy. He spoke in a soft, soothing voice that almost sounded like a beloved childhood lullaby.

"Listen, Adrienne, you don't have to lie to me. You know how I said I could see the whole picture? Well, I figured you had some sort of emotional burden you're carrying and that you put on a brave face for the cameras and nosy kids while you are silently screaming for help. That's why I kind of hesitated telling you when you asked. I want to believe that you aren't, but now there's no other way around it. Whatever you do, don't lie to me. I can tell when somebody's lying, especially when it's somebody as open as you."

I looked down for a moment and looked back up again. There wasn't any other option than to tell him, especially now that my cover was blown—Mother's cover, that is. But where would I begin? It was a subject that I didn't even bring up around Richard! In fact, the only time I'd ever spoken of it with somebody else was with Leah when she'd driven me home that night, and even then, I didn't go into full detail of what I'd seen that day so many years earlier. I didn't know how to tell somebody about that day, considering that it was one of those things that was supposed to be forgotten and was just as forbidden at dinner table conversations as the topic of Aunt Margaret. Everybody had some kind of baggage or secrets they had to haul around for the rest of their lives—secrets they couldn't share to protect the people they loved from heartbreak, like how some married men slept around with women when their wives left for vacation or teenagers who hid secret stashes of vodka in their sock drawers.

Honestly, I'd never thought that I'd talk to anybody about it, even if the burden grew so heavy that it slowly ate me alive. Yet here I was, attending a strict boarding school worlds away from home, telling things I've never told anybody else to a bizarre boy with gems for eyes and snowflakes for skin and a scar that no one else could bear to look at.

I felt tears form, but I held them back, because I didn't know how he'd react if I did start crying. "I've never been hit by her in my life. My sisters are the ones abused verbally and physically every single day of their lives. That's why they all hate me so much." "Why?" he asked with a voice as soft as velvet.

"Because I'm so much better than my sisters—in my mother's eyes, at least. I'm the heir to my family's business while my sisters won't get a single dime of inheritance." I paused, knowing that a change in subject was a good idea. "So that's a glimpse of my dreary life. Tell me a little bit about you."

He looked down but smiled a little. "There's not that much for me to tell you."

I shook my head and squinted at him. "Come on, Jeydon, we both know that's an obvious lie! Every single little detail about you is so intriguing—the way your eyes shine, the way you handle situations, the way you speak with so much intellect. I can go on and on."

"The point being?" he asked, obviously agitated.

"The point is that there are so many things for you to tell me ... things that I am dying to learn about you. I told you a little about myself, anyway, so you should tell me a little bit about you now."

"That depends. What do you want to know?"

I thought for a while, trying to think of a question worthy of asking. Then as soon as I started thinking on the topic of family questions, I knew what I was going to ask. "You said that you have no family besides Anthony. So what happened?"

His face grew the slightest shade of pink, and I knew that was a hot spot. "That's none of your business!"

It was finally time to get sassy again "It was none of your business that my mother abused my sisters, either, but you asked me, and I was honest about it."

I guessed that he'd totally ditched the sassy act, because he'd figured out that logic worked better on me. What could I say? I was a sucker for logic.

"That's different. I had a clue as to what was going on. You, on the other hand, have not in the slightest idea what's going on in my head as we speak."

"That is why you'll have to tell me! We all can't be as perceptive as you are!" I replied with a hint of frustration. "And by the way, I've not told anyone that my sisters have been abused, so you should tell me something you'd normally not tell anyone else. Like you said to Mr. Blake in the office, 'What goes around comes around.'"

His eyes widened in surprise. "Really? No one?"

I nodded, and he went on, "Don't get me wrong. I'm glad you told me, but of all the people you could tell, why did you tell me? It was only because I'd already figured it out without you needing to tell me, wasn't it?"

I shook my head. "You're wrong again. I don't know exactly what it is about you that made me confess, but I know it's not because of your borderline psychic ability to read people. If you were anyone else but still made assumptions, I'd deny it to my wit's end. I can't quite put my finger on it, there's just something about you that's ... different."

He nodded. "I know this is not what you asked me to say, however, I think it counts as information about who I am. There's something different about you too that's so unique that I can't ignore it. If you were anyone else, I'd have no problem attempting to shut you completely out of my life, but I can't, no matter how hard I try. This is a first for me, but I've given up on trying tremendously to force you out of my life."

I was at first shocked, but after that came joy. I felt as if I'd won a war—and, in a way, I had.

Jeydon finished unpacking all the contents of my bag, and we said our farewells. But as he headed out, I felt twenty times more fulfilled than I'd ever felt in my life, and I wondered what exactly that feeling meant.

CHAPTER 14

Betrayal

I couldn't sleep that night. I tried to toss around, hoping that my energy would eventually burn out, but after I don't know how long, I figured out that getting my heart racing wouldn't get me sleeping anytime soon. I tried to find a position where I was comfortable, but every position in which I lay down felt as if gravel had been stuffed into my mattress. I even considered reading, which was something I did very rarely, but I knew that Mrs. Kelli would have a cow if she discovered that I'd turned on my desk lamp to read.

Since I grew very tired but still couldn't find a way to shut my mind off, I decided to be productive at that hour. I turned on my laptop and got onto my e-mail account, which I hadn't checked in at least two weeks. There are a number of excuses I could make as to why I didn't get on it regularly, all my loved ones being so far away and all, but the only one that was legit was that I was too busy obsessing over Jeydon and forgot completely about Richard and then after about a week was too afraid that Richard would be angry at me for not contacting him—just like how he should've been angry about me leaving him after he's said that he loved me.

As I skimmed through my inbox on my laptop, I noticed two e-mails—one from Richard and one from Mother. I clicked on the one from Mother first, knowing that she wouldn't send me a message unless it was something urgent. She was always on the move and had too little free time to sit around messaging people, even if they were her own flesh and blood.

> I forgot to tell you that I scheduled an appointment for your wrist on Thursday at Palm Springs Medical Clinic at 8:30 a.m. I've already informed your first-period teacher and the headmaster that you'll be absent, and the headmaster said that some boy named Jeydon in your chemistry class will bring your homework for you. Love you.

I went ahead and absentmindedly typed in "Thanks, Mother! Love you too." Then I pressed Enter to send it. After an icon popped up verifying that I'd sent the message, I went on to click Richard's older message.

I hesitated reading it for a second, because in the three weeks that I'd been at Tampa Bay, I hadn't bothered to message him once, even though I'd promised that I would message him with regular updates no less than once a week. I thought about messaging him sometimes, usually whenever I wasn't thinking about Jeydon, but I told myself that he'd message me.

I'd even gone as far as to type up a handful of drafts a couple of times, but I never sent them, because I couldn't think of anything good to say that didn't involve Jeydon. I had an urge to tell him about my roommate situation and complain about my awful new friends, but I reminded myself that whenever something was going wrong, Richard always wanted to fix it, and he became discouraged if there was nothing he could do.

Even though we'd grown apart, the last thing I wanted to do was discourage him, especially after how he was still so good to me even though I'd done so much wrong to him. The question I wanted to ask him was why he hadn't e-mailed me more than once. Was he waiting for me to e-mail him as I was waiting for him to e-mail me? Was he angry because I'd broken my promise to keep in touch with him? If he was mad at me, he had a right to be, because I was in the wrong, as I always was. And I wouldn't be shocked if he was mad at me, either. I hastily read the message and winced at every kind and loving word I read.

September 17, 2014

Adrienne,

Miss me already? I already miss you, even though it's only been two weeks without you. I guess it's going to be a pretty long, sad year for me, considering the past few days have felt like a millennia. Oh well, enough of the pity party. I don't want you to waste your time and energy feeling sorry for me.

Besides, I am dying to know all about how life at Tampa Bay is working out for you. Who are your new friends, and what are they like? Whoever they are, they'd better be a tad bit more decent than the gang, or at least I hope so. If, God forbid, you aren't fitting in because you're too gorgeous for all the other girls to handle, remember that I'm here for you and always will be. You might find it hard to believe because I'm so far away, but please remember me if you ever feel alone or forgotten. Remember the day of the Anticipation right before the event, the kiss we shared. Feel free to call me whenever you need me, considering I'll have nothing better to do than sing the blues until you come home.

I know I'm asking a lot, but promise me that no matter how much fun you're having with your new friends, you won't forget me, because that's my biggest fear.

I love you,

Richard

After reading his message, I sprang up and rushed over to my phone. Even though it was late, I was sure that Richard wouldn't care. Like he said in the e-mail, he didn't have anything better to do at that hour except for sleeping, and that wasn't very important considering that he had already spent a full one-third of his life in bed, anyway.

I knew him well enough to know that he'd put me before a good night's rest. I dialed in his number fairly quickly, and as it started ringing, I thought about how lucky I was to have such a good friend. I rolled my eyes at my flawed thought process. *He's your boyfriend, not just your friend! Get it right!* I rhetorically told myself, even though I knew that if it were up to me, he'd be nothing but a good friend—my *best* friend, the kind who ate glue with me and played hide-and-seek on the jungle gym when we were kids.

The kind of friends we used to be.

Maybe one day, if I was lucky enough, we could have that same friendship again.

Yeah, right, like that will ever happen, I thought as I reminded myself again about our current relationship.

It took about three rings before he picked the phone up, but I didn't think anything about it. I knew for a fact that he was a deep sleeper from the naps we'd taken together when we were little.

"Hello?" Richard asked groggily as he answered the phone. I could picture him sitting up in his bed with some major bed head, and I smiled at the image.

"Hey," I greeted cheerfully. "Sorry for not e-mailing you like I promised and randomly waking you up in the middle of the night, but I've got to tell you some stuff."

"It's okay," he answered forgivingly, sounding more alert. The tone in his voice turned into an uneasy one. "Listen, Adrienne, right now's not a good time to talk. Can we talk tomorrow or something? I need to get back to bed; I've got a … test I have to take tomorrow."

I wrinkled my brow in confusion. "Since when are you so studious?"

"I'm trying to get a scholarship. Got to go. Talk to you later."

Even more confusion troubled me as I wondered why he was acting so odd. His parents weren't nearly as rich as mine, but they could still well afford to send Richard off to an outstanding college, even though—like me—he wasn't the sharpest knife in the drawer.

"What's really going on here?" I asked accusingly.

"Nothing!" he denied with a hint of panic.

What was he up to? What was happening at three o'clock in the morning that was so important that he was trying to skip out on my phone call?

That was when I heard a very familiar voice that wasn't his ask, "Baby, what are you doing up? Come back to bed; I'm keeping it warm just for you. You don't want all my kindness to go to waste, do you?" the girl purred with lust.

I felt as if I'd been electrocuted, because I knew exactly who the voice belonged to.

Tori, my "best friend."

"Tori! What are you doing there?" I yelled, forgetting about how I was supposed to keep a low profile to keep Mrs. Kelli from kicking me out. Tears started forming in the corners of my eyes. I was seeing red, and what I was mad at most of all was that I wasn't there in person so that I could kick him straight where it hurt him the most. All I wanted to do was hurt him like he'd just hurt me.

"It's not what you think!" Richard assured loudly, I think to the both of us.

I had a dozen curse words on the very tip of my tongue that I was more than eager to say to the both of them.

I could picture Tori's awful face as she said, "Are you talking to *Adrienne*? Baby, I can't believe you're still in love with that stuck-up whore! You know what? There are twenty other guys going after me that are ten times hotter than you, so you can have her, you jerk! Whore and jerk sitting in a tree. K-i-s-s-i—"

"Shut up, Tori! Nobody ever listens to a single word you say, so there's no point in it!" I screamed at the top of my lungs as gallons of tears began pouring down my cheeks. Despite the soggy situation, I went on with my rampage. "Well, it's true! You act like you're all that, but everybody knows that all you are is an insecure, lonely girl who's jealous of me because I'm the one who gets all the boys and attention and compliments on my body! I'm better than you when it comes to appearances, Tori, so get over it, and get a life!"

Tori called me the one word no girl ever wants to be called, and judging by her big heavy footsteps, I think she exited the room, which left Richard and me.

"A jerk's looking very good right now compared to you! How could you do this to me? And with *her,* of all people! Who else have you slept with while I've been away? My mother?"

"Adrienne, please. At least try to understand," he pleaded as he started crying, which only added more fuel to the furnace of my fiery rage.

I scoffed in disbelief at what I was hearing. Had he completely lost his mind? "What is there to understand? We're over, and I don't care if my mother will punish me to the extremes to get us back together! You could go outside and hang yourself for all I care! In fact, go ahead and do that, because everybody knows you are nothing without me! So go out and do us all a favor by removing yourself from this world, and never, *never* even think about talking to me again!" I called him every single curse word

I could think of before finally hanging up and throwing my phone across the room.

I heard footsteps and a knock on the door and immediately got into my bed, making sure not to face the door where Mrs. Kelli could see my tears if she peeked in to make sure that somebody hadn't been murdered. I heard the door creak open, and a bit of light seeped into the room, but after a moment, she closed the door and went back to bed.

I lay awake with my head on my pillow, weeping intensely and trying to get over the initial shock of what had just happened. I thought back to all the foolish things I had been thinking when I was waiting for him to pick the phone up. Was it really only a few minutes ago? I went all over the pitch-black room and felt for my phone. When I finally found it, I went through all my recent calls and found out that our conversation had only been three minutes and fifty-seven seconds long.

Three minutes and fifty-seven seconds in hell.

I sat and stared at the phone, crying so loudly that I was surprised that Mrs. Kelli hadn't come back in again to check on me. About fifteen minutes later and after some more nonstop crying, I heard footsteps again.

Oh, well, I thought as I shrugged my shoulders. *It's not like getting one extra detention would make things any more hellish than it already is.*

But the person who walked through the door wasn't Mrs. Kelli. It wasn't any member of authority, in fact. It wasn't even another concerned student that heard all of my constant shrieking and crying from down the hall.

It was Laine.

The light of the hallway peered into the room and temporarily blinded me. As soon as I got over the shock, I managed to stammer, "W-what are y-you doing up this late?" as if there was a ghost standing in the doorway instead of the annoying, skinny girl that everybody picked on.

"I was about to ask you the same thing," she said as she threw her bag on the top bunk she normally slept on. I saw that Rosie was still somehow sound asleep in the bottom one. Laine turned the desk lamp on and then quickly shut the door. She put a finger up to her lips as if to say, "What Mrs. Kelli doesn't know won't hurt her."

She sat on the floor next to me. "So what's wrong? Did the world run out of stilettos and red lipstick?"

While she laughed at her own joke, I looked at her bitterly.

"Obviously, you've been hanging out with Jeydon too much, going around making jokes like that," I mumbled to myself.

She nodded and grinned mischievously. "That observation just proves that you've been talking to him."

I felt as if I was a kid caught with a hand in the cookie jar, even though I knew Laine was a friend to Jeydon, and she wasn't going to ridicule me for it.

"Fine, I admit it, you were right. Are you satisfied now?"

She laughed. "Of course. So, putting jokes aside, what's the matter?"

I rolled my eyes. Was she this way with everyone? It was odd enough she acted this way with Rosie, where she only played a small part in making her cry. But I'd intentionally gone off on her in an effort to hurt her feelings just twelve hours earlier and didn't even bother to say sorry, yet she was concerned about me.

"Do you have bipolar disorder? Short-term memory loss? A possible case of multiple personality disorder, maybe?" I asked impulsively.

She glowered at me with her eyes widened, and I noticed that her eyes weren't just plain brown like I'd thought they were earlier; they were a tawny hazel with a few specks of gold mixed in here and there.

"Oh, so you're saying I shouldn't be concerned about another human being's feelings?"

"Not if they went off on you like I did today," I replied.

"One thing I've learned with Jeydon is how to forgive others very quickly, even if they don't apologize. Besides, I was kind of at fault today too. I shouldn't have gotten all up in your space, but I was so curious. I heard rumors, but I never thought you guys were actually speaking to each other, especially after Jeydon was complaining about you a couple of weeks ago," she informed me.

I shrugged. If she could forgive me after I'd said all those awful things, then why couldn't I? "It's okay," I said. I thought of a question that would break the ice, preferably a question about Jeydon. "So what do you mean when you say that you learned how to forgive quickly because of Jeydon?"

Without any form of hesitation, she answered, "You know how he tells you exactly how he thinks it is? If you think he's bad at keeping his mouth shut now, he's not nearly as bad as he was when we were kids."

I lingered on the word *kids*. It was too difficult for me to picture Jeydon as a child. He was so different that I honestly wouldn't have been surprised if he'd come out of the womb as a fully grown teenager instead of an infant. I wondered if he'd had the scar back when he was a little boy too. I was going to ask her that, but instead, I took a safer approach by asking, "How long have you known each other?"

"Somewhere around four years. The day we met seems like it's even longer ago than that. I mean, it feels like the three of us have been friends forever," she answered.

I was so used to everybody—including me—being so secretive that it shocked me to hear somebody opening up to a stranger.

"The three of us?" I repeated.

She nodded and smiled in remembrance. "Yep, me, Jeydon, and his brother, Anthony. You'll know him when you see him. He's got black hair, freckles, and is always at Jeydon's side. Anyway, we're sort of like the three musketeers."

"Wait," I said, trying to figure out the suspicious element to this group of friends. It was there and on the tip of my tongue, but I couldn't quite figure it out. Then I remembered. "Aren't the three of you new kids, like me?"

She nodded and wrinkled her brow. "Yeah, we came together. Why?"

I shrugged. I wanted to ask her why, but I figured that since she'd had already told me, an outsider, an ample amount of information, I shouldn't overstay my welcome. "Just wondering," I remarked. I paused, very tempted to ask her another question and trying to think of one that wasn't too invasive. "So how did you guys meet, exactly?" That was an okay topic, wasn't it?

She sighed, and I knew I had my answer. "It's a long story. It's kind of boring, actually. I promise I'll tell you some other time."

The way she said *I'll tell you some other time* made me think of my conversation with Richard when he'd said, *Right now's not a good time to talk, maybe later.* Jerk.

Though I knew it was wrong, I still had an urge that I couldn't explain. I just had to know. "I like stories," I persisted.

I could tell that she was annoyed at the constant questions, just as I had been earlier that day. I saw that part of her wanted to tell me just to get me to stop asking about it. "You know what? I'll make a deal with you. You tell me what all the crying is about, and I'll tell you how we met. Does that sound okay?"

I silently groaned and thought, *Man, this girl needs to stop hanging out with Jeydon if she goes around acting like this all the time.*

Still, I needed to get it off my chest, and there was nobody else to tell, really. I couldn't tell Mother, because she would do nothing but force me to make up with Richard. I couldn't tell any of the gang, because Tori would turn them all against me after she shared with them what I'd said to her. Obviously, I couldn't tell Richard. None of my friends at Tampa Bay would care.

The only two people I could think of that I'd even consider telling were Jeydon and Laine. Jeydon, though, was unpredictable. And after sharing with him my deepest, darkest family secrets, I didn't feel up to telling him anything else for a while.

Laine, on the other hand, I'd told nothing, and after sharing with me—almost a complete stranger to her—a little piece to the puzzle that was Jeydon, I knew that I had to tell her something in return.

So I told her everything that happened. I managed to include every single curse word I'd screamed at both Tori and Richard and every detail about how betrayed I felt, and I even showed her the e-mail that Richard had sent that made him sound like such a loving and considerate boyfriend that treated me like a fairy-tale princess.

That was how everybody, including me, viewed our relationship. Because while I never could get over the dull emptiness I felt every time he crossed friendship boundaries, I felt glad to know that out of all the other gorgeous girls—Tori included—he'd chosen me to be his.

But now I knew that every single move he'd made on me was a twisted, tangled up web of lies, including the first kiss we'd shared backstage right before the Anticipation, the eloquent toast at the reception, and every single word of love he'd whispered in my ear at the party. Because while he mindlessly typed in the words *I love you* on the keyboard, he was probably screwing around with Tori.

No, not just Tori—he was probably screwing around with every other member of the gang, even pudgy, insecure Katy, just because she wasn't me.

Heck, for all I knew, he could've been the one who had given Madison Huffington HIV.

I couldn't help but smile deviously at the thought. *Ha-ha, that's what you get!* I'd tell him if that was the case. *Like my new-and-improved friend Jeydon says, "What goes around comes around!"*

As fun as it was to picture Richard suffering, I very well knew there was a little part of me that still cared tremendously for him. I didn't know how dominant that part of me was yet, but I feared that as time went on and my anger toward him began to decrease little by little, that I'd learn to forgive him—like Laine did so easily—and end up back in his arms.

We'd get married, of course, live in a mansion somewhere, and have kids just to point out their flaws. But our whole marriage would be a lie, because after the demons that drove my mother finally ceased and I was always on the go running the business she left behind for me to pick up, Richard would invite a middle-aged Tori and all of her future hooker friends for a little bit of fun.

Just as my dad did.

Then I realized that I'd spoken out loud all of these thoughts that were meant to be rhetorical to Laine.

Everything.

And that only made me cry again. But unlike the last bitter weeping, which was a toxic mixture of rage, disbelief, and betrayal, these tears were out of embarrassment and regret. Was I losing my mind, going around telling all my secrets that I never dared to tell my best friends to almost complete strangers?

It turned out that Laine's shoulder was a great place to cry on, though, so for what seemed like an eternity, I sobbed on her bony shoulder while she ran her fingers through my hair and reassured me that everything was going to be all right. It reminded me of when I sat in Mother's lap crying all those years ago after witnessing Mary's unfair treatment—except there, I was afraid.

Here, I felt safe and secure for some reason. Maybe the fact that I felt more comfortable crying on a stranger's shoulder than on my own mother's proved that I was losing my mind.

When I finally ran out of tears to cry, I dryly asked her not to tell anybody, and she nodded with agreement.

"I promise," said Laine. "I'm like a well. If you throw something inside me, it will never come back out."

I actually managed to smile, even though I was still close to tears. "Good to know. Now that I've told you about all that, will you tell me how you and Jeydon met?"

"That," she said, "is kind of a funny story."

CHAPTER 15

Chance Meeting

Told from Laine's Point of View

The day I met Jeydon and Anthony, there was a cool breeze that blew through the palm trees of Miami, even though it was late May and the temperature had been well over eighty degrees. I didn't really notice this oddity at the time, but now that I look back on it, I should've known then that something was about to happen.

It was somewhere in the late afternoon on a Friday. I didn't know how late it was, but when you have nothing better to do than stare out the window of the seventh story of a building and count cars for twelve years, you develop a sense of timing by watching the amount of traffic. Yellow school buses and a sun positioned high in the sky meant that it was a little after three o'clock, and all the normal kids were coming home from school.

I drifted off into thinking how great it would be to go to school, talk to friends, go to the movies, stress over a math test, and thousands of other things that normal kids take for granted every day. But then I reminded myself that it was no use to wish for such things. I'd figured that out long ago when I'd wish on stars that my mom would find out where my dad ran off to, and they'd come back, and we'd live the American dream as a big old happy family. Sometimes you don't get what you wish for, especially when it's a problem that no amount of star power can solve. Like every aspect of my life.

As soon as I learned how to walk, my dad learned how to run, and my mom went after him, not caring that she'd have to leave me behind with nothing but the man she paid to clothe, shelter, and feed me. She obviously hired the first guy who accepted the job, considering he was a nasty doorman whose thumbnail was larger than his heart. Mom had a small set of rules that she made sure he made me follow. One of them was that I was never allowed to set foot in a public school—or even a private one, for that matter—and a woman named Mrs. Delarosa who lived in the same apartment complex came over and tutored me in every subject known to man.

A knock on the door sent me back into reality, and I smiled, knowing exactly who was there, mainly because he was the only person who would even think about paying me a visit without getting bribed by my mom; David Thorne, the thirty-one-year-old engineer who lived a couple of stories below me. Go ahead and mock me, but he was my only true friend.

He was more than a friend, actually. He was like the father figure I never had, and he'd told me a few times that he thought of me as the daughter he always wanted but never found somebody to settle down with and start a family. He told me that I—the scrawny twelve-year-old girl that nobody else wanted— helped him fill up the void in his life.

He held a couple of chocolate bars in his hand and a deck of his finest playing cards in the other.

"I'm back and ready for a rematch," he said, his eyes light with amusement.

I laughed. "Two chocolate bars, huh? See you're bringing out the big guns this time."

I recalled the last Wednesday when I'd beaten David at poker for the fourth time in a row. He'd only brought one candy bar to gamble on, and even before it was rightfully mine, I'd already eaten half of it, because I was just that skilled. Yes, I failed at all the important things yet was gifted in something as meaningless as poker. No wonder my parents ran away from me.

"You know I can't back down from a challenge," he said with a grin.

Somewhere around ten minutes later, our game got intense. I had a gut instinct whenever I knew that I was going to win, and that instinct had yet to fail me.

I pushed all of the little bite-sized pieces of the candy bars that David had brought, and I broke up toward the center. "Going for all or nothing!" I proclaimed despite the risk.

"I hope you're preparing to lose," David joshed gently as he studied his cards closely with his eyes.

As he widened his eyes to study them a bit more clearly, I could see that his age was starting to take a toll by the creases on his forehead and fine lines underneath his eyes. Still, he looked a lot better than most aging bachelors did as they reached the three-decade mark.

I remembered three years earlier on the day he'd moved in. Since I was only nine back then, I hadn't remembered a whole lot. I do remember, though, how I'd thought he was handsome and heard all the old dowdy housewives wondering in hushed voices how a guy who looked like that couldn't catch a woman by the time he reached his late twenties.

He told me he was waiting for the right woman to come along, but after he dated a perfectly fine woman named Brittany for five months and dumped her because she "just wasn't the one," I couldn't help but wonder if he was being too picky. All the nosy housewives thought he was.

"I think *you* should be the one preparing to lose," I teased.

He chuckled. "Those are fighting words."

"What are you going to do about it?"

He reached his hand out over the table, and I knew exactly what he was going to do. He'd figured out a couple of years earlier that I couldn't stand to be tickled right below my prominent rib cage, and ever since then, he had used it against me. "Don't make me."

As I prepared to receive the tickling of my life, I was saved by the bell. Literally.

David got up to get the door. "Who could it be?" I asked him.

He shrugged. "Don't know. It's probably just Mr. Blake checking on you again."

Mr. Blake was the name of the mean apartment doorman my mom had hired to raise me.

I could tell that David was sure that it was Mr. Blake—and nine times out of ten, it would have been—but this was no normal case.

At the door stood two young boys. You could tell just by looking at them that their situation at home wasn't good, but the taller, older one still managed to appear healthy with tanned yet freckled skin and cropped hair almost as black as mine. He looked to be about my age, somewhere around twelve or thirteen. He smiled a shy toothless smile at me, so I grinned back with my crooked one.

The smaller one was a cat of another color. His skin was a white so bright that it made my eyes kind of hurt, and I wondered if he was on death's door, which wouldn't have surprised me; he had large purple circles under his equally large eyes and a body like a couple of pipe cleaners twisted together to make a stick figure. His masses of pale hair told that he was long overdue for a haircut, and he could've used a shower, as well, to remove the smoky smell from his clothes and smudges of dirt on his face.

I didn't pay much attention to any of that, though, because I was too busy staring at the scar on the left side of his face. I couldn't help but stare at it, for I had never seen a sight so horrid. All I wanted to do was look away, but somehow I couldn't. Were those the type of things that Mom sheltered me from? Would I go running outside to find mobs full of boys like this one with horrifyingly disfigured, heinous faces that resembled Halloween masks?

For Pete's sake, Laine, it's just a boy! It's not like he's a devil, so you don't have to treat him like one! I told myself as I still tried to stop staring.

When I looked over at David and saw that he was completely speechless and staring also, I didn't feel half as bad as I had.

"Hello. What are you boys doing here?" David managed to ask after getting over the initial shock.

"Our toilet broke, and we were sent down the street to ask for a plumber. Somebody told us there was a plumber who lived in this building and that we'd find them in this apartment," the one with the scar explained fearlessly.

His voice was a beauty, though—probably his only beauty. I say *probably* because his eyes could have counted as one too if they hadn't been as large and angry as they were.

It was a bit comical to watch the older one step back without a fight and let the younger one take the lead, but I didn't know how Jeydon and Anthony worked yet.

"Oh, you mean me?" David asked, pointing to himself.

"Yeah, so are you the plumber or not?" he asked with cockiness.

I tried to focus on his eyes, but I couldn't get over the scar.

"Not really; I'm an engineer," said David.

"Do you know how to fix a toilet?"

He nodded. "I suppose."

"Then it's the same difference," he replied back in a smart-alecky manner. There was something about in the way he spoke that told me that he knew what he was talking about. "Anyway, just give me some kind of wrench, and we'll be on our way. Out of your life painlessly."

David dropped his jaw, obviously not sure what to think about this strange child. I didn't blame him; I wasn't sure what to think about him, either. It was as if a rebellious seventeen-year-old had been trapped inside the body of a nine-year-old at oldest.

"Listen," David began in the fatherly tone he usually spoke in with me, "I'll just come over and fix your toilet for you. A boy your size who doesn't know what he's doing—"

"I'm a fast learner, and if size is what you're worrying about, I'm fine. I'm stronger than I look." It sounded like he was trying to act sweet to get his way, but it was obvious he just wanted to get out of here.

Manipulative or not, it didn't matter to David. He found it hard to find fault in a child, even a child as bizarre as that one.

"Please, kid, any little boy under the age of ten—"

"I'm eleven!" he growled, dropping the sweet act and launching into the full-blown, agitated one. I couldn't say I blamed him; I looked younger than twelve, and I had my many shares of people underestimating my age and potential.

David's face grew flushed with embarrassment and cluelessness. "Sorry, but that doesn't matter. I'm not going to just let a couple of little boys grab one of my tools and leave with it. I'll still be happy to come over to your house and do it for you, and it won't cost a penny."

"What do you think I am, some kind of joke? I'm not a bum shaking a cup in front of your face, so stop treating me like one!" He balled his hands into fists, and I could see that there was strong hatred in his eyes—a hatred of not only David but of the world.

Confusion struck David's face. "Who said I was treating you like a bum?"

"Me, obviously."

The older one—who, up to that point, I'd totally forgotten was in the room with us—came out of his frightened mute stage. "Jeydon, please stop. The poor guy's just trying to help us."

Jeydon sighed like an exasperated parent would at their troubled child. "You trust people too much."

"No, you try your best to see the bad in people," he argued, noticeably scared as they inched up until they glared at each other in the face, quivering with fear even though he towered over him.

How could such a small kid be so threatening?

"I only see the bad in people because it's there! Maybe you'd figure out whom to trust if you used your brain for once instead of following me around, trying to be my Jiminy Cricket!" he snapped so loudly that the old lady across the hall peered out her door to see what was going on.

The older one looked truly lost. "Who?"

"That does nothing but prove my point!" He turned all his rage back toward David. "You know what? You can just pretend that I never came by here. I'd rather go out and steal a wrench than borrow one from you."

He stormed off, not noticing or caring that his counterpart was still standing at the doorway with downcast and nervous eyes.

"Sorry for my brother," I heard him say so quietly I had to lean in a little to hear it. "He gets angry easily; you have to be really careful what you say around him."

David gave him a reassuring smile. He always had a soft spot for boys, especially around the age group that this boy seemed to fall under. "No problem, kiddo. It isn't your fault, you know. I can tell you're trying your best to steer him in the right direction."

He looked up at David with sincere but hurt and nervous eyes. "I know. It's one of the few things I do know."

"What's your name?" I boldly asked, getting up from my seat and going over to join the two of them.

It took him a moment to answer, and I wondered if he was either extremely timid or not capable of remembering his own name.

"Anthony. My brother's name is Jeydon," he finally informed me as he held out one speckled hand out to the both of us.

David shook his hand first and introduced himself, and I did the same.

"Would you like to play cards with us?" I invited right after I was done shaking his hand. He seemed nice enough and totally innocent, not a bit explosive like his brother. So why not?

He shook his head repeatedly and acted as if he were going to have a panic attack. "I can't. I have to be Jeydon's Jiminy Cricket. Still have no idea who it is, but I still have to be that for him. I need him, and he needs me; he just doesn't know it yet."

I heard Jeydon holler for Anthony to come on, and as he left, David stopped him, saying, "Here, take this," and he gave him the pieces of chocolate. Anthony objected to his gesture of kindness more than once, but he gave up, said his thank-you, and ran back hastily to his brother as an obedient puppy would for its master.

They're probably out of our lives forever, I thought, *just as Jeydon said.*

But little did I know that in the near future, we four people with completely different points of view would be joined together as one powerful family.

CHAPTER 16

Games

"Wow," I said after Laine shared her flashback with me. I stared down at the floor and back at her face, assessing all the information she'd given me. "I never thought I'd say this, but he was worse back then than he is now. How exactly did he change?"

"Soon after we met, David started looking after the both of them as he did to me. Anthony was grateful for his help, but Jeydon did his best to drive David away. David kept persisting despite all of the rejection, and eventually, Jeydon gave in. David sure can work miracles; he's changed him a lot."

"He did the same thing with me when we first met," I recalled in remembrance of the bitter boy I knew at the Plaza on the first day of school—the boy I still cared about deeply even after he'd pointed out every single bad quality about me. The boy whose heart softened toward me a bit with a simple acknowledgment and who admitted that he gave up and was going to let me into his life.

She nodded. "I figured he did. That's kind of how we became friends, too, except I didn't go out of my way to help him like you and David did. It kind of just fell into place. I have to say I'm very surprised that you two are friends. I've seen for myself how stuck-up you can be, and he hates people like that with a passion. I know this is going to make me sound two-faced and so judgmental, but how can you accept Jeydon for his face when you're so conceited about yours?"

Even though she'd said that she didn't mean it in any bad way and I knew she was nothing but curious, her question still made my veins throb and blood boil in pure rage, made even hotter by the unhealed wound caused by Richard.

When I remembered what Jeydon had said about how frustrated he got when other people judged him for his appearance and what she said she thought of him the first time she saw his face, I wanted to punch hers in really badly. Why was Jeydon her friend if she was just as judgmental about him as everybody else was?

Still, my anger for her was almost nothing compared to my confusion and frustration. Was I the only one who wasn't squeamish or revolted or dry-heaving or anything else of that sort? Was there something wrong with me? There had to be; even David, with his supposedly good heart, was still shocked by Jeydon's so-called harrowing face. I'd thought Jeydon opened up my eyes, but he didn't, because I couldn't see the exterior ugliness that scared everybody away, including his friends. I couldn't see any ugliness, something I had no problem in doing before I met him.

Was this a blessing or a curse? If he really were that ugly, then I should've been glad that I was able to see who he really was. I'd told him myself that I desired nothing more than for people to look beyond my beauty and see who I truly was ... or at least he knew that was how I felt.

Why couldn't everybody else see him the way I saw him? That question made me a little depressed—three strong emotions mixed up inside one weak, hollow shell of a girl.

Before I could get enough hold of my emotions to say anything, she did. "I'm sorry; I shouldn't have asked that. I just have no idea what to think about this and want to understand so badly."

I shook my head and took a few deep breaths in an effort to calm myself down, but it was no use. "Is there something wrong with me?" I cried out in anguish.

Laine looked at me like I'd gone completely mad and needed to be sedated instantly. "Come again?"

"I don't get why everybody, including you, thinks he's so ugly! I try to look for it, but I just can't see any ugly in him, even though it's so easy to find ugly in everybody else. So that comes back to my question. Is there something wrong with me? Why can't I see him the way he's rightfully seen?"

Laine's expression eased back into a soft one. "I don't think he's ugly; I'm sorry if I misled you. I did, but that was only a first impression. When I got to know him for who he was instead of a face and an explosive temper, I didn't care what he looked like. You're different from the rest of us, though. You can see past his appearance without getting to know him. I've never seen anything like it, but I can tell you that it's not anything bad. It's actually beautiful in its own way, and there's no need to get frustrated about it."

I took a few more breaths and finally succeeded in calming myself. "I'm sorry. I guess I just thought you saw him in the same way I did. I must've forgotten that you're a normal person."

She shook her head in a way that told me how wrong I was. "There's no such thing as a normal person, and if there were, I would definitely not be considered one—or Jeydon, Anthony, and David, for that matter. But there is no such thing as normal, so it doesn't matter. And remember that no matter how normal people seem, they hurt, cry, love, and laugh just like you do. Never put somebody else above you or vice versa."

Crap. She knows just how narcissistic and stuck up in the clouds I am.

But on a second thought, who wouldn't know that? Especially after I'd gone off on her like that and how Jeydon talked about me after that big blowout we'd had a few weeks back. In fact, she could've been so much rougher on that matter.

So much more like Jeydon.

We talked for a couple of hours after that. Some conversations we had were nothing but a blur of laughter at five o'clock in the morning and fondly shared childhood memories. I didn't tell her about any of the bad stuff, of course. Instead, I told her things like the warmth I felt whenever my dad found time to hold me in his arms and all the exciting bedtime stories Mary came up with to feed my imagination as a child.

I left out everything that included Richard and the gang, which was the factor of about 90 percent of my cherished childhood memories. My childhood must've sounded pretty pitiful, but it would've sounded a whole lot worse if I had gone on and on about how manipulative and abusive my mother was.

I'd already managed to put Jeydon through the wringer by telling him all about my dreary existence. Putting Laine through the wringer as well would do nothing but bring shame on me.

Besides, there were some things you just couldn't share with another beating heart, especially if they were a lying jerk like Richard was. I was sure that he'd told Tori all about the deepest darkest secrets I'd told him throughout the years while he kissed her in places he'd never found the strength to kiss me. The worst part of it all was that I'd believed every single one of his lies. I felt so guilty for so long about running out on him when I shouldn't have been, because he was the one who was in the wrong for going as far as to say he loved me.

I did the right thing by running away, even if it was only temporary.

I looked over and glanced at Laine, who was a bit more than half-asleep with all her hair tousled over her face. I leaned and brushed the long pieces of hair away from her eyes.

"Laine?" I whispered.

Her eyes were still closed, but I heard her mumble, "Huh?"

"I don't think I'm going to school tomorrow," I announced not only to her but to myself.

She pried her eyes open just enough that I could see the gold specks in them. "Why?"

I touched the skin under my eyes, which was puffy from all the incessant crying. "Can't go to school this way. Facing school is hard enough as it is; it sounds impossible right now for me to go back there. Besides, I need sleep."

She just shook her head and mumbled, "Okay, hang in there." Her eyes fluttered shut to where it looked like she was batting her extremely thick, dark, long eyelashes at me.

"I will," I promised her, but when she responded with nothing but deep breathing, I could tell that she'd fallen back to sleep. I lay there for a minute and studied her appearance as she slept. She looked younger and content in her sleep, and I thought that maybe she would've been pretty if she were not so thin and if her teeth weren't crooked.

Then I rolled my eyes, because I remembered that I was seeing the ugly in people and not the good. If I could see nothing but the good of somebody as appalling to the naked eye as Jeydon, I could certainly find a few good qualities in others. Then again, if Jeydon wasn't who he was, he wouldn't be any different from any of the other few disfigured faces I'd laid my eyes across.

But why? Did we have some sort of special connection that was a rarity, like Laine said, or was it a curse because I couldn't see him for the trouble that he was?

These were the things I thought as I went to sleep, and the dream I had that night was the scariest one of all. I couldn't remember what it was except I knew Jeydon was in it—as all my dreams were at that time—and all I knew was that I woke up with a cold sweat coating my forehead and a racing, erratic heart that kept skipping beats.

As soon as I realized that it was only a dream and tried to calm myself down, I heard a voice that was too well known say, "It's about time you woke up."

I jumped at the sound of his voice and then sat up and saw Jeydon sitting down on the bottom bunk with a book in his lap.

"Jeydon, what are you doing here?" I asked him out of surprise.

He snickered. "Good morning to you too. Or should I say good afternoon?"

"You still haven't answered my question!" I pressed as I rubbed the crud from my eyes. I was in the usual grouchy mood that I always was when I first woke up and didn't want anybody to bother me. Not even him. I took that back pretty quickly. I was glad for his surprise visit.

"I figured since you were sick, I'd tell Mr. Blake that I was helping you catch up on schoolwork and get out of cafeteria duty," he explained, putting the word *sick* in air quotes.

Great; he'd figured out that I wasn't really sick but just didn't want to go.

"So you've just been sitting here watching me sleep?" I asked, not knowing what to think of that. What if I said his name in my sleep and he'd heard? What if he'd figured out that I was dreaming about him? He was perceptive enough to figure out that I was skipping school, so there was a good chance that he'd figured out my dirty little secret in the same way that he'd figured out the secret about my mother.

He gestured to the book on his lap. "Nope. I've been reading a book waiting for you to come out of hibernation."

I perked up a little at the word *hibernation*. I looked over at my clock and saw it was four thirty. Wow, I'd been asleep for at least ten hours. "Why didn't you wake me up?"

"I tried everything I could to wake you up, but you were knocked out cold. The next time this happens, make sure there's a bucket of ice-cold water somewhere near."

I laughed. "Still trying to force me out of your life, I see?"

"No. Why? Is it working?" he asked with a microscopic grin.

I shook my head and smiled sheepishly. "Nope. In fact, it just draws me in more. There's nothing you can do to kick me out of your life, especially now after I told you about all that crap yesterday."

"I was afraid of that," he said as that tiny grin turned into a scowl that made the corner on the left side of his mouth droop down farther than the right side. "Do you really trust me with that, Adrienne? Or are you every bit as stupid as you're sounding right now?"

He was catching me off guard as usual, and my face grew red and hot. "I'm not stupid for trusting you, especially after some of the other people I've trusted in the past," I said, thinking mainly about Richard.

"Yes, you are!" he snapped. I did nothing but stare at him in disbelief. "I apologize, but I don't know how else to make it clearer. I can tell you look up at me with admiration like I'm this superhero in disguise, but I'm not! If anything, I'm the bad guy, so whatever you might see in me, it's not there! I want you to see my true colors, for your sake. A goody-two-shoes girl like you shouldn't be looking at a guy like me the way you do."

I couldn't believe he was saying this. Why was he saying this? Just the day before, he'd told me that he was going to give up on trying to drive me away and let me into his life, but now he was trying to drive me out again.

It made me so confused and angry that I felt like I was going to cry. "Uh, hello? Did you listen to a thing I told you yesterday? I'm not anything close to a goody-two-shoes! I've been arrested!"

He narrowed his eyes at me, but I could still tell that there was pain in them. "I've been arrested for things far worse than you."

I shook my head side to side and tried not to judge even though I'd been in his shoes. "It doesn't matter. I still want you in my life. Like I said, it's no use trying to drive me out, because it's impossible. You might as well give up these mind games now like you said you were going to do yesterday, because I'm always going to come back no matter how unforgivable you are."

He closed his eyes and sighed, and as he did so, I could see the scar clearly, but it still didn't bother me as much as I thought it would. I observed that, in a way, it looked like a single tree limb that branched out into multiple hard, thick twigs that twisted up with each other so much that they made knots.

I desired walk up to him and feel the scar, wondering if the texture would feel as rough and bumpy as it appeared. I pictured it feeling sort of like my grandma's hands after her arthritis set in, but not quite as bony. It probably had its own texture, and I wanted to learn what it was.

After a few moments of me staring at him, he finally opened his eyes and said, "Sorry, but I've got to get going. I put your homework on the desk. See you around."

I smiled weakly and foolishly wondered if we'd ever speak again. I knew I should've told him to stay or how important he was to me, but instead, I waved and said, "See you around."

After Jeydon left, I got to work on my homework. Jeydon left a note that explained what lessons and questions I was supposed to do, and since the note explained things so well, I got done with everything in about fifteen minutes. When I was done, I glanced over at the clock and saw that it was 4:49 p.m. and wondered what Jeydon was doing.

Probably getting into some kind of trouble, I thought.

Whether it was ditching cafeteria duty or smarting off a member of authority, I knew that he was probably getting kicks out of it. Then I understood what he was saying. He didn't want me to get involved with him because he knew that the idea of him and me was a bad one. He was trying to protect me from doing something I'd regret, and I couldn't help but smile at the thought of him being so selfless.

On second thought, maybe he was trying to protect himself from me, because the thought of me trusting someone like him was frightening. Maybe he didn't know what to think when I'd said that I wanted him in my life.

Why was it so hard to predict what he was thinking? Because he was unpredictable, that's why. I could dig for a thousand years and still not unearth the bottom of his mind. I wished that he was a more predictable person, but then I took that back because I knew that was what drew me to him—or at least that was the best reason I could think of, because I didn't really know what drew me to him. For all I knew, even fate itself could be responsible. I scoffed at the idea, because I already knew what my fate was, and nobody could change it. That was when I caught something on the bottom bunk: Jeydon's book. For a brief moment, I wondered if fate was bringing us together.

* * *

I slipped on a pair of shorts and a tank top and literally ran to the boys' dorm with Jeydon's book at hand. The book probably weighed more than my head, so by the time I made it to the dorm, I was sweating buckets even though the two buildings were relatively close together. All the sweating and fatigued thigh muscles would be worth it, though, because I'd get to see him again.

I walked inside the boys' dorm, and all eyes were on me, like how everybody had stared at Jeydon in the girls' dorm the day before. I could tell that everybody thought of my unexpected appearance as a pleasant surprise by their crude remarks and long, lustful glances. The boys from my table seemed especially excited that I was there.

The four of them were together, as they always were, all with facial expressions that warned me there was hate in their heads.

"Hey, eye candy, I didn't expect to find you here!" Mark hollered across the hall as Connor ran up to kiss my cheek and declare dibs.

I pushed him off of me, and the other guys laughed.

"See? I told you she didn't like you. She's too busy digging the Kodester!" Kody sneered, turning to me and squeezing me in closer to him with hands that felt like they were jabbing into my lower back. I tried my best to pull back, but I was easily overpowered by him and brought back even closer, his nails digging into my butt even more.

"Right, baby?" He basically yelled it in my ear.

I was close enough to him that I could see the light-brown stubble on his chin and smell the alcohol on his breath.

"Seriously?" I said, trying to think of what Jeydon would say if he were in this situation. "You must be either really drunk or really stupid to think something like that!"

A couple of the boys laughed and yelled, *"Burn!"*

Kody shoved me so hard that he knocked me onto the floor like I was a house of cards facing a deadly earthquake.

I hazily looked around, expecting eyes to be on me for an entirely different reason, but nobody even noticed that the same person they were staring at a moment earlier was collapsed in the middle of the hallway. The people who did see it—like Connor, Mark, and Jacob—either left and pretended that nothing had happened or were applauding and placing bets like it was a professional wrestling match.

Kody cocked his head to the side for a second and then continued the drunken rampage by picking me up by my hair. I shrieked in pain, but nobody seemed to pay attention except for two figures that came up behind him—two figures that I could distinguish from far away.

Jeydon stood there menacingly with a flame in his eyes and hands balled up into pointy-knuckled fists that screamed that he'd found blood in the water. Anthony trailed just a little bit behind him, shuffling his feet anxiously as he trudged after Jeydon. He kept his head down along the way and didn't look up at me until they got a bit closer, but I could still see the abundance of freckles that splattered his face like how paint would splatter on a blank canvas and eyes that were the color of ice, which looked odd compared to the darkness of his skin and even darker freckles. He would've been good looking if it wasn't for those two things.

Great; now I was seeing the ugly in people again. Don't get me wrong—he was far from ugly, but he wouldn't be considered a stud by anybody, either. It might've been possible that some people thought he was cute, but because of his freckles, it would be in a little boy sort of way.

Kody didn't see they were creeping up behind him, so he continued with his scene by threatening, "You listen here, whore. Nobody talks to me that way! So shut your trap now, because it would be a shame to ruin such a pretty face!"

I could see Jeydon and Anthony in the background gesturing to each other, probably in some secret brotherly language I'd never understand. Jeydon, of course, was the one who stepped up.

"No wonder she doesn't like you, considering you go around talking to girls like that," Jeydon said, and a few people around us who were listening chuckled.

I heard someone murmur, "Hey, that scar-faced kid has some gut!" and I smiled, hoping that people would look past the scar and see how admirable he really was. Then I reminded myself that I was the only one who could do that, because we supposedly had some sort of special connection.

Kody scoffed with arrogance. "I don't think you should be the one talking, since you're the one she can't bear to look at."

"At least I'm not the one she's trying to run away from," he argued as his fingers that had been loosened curled back into tight and potentially deadly fists again.

I didn't understand why Kody didn't run away and hide just from looking at the rippled muscles of Jeydon's forearms; they were a clear warning sign that he wasn't a kid to be messed with.

"You're pathetic if you think you can possibly have her," Kody spit out with fury.

You're the pathetic one if you think you can have me, I wanted to say, but I kept my trap shut, because I didn't want him to deliver his threat to punch my face in. Besides, I knew that Jeydon could handle it.

Jeydon laughed meanly as if he were a lion and had found a limping antelope. "We all know you're the pathetic one, going around smacking every innocent girl who rejects you, and rightfully so. You obviously have some type of void that you're trying to fill, and going around sexually harassing girls isn't the way to fill it."

Kody finally released his agonizing grip on me, held this fist up in the air, and waved it around like it was the American flag. "Do you want me to use this?"

"Go ahead. I dare you to see what happens, but if you back down, it'll do nothing but prove my point that you're pathetic," Jeydon spit out without hesitation, obviously more than happy to start a fight.

I realized that he was fighting Kody because of me, and I felt both a sense of pleasure and guilt—guilt because it was all my fault and pleasure because, in his eyes, I was something worth fighting for.

The pleasure was overthrown by the guilt. "Jeydon, stop it right now! You've obviously proved your point!" I warned desperately, forcing myself in between the two of them before either one could do damage to the other.

Jeydon restrained a bit with me in the center, but Kody just threw me out of the way and punched Jeydon on the cheek. Jeydon didn't seemed affected by it in any way even though it made an awful smacking sound, and he socked Kody back so hard that Kody fell on the floor with a bloody nose and stars in his eyes. There was dead silence as he struggled to stand up, and when he finally managed to do so, he looked at Jeydon with a sense of shock, hatred, and defeat and then darted out of the dorm.

After he was finally gone, Jeydon looked over and appeared to analyze me to see if I'd been damaged in any way. I don't know what overcame me, but I flung myself into Jeydon's arms before he had any time to object. He was every bit as warm as I remembered in my dreams, and I inhaled the scent of his threadbare T-shirt.

It was the scent of him—a mixture of fragrances that wasn't at all like Richard's God-awful cologne and aftershave that I'd learned to tolerate. I instantly loved it like I loved his laughter and his eyes and the goose bumps on my forearms and all the other feelings he gave me. At first, he was startled, and I thought he was going to throw me out of his arms, but then when he got over the shock of me touching him, he hugged me back gently like I was an injured three-day-old kitten.

"I told you I'd come back," I whispered in his ear.

"I knew you would. I left the book there on purpose," he whispered back as he released his grip on me.

His face lit up in a dazzling smile even whiter than his skin, and I beamed at it for a moment, knowing that I was the reason his face was a thousand watts brighter. And just like how I wanted to hear his laughter, I wanted to see him smile like that so much more, because I felt sparks fly when I saw him smile or in any other sort of happiness.

It felt so much colder to be out of his arms, and I was getting chills. I wanted more affection from him.

"Why?" I asked, dumbfounded, as I hugged myself, trying to fight away the cold. I should've known that it wasn't fate bringing us together, and I was stupid to think so, because it was just one of his mind games. Maybe our whole relationship was one of his mind games.

"To see if you were just saying you'd come back or really meant it. My gut instinct told me that you were going to return, but I kept telling myself you weren't because I had to drive you away. However, you did, so I guess you actually want me in your life."

More logical talk, but like Laine said, I could tell that he knew what he was talking about.

I nodded, hoping that this time he'd actually meant that he was going to let me into his life and not push me out again. "I wouldn't say it if I didn't mean it," I said.

I caught the sight of his right cheekbone and studied it, because it was already starting to bruise and swell up from the force of the punch. "Are you sure you're okay? He hit you pretty hard. It made a really nasty sound."

"The real question should be if *you're* okay. You're the one who got shoved around like you were a rag doll in a washing machine. I couldn't stand watching it even for a second." He rubbed his swollen cheek. "The only bad part about it is that he punched my good side. Now they're even."

"You don't have a bad side," I said with a smile.

"So you're saying I'm 100 percent perfect just the way I am? Do us both a favor and drop the act now, because you know I'm not stupid enough to believe it for a second," he retorted with the same lopsided scowl that made other people run for cover while I actually began to think it was kind of becoming.

"I don't have an act; I'm saying what I really think. Call me insane, but I wish everybody could see you in the way I do—" I began, but I was interrupted by a small tap on my shoulder.

I turned around, and Anthony was standing there with icy eyes every bit as nervous as Laine had described them. In his shaky hand was Jeydon's book, and he handed it over to me.

"You dropped this," he said very quietly in a husky voice that sounded like he was croaking instead of talking.

Honestly, I'd totally forgotten that he was there or that he even existed. He was just so invisible, because while Jeydon stuck out so that it was impossible to overlook him, Anthony was always overlooked by everyone and everything, including me, the girl who knew his name only because she was so captivated by his brother. My heart dropped a little at the realization that he might've been eavesdropping on us, because even though I tried not to care that people thought I was insane for seeing Jeydon in the way I did, I still didn't like anybody listening to us conversing about such a delicate topic.

"Thanks," I said as I forced myself to smile at him because I was afraid I would've spooked him if I didn't. "You must be Anthony."

Anthony nodded but looked at Jeydon with question marks in his eyes. "This is Adrienne," Jeydon informed him.

He wordlessly raised his eyebrows at me and nodded like I was a very friendly cocker spaniel instead of an attractive bikini model that had every single boy's undivided attention, and then he looked back at Jeydon. I could tell by then that every time he looked at him, there was more than a glimmer of admiration in his eyes. "You mean the girl you were talking about yesterday?"

I laughed and playfully punched Jeydon on the arm. "You've been caught red-handed, Jeydon Spears! Now for your punishment, you'll have to take a walk with me around campus."

He laughed wonderfully. "I just saved your skin from a drunk, perverted football gorilla if you've forgotten about it already."

"And I saved your skin from being expelled, so we were even, and you'll be even with me again after you've gone on a walk with me. It's a cruel and degrading punishment, I know. I don't know how you'll live through it," I teased in an effort to get him to sport a big, toothy grin like he had a moment earlier.

He did smile, but not the big smile he'd worn a couple of minutes before. It was the usual ghost of a smile that came and went in the blink of an eye.

Still, I felt compassion with every split second his face was lit up, because I felt like I was changing him almost as much as he was changing me.

"A walk around campus it is!" I exclaimed as I took him by the arm, and we headed outside to experience the great outdoors, me totally forgetting that we were leaving Anthony alone by himself in the dust.

CHAPTER 17

Small Sacrifices

As soon as we got outside and I thought the coast was clear, I said so that we wouldn't have to resume our previous conversation, "Anthony seems nice ... a little bit on the quiet side, though."

He nodded. "He has really bad social anxiety, and that's why he never talks. But he's downright friendly after he gets over it and warms up to you." He unhooked his arm from mine, and I backed up a bit because I didn't want him to feel uncomfortable with my desire for his undivided affection.

He stopped in the middle of the path and looked at me like he was going to bring up something delicate, and for once, I knew what he was going to say.

"Listen, Adrienne, I don't really want to talk about it, but I think it's necessary. What you said to me, about seeing me in a different way than everybody else ... I'm just wondering how you see me, because I've never met somebody who sees me in the way you do."

I looked up at him and couldn't help but smile when I saw his face, even though it was the face I should've been running away from. "I see a boy who—like me, in a way—has been misunderstood all his life. He has gems for eyes and snowflakes for skin and a dazzling smile that should be used a whole lot more. He's a little rough around the edges, but I know that he has a heart as good as gold. I should be afraid of him like everybody else is, and I know he can cause a lot of trouble when he puts his mind to it, but I just can't see the part of him that everybody else focuses on. I can only see his good qualities even when I try to see his bad. I guess I can see the whole picture, but only with you."

He looked down at the brick path and laughed louder than I'd ever heard him laugh before, though it was still quiet. When I gave him a confused look, he looked back at me, and his face turned solemn again.

"Sorry, it's just a little comical. You can pick out every tiny bad quality in a perfectly fine person and can see something good in somebody as screwed up as I am."

I shook my head, and we continued walking along the path. I made sure that we were still far enough apart that we weren't touching even though I would have preferred that we were. "You're not as screwed up as you think you are."

"You don't know me, obviously. And the hints I've given away through my actions you've been completely oblivious to. I just got in a fight, for God's sake!" he said as he pointed to his bruise, which had turned a shade of dark purplish blue. The bruise was round and circular, the same shape and size as Kody's enormous catcher's mitt of a fist.

His bruise only reminded me of his bravery.

I said, "Yeah, but for me. You could've walked away like the rest of the boys did and let him do God knows what, and you got hurt while doing it. You said that I thought of you as a superhero. Well, I think of you as one now."

He shook his head slowly and looked down, but this time he wasn't laughing. "I'm no hero. Yes, maybe compared to all those juvenile imbeciles I am, but I'm still not the definition of a hero. I'm just a kid that had enough guts to do the right thing, even if it meant getting hurt a little in the process. I don't mind getting hurt that much, because I'm no stranger to hurt. But you aren't, either, Adrienne. And let's be honest, you would've gotten hurt a whole lot worse than I did if I hadn't been there to stop him."

I considered what he'd said. Yes, it was true that we were both acquainted with hurt. What person wasn't? But still I didn't want him to get hurt, even if it meant me getting hurt worse. That had to be the same way he felt about me, or else he wouldn't have done what he did or said what he'd said.

I still had to smile at the thought of him being a sacrificial lamb for me. "Yes, you're right, but I still feel responsible. I would rather me get hurt a lot than you get hurt a little bit."

He looked at me with surprise and then remorse. "Well, then this will be a bitter news flash for you; I'm already hurting." His voice sounded more like Anthony's than his own melodious one.

I had thousands of questions to ask. Was that a confession? Was he screaming silently on the inside and hoping that somebody would come to the rescue just as I was? No, that could never be Jeydon. He was too strong. Instead of doing nothing but scream, he would face his problems in the same way he'd saved me from mine. Everybody was hurting, and I shouldn't judge him because of it, because like he'd said, I was hurting too.

I put my hand on his left arm and noticed the scar on it. It wasn't all over the place and asymmetrical like the one on his face was but rather a faint, thin line that looked more like a pink ribbon that adorned his bland skin than something I was supposed to be grossed out by.

"You don't have to be," I told him as I traced the scar on his arm with my finger, which began at the rippled muscles of his bicep and ended at his forearm. It reminded me of a line made by a stick dragged in the mud for too long.

He nodded and said bitterly, "Yes, I do, because apparently that's what makes the world go round."

He looked away, but I could still tell that there was pain in his eyes. I wondered again what his story was and why he refused to share it with me. What had happened that made him lose his trust in people and the world? What could I do to gain that trust?

I looked down and wondered what to say. When I looked up, I had a question to ask, even though I knew it was a question that would put our relationship on thin ice. "You told me that you'd gotten arrested for things far worse than I have, so tell me what you've been arrested for."

He hesitated, and I thought he wasn't going to tell me just as he wouldn't tell me any other detail of his life, but to my surprise, he started telling me little tiny chapters of his story. "I've been arrested seven times in total. The first time was when I was nine and another kid no better than I was tried to mug me when I was walking down a street alone one night."

"Why were you walking down a street alone if you were only nine? Why didn't you bring someone like Anthony with you?" I asked impulsively.

"Because the state kept us apart," he explained. "It was a way of breaking us, I guess. We were sent to different boys' homes, and I managed to escape from mine, and after that, I was out on the streets."

He shuddered, and I wondered if he'd seen some horrible sights out there, kind of like how I'd seen Mother beating Mary.

"Well, anyway, so when that kid attacked me, I used a knife on him that I kept in my pocket for safety. I didn't hurt him that badly, but the kid went crying to the police, and because of my scar, it didn't take that long for the cops to track me down. I got arrested and was sent to a reformatory school for a couple of months, and it went all downhill after that." I didn't know whether it was the neutral tone he used to explain this or the lack of any sort of light in his eyes as he explained it, but whatever it was, it made me wince like I had when Kody dug his talons into my skin.

"What do you mean?" I asked. He was exasperated by my questions, I was sure of it. "After I got out of that boot camp, I was put in another boys' home—which I also escaped from—and then I got in another fight where I dislocated a kid's shoulder. After I got out of jail again, I stole stuff I shouldn't have stolen, got in more fights, and took up smoking underage and got busted for that. Anyway, here I am today, your average fifteen-year-old juvenile delinquent with seven arrests and several more violations of the law under his belt."

I just stared at him for a little bit. Sure, I knew for a fact that he was a good fighter from witnessing him beating the crap out of Kody, but I couldn't picture a kid no older than ten having enough will and strength to dislocate a shoulder, not even if that kid were Jeydon. Then again, from what Laine had said, Jeydon was a bizarre little terror with a fuse shorter than a fruit fly's life span. Nonetheless, I knew all of the crap that had happened to him was horrible, though he deserved his punishment a couple of times from what it sounded like. But something about the way he said how he was fifteen stuck with me.

"You're only fifteen, and you're a junior?" I finally asked.

He gave me a weird look. "Yeah, why does that matter?"

I wanted to slap him silly. Did he not think a fifteen-year-old junior that took advanced classes was a bit out of the ordinary? Then again, he was probably used to being out of the ordinary, and compared to some of his other qualities, this one may have made him feel like an average joe. Maybe he was just surprised that I was shocked by that little detail I should've ignored.

Yes, that had to be it.

It made me feel a little guilty, knowing that he'd finally opened up to me about his elusive, checkered past, and I'd focused on a little detail that wasn't even relevant.

Still, I explained myself even if it was a dumb question. "Because you should be a sophomore, and from what it sounds like, you've also missed a lot of school because of all the arrests and reform schools. I figured that you were smart, but you must be even smarter than I imagined."

He shrugged humbly. "I'm not that much smarter than the next guy. Besides, I decided to be street smart over book smart a long time ago. I would've been eaten alive out there if I hadn't."

I grinned mischievously. "Was that you admitting that you have brains?"

He smiled a little, and I could tell that he was hiding the vastness of his intelligence—either that or he was just being modest, the trait I miserably lacked. "I guess it was."

"How smart are you, exactly? You must be a pretty sharp tack if you had to make a decision between the two. You're also in both my chemistry and accelerated language classes, so that means that you must be above the average junior standards."

"I've not been officially tested since I was eight, if that's what you're asking."

"They do IQ tests on eight-year-olds?" I asked stupidly. "What do they do differently—give the kid a crayon to write with instead of a pencil?"

The light went back into his eyes as he had a good, quiet laugh. "Obviously, your IQ level wasn't worth getting checked out."

I, on the other hand, laughed out loud for all to hear. "Well, what can I say? My mother always told me that I'm a beauty and not a brain. And that's not just me being conceited; she thinks all women should be beauties instead of brains. That's why my eldest sister, Mary, got the worst beatings; what she lacked in looks she made up for in academic success."

He scowled his usual lopsided scowl. "Your mother's a witch. No offense."

"None taken," I dismissed abruptly and then realized that I was talking about myself when I should've been learning things about him now that he was opening up a little. "But seriously, what do they do differently?"

He chewed on the inside of his lip as he said, "Since I'd only been tested that one time, I'm not really sure what the adults' version of the IQ test is, but when I was tested, I was put in a small, vacant room with nothing but a desk and a chair in the corner. I was given an extensive test full of riddles and math equations and had an hour to complete them or do as many as I could."

"How'd you do?" I asked stupidly, not knowing what else to say.

"I did okay," he answered in a tone that almost sounded like the flat line on a heart monitor.

"What do you mean by *okay*?" I asked with a cocked eyebrow. Just like when the gang and I broke into the medical records to discover Madison Huffington's weight, I was expected a number larger than life itself.

"One hundred forty-three," he said as if he were coughing something up.

I gave him a weird look, because I couldn't understand what he'd said. It reminded me of the one dream I'd had at the beginning of the school year where I couldn't understand a word he said and wondered if it was just a coincidence or something more. "What?"

He took another breath, released it, and then clarified. "I scored an IQ of 143."

"Oh, is that good?" As soon as I asked that question, I felt more ignorant than ever. My cheeks became hot due to embarrassment and insignificant feelings as I told him, "You don't have to answer that. Sorry, I guess we all can't be as smart as you."

He shook his head with a scowl and retorted, "I'm not that smart, at least not anymore. I make good grades and am in advanced classes, but it's not like I'm some freaky kid genius."

His attitude, whether it was from extreme modesty or spending too much time in a cell and not enough time in a school, made me mad, and I was determined to prove him wrong. "Apparently, you were if you got an IQ score of 143 when you were only eight. I've heard than an average adult can't land a score anywhere near that high!"

"Like I said yesterday, things change," he retorted again in the same flat tone.

I sensed an opportunity to use reasoning. "Things may change, but people don't."

The small twinkle that was still in his eyes faded again. "People can change if they want to. I didn't really have an option. I had to change, not only for my sake but for Anthony's. I wouldn't be able to be there for Anthony if I were away at some fancy college with a bunch of preppy rich kids right now."

His words shocked me. Why would anyone throw away a chance for a better life? Was he as crazy as I was, or did Anthony need his attention that much? I remembered the way Anthony clung to him and looked up at him with admiration, and I wondered if Jeydon would feel possibly guilty if he left him on his own so that he could make something out of his life.

"You mean you've gotten offers even with all your arrests?" I asked in both fascination and horror.

He nodded and answered, "A few from various colleges who think I'm some kind of diamond in the rough, but that's beside the point. I've had a few opportunities to be the freaky kid genius who's attending Harvard at fifteen, but I'd choose my brother over that life any day. They don't need me; he does. Also—and this may be the rebel without a cause in me talking—I don't think I could stand it. Following everybody else's rules and doing whatever everybody else wants you to do, you know?"

His words hit me hard. "I do know, more than anybody else."

He gave me a look that was a mixture of concern and confusion, so I continued, "I never really asked to be the heir of my mother's company. I was just chosen, and since she chose me, she also chose every aspect of my future."

"Like what?" he asked with a scowl, clearly horrified at the idea of my planned-out future.

I didn't know what to think about Jeydon's curiosity about my life. Was he every bit as captivated by me as I was by him? No, nobody could be nearly as captivated by somebody as I was by him, not even Jeydon Spears himself.

I told him about it, anyway, despite my concerns, because it was too hard to keep a secret from him. "For instance, I was forced into modeling, particularly bikini modeling. She made me exercise vigorously to get thin enough to do that. Also, I'm being forced in a relationship with a lying, cheating jerk that I have to marry someday."

As I was telling him all of this, I knew that I was adding gasoline to the fire and waiting for an explosion, and it finally happened.

"Okay, I'm stopping you right there, because I can't hear any of this crap anymore!" He got hold of his temper with a couple of quick breaths. "Sorry, but it makes me so mad that this woman thinks she can physically and psychologically abuse and manipulate you and your sisters like you're her string puppets! It makes me even more furious that you let her! It's your life, not hers."

"I know, but ..." I began timidly as I bit my lip to hold back tears, but Jeydon didn't stop ranting, because he was on a roll. I wanted to ask him what he had to be angry about. She was doing this to me, not him. Did he actually care? He had to, or else he wouldn't have saved me from Kody's painful grasp.

"She's nothing more than a corrupted, sadistic sociopath from the sound of it! She's nothing to be afraid of!" he said, enraged at a woman he'd never even seen in person before. Then again, he didn't need to know her to hate her, especially after all the awful things I'd told him about her and his freaky perceptiveness.

I was able to hold back my tears for once, only because I'd cried my eyes out the night before. "You don't know her; I do. And she's everything to be scared of. Let me remind you how much power she's got."

"It's mostly in your head."

"And in her fists and bank account," I interrupted hotly. "I've seen some of the things she's been able to do to anyone who crosses her path the wrong way. She can destroy you."

"She can't destroy you if you don't let her," he said as he calmed down a little toward me, but I could still tell that he was very angry at her. I told myself the reason he was so mad was because he cared about me and didn't want her to hurt me, just like he hadn't wanted Kody to hurt me. Would he do the same thing he'd done to Kody to my mother if she were there with us? I liked to think that he would, even though the thought of my own mother getting beaten like Kody had did made me wince, no matter how abusive and manipulative she was.

I felt joy all around at the thought that Jeydon, the fiery-tongued juvenile delinquent who was capable of dislocating a kid's shoulder at the age of ten, could emit an emotion toward me besides anger.

"She'll only keep persisting and persisting until you crack if you act like it doesn't bother you. She never gives up, Jeydon; you don't understand what demons drive her," I said, my voice wavering.

"I think I have a pretty good idea. You don't have to be afraid anymore. She's not going to hurt you now that she's so far away, and if she does, I'll give her something to be afraid of," he assured me softly, but there was still fire in his eyes. The lull of his voice still soothed me, though, even if it was a bit angry, because I knew his anger was toward her and not me.

I shook my head side to side rapidly. "No, Jeydon, don't. I've already gotten you in enough trouble for a lifetime."

"I've gotten *myself* in enough trouble for a lifetime. You were the one who saved me from trouble I'd gotten myself into, and that was the least I could do to pay you back," he corrected with the usual sense of intellect to his voice.

"I got myself into trouble when I went into the boys' dorm room to give you back your book."

"I left that book at your dorm on purpose, so I got both of us into trouble," he argued, but this time, he seemed to be having fun debating this matter instead of being engulfed in anger.

"I could've stayed in my room wallowing in my own self-pity."

He smiled a little wider than usual, but it still wasn't the big, toothy grin I strived to see him wear again. "I'm glad you didn't."

I nodded and smiled back at him. "Me too."

When we entered the Plaza, I suggested that we stop and play with the few flowers that weren't scorched out by the heat. We spent a few minutes playing with the flowers instead of talking. Soon enough, I got tired of the silence, and I also had something that I needed to get off my chest.

"I lied to you," I told him as he was plucking all the petals of a particularly delicate daisy one by one.

He stopped mutilating the daisy and looked at me with a head full of thoughts that would remain locked up tight with the key just out of my reach. "What do you mean?"

"I told you I could've stayed if I wanted to, but the truth is, I couldn't," I confessed with actual shame. No, it wasn't exactly shame, but it was an emotion that I couldn't quite put my finger on. I might've been unsure of what it was, but since Jeydon's radar for emotion was so sensitive, he could probably categorize it in the blink of an eye.

He closed his eyes. I guessed the reason was because he was in deep thought and didn't want any visual stimulation to be a disturbance. While he was contemplating whatever was in his head, I studied his face as the light shone off his ivory skin, which appeared to glisten in the sun. It reminded me of what I thought an angel's skin would look like, if by any chance I made it to heaven and actually saw one.

Who knows? Maybe Jeydon was an angel in disguise, like how I'd thought he was when I first met him. I didn't really think of him any differently from the way that I had back when I'd had my first dream about him, except I knew now that he had other flaws besides his outward appearance. While flawed outward appearances were on my mind, I tried for the thousandth time to focus on the scar. It still didn't bother me. To show the world that I didn't mind, I scooted toward him until we were just far enough away that it wouldn't make him uncomfortable and traced the ribbon of a scar on his arm.

He opened his eyes, and I was once again astounded by their unusual, vibrant shade of green that were as pleasing to the eye as his voice was pleasing to the ear. He looked at me with a twinkle in his eye that I'd never seen before. And of course, I loved it like I loved everything else about him, which was starting to become a very extensive list.

"I know," he said.

I picked out the flower nearest to me that was worthy enough to be given to him. "Here," I said as I handed it to him. "To make it up to you."

He took the flower delicately between two fingers, not at all how he was holding the other flower he had just finished maiming a moment earlier. After analyzing it for a moment, he smiled and said, "If you really want to make it up to me, you should let me drive you to get your wrist checked out tomorrow."

I wondered how he'd even found out about that, but I would never object to spending more time with him, so I just nodded and said, "Okay."

CHAPTER 18

Part of Me

I had another awful dream that night, but I still didn't have any clue as to what it was about except that Jeydon and Richard were in it. All I knew was that I woke up with a cold sweat on my forehead and terror in my heart.

I didn't feel like going to breakfast, and I told my roommates that I wasn't feeling well again. After I verified with Rosie the night before that Jeydon and I were friends, she told me that I was dead to her, which didn't crush me nearly as much as I'd thought it would. Actually, I was relieved. And I should've been, because I traded in my fraud friendships with Rosie and Emily for something so much better.

Laine pretty much knew that I was faking again, and as soon as Rosie left, she told me that I could sit with her, Jeydon, and Anthony, but I declined. I explained to her briefly that I had an appointment at the doctor's for my wrist, and Jeydon was going to take me to it, and she understood. She asked me about the fight, but I told her that I would tell her later even though I wasn't going to tell her. I don't know why exactly other than that I didn't feel up to it. Besides, she'd probably hear all about it from multiple nosy kids by the time the day was over.

As soon as everybody was gone, I took a shower, thinking that a rich lather would help calm my nerves a little. I spent about fifteen minutes or so in the shower, because I wasn't really in that much of a hurry. In fact, I didn't really mind being late or not showing up at all to chemistry class, because I was only going to be there for fifteen minutes. When I got out of the shower, I wrapped a towel around my body and went back into the bedroom to put some clothes on.

Of course, Jeydon had to be there, patiently sitting on my bed. He seemed to pay no attention to the fact I had nothing on except a towel.

"Ready to go, or do you need another five hours to do a complete spa relaxation treatment? If I were you, I'd suggest that cucumber facial, considering the dark circles under your eyes," he said.

At that, I smiled and forgot that I was almost completely naked in front of the only boy I wanted to make an impression on. "Sorry I'm not presentable enough for you."

I thought I heard him laugh, but I wasn't sure. "So I'm guessing you couldn't sleep last night."

My smile faded. "Nightmares," I answered with a nod.

"Were they about me?" he asked quizzically with a half smile and one eyebrow raised.

I looked at him with wide eyes and wondered if he was some kind of mind reader. "How'd you know?" I asked, both aghast and a little embarrassed.

He was so unpredictable, so I didn't have the slightest clue as to how he was going to react to something like that. Was he going to call me out for the obsessed freak that I was, or would he somehow understand? He understood with all of my other secrets, so there could've been a good chance that he would. But I didn't want to find out how he'd react, because it was the only thing that was still my dirty little secret.

Strangely enough, Jeydon didn't seem to think that I was weird or crazy like I feared he'd be. Instead, he laughed and said, "I'm the cause to a lot of people's nightmares, so I just figured I was the cause of yours too."

I giggled. "Wrong again. The main cause of my nightmare was the jerk my mother's making me date. You were just in it."

"That's a little less flattering," he said with a tiny smile. "So tell me, did the jerk and I slug it out? If we did, who won?"

I laughed. "Can't remember, but it wouldn't surprise me if you did."

I finally came to my senses and realized again that I had nothing on me but a towel and that there was a teenage boy in the room. "Um, Jeydon, do you mind?" I asked awkwardly as I gestured for him to leave the room.

Jeydon left the room without a fight, and I wondered if he needed his vision checked. Of course, it had never bugged me before that he didn't suck up to me and tell me how beautiful I was like everyone else did. In fact, I kind of admired it. But I didn't understand how a fifteen-year-old boy could stand to be in the same room with an almost naked bikini model and not even sneak a look with the slightest bit of lust. Probably because he wasn't like any other fifteen-year-old boy. I should've figured that out by then.

Still, it made me a little insecure and self-conscious that he didn't find me beautiful—or if he did, he sure didn't show it. I sort of wanted him to look at me the same way everyone else did, but I reminded myself that if he did, we'd have no relationship. He'd be nothing more to me than one of my many admirers who I wouldn't talk to if my life depended on it.

But since he was exceptional, he managed to captivate me, and I in return somehow heightened his interest. We could see each other clearly—or the whole picture, as Jeydon would say—for who we were as people and not our appearances. It was something I'd wanted for what seemed like forever, and I finally had it, so it was foolish to wish it away.

I threw on denim shorts and a tank top, and we were ready to go. Jeydon somehow convinced me to leave my stilettos behind, and for the first time in months, I wore sneakers—or *actual shoes*, as Jeydon called them. My feet ached because I was so used to wearing my high heels, and I made sure that I complained about it on the walk to the parking lot.

When I complained, Jeydon replied back, "You'll thank me one of these days when I save you from a broken leg."

I gave him a weird look even though I was pretty sure I knew what he was talking about. "How could I break a leg from wearing heels?"

He chuckled. "Have you noticed how you walk in those things? I'm not saying this to be rude, but you look like Bambi did when he took his first steps. I'm telling you, one of these days, you'll fall, and your leg will snap like it's a piece of spaghetti."

I glared at him with a look that showed him that he was testing me again. "Well, thank you for your consideration."

He smiled mischievously and said, "Anytime."

I giggled all the way to his car, a beaten-up old Toyota with more rust on it than red paint, countless dents, no windows, and a hole through the windshield that I was 90 percent sure was a bullet hole. Still, because of his age, I didn't think it was his and asked if he was going to hot-wire it.

He laughed. "Don't have to; this is all mine."

I looked at him with eyes that screamed questions.

"What did you think my mode of transportation was? A bike?" he asked with a light scoff.

"It wouldn't surprise me if that was the case," I said as I stared at it, trying to find a little bit of good in it. Crap, now I was seeing the ugly in cars, which only proved that I was losing my mind. I was losing my mind over him. "How do you have a car if you aren't even old enough to get your license?"

"Where there's a will, there's a way," he answered as he unlocked the car and we both got in.

I went to get in the driver's seat, but he stopped me.

"Oh no you don't. My car, my rules. I'm driving."

"You don't even have your license!" I objected as I wondered whether his driving me to the doctor was a death sentence.

"Two words. Learner's. Permit. Passenger's seat, now!" he ordered in a teasing fashion.

I asked myself what Jeydon would do and smiled deviously when I found my answer. "I will as soon as you tell me why you even have a car at fifteen. Are bikes just not cool enough for you?"

He smiled approvingly. "I see my little girl's growing up. Get in the car, and I'll tell you."

I started to object.

"Oh, so now you don't trust me? Think I'm going to drive off without your questions answered?" he asked with amusement.

I shook my head and swiftly got in the passenger's seat.

"That's what I thought," he said with a satisfaction he'd never shown before. It was the satisfaction of getting his way.

When I got in the truck, the first thing I noticed was that the driver's seat had curse words roughly and crudely carved into it, but I didn't even bother to ask. *One story at a time,* I thought. Honestly, after hearing about his past and witnessing some of his impulsive, reckless actions with my very eyes, I wasn't that shocked to see something like that carved into his car.

He was starting to put the key in the ignition, but I stopped him by putting my hand over his. "Oh no you don't. Tell me the story about the car first."

"Fair enough," he remarked slyly as he moved his hand away from mine and put the keys in the cup holder. "This is technically Anthony's car, not mine. But Anthony has always sucked at driving, and I'm not a safety hazard, so I've always been the one who drives."

"Exactly how much older is Anthony than you?" I asked in disbelief. Of course I'd heard whispers on the street that Anthony was a dunce, but I figured that he could get the basics of driving down like every other junior.

"Almost two full years. Twenty-one months, to be exact," he informed me. "He got held back in kindergarten and I, as you know, advanced a couple of grades."

"You seem like you should be the older one, if you ask me, especially if you're driving," I told him.

He nodded in agreement as he put the keys back in the ignition and switched the gearshift into reverse. "I think I should be too, but I'm not, so there's no use wanting to change it."

He had a tone with a bitterness that made me wonder if he felt that way about something else instead.

"Is that …" I began to ask him if that was how he felt about his scar, but in midsentence, it occurred to me that such a question would do nothing but anger him and make me sound like that was all I saw when I looked at him, just like the rest of the world. "Never mind," I dismissed.

He looked at me not with anger but with no apparent emotion at all. "I knew what you were going to ask, so go ahead and spit it out."

I shook my head neurotically. "I don't want to; it makes me sound no better than all of those other judgmental kids," I said as I held my face in my hands, despising myself for even bringing it up.

"You aren't," he reassured with gloominess to his voice that reminded me that it wasn't a subject to be tampered with. "In fact, it sort of amazes me how you aren't like all those other kids when it comes to that matter."

"It amazes me that they aren't how I am. I know I've said this before in so many words, but I think it's worth repeating. I can't see what everybody else sees. However, I wouldn't trade it for anybody else's dumb judgment of you if my life depended on it., because what I see is so much better than what everybody else sees," I said, knowing that I was speaking from my heart instead of my head.

I found out that when I spoke things from my heart, it was so easy to communicate. It was when I spoke my mind that I choked on my own words and said things that I later regretted. But with Jeydon, I didn't have to even think about the transition; I just automatically spoke from my heart every single time. I didn't have that with anybody, not even Richard. But I had numerous things I felt with Jeydon that I'd never felt with Richard. That was one of the many reasons why I'd traded Richard in for him.

"I figured that out on my own," he dismissed with the slightest bit of gratitude as he took the nearest exit onto the highway. His driving might have been flawed, but I still had to admit that it was better than mine. "What I'm confused by is how you can be so open-minded when it comes to me but be so rude, judging, and arrogant when it comes to other people even if they have the heart of Mother Teresa."

I shrugged. "I'm confused by it too," I confessed. "I actually talked to Laine about it the other night." He took his gaze away from the road and analyzed my casual expression with his brow arched. "I thought you two were sworn enemies."

"I thought you two told each other everything," I shot back at him as I saw out of the corner of my eye a silver sport-utility vehicle back out right in front of us. I gasped.

He stepped on the brakes just in the nick of time. As I caught my breath, he shrugged it off as if he'd almost hit an ant instead of an SUV and said, "Correction: Laine tells everybody everything because she has no secrets, which is only going to come back someday and bite her in the butt when she tells the wrong person. She may be my friend, and we may have known each other since we were little kids, but you know a lot more about me than she does."

Honestly, I wasn't really all that shocked that Jeydon didn't tell Laine anything. What I was shocked by was that I knew more about him than she did, when my knowledge of him was like the tip on an iceberg, "That's actually kind of sad, since you guys have known each other for so long."

He shook his head. "What's even more tragic is how she goes around telling all of her deepest, darkest secrets to girls who will do nothing but break her. Like you, for example."

"Are you implying that I would stoop down to that level?" I asked hotly even though I knew that I had already when I was in cahoots with making her cry. She'd probably told him all about that too. Maybe that was another reason why he'd hated me the first time I'd met him.

"No, but she didn't know that you weren't. I'm also assuming that you guys had this chitchat after your fight, so every other girl would steer clear of talking to you, much less telling you their secrets."

At that point, I figured out that—for once—Jeydon's assumption was wrong, and I had to correct him. "She didn't just walk through the door and blab to me all her secrets."

Confusion and the shame of being wrong—a feeling he'd probably seldom felt before—struck his face. "What do you mean?"

"You know that class-A jerk my mother's making me date?" I asked.

He nodded. "Yeah? What does he have to do with anything?"

"I only found out that he was cheating on me recently." That was how I began to tell him all about what had happened with Richard and me. I told him how we were childhood best friends and how close our mothers were. I told him all about how much I trusted him and loved him but still couldn't stomach the thought of us being a couple. I told him how he'd treated me like a princess, that I was so sure that he loved me from the kiss backstage and the slow dance at the party where he went as far as to confess his love for me and the loving e-mail he'd sent. I found myself also telling him all about Tori and the rest of the gang. I told him how cruel we were, even going as far as to tell him the Madison Huffington incident. He listened thoughtfully as I told him how I'd found out that he was cheating on me in detail, including all the curse words that Tori and I had shot back at each other.

I explained how Laine came in when I was crying, and she'd consoled me. I explained how I'd felt more safe and secure crying on her shoulder than my own mother's.

I asked him if that was weird, and he replied, "When your mother's the identical twin of Mommy Dearest, it isn't." His face brightened up a little even though he wasn't smiling. "I think that's what I'm going to call her for now on."

I giggled. "It has a nice ring to it."

He grinned almost as widely as he had the day before. *Was it really only yesterday?* And just the day before that was when I'd had my big fight with Richard. Why were things going so fast? I wondered if Jeydon was thinking the same thing.

I don't think he was, because he always said what he thought.

Instead, he said, "So I think you've been caught red-handed, Adrienne Hudson, talking about me behind your back. What did you say?"

"I told her some of the things I've told you, like how I didn't notice your scar the first time I saw you. She thinks we have some kind of a special connection," I answered, feeling sort of stupid for making a big scene out of him talking about me to Anthony when I was guilty of the same crime.

He raised his eyebrows and considered it for a moment. "I suppose we could, or you just might have a thing for severely scarred juvenile delinquents," he said it in a lighthearted manner.

It still struck the wrong nerve.

"Jeydon, stop talking like that." It was bad enough that I had to hear that crap from other people. I couldn't listen to him say it. "We both know you're so much more than that."

"I know," he said quietly with a small smile on his face. He looked at me with eyes shining brighter than the sun. "And to answer your question, that's how I feel about my scar. I'm so much more than just a face, and people are too stupid to see that, so that's why I don't any pay attention to them. They're not worth listening to. There's no use in wasting all my life locked inside an attic somewhere, hiding from the world and wishing that I'll wake up one morning with my face completely healed up and normal. It's a part of me that can never be taken away, and I've learned to like it just as I've learned to like all the other parts of me that people aren't too crazy about."

"Why did you say that about yourself, then?" I asked, wondering the motivation behind his logic. Perhaps it was another mind game, or maybe it was something more. I rejected my philosophies and logics and paid attention to his.

"Because that's the single-minded illusion as to who I am, like how yours is the conceited, arrogant heiress. Even though you've said to me numerous times that you didn't see me in that way, I wanted to make sure." He explained it as if everything was as simple for me as it was for him.

"By playing more mind games?" I asked, already exasperated by them.

"You know it," he said with a mischievous smile.

After a couple of more minutes of talking a little bit more about my miserable life, we finally arrived at the clinic. I asked Jeydon to go in with me, and he looked bewildered, but he didn't object. We walked into the clinic with my hand wavering toward his like it was a piece of iron to a magnet, and I went to check in for my appointment.

The receptionist behind the glass window was young and pretty with silky brown hair and plump, perfectly pink lips. "Hello, how can I help you?" she asked as she gave me the usual patronizing smiles grown-ups give little kids.

It aggravated me a little, because she didn't look a day over five years older than I was. "Yeah, my name is Adrienne Hudson, and I have an appointment with Dr. Hourani."

She nodded and smiled in a patronizing way again, but when she nodded toward him, I realized that she didn't think of me as a little kid but rather thought that I was insane. Awesome—yet another person whose face I wanted to punch in.

"Okay, get checked in, and the doctor will see you shortly," she said.

I sat down in a chair next to Jeydon and quietly filled out the forms while he flipped through the pages of some science magazine at a record speed. Soon enough, the doctor called me up and he gave me a weird look when I made Jeydon come into the exam room with me. The doctor asked me who Jeydon was, and when I told him that he was a friend, he looked at me even more skeptically.

The whole time the doctor—a short, balding man as skinny as a rail—was supposed to be examining my wrist, he was looking at Jeydon's scar, giving him stares so long that it annoyed the crap out of the both of us. After spending a few moments running a couple of simple tests to determine the strength of my wrist, he declared it fully healed.

Right before we got up to leave, he stopped us and turned to Jeydon. "I'm sorry to bother you or even bring it up, but one of my old med-school buddies is a plastic surgeon. I was wondering if you'd like his business card so you can make an appointment to get that ... thing checked out."

I gave him a *how-dare-you-say-that* look and expected Jeydon to let his temper get the best of him, but he just shrugged it off and said, "It's not necessary. Thank you, though."

The doctor raised his dark thick eyebrows, which extended toward the bridge of his nose to the point where they almost formed a Frida Kahlo-style unibrow. "Are you sure? Keep in mind that it could change your life."

He nodded politely. "I'm sure."

The doctor insisted he take the card, anyway, and the minute we walked out the door, Jeydon ripped the card straight down the middle and threw it on the sidewalk.

"I'm surprised you didn't make a scene in there," I said to him, feeling a gravitational pull drawing me toward his body.

He shrugged. "Didn't have the steam. All of it got used up yesterday thanks to you. Besides, I think that doctor needs to get that unibrow fixed before I get my scar checked out."

I laughed at this, and then I did the unthinkable: I grabbed on to his hand without considering how he might react and felt his warmth. He didn't seem to mind, and I kept telling myself that he was enjoying it. Who wouldn't?

But it was kind of hard to focus on that, because another startling realization that had slipped my mind before came into my thoughts. He was every bit as soft to the touch as he was in my dreams.

We got into his car, and he started it back up again. The wheels were turning in my head in sync with the wheels of his car.

I looked out the window, but for once, I wasn't paying the slightest bit of attention to the scenery moving by. Of course, I was thinking about Jeydon and what had just happened in the doctor's office.

Jeydon must've really not cared what other people thought, because that doctor gave him an opportunity to blend in with everybody else. Of course, he probably didn't want to blend in with everybody else. He probably liked sticking out just fine.

I knew I did, because if he didn't stick out, he wouldn't be himself, and I loved him for who he was. *Did I just say love?*

I replayed his words from before in my head. *It's a part of me that can never be taken away.* What exactly did that mean? Did he mean what I thought he meant, or were these words too complex for a simpleton like me to understand?

I looked over at him. "Jeydon?"

His eyes met mine, and I felt the usual chill down my spine. "Yeah?"

My nose cringed in disgust at myself as I tried to find the right words. "What you said before, about it being a part of you that can be taken away ... it got me wondering. Isn't there anything you can do to ... fix it?"

Why was I even asking this? I didn't care if Jeydon was okay with it or not. I still felt like a hypocrite, just like all those other awful kids whose faces I wanted to kick in, including Laine.

He shook his head; it wasn't in sadness, but strictly matter-of-fact. "When I was younger, I was taken to several different plastic surgeons to get it checked out, including that same one Dr. Unibrow mentioned today. Turns out a major artery lies right beneath the scar tissue, and if anybody attempts to fix it, there's a risk I'll bleed out. They all said they were sorry but that there was nothing they could do. So, yeah, that's what I meant when I said that. I'm stuck with this thing for life."

I looked at him with cautious eyes, knowing that I was once again asking questions that pushed boundaries. "If you don't mind me asking, what happened?"

He returned my gaze with cheeks that possessed the slightest bit of color in them—a shade of chalky, pasty pink that I didn't know existed on the color spectrum. "When I was five, my mom was driving with Anthony and me in the backseat. One minute, everything was fine, and the next minute, she drove the car off the road, and the engine burst into flames. Anthony was lucky; he got thrown out of the car before it exploded, and he escaped with nothing but a broken femur and a tiny scar on his leg where the bone stuck out."

His voice started wavering with anger and bitterness. It hurt me to see him hurting, but I figured it was better than him explaining it to me with no emotion whatsoever. That hurt me even more because I hated seeing the life sucked out of him like that.

"I stuck around the flames just long enough to burn my legs, chest, and half my face off, but then the fire must've thought I tasted bitter, because it spit me back out as soon as it was able to leave permanent damage. My mom, though ..."

He didn't need to finish it. I tentatively put my hand over his free one and instantly felt like I had everything in the world. "I'm sorry."

He shook his hand off of mine and scoffed rudely. I was about to ask him why he was treating me exactly how he did the first time he met me—back when he hated me—when he looked up at me with pain-inflicted eyes that resembled mine when I talked of my own mother.

"Don't be," he said. "They did an autopsy on her body after the car crash, and the lab results that confirmed her blood alcohol content was higher than Stephen Hawking's IQ."

"So it's ..." I began to ask slowly.

"All her fault?" he finished for me briefly as if it didn't matter that she was his mother.

He probably didn't care about it, though, like how he didn't care about anything else in the world, with an exception of me, his brother, and maybe Laine. The question I wanted to ask him was why he cared about me, but I didn't, because I couldn't put into words how glad I was that I was one of the few things he cared for.

He continued, "Yes, it is. The funny part is, though, a lot of people at the hospital said she was the lucky one."

He laughed lightly at that, but I could tell that it was out of his own ignorance, if there really was such a thing. "I had no idea why they were saying that; I was obviously the lucky one because I'd escaped death. Then I saw myself in the mirror and understood what everybody was talking about."

I felt a sickening feeling in the pit of my stomach. "Please don't start that."

He wrinkled his nose like he'd smelled something bad, and I could tell that his blood pressure was rising. "I'm not starting anything. I thought you wanted me to open up to you, but here I am doing exactly that, and you're rejecting it. This is why I never tell anybody anything."

"I'm not rejecting you. I just don't like hearing you put yourself down!" I told him, hoping he'd believe me. I obviously had earned his trust if he was telling me things he'd never told anyone before, and I wanted to keep that trust as a soon-to-be amputee wants to keep his leg.

"I'm not putting myself down! I'm just telling you how I felt about it back then. If you were me, I'm sure you'd feel like your life was over too," he said in a raised voice full of irritation.

His eyes were full of an anguish I'd never seen before, and I didn't want to see it. I'd rather him be emotionless like a robot again so he wouldn't have to feel any pain. Then again, he probably did feel pain, and he just didn't show it. Like he'd said the day before, everybody hurts. I didn't know what hurt me worse, though—the realization that he was in pain or seeing him in pain.

All of the little anger I had toward him suddenly disappeared, and a sense of remorse took its place. He was right, as he always was.

I remembered my first photo shoot when I'd thought the world was over just because I'd gotten that cut. If I had a panic attack over a little cut, which was nothing compared to his scar, I couldn't imagine how awful it would be to carry something around like that for the rest of my life.

I'd probably do exactly what Jeydon said was a waste of time—hide up in an attic somewhere to escape the harsh world's criticism. Every night, I'd wish on a star that my face would heal completely overnight and cry the next morning when my wish hadn't come true. Good thing Jeydon wasn't weak like me, because if he were, maybe that would be his fate. He'd be up in that attic wasting away instead of sitting in the car with me here right now. I would have no idea what a wonderful person he was.

Thank God for that.

This wasn't one of my prouder moments, but I had something I felt like I needed to get it out of my system before I exploded. It had been a slow countdown to explosion, because I'd had it buried deep inside of me for the past ten years. But Jeydon speaking about such a personal matter was the shovel that dug it straight up, and it needed to get out.

The words came up like vomit. "I caught my mother beating one of my sisters when I was six. I've never told anybody about it before, not even my other sisters."

He made a soft, understanding smile, and I wondered if he'd known that I'd been hiding a traumatic experience like this from him and everybody else the whole time.

"I'd like to hear about it," he said.

So I finally told him the whole story, not holding back a single word.

CHAPTER 19

Discovery

After we returned to the campus, Jeydon invited me to sit with him at lunch, and of course I accepted his invitation. But as we entered the cafeteria hand in hand, I could feel people staring at us more than ever before.

I felt my cheeks get red, and my heart started beating like it had in my nightmares. I let go of his hand and staggered nervously behind him, and he slowed down his pace so I could catch up with him.

When I did, he whispered in my ear, "Just ignore them. They're a bunch of stupid kids that are trying to ruin things between us because they have nothing more important to do."

I looked at him straight in his eyes and gave him a smile that was both an apology for letting them get the best of me and a thank-you for everything you've done wrapped in one. "Why do you always have to be right?"

He laughed. "It's what I was put on the face of this earth for."

I laughed at this too, and I knew from then on out that he was definitely one hundred times over worth the ridicule.

* * *

Over the next couple of weeks as September turned into October, I began to love Jeydon a little bit more each day. Laine and I became friends, and even though Anthony and I had only a handful of conversations, I thought of him as a friend too.

I'd learned—mainly because it wasn't that hard to figure out—that Anthony was nothing like Jeydon. While Jeydon couldn't keep his mouth shut about things, Anthony found it hard to speak up about anything, and when he did, he only spoke a handful of syllables, but he made sure that each one counted for something. Jeydon loved a good fight, and Anthony shared with me that he hated fights or any type of violence. While Jeydon could look fear straight in the eye without a single nerve shaking, it wasn't hard to tell that Anthony was always nervous and afraid.

It was clear that Anthony lived in the shadow of his younger brother. Anthony was the kind of person who needed a strong individual's shadow to dwell in, and that individual was Jeydon. He was right when he'd said that Anthony needed him.

Yet it had to be an even greater connection than just that, because every time they looked at each other, I could see what they thought just by how their eyes lit up.

Jeydon's eyes had a sense of intensity that spoke just how protective he was of him, and he wouldn't in a million years let anything hurt him. And every time people even looked at Anthony the wrong way, Jeydon always made sure that they'd never look at him in that way again.

Anthony had admiration in his deep-set icy eyes that told everyone that he worshipped the ground Jeydon walked on. Whenever everybody else was absent was when he actually started to speak his mind, and he always made sure that his brother was the one to hear it.

That look in Anthony's eyes always reminded me that no matter how different he and I were, we both had one major thing in common that helped us bond.

We both needed Jeydon, and just that reason alone was enough to make us friends.

As the days passed and we spent more time together, I could sense that I was changing Jeydon almost as dramatically as he was changing me. His face lit up like a lightbulb sometimes when he talked to me, and he was laughing an actual laugh and smiling a thousand-watt smile that made the stars look like they weren't shining. He also didn't explode as much as he used to, and when he did, he didn't blow up on me. There wasn't much need for him to blow up, because after word got around about Jeydon and Kody's fight, everybody learned to shut up and respect him just as they learned to respect any other person. Jeydon might not have cared if they were talking crap about him or not, but it made controlling my blood pressure a lot easier.

I wasn't the only one who noticed that he was changing, because one evening in the middle of October, Laine and I were hanging in our dorm when she said, "I was wrong. Remember how I said a while ago that David was a miracle worker? He's not the miracle worker; *you* are. I've never seen Jeydon this happy before, and it's all thanks to you."

I couldn't help but smile ear to ear at this, but I knew that she was wrong and needed to be corrected. I shook my head and said, "I'm not the miracle worker. Jeydon is."

It was true.

A couple of months earlier when I'd looked at a shady kid like Jeydon roaming through the streets with ripped jeans and a cigarette butt hanging from his mouth, I would've thought of him as nothing but a waste of oxygen. Now after I knew how great Jeydon turned out to be, whenever I looked around at all the kids in the hallway scurrying to class, I didn't look at the preppy jocks like Connor or mean girls as skinny as a toothpick like Emily.

I looked at the kids who nobody else—including me a few months earlier—would give the time of day. If I actually gave people a chance, who knows what I'd find?

I struck up a conversation with Mrs. Kelli one evening when I went with Laine to get an extra room key, and I learned that the woman I used to call the Dorm Nazi was not anything near a Nazi but a bighearted woman with an even bigger love for romantic poetry.

That discovery made me jump for joy as if I'd struck gold. Even though I'd felt like I'd been transformed, I knew very well that it only had to be the beginning of my transformation.

I made sure that Jeydon was by my side everywhere I went, even in places like the girls' dorms—at the appropriate times, of course—and whenever I had to go to the bathroom, I made him wait right outside. I didn't know what, but something about that boy made me want to be with him 24-7. I couldn't put my finger on it, but if I had to narrow it down to two choices, they'd be Laine's theory about the special connection or the fact that I was hopelessly captivated by him.

There could be a third option too—that I was just losing my mind over him.

Whenever we—God forbid—were apart, I could always find him in my thoughts and dreams and take comfort in them, imagining that he was with me then too.

I longed to feel his soft, tender embrace again, but I always restrained myself, because I knew that if I kept up with my borderline-psychotic clinginess and excessive touching, I might scare him away and have nothing again. I didn't want to go back to having nothing, especially now that I knew what everything I needed felt like.

Come to think of it, I was surprised that I hadn't scared him away already with my constant hand-holding and heart-wrenching stories of the things Mother had done to my sisters.

I couldn't help sharing my secrets with him, and soon enough, he became the keeper of them. He was the only person I trusted enough to take that position. Sure, I gave a few hints to Laine every now and then about how bad things at home really were, but she couldn't figure out the whole puzzle like Jeydon could, so she didn't know nearly as much about me as Jeydon did.

But like I'd said to him before, his freaky sensitivity to emotions wasn't the reason I told him everything. I couldn't tell if it was the sincere and earnest look in his eyes as I told him all the horrible secrets I'd successfully hidden from the rest of the world or the soothing lull of his voice he used to comfort me with, but whatever it was, it made all my secrets slip out of my mouth one by one.

One morning—the morning of Halloween, to be exact—when the four of us were walking to breakfast together, Laine looked over and eyed me as Jeydon and I walked with our arms linked. She had a mischievous smirk on her face that apparently bugged Jeydon. I learned that he was very abrasive when it came to Laine, but besides that, he was a good friend to her. I knew this because I'd found out from Laine that Jeydon was the one wiping her tears when Emily made her cry. The only reason she sat there was because—like me—Rosie made her, and as soon as she'd told her she was friends with them, she was instantly out.

"What?" he demanded with agitation the exact moment it started getting on my nerves too.

She gestured toward me with a few hyena-like giggles escaping from her mouth. "He wants to meet her tonight."

He released an annoyed and angered sigh as I wrinkled my brow in confusion. "Laine, I told you exactly not to tell him about her!"

My expression didn't change, "Who's him?"

"David," Jeydon answered, briefly turning to me. He turned back to Laine and asked, "Why didn't you just tell him what I told you to tell him?"

At this point, I was totally lost about what they were talking about. I glanced over at Anthony to see how he was taking it. He was walking along, speechless as he always was, but he obviously had a clue as to what was going on.

Laine looked at him in disbelief. "You really think I was going to tell him that you got arrested again? The poor guy worries about you enough as it is."

Anthony lifted his head up and looked at him with guilty eyes. "I was the one who told him." He confessed so quietly that

I'd barely heard it. Still, everyone stared at him in shock, because nobody really expected him to say anything, much less confess something to the person he was afraid of disappointing the most.

Jeydon dismissed it after a second and rolled his eyes because he was more used to hearing his voice than the rest of us. "Of course you did."

At that point, I was tired of being silent and needed to say something before I exploded. "Seriously, Jeydon? Why is it such a big deal that they told David about me? And when did they even tell him this?"

I guess my second question was the easier one to answer out of the two, because Laine automatically explained to me, "Friday night when he stayed with you instead of coming to dinner with us."

I remembered that the group had plans for the previous Friday night as they always did on Fridays, but I'd wanted somebody to stay with me for a change, and I made sure that somebody was Jeydon. He seemed more eager to spend time with me than wherever they were going, so I figured it wasn't that big of a deal—some old tradition they'd always done together that a newcomer like me wasn't allowed to partake in yet.

I had no idea that David was involved with these plans. I felt sort of guilty taking Jeydon away from the only father figure he's ever had—or at least that's what Laine had told me—but it wasn't like I'd held on to his leg and said that I'd never let go unless he stayed with me. He was more than willing, so he obviously didn't care. Maybe he was even trying to avoid David, though for what reason I didn't know. From what had Laine said, he had a heart of gold.

"Adrienne," I heard a familiar but still harmonic voice call out.

It startled me. "Huh?"

"Laine asked if you were going tonight. Didn't you hear her?" He wasn't going along with the idea of me meeting his faux father as well as Laine and Anthony were. Why did it matter that I might meet David?

I shook my head in an effort to transport myself from my fantasy world and back into reality. "I spaced out at bit there, sorry. I don't know if I'm going, because you're obviously not okay with it."

His eyes were filled with unidentifiable emotions. "No, it's not that. It's just—"

"I'm not good enough for you? For David?" I shot back at him.

He took the emotional punches even better than he took physical ones. "Do you honestly think that's what I think about you? Yes, Adrienne, you've discovered the truth; I totally think you just aren't cool enough for me." He rolled his eyes as he mumbled, "Be real."

"Then why don't you want me to meet him tonight?" I asked, still not convinced that it wasn't the reason. That had to be it; there weren't any other logical explanations.

Well, there *were*, but I didn't like any of the others.

He sighed. "I don't know why exactly. I just have a gut feeling."

I tried to believe him. "If that's your only reason, then I'm going."

"I thought you said you weren't." He groaned in a way that made me more suspicious.

I shrugged my shoulders. "Things change," I said as I tried to make my voice soft and melodious like his. Of course, I failed miserably.

The whole day at school, I was on the edge of my seat in nervousness. What if David didn't like me like Jeydon's gut instinct predicted? What if I made a total fool of myself and proved that I wasn't good enough? What if I embarrassed Jeydon so much that he abandoned me and I'd have nothing again?

On the way to science class, I asked Jeydon if he thought I'd embarrass him, and he tried to assure me that it wasn't why he was uneasy about me going. But I wasn't reassured. He realized that from the beginning and kept saying throughout the day that it had nothing to do with me, but he never convinced me even though usually he could get anyone to believe anything.

During lunch, I made Laine go to the restroom with me, and when we got in there, I asked her if she knew why he didn't want me to meet David. She shrugged.

"I think he's telling the truth when he's saying that it has nothing to do with you. I think it's somewhere more along the lines of David."

"So he thinks David won't like me?" I asked.

She shook her head. "No, it's not that. Honestly, David wouldn't care if you spoke through a sock puppet or had a leg growing out of your forehead. He's just so glad that Jeydon's found someone. Sure, he had Anthony and me and him, but Jeydon's always kind of been on his own, you know? And it always pained David to see him like that."

I thought of how Jeydon had told me that he'd never told anyone anything, and I knew what she was talking about. He finally had someone to be his significant other—whatever that meant—so it didn't matter. I was there for him and happy to do so, because he was there for me too.

I nodded, and we exited the bathroom. When I reunited with Jeydon, I sat down next to him and squeezed his hand tightly. He squeezed back, and I knew that though I thought it didn't matter, I wanted to be more than his friend.

* * *

That evening, Laine and I met the boys right outside their dorm. When they saw us, Anthony smiled widely and tapped Jeydon on the shoulder. He whispered something to him, and Jeydon rolled his eyes. I had a feeling that they were talking about my choice of attire—a lacy white dress that was short in the front and long in the back.

"You look pretty," Anthony complimented, for the first time seeing me as something more than a cocker spaniel.

"Thanks," I mumbled halfheartedly, mad that the words came out of his mouth instead of Jeydon's.

We all piled in Laine's car—a black Chevy that at least had windows, minimal rust, and no bullet holes—and soon enough, we arrived at the restaurant. It was a grill and bar named Rodney's. I remembered the name, because Jeydon told me he used fake IDs to buy liquor there religiously.

I could single David out even though he was a few yards away. Laine was right about him being handsome. He might've been in his thirties, but he wore the years well. There were creases of stress under his eyes, though, probably from dealing with a young, bloodthirsty Jeydon. His chestnut-brown hair and stubble also had little signs of gray in them, like a few grains of sugar mixed in with a ton of cinnamon. He was tan, and the muscles under his flannel shirt were rippled. I could tell from the kind, caring look in his brownish-green eyes that he had to be a father in some way or another.

Laine didn't hesitate to run up and plant a kiss on his cheek, and Anthony followed by giving him an affectionate hug. When they were done with their lovefest, Jeydon and I gingerly approached him hand in hand.

The look of shock on David's face when he saw me was priceless.

"David, this is Adrienne," Jeydon said as he introduced us and let go of my hand as if to present me.

I gave my politest smile and held my hand out for him to shake it. He rejected my gesture and gave me a friendly hug instead. I liked to think that he smelled like a dad too, but since my own father was never around, I had no idea as to what a father smelled like. He smelled like burned tobacco; I guessed that was fatherly enough.

"Hey, Adrienne. I've heard so many wonderful things about you," he said.

I smiled, but my smile faded into a flat line when I remembered that he'd only heard what Anthony and Laine had to say about me. "I've heard so many wonderful things about you too."

We went inside and were seated at a large round table with chairs that squeaked against the linoleum floor. I sat between Jeydon and David, and I scooted my chair a little toward Jeydon's until he was just a touch away. He made a gesture as if he were going to touch my leg, which made me hopeful for a second, and when he pulled back swiftly, I punched him in the arm with some force. It didn't shake him any, and we both laughed out loud.

The whole time, I felt David marvel over how this could be. Jeydon saw him staring at us and gave him a dirty look.

He winced at the look and cleared his throat. "I'm sorry for staring." I turned all my attention toward him. "I have to admit that you're a lot better looking than I'd thought you would be."

"Thanks," I said flatly while Jeydon shot him another dirty look, which David ignored because he was studying my face. "You look oddly familiar. I know this is a dumb question, but do I know you, by any chance?"

Before I could answer, Jeydon answered for me. "You've probably seen her in magazines. Adrienne's a model."

"*Used* to be," I corrected as I took a nervous sip of my water. "My contract got suspended a few months ago."

This must've spiked his interest somehow. "Really? Why? Did your mom not want you to do it at such a young age?"

"Yes," I said as I nodded along with it.

Laine and Anthony did the same thing even though they had no idea why my contract got suspended. Only Jeydon knew that.

I glanced at him, and he gave me a small, uncomfortable smile, and I smiled back with my nervous one. He put his hand over mine, and that helped steady my nerves a bunch.

After a grueling round of twenty questions by David, he turned to Laine and Anthony and spoke in low whispers about people I didn't know. I asked Jeydon in a whisper who they were talking about, and he said that they were people from back home. Jeydon and I carried a separate conversation from the rest of the table, and I could really see what Laine was talking about. He might've been a part of this group, but he didn't really feel all that comfortable sitting at a table drinking sweet tea and gossiping about people he didn't give a crap about. That wasn't what either of us called an interesting conversation. It might've been harmless, but it still reminded me of the gang's constant trash-talking, and the neurons in his brain just weren't aligned in the order where he liked to talk about who was dating whom and who'd died of an overdose.

But whenever Jeydon laughed at something I said, they always paused their conversation and looked at the two of us, probably thinking somewhere along the lines of how they were so glad that he'd finally found somebody. I could see David's eyes shining at me as if to say a big fat thank-you, and I could tell that he thought of me as an angel sent from heaven to make his son happy in a way that he couldn't. I felt like I needed to correct him, because Jeydon was the angel that was sent to save me. He just had a broken wing.

The buxom waitress with a waist the size of a pencil flirted with David throughout the whole time, but he was too much in a daze to notice. She came back with our food, and "accidentally" spilled some whiskey all over his lap. "Let me get that," she offered with a goofy grin on her face.

"No, it's fine," David assured her with the slightest bit of irritation.

"At least let me wipe it off a bit," she said, blushing a shade of red as deep as my lips. She giggled in a nasally high pitch the whole time she wiped his lap off with a towel. David didn't seem to notice that her boobs were basically falling out of her shirt as she did this too.

As soon as she was gone, Laine chuckled. "That was fairly awkward."

Jeydon reached across the table and took the bottle of whiskey that the waitress had given David on the house. "And revealing," he added as he took a drink.

She laughed a little bit more. "Yeah, almost as bad as Keri's. That waitress reminds me a bit of her, doesn't she, Jeydon?"

He did nothing but nod, probably flustered that they were talking about people he didn't give a crap about again. I gave him a confused look, and he told me that she was the neighborhood's slut. David's eyes reflected the same type of pain I felt whenever somebody trash-talked about Jeydon's scar.

He cleared his throat again, and I could tell that it was a serious matter, because his voice dropped an octave. "Speaking of your mother, I have some news I want to share with you if you're willing to hear it, Jeydon."

Anthony's face grew pale under his tan, and the tips of his ears got really red. Laine dropped her fork clear under the table. Jeydon was holding himself back from getting out of his seat and slapping David smartly across the face.

I was too baffled to notice these expressions at the moment. "What do you mean by news? She's dead."

David looked at me with confusion. "No, she isn't. Who told you ..." His mouth opened, and he shifted his widened eyes toward Jeydon. "You didn't!"

Jeydon had enough anger to enrage everybody else in the restaurant. "You're an idiot," he growled at David. "Why did you even bring it up? You know nobody here gives a crap about her besides you!"

Before David could speak, Jeydon snatched a beer bottle and threw it across the room, narrowly missing our waitress's head. Everybody was startled by the flyaway bottle, and all stared at our table like it was floating in midair. The waitress stumbled and crashed the tray full of dirty dishes that she was carrying onto the ground. She looked at him with bewildered eyes.

"Oops. I thought there was an apple on your head, and I wanted to see if I could knock it off," Jeydon mocked through gritted teeth.

David, who should have been used to such behavior by then, looked extremely embarrassed and aghast. "Jeydon, cut it out! Tell that poor girl you're sorry, and clean that mess up!"

Jeydon didn't respond with words, sweeping his arm in one swift movement across the table, crashing everything that was on the table onto the floor.

He looked up at him with furnaces for eyes. "I bet you expect me to clean this mess up too."

I couldn't take it anymore. Nobody noticed that I'd fled from the building with tears rolling down my cheeks. I wasn't that shocked about the scene that Jeydon had just made like everybody else was; I was shocked at the fact that he'd lied to me.

I'd trusted him, told him everything I was too afraid to tell anyone else. And what did he do? He'd lied to me just like Richard did. This was an even worse feeling, because Richard wasn't the keeper of my secrets; Jeydon was. Richard might've thought he'd known me, but he couldn't see through my eyes and into my battered, terrified soul like Jeydon could. Richard was wrong about me, and Jeydon was right about me as he was right about everything.

I wondered if Jeydon had been right when he'd said that I was stupid to trust somebody like him.

But despite his warnings, I'd trusted him, and I came to love him with all my heart. I continued to tell him everything and thought he'd told me everything, but for all I knew, everything he said could've been a lie. Even worse, it could've all been a mind game. I knew how much he loved those.

There was a small fountain with a swan on the top right outside the building. I sat down there and cried bitterly for what seemed like forever, even though it was only a few minutes.

I heard sirens and saw red-and-blue lights flashing that signified police, and I shouldn't have thought that much about it, because Jeydon truly deserved a good punishment for his ugly, raging fit. But still I felt a sickening feeling in my stomach, and I realized that I still cared for him. With that realization, I decided that it wasn't like Richard's deceit at all, because it wasn't just a small part of me that still cared for him.

I loved and cared for him with all my heart. Also, I could never say I loved Richard, but I'd be lying if I said that I didn't love Jeydon. I still thought of him as the angel with a broken wing that was sent from heaven to save me from falling through the clouds at one hundred miles per hour.

I heard his voice. "Adrienne."

I saw a pair of ratty sneakers and looked up, and he was there in front of me.

All my anger vanished as he sat down beside me and spoke with a soothing voice. "I'm such an idiot for lying to you. I know you've probably lost all your trust and hope in me, but I swear that I hate myself for hurting you."

I speechlessly moved in toward him and rested my head on his shoulder. He held me in his arms and gently stroked my hair as I cried. While he did this, he explained the whole thing to me.

"I only told you that she was dead because I didn't think you'd ever figure out the truth, and I didn't want you to. She's dead to the three of us, and we can't stand to talk about her, so David knows to shut his trap about her. Still, I was wrong to make a scene in there. It terrifies me what I'm capable of doing when I let my anger get the best of me."

"Did you get in any trouble? I saw the cop cars," I asked, not taking my head up from his shoulder. I wanted to keep it there forever.

"I should've, but they let David decide what to do with me, and he didn't press any charges. I was given a warning. The waitress was pretty ticked off about that," he said.

"You're lucky to have him as your dad. He cares about you and loves you so much no matter how awful you are. I wish my dad were like that." I'd already told him all about how my dad was never around to hold me in his arms.

"He's not my dad," he retorted with anger. "He loves Keri; that's the only reason he took me in."

He went on to explain how his mom was a drug addict that sold her body for money. She was usually very fragile and scared to hurt a fly whenever she was sober, but when she was drunk or high, she became very aggressive and hit Anthony every time she was able to get her hands on him. Jeydon soon became Anthony's protector, because he easily overpowered her, but whenever he turned his back for just a second, he'd come back and find Anthony lying on the floor beaten to a bloody pulp.

One night when a couple of her drug-addicted clients started attacking them, they had no choice but to flee over to David's house, and he promised to go over and tell her to knock it off or else he would contact the authorities in a heartbeat.

He didn't do as he promised, though, because he fell in love with her the first moment he saw her.

"Maybe he saw some hope in her, like how you saw some hope in me," I said as I took my head off his shoulder to look into his eyes, which I melted into like butter in a fire.

He scowled. "She's one of those people who has wasted all their hope. When she was arrested after the car crash for DUI, she promised us that she was going to rehab and would change. At first, I believed her, but after rehab, she relapsed before she was able to gain custody of us. She promised the same thing again, and I believed her, and she broke her promise again. That cycle repeated a few more times before she wasted up every last ounce of her hope, and my life spiraled down the drain with arrests and all that crap. After my third arrest, they told me that I was going back into her custody. Anthony was thrilled, but I knew it was a disaster waiting to happen. And I was right. Soon after she saw what she did to my face, she went back on drugs to cope with her guilt. After living four long years with her, I got sick of her crap and ran away to Tampa Bay with Laine, Anthony, and a lovesick David."

"From what it sounds like, he loves you more than he loves her, because he helped you run away," I reasoned, not believing that David only wanted him for his mom. But what did I know?

He shook his head. "That's impossible. Didn't you see the way he looked when Laine mentioned her name? Cupid could shoot him with an arrow, and it wouldn't make any difference. He doesn't focus on any other person but her."

I knew I was taking a risk when I said, "Like how I am about you?"

He laughed and nodded. "Yes, exactly. Come to think of it, you and David have a lot in common. You both find hope in the hopeless."

I smiled and rested my head on his shoulder again. "I'm glad I can."

"Me too."

Since that had gone well, I wondered what else would go well. It was two months already, way over the time for me to find out.

I looked down at his hand and put mine over his. I might've done this a thousand times in the past month, but the feeling never got old. "So if you promise not to throw any more beer bottles, I was wondering if you'd like to, um ..."

He smiled a little, and I knew he could tell what I was thinking. "Yes, Adrienne, I'd love to go to dinner with you. Is Friday okay?"

I laughed. "You took the words right out of my mouth."

CHAPTER 20

Together

I told Laine about my plans with Jeydon later that night as we walked to the dorm together, and of course, the first thing she asked was whether it was a date or not. I stopped walking with a skip in my step at that question. I told her that I had no idea. I never have any idea what was going through his head.

Even after we'd long dropped the topic, I lay in my bed for hours tossing and turning thinking about whether it was a date or a friendly outing. The eagerness in his voice and twinkle in his eyes said yes, but there was a certain factor missing: every other boy would max out if he were lucky enough to go on a date with me.

What was it? Oh yeah—attraction.

It was no secret that there was something in him that I found extremely irresistible—probably his fearlessness, the way he could always calm me down if I was having a panic attack over Mother, how he could always turn the course of the day completely around by making me laugh, or even the fact that he didn't fall head over heels for me like everybody else did.

Who was I kidding? I found everything about him attractive—even the scar—and if he had the slightest bit of attraction toward me, he concealed it well.

But I could tell that while everybody else looked at my face, he looked into my soul, and that wasn't nearly as pretty. I should've given him gratitude that he didn't run away screaming. But then again, Jeydon never ran away screaming from anything, not even the hollow shell that was my soul—or at least that's how I pictured it to look, but I had no idea as to what it really looked like or if it even existed. If it did, only Jeydon could see it.

Yes, a couple of times, I'd tried to see my soul for myself, but every time I looked in front of a mirror and stared at myself, I couldn't get past the plump red lips and large, mahogany eyes that lacked any shine or glimmer whenever Jeydon wasn't around. I liked to think that his eyes were the same way, and Anthony verified that it was true.

That week, I was on pins and needles. I was always the one who brought up our plans whenever I was conversing with Jeydon. That was a bad sign. But for the first time since the day of the fight, he let me hug him and said that he didn't care if I never let go. I guessed that was a good sign. But he didn't say anything about wanting me to be in his arms forever and ever, so that had to be a bad sign.

By the time the sun set on Tuesday, I was both mentally and physically exhausted from all the rhetorical debates over Jeydon's attraction level for me.

I asked Laine what I should do, and she advised me to just ask him.

"Yeah, if it were only that simple," I sneered as I picked up a wrinkled-up pile of Rosie's stinky clothes and threw them onto her bunk. At that point, we'd almost completely driven Rosie out of the room, and that was just the way we liked it.

"It is."

I wanted to scoff at that, but I knew only Jeydon could pull off the smart-alecky act with her and get away with it. "Nothing about him is simple."

She nodded. "That might be true, but do you know what is simple? Love. In fact, it's the simplest thing in the world, even when it involves Jeydon."

"What are you trying to say?" I asked skeptically.

I didn't need to ask her that, because I already knew what she was saying; I just thought it was too good to be true.

"Isn't it obvious what I'm saying? He loves you, Adrienne, for who you are and not your body," said Laine.

I plopped down like a brick onto my bed. "How do you know he's in love with me? He never tells you anything," I said, still skeptical.

She giggled. "Please. It's almost as obvious as your love for him."

"It's not that obvious, because I've never noticed it," I mumbled.

"He displays his love differently from the way you do," she explained as I leaned in closer, not wanting to miss a single word. "You should've seen how worried Jeydon was on Friday after you ran off like that. He almost tackled a couple of the cops who were blocking the exit to get to you. I've never seen him that protective of anyone before, not even Anthony."

"Wow," I whispered as I tried to wrap my head around the idea. It seemed absurd, especially after Jeydon had told me tales of what he had done to kids who'd picked on Anthony when they were younger. There was a time when a couple of kids jumped Anthony and beat him pretty badly. Jeydon found out where they lived, broke all their windows with rocks, and wrote some things I won't repeat on the wall of their house using a can of cheap spray paint.

That would've been arrest number five if David hadn't bribed the kids' parents—who were drowning in mortgage payments—to not press charges. I learned that if it weren't for David, Jeydon would've been arrested a dozen more times without exaggeration.

But on a second thought, I could see what Laine was talking about. My mind went backward to the previous week in science class when Emily said that I had some severe self-esteem issues for touching Jeydon without dry-heaving.

I smiled as I remembered what he'd said to her. "I'd shut that butthole you call a mouth if I were you, because everybody knows you've got major issues with self-esteem." That shut her up.

I also thought of the hateful looks he'd given Kody. Now all the other football jerks were scared of Jeydon, much in the way that I had been scared of Tori for all those years. That only made Kody resent him even more. He figured out that the way to make Jeydon mad was to trash-talk me instead of his looks, and he made crude remarks about me in science class. Eventually, Jeydon turned around and growled, "Say one more word about her, and I'll pound your face in twice as hard as I did last time."

Of course, Kody had continued, and they went outside to "settle things" during lunch. Kody came back sporting another broken nose and a nasty shiner while Jeydon wore a triumphant smile.

These were the little things that Jeydon did that made me realize that he just might be in love with me.

* * *

Jeydon said to meet me in the parking lot, and I told him I couldn't wait. Right after class was dismissed, I ran to the dorm, and Laine ran after me. Eventually, she caught up to me.

"What's the hurry?" she asked as she tried to catch her breath.

"You know what the hurry is; I've got to get ready for tonight!" I said, panting also.

"Why? You know appearances don't matter with Jeydon."

"They matter to me!" I retorted loudly but then I realized that what I'd said made me look like a hypocrite.

She didn't pay much attention to my hypocrisy. Her voice lowered, though. "Wear exactly what you're wearing right now, and tell me what happens. If everything is exactly the way it was before, then from now on, you can pretty yourself up to your little heart's content. Do we have a deal?" she asked as she held out her hand.

I thought about it for a second. "Deal," I said as I shook her hand.

An hour later, I was in the dorm alone. Laine left because she and Anthony had plans to study in the library. After she left, I worked on my appearance; I at least had to fix myself up a little bit. I never needed that much makeup, anyway, so all I put on was the tiniest touch of mascara to lengthen my thick, dark lashes. My outfit was the thing I wished I could work on. I was wearing a white T-shirt with the smallest smudge of BBQ sauce from lunch and Jeydon's flannel jacket that he'd let me wear so that I could hide it. My jeans had a rip in them, and now I was wearing sneakers on a regular basis instead of heels.

At first glance, I looked like a disaster, and I wondered what Mother would say if she saw me dressed like this, but when I took a second look at myself in the mirror, I saw something different.

I saw Jeydon looking back at me with beaming eyes and a smile on his face. He mouthed the words *I love you,* and then I was looking at my reflection again.

It dawned on me what Laine was saying. Appearances didn't make me any better of a person, and getting all dolled up for him didn't give me an edge. In fact, I might go further with him looking like this, because he'd get to see how much he was changing me.

With that, I left the dorm, not even bothering to brush my hair.

I met up with him in the parking lot, where I saw him leaning against his car smoking a cigarette. I leaned on the car next to him and could feel his hip touching mine.

"I thought you quit."

He gave me the classic kid-caught-with-his-hand-in-the-cookie-jar look. "I did, but once in a while, I need one, because it helps steady my nerves."

I didn't fully know what to think of this, because I knew how much he hated the smell of a burning cigarette. He hated it so much that I wondered why he'd started in the first place.

"What are you so worried about that you need one?" I asked.

He looked at me with eyes that I always melted into. "Things you wouldn't understand."

I gave him a tiny smile and traced the scar on his arm. "Try me."

He smiled weakly and threw the cigarette butt on the ground. "Get in the car, and I'll tell you."

As soon as we got in the car, he started it, and he drove out of the parking lot before he began. "It's them—David and Laine. Every single conversation they've had with me for the past week has been about you. It drives me insane."

"So what? You don't like talking about me?" I asked, slightly insulted.

He shook his head. "Not when it's all they ever talk about."

"They're just really thrilled that you've found somebody. Laine and I talk about it a lot," I began.

A ghost of a smile flickered across his face. "You do? All Anthony and I talk about is that too. It's okay when I talk to him, because he doesn't get all up in my face about it. I wish he'd get over his anxiety and talk around you. You'd love what he has to say."

I was flattered that he talked about me a lot, but more than anything, I was intrigued. "Really? What does he say?"

We took turns telling each other what we talked about. The difference was that I found a way to work my conversations with Laine into my conversations with him, and he told me things that Anthony said that I never would've guessed. Apparently, Anthony was a big push factor of our romance, finding a way to work into it and making it move faster. He was indeed attracted to me, but when he saw me clinging on to Jeydon, he completely set that aside, because he knew from then that Jeydon and I would be together.

"So," I asked cautiously, knowing the answer might hurt me, "are we together?"

He smiled mischievously, and I think he liked the thought, but I wasn't sure.

"That depends on if you want us to be."

I laughed but knew that wasn't the best thing he could answer because he was so sensitive to emotions that he'd have to notice I had feelings for him. "Yes, if you haven't noticed. The big question is if *you* want us to be together."

He laughed too. "I've wanted to since that day when you said hi to me. I didn't notice the spark at first, but it was there. Then after you told me everything even when I told you nothing and showed me the kindness the world never did, you kept growing on me more and more each day. You're the best thing that ever happened to me, Adrienne, so I say yes a hundred times over."

I felt tears forming in my eyes. When he scowled and asked, "What's wrong?" I knew I had to dry them up and did exactly that.

I grabbed hold of his hand and smiled. "I'm so happy. You don't understand how long I've wanted this."

He appeared extremely intrigued. "You've got to be kidding me."

I shook my head, and he laughed like it was some kind of joke.

"How long?" he asked.

"Since the first moment I saw you," I answered, but I knew I wouldn't be telling the full truth, and I always told him the truth, so I added, "No, even before that."

He looked so lost, and since he understood everything so well, I wasn't used to seeing that expression. "How?"

I took a deep breath and knew that after some of the things I told him, it shouldn't have been that hard to say, but the words still came with difficulty.

"I had dreams about you before I met you. I have no idea why or how. All I know is that I fell asleep on the plane ride coming over here, and I had a dream about you. Ever since I found out that you were a real person, you've been all I could think about."

He turned away from me, took a few deep breaths, and appeared to be concentrating on driving—something he almost never did. He didn't have to pay that much attention, like how he didn't have to pay any attention in class to get straight As on the midterms.

I was about to ask him what he was thinking when he said, "I've never believed in fate, but now I do. I mean, let's be honest, if you hadn't had dreams about me, you would've run away like everybody else does."

I shook my head. I didn't even like thinking about that thought before I met him, and now it pained me. "No, I wouldn't have."

He sighed. "I'm not saying you're a bad person; I'm just stating a fact. It doesn't matter." He looked at me with a look of affection and gratitude, and it didn't matter to me anymore if he found me physically attractive or not.

He caressed my hand gently. "You're here, and we're together. That's the only thing I care about right now. I swore that finding someone who could see past my scarred face and love me for who I am would only happen in my wildest dreams."

"Oh, Jeydon." It was all I could think of to say. I was more than aware that I was falling hard for this boy.

He continued, "Last night, while I was staring at the ceiling trying to fall asleep, I wondered if I'd wake up and you'd be gone. That's my biggest fear."

I held up his hand and kissed the warm, soft skin on the center of his palm. "I thought you weren't afraid of anything,"

He shook his head. "Everybody hurts. Everybody fears. I'm no exception."

"Yes, you are," I replied. "And that's why I love you."

Instead of saying *I love you too,* he looked as if he'd had an epiphany. "See, this is what I'm talking about. It was fate for you to go to that party and fate for me to have a huge blowout with Keri that sent me running. It was pure fate for us to find each other."

"I've thought about it many times before, but all I know is that whatever it is, I couldn't live without it," I said, and I knew it wasn't an exaggeration.

He gave an understanding smile. "Me, either."

He looked out the window and then back at me excitedly. Up to that point, I'd never really seen him excited before, so I knew this must've been important to him.

"We're here," his voice rang out.

I looked outside and saw nothing but sand and palm trees. "I thought you were taking me out to dinner downtown."

"No, I said I was taking you out to dinner. I didn't tell you where," he said as he smiled mischievously.

"Where?" I asked stupidly.

"That's classified information. Come on, and I'll show you."

I didn't know what to think, but as soon as I got out of the car, he took me by the hand and instructed me to close my eyes.

"Where are you taking me?" I asked again.

"Trust me," I heard his voice say. It sounded even more angelic with my eyes closed. "You'll love it."

He led me to the secret destination with me giggling the whole way. It started raining down on us all of a sudden—typical Florida weather—and I said, "We're definitely going to have to kiss now."

He laughed but didn't say another word. I opened up my eyes a little to see his expression, and he caught me in the act.

"Not so fast," he said with a chuckle. "We're not there yet."

I squeezed my eyes shut. "How much longer?" I asked in a way that made me feel like a whiny six-year-old.

"To the place or until we kiss?" he asked.

I didn't need to open my eyes to know he was smirking as he said it.

I wanted to laugh, but I couldn't—not when we were talking about something that I wanted so much from him that he didn't want as much from me.

"Both," I answered.

"We're almost to the place, and we'll see about the kiss."

He might've been joking around, but I didn't think it was funny. I wanted to know what he was thinking, and since I couldn't get into his mind, I had to think of another way to get this information.

Maybe Laine was right. Maybe I should just ask him. Maybe things were just that simple. Maybe he was just that simple.

"Jeydon, do you even want to kiss me?" I asked timidly.

At first, I beat myself up over not being bold, but I stopped, because I could've easily chickened out.

I still had my eyes closed and couldn't see his expression, so I had to listen closely to the tone of his voice. He sounded sincere.

"Yeah. I do. What makes you think that I don't?"

"You just sound like you don't, like last week when you didn't want me to meet David," I said as I felt a particularly large drop of rain trickling down the back of my neck.

The urge to get closer to him was even greater than it had been most days, and I wondered if the electricity of the lightning had something to do with the extra electricity between our bodies—which, by my guess, were six inches apart at the closest.

His voice had a hint of uneasiness to it. "I want to really badly, but I want to do it when the time is right. I've never kissed anyone before. My scar isn't exactly what you'd call a chick magnet."

I was almost positive that his history of romance was nonexistent already, but I didn't blame it on the scar like he and everybody else did. I blamed it on the fact he had no interest in anything but mind games and troublemaking. He never once gave a girl a look of lust, desire, or even interest.

He never gave a girl a look of interest—that is, until he met me.

I didn't say anything, and I don't think he expected me to, because he continued, "It's probably not as special to you as it is to me. Only God knows how many boys you've kissed."

Was that him implying that I was attractive or a slut?

"No, I've just kissed a jerk and another guy whose name I don't remember. And I shouldn't count either of them, because I didn't feel anything."

"You mean you didn't feel a spark?"

"Exactly," I said a little bit too eagerly. "And that's why I want to kiss you so much, because I feel like I have everything right now just because I'm holding your hand. I want to kiss somebody I actually love and be kissed by somebody who loves me. At least I pray to God that you love me."

For a moment, the only sound that came out of him was the whoosh of his breath, and I could barely hear that because of the violent downpour of rain. "Promise to keep your eyes closed?"

"Why?" I asked as my heart sank to my toes. "You should know by now that it doesn't bother me."

He sighed heavily, and I knew that he had pain in his eyes though I wasn't looking at them. "It bothers me right now. I guess when it comes to something like this, I care that I look like something straight out of a horror movie. You can open your eyes if you want to. We're here, anyway."

I opened my eyes cautiously and faced a sight I thought I'd only see in postcards. The most perfect beach was before me, with sand that looked more like crushed-up crystals of diamond than actual sand and a true-blue ocean that formed a crashing lull of waves.

I turned to him and inched toward him until my perky nose touched his delicate angular one. They would have met each other perfectly were he not about four or so inches taller than I was.

Noting this height difference, when I hugged him, I tucked my head in the space between his neck and chin, not caring that part of the skin was rough and scratchy from his scar. Instead, I listened to his rhythmic, fast heartbeat. I could feel my heart beat fast in my chest also, and I wondered if our hearts were in sync with each other—like how Richard's heart failed to do with mine.

I released my grip on him and prepared to do something more than just hug him. Don't get me wrong: having his arms wrapped around me still felt amazing, but first I had something on my chest I had to tell him. No, it wasn't on my chest. It was coming straight from my heart.

"This place is beautiful, and so are you. You know how a few weeks ago you told me that you've learned to like every part of you? I love all the parts of you, and I didn't need to learn; it just comes naturally."

At that, he looked at me with the same look I'd seen on his face in my first dream of him. I realized that I was inaccurate about that dream, because it wasn't a look of confidence but a look of love.

Right then and there, on a beautiful beach in the pouring rain, was where he kissed me for the first time. His lips were so soft and delicate against mine, and I wondered how he could have possibly never been kissed before and be that good at it. Any other idiot would say that it was just technique or beginner's luck, but I know it was so much more than that. As we were kissing, I could feel electricity soar through my body as if lightning were striking down on us, but in a good way that instantly woke up every cell out of which Mother and Richard had sucked the life.

And, yes, I did feel sparks fly. In fact, it wasn't just a couple of random sparks flying aimlessly around but a captivating fireworks show with a vivid array of brilliant colors.

When his lips left mine, I was taken away from euphoria and sent back to reality, but it was still a happy reality, because he was standing there so close to me with his arms gently placed around my waist.

"Did you feel what I just felt?" I asked him.

He grinned wider than he ever had before, and his features glowed along with it in the way that made him look like an angel. "If you felt like you left the earth and went straight into heaven, then yes, you felt what I felt."

I laughed and said, "No, it didn't feel like that. It felt twenty times better. I feel like I've not lived until just now, and I know that I'd never truly loved anybody until I met you."

He kept his large smile and beamed at me. I could tell that he was thinking about something, and he finally said it. "It astounds me that out of all the flowers in the garden, the rose would fall in love with the thorn."

At first, his metaphor went above my head. "Either she's a really stupid rose, or the thorn isn't as sharp as he thinks he is."

He shrugged his shoulders and said, "I think it's the third option."

I laughed in remembrance. "Which is?"

"That their love is more than what meets the eye."

Since I had no words to tell him exactly what I thought of him, I kissed him tenderly on the lips, and even though I'd been kissed many times before by Richard, I felt like I'd never actually been kissed before until that moment. I guess I'd never had a genuine kiss with Richard, really, considering that half the time, it felt like he was trying to shove his tongue down my throat until I vomited—or at least that's what his kissing felt like compared to Jeydon's.

As soon as I was done sampling a little bit of heaven, I replied, "I think that too."

CHAPTER 21

Shadows

Eventually, the rain grew old, and I wanted to go indoors, so Jeydon led me to a small, homey beach house the color of a robin's egg that was about one hundred yards away from the shoreline. I saw how the rain concealed our footsteps as we walked, and I wondered if walking on the beach with him would someday be a distant memory.

No, I would never let him fade away from me like all of my other relations had. Never. Like I said, I couldn't live without him. I didn't know how I'd spent the first sixteen years of my life without him. The answer was actually pretty simple, though. I lived those years miserably. But all those years were worth it, all because I was with him. We were together—whatever that meant—and his extra-tight grip on my hand reassured me of it.

Jeydon went to open the door of the beach house, but I stopped him and asked, "Whose house is this?" because I wanted to make sure he wasn't breaking and entering. He'd done that several times before.

"David's. He bought it after we moved down here," he informed me.

"It's nice," I said, though I wasn't one to make small conversation like this. I called it small and meaningless; everybody else called it normal.

Of course, he wasn't, either, but he nodded along and gestured toward the ocean. "Yeah, but he bought it for the view."

I looked over and saw that the sun appeared to be in the form of a hemisphere as it was setting over the ocean, bursting the reflections in the waves and the sky into a kaleidoscope of pinks, oranges, yellows, and blues. "I can see why."

We went into the house, and the first things I realized about it were that it appeared to look a lot more compact on the inside than the outside and that while the walls on the outside were blue, the walls on the inside were a cheery shade of yellow.

Jeydon took a seat at the small table in the kitchen that was meant to be only for two people but somehow managed to accommodate five chairs crammed around it.

"Jeydon, I have a question."

He looked alarmed and interested at the same time. "What is it?"

I took the seat directly across from him. "What are we doing here?"

He blinked a couple of times before answering. "This," he answered, "is the cheapest and most efficient restaurant there is. Not to mention all the free bait."

I found myself yet again puzzled by him. "What? We're eating here? And what do you mean by live bait?"

He held out his hand. "Come on, and I'll show you what I mean by that."

He led me outside to a boarded-over and unsteady-looking deck that at first I was reluctant to get on, because I didn't think it would support my weight. When he finally convinced me that it was safe to stand on, I first tested its stability by putting one foot on it, or at least I was going to before he fearlessly jumped on to reassure me there was nothing to be scared of.

The deck was slick from the rain, which was still pouring down, and I was cautious to place one foot after another, but it was structurally sound. At the end of the deck lay a small rowboat floating in the water, and I had a feeling that I knew what he'd meant by live bait. My suspicions were confirmed when he reached in to the boat to grab a small tackle box and opened it only to reveal a can full of live worms squirming around.

I grimaced and dry-heaved a little at the sight of them, and he laughed.

"Hop on board," he joshed.

I made a sour face and asked with a groan, "Why are you making me do this?"

He smiled deviously. "I want to show you what my idea of having fun is."

I grimaced and replied, "I thought your idea of fun was causing trouble."

He laughed and nodded. "Yes, it is, but that wouldn't be fun for you, now would it?"

He was right; spending time locked up in a cell for doing reckless things that were enjoyable at the time wasn't my idea of fun. I'd already experienced enough of that.

"What makes you think touching a bunch of slimy stuff is my idea of fun?"

His expression became a little more serious. "How do you know that it's not fun? Have you ever tried?"

Again, he was right. I shook my head and felt like an insignificant baby for being me. I remembered, though, that Jeydon was especially bulletproof when I was weak, so for once, being insignificant and vulnerable was okay.

I still felt small, though, probably because I knew that if Mother saw me acting like such a coward, she'd snarl her upper lip at me in disgust. Then again, she'd probably not be paying attention to me, because she'd be too busy snarling at Jeydon's scar in disgust. I didn't like thinking about how Mother would react if she found out that I was in love with him, because the very possibility of the thought caused me discomfort. I pushed the thought into the back of my mind and focused on what was in front of me.

Jeydon had a look in his eyes that made me wonder if he knew what I was thinking, and to think that he knew the depth of my incompetence made me lean over to kiss him again. As soon as we were done with that, he asked me if we were going to get in the boat, and I simply nodded.

Jeydon hopped in the boat first, of course, and when I lost my footing while trying to get in and let out a squeal, he caught me in his arms and pulled me in. "Are you okay?" he asked.

I nodded, and he went to work putting his worm on the hook. As he was doing this simple task, I marveled at him wordlessly. The rain was beginning to cease, and the sunlight was starting to peek through the clouds again, so his skin and eyes started shining along with the sunlight a little more than they usually did.

Most people would say that it was because of how the light shone down on his features, but I knew better. It was because he was happy. I smiled at the thought of him being happy instead of miserable for once. If anybody on earth deserved to be happy, it was him. People like Tori and Richard were those who should've been miserable, and in a way they were. At least I wished they were, but something inside me knew that they were probably perfectly content running around screwing up other peoples' lives.

But not Jeydon. He'd told me once that he'd never in his life been happy because he deserved to be that way, and that was the only time he'd ever been wrong about something.

Despite all his flaws and the reckless decisions he'd made in the past, he deserved to be happy. He didn't deserve to get in that car crash at such a young age that left him with a scarred face that he and the world obviously thought to be unlovable. He didn't deserve to be abandoned, rejected, and ridiculed about something he couldn't help to the point where he became angry at the world. He didn't deserve to be jumped that one fateful night that would sentence him to prison for the first time, which only hardened his heart instead of helping him.

His knife for a voice cut in to my deep thinking. "Adrienne, are you there?"

I blinked fast a few times to snap out of my daze. "Yeah. You just look so happy that I couldn't help but notice."

He smiled gently and put his fishing pole aside to caress my hand. "Why wouldn't I be? I'm experiencing the joy of first love, something I never thought I'd experience. Also keep in mind how miserable I was before I met you." His smile faded and was replaced with a look of pain.

I tried to deny that he was in any pain by retorting, "Yes, I do. You told me that you've never been happy before you met me." That look of pain in his eyes always caused me discomfort, but now that I loved him so much that I couldn't bear to see him in any pain, and I wanted him to be happy forever.

But that would never be, because everybody hurts.

He gently raised my hand up to his lips and kissed it. "You only know the half of it, but don't get me wrong. You still know me better than everybody else, even my own brother."

For some reason, I felt like I was going to cry. "Please tell me, Jeydon. You have no idea how badly I want to hear it." I didn't know which one hurt worse—knowing the fact that he was hiding things from me again or that he had things that were so dark that he felt a need to hide them from me.

For the next hour as the sun set along the horizon, Jeydon and I fished while he told me all kinds of horror stories from his past. It didn't matter to me if they were about what he had done to other people or what people had done to him, because it was all awful, and it made me want to hold on to him and never let go—which is what I basically did.

I had no clue why he didn't shed a single tear as he talked about all those horrors, but I reminded myself that this was Jeydon. He had to remain strong even when there was nobody to be strong for.

When he was in the hospital after the car crash, every doctor was convinced that Jeydon was as good as dead. Even after he became a medical marvel that somehow pulled through, doctors condemned him to having the same quality of life as a vegetable because his lower body was so burned that he'd have to be catheterized and in a wheelchair.

That made him determined to prove them wrong, and within the next three months, he could walk and use the bathroom without any aid from a machine or crutches, but there was something else doctors realized about Jeydon that made him even more of an exception. Despite having little schooling, he could read at the level of an eighth grader. His brain absorbed information like a sponge, and people began to closely analyze him, but Jeydon went through a stage where he didn't talk, because the bulging scar tissue on his face made it difficult to pronounce words correctly, so some people tried to pass him off as retarded.

When he was seven, there was an opportunity for experimental surgery that would cut around the artery that was preventing him from having restorative surgery. He wanted the taunting of his much-older classmates to stop, but what he wanted more than anything was to talk normally again. Jeydon ended up getting his wish, but that's where the luck ended. The surgery was otherwise a complete disaster, because all they did was remove as much scar tissue as they could around the artery until it bulged out from underneath. The effect gave him the ability to use his jaw for daily tasks like speaking or eating, but it caused his face to look ten times worse than it had, because while his scar was a grotesque mass of puffy, discolored flesh before, it caved in to his cheekbone like a huge bite of his face had been taken out afterward. I hadn't even noticed that his scar caved in until he pointed it out.

For five months, he said that he had mono, and he hid from the world. His foster parents respected that at first, but after a while, they got tired of his moping around and moved him to the next home.

When he went to the next school, which was a special school for exceptionally bright children like Jeydon, most kids did exactly what he'd expected them to do. One kid was relentless, though, and he lived to make Jeydon feel like crap about his face. Jeydon finally lashed out his pent-up anger and punched the kid in the face so hard that he broke the bone below his eye, leaving him with a deformed face, as well.

After being sent to a mental hospital for six grueling months and a rehabilitation camp for another four, he was kicked out of that school, and since nobody wanted an eight-year-old with a diagnosed anger disorder and a disfigured face, he was sent to a boys' home.

He escaped and was out on the streets when he got jumped. He was sent to prison with the charge of attempted robbery and manslaughter, and an older boy took him under his wing and taught him how to fight. Soon after, he was released, but he got right back in again at nine when he dislocated a kid's shoulder. He spent another year in prison and a year out on the streets as part of a gang of older juvenile delinquents who convinced him to take up smoking and wreaked havoc with him.

A boy who was a part of his gang found out about his secret intellect, and after Jeydon decided that he wanted to rid himself of it, they stole narcotics from a local CVS, and he got hooked on those for a while. But eventually he got busted and arrested for the third time. That was where Keri took responsibility for Jeydon and regained custody of her long-lost son.

By the end, I felt tears coming on as I clung to him tighter than ever before, and Jeydon's voice wavered in rage. "I wanted to believe that it would get better once I reunited with Anthony and met Laine and David, but it never did. I still got arrested and in fights and woke up every morning enraged. Some days, I was angry because of what could've been, but the majority of the time, I woke up just plain mad at the world for being so cruel and heartless."

His voice grew softer, and he looked at me with loving eyes and a gentle smile. "But I guess the world's not as heartless as I thought of it to be, because it was generous enough to give me what I thought I'd never have—somebody like you. I apologize that I've never told you in words exactly what I've been through or how much I love you, because I never really could until now."

A tear trickled down my right cheek, but the tears weren't over the injustices of Jeydon's past anymore. "You really love me?"

He laughed a little and nodded. "How couldn't I? You're everything I ever wanted plus more. The fact that you're open-minded enough to love me alone makes me love you like I've never loved anyone."

I loosened my embrace on him so that I could raise my lips up to his, and I kissed him over and over again. This was interrupted by a tug on his fishing pole. He released his grip on me and reeled it in.

In the hour that Jeydon told me his life story, he'd managed to catch four whoppers while I caught nothing, which was just another thing to make me feel inadequate. It turned out that Jeydon also knew how to build a fire from being out on the streets, and while he put the fish on a spit he'd made out of a couple of sticks, I cuddled up to him because I preferred him to keep me warm instead of the fire.

He took the fish off the spit and gave us each a serving and told me tales about fishing while I listened with eager ears and a belly full of delicious fish. He told me that David was the one who had taken him fishing for the first time and told with guilty eyes how David told him that he loved Keri on one fishing trip. He got so mad that he shoved a fishhook through David's lip. He said that it wasn't one of his prouder moments.

For a moment, we both stared into the fire with our arms wrapped around each other instead of talking, and while I stared at it, a thought popped into my head. "How bad does it hurt to be burned?" I asked as I winced at the sight of his bare, gnarled legs that had ripples over ripples of scars on them. I'd never even noticed the scars on his legs before he'd pointed them out, but since he usually wore jeans, they was hard to notice. I ran my finger down his leg and felt the cool, almost leathery skin that was such a different texture from the soft, warm unharmed skin on the rest of his body.

He looked at me with a reflection of the orangey flame in his eyes. "The pain is so excruciating that you forget who you are and what matters the most, because all you want to do is stop burning. I've been to hell and back, Adrienne."

I felt very guilty for asking and couldn't help but shudder at the thought of him—or anybody else—in that much pain. "I'm sorry; I shouldn't have asked."

He went back to staring at the fire for a minute, and I was surprised to hear his voice. "What's the worst pain you've ever felt before?"

"The sixteen years of life that I spent in misery before I met you," I answered without any thought or hesitation.

He smiled a little, but compared to the other grins I'd seen, it looked like a pathetic weakling. "You have no idea what true misery is until you've felt it."

I would've normally argued this with him, but now that I knew his story, I knew better than to quarrel with him about the meaning of misery. Instead, I asked, "What does it feel like?"

He breathed heavily before answering, "Every day was like black, heavy storm clouds came in and blurred the world and everything in it. Even when people who actually cared about me came, my life stayed black and roaring with the thunder of my rage until you took my hand and showed me a way out of it. I can never thank you enough."

I shook my head and kissed him again, but like holding his hand, the feeling would never get old. I thought about what Mother would think if she found out that I was having such enjoyment out of kissing a boy who'd had a huge bite taken out of his face, but I pushed that thought aside again.

"Don't thank me," I told him in between our kisses. "It's not like I'm trying to be nice by loving you."

I kissed him on the lips again, and this time felt a pleasure that made the words I'd been thinking for the past month slip out of my mouth. "You're the most beautiful boy I've ever met, and you're perfect. Everything about you amazes me."

He kissed me on the cheek and whispered in my ear, "I'd say that I loved you, but those three words just aren't enough for me. Everybody says them, and I don't want to be like everybody else, so what I will say is so much more. I promise to do anything for you, because you're the girl who somehow managed to steal my heart, something I thought would never be taken."

I beamed at him, barely able to believe my ears. This was Jeydon Spears talking, the rebellious delinquent that once loathed me with a passion, but now he pronounced that he loved me with all his heart. And how was I—the spoiled-rotten narcissistic heiress—able to win his heart?

Most people may have thought that I was too good for him, but the truth was he was too good for me. I didn't deserve someone like him, but somehow he was here right now, kissing my neck and whispering words of love into my ear as I felt like I was soaring through the clouds.

Was this all because I loved him? Did he actually love me back?

Of course he did. Jeydon wasn't one to bluff or say something just to make me feel better. I guessed it was just too good to be true. He loved me, but for once, I knew for sure that I felt the same way.

No, I *didn't* feel the same way; I loved him forty times more than he loved me. I was sure of it, because nobody could love anybody in the way I did.

Nobody else could feel the spark that I felt deep within me whenever I made him laugh or smile.

Nobody else could experience the array of fireworks I felt whenever I kissed his soft, delicate lips that I had come to believe in the past couple of hours were created to kiss mine and nobody else's.

I could never think of kissing or being with anybody else besides him now, and even if I did, Richard would still be definitely out of the question. I hated Richard almost as much as I loved Jeydon.

If I could have had one wish, it would have been to stay there forever, on that beach, with my head on Jeydon's chest. I could have almost cried that at some time, I would have to be back in my dorm trying to block out Rosie's harsh words against our relationship. I always took Jeydon's advice and tried not to listen to her, but sometimes it got too hard. I didn't understand how it was so easy for him to tune people like her out.

I couldn't think about the school year ending, knowing that my life would return back to the way it was, with Richard shoving his filthy tongue down my throat as I listened to Angela's screams as Mother threw her into the coffee table. That happened more than once.

But right now, we had this moment, and I had an idea to make it last longer. I cleared my throat. "Jeydon, can you do something for me?"

He sounded like he was singing. "Yes. Anything."

"Can we stay here tonight?" I asked as I cuddled up even closer on his chest and listened to his heartbeat. I was sure that our hearts were in sync now, if they weren't before.

I could see the corners of his lips curling up into a gentle smile just by the lull of his voice. "If you're prepared to forget the world and lie here with me forever."

I smiled and buried my face into his warm, solid chest, considering that maybe the reason I was born wasn't to be the heir ... but to be with him.

CHAPTER 22

The Spark

22, 23 & 24 are told from Jeydon's perspective

I didn't sleep at all that night, because my mind just wouldn't shut off. I used to have really bad insomnia that kept me up for weeks at a time, but after I ran away from Keri, the first thing I did was sleep for two days straight. Needless to say, that problem got solved with her absence, along with a lot of others.

As I stared up at the stars and felt the warm, steady whoosh of Adrienne's breath on my chest, it sort of clicked to me why I wasn't asleep having the usual nightmares that turned me into an insomniac in the first place.

I was so used to sleeping alone. I was so used to *being* alone. But now I had a feeling that my life had changed, because there was a sweet-smelling furnace of a body on top of mine with her arms wrapped around me, showing no sign of any emotion but contentment.

What exactly did this girl see when she looked at me?

Was she the tiniest bit afraid? I wouldn't blame her if she was, but I knew that wasn't it. She didn't give herself credit for how brave she really was.

Did she pity me? Why was I even considering that? I knew that she hadn't pitied me at all from the very beginning, but I'd tried to convince myself that was it because I'd had no idea what else to think about her.

Then what did she see, exactly? Let's be honest, I'm no prince charming, but she acts like I am.

Whenever I made the smallest comment about my scar—which I don't bring up often—she acted hurt, so obviously it bothered her, but not in the way that it bothered everybody else. She looked at me with a look I'd never seen anybody give me before. She wasn't at all afraid to touch me; she actually found enjoyment in it, and she didn't get disgusted when I wore shorts that revealed my mutilated legs.

I'm not ignorant. I knew that she loved me, and I should have just left it at that—believe me, I was more than happy that this girl I'd come to adore loved me—but I've always been the one who ended up killing the cat. That's not me talking, either. Soon after I was locked up in the loony bin, I was taken to see a psychologist who wrote those exact words down along with multiple anger and personality disorders I possessed, so I guess I had an excuse to wonder aimlessly about questions.

Why did she love me? If only I could get into her mind like I could get into everyone else's, then that would be an easy answer.

Yet what could I say? Life hadn't really been easy for me before she saw something more in me that the world didn't, and it's not like my life was anywhere near hell, because I didn't know the answer as to why she was in love with me.

And also, the things I knew about her without a doubt outweighed the things I was unsure about. In fact, I knew almost everything there was to know about her. Any other time—like with Laine, for example—whenever I got to the stage where I knew any personal matter about people, I'd get bored and bluntly tell them to shut up, but Adrienne was different.

I wanted to know more and more about her, because I was the one to kill the cat. I didn't understand why that lady who needed more counseling than I did wrote that about me all those years ago until the day Adrienne greeted me with that warm, sweet smile that made the insides of my stomach twist like they never had before. At first, I didn't like that feeling in my gut that I'd eventually figure out was the spark between us.

But for once, there was nothing I could do to drive her away. So my interest grew into captivation, and my captivation became the four-letter word I thought I'd never use to describe my feelings about anything or anybody.

Yes, I just admitted that I loved Adrienne.

And, yes, I'll also admit that she's beyond beautiful, but that's not why. After having a severe facial deformity for the majority of my life, I'd learned to focus on the inside and hope that others would do the same to me.

I loved her because whenever I was with her, I forgot about the ghosts of my past and could actually feel something more than pain. She was also charming in her own way, or at least I thought so. She trusted me to keep all her secrets, and she'd somehow managed to open me up for once and let all the dirty contents inside pour out.

But mostly it was because of the little things that attracted me to her, like her fragrance. I didn't compare her to a rose for nothing. The way she looked at me with almost childlike, dark loving eyes that were light with affection that she only showed me—the person who needed it the most—and a smile sweeter than honey.

I'd always been one to scrutinize every illogical theory Laine came up with, but for once, I think she was right about something, considering that Adrienne could see something more out of me than a bunch of scars and an extensive arrest record.

This special connection we had was an electric one, and with every kiss and touch, I could feel every single aching cell in my body that had been dulled by pain wake up. I could tell that it was doing the same for her without her needing to say anything.

Even though I found it hard to get inside her head, sometimes it was so easy to feel her feelings. Whenever she laughed, it was so contagious that I had to laugh too, although I'd barely ever let out a chuckle before she came along.

While she told me all of the stories about how her mother abused her, I felt a new rage that began in the pit of my stomach and spread throughout my whole body until steam came out of my ears. I didn't even feel that when Anthony was oppressed. Did that make me a horrible brother or a fool for love?

When she cried in front of me for the first time, I developed a hatred for myself for hurting her like that. I didn't expect her forgiveness. I didn't deserve her forgiveness, and as I held her in my arms while she sobbed on my shoulder, my head was spinning around with the realization that I was hopelessly in love with her.

How could I not have realized it before?

Looking back on it, there were multiple signs that I had somehow managed to catch the epidemic known as lovesickness— one of which being that I didn't care whenever people talked crap about my appearance or any other flaw they could find, but if they talked crap about Adrienne, it made me want to show them just how much force I could put into one punch.

The first time she ever held my hand, I could feel the blood rushing to my face and my soul stirring from a long hibernation, but I denied that I had any feelings for her.

Sign after sign after sign after sign all piled up in my head, each one making me feel a little bit more like an idiot. But I wasn't going to be a fool anymore, because I knew there was no use denying that fact any longer.

I loved her. I couldn't imagine loving anyone else. I couldn't imagine anyone else lying here with her head on my chest, because I doubted she'd smell like roses or patch up my damaged soul or love my scars in the way Adrienne did.

For a while longer, I lay there, and think I might've dozed off once or twice. I heard a gentle, familiar voice that wasn't exactly the one I wanted to hear.

I opened my eyes and saw David standing there beside me, crouched over us and looking straight into my face. He looked at the two of us as if we walked on water.

"I didn't think you would still be out here this late," he said.

I nodded and tried to forget the extra tension that had been between us since the week before at that restaurant. "She wanted to stay," I said. My mind wasn't focusing that much on Adrienne but on David and all of the things he'd done for me.

And what had I done for him? Pierced his lip with a fishhook? Bit him so hard that he'd bled because he'd said he wasn't going to report Keri to the authorities? Worried him to the point where he almost had a stroke over all my arrests? Cleared his wallet multiple times with bails and bribes to keep me out of jail?

It's a good thing that my real father ran out on Keri while she was pregnant with me, because I'd have made a horrible son.

"You guys can come inside if you want to. It's getting cold out here," I heard him offer, but I was too deep in thought to listen to half of what he said.

I just shook my head. "No, it's fine."

I hoped that he'd leave after I said that, but he didn't. "It's more than fine, because you're out here surrounded by the stars while cuddling with a girl."

A normal kid would have laughed, but since I'm not normal, my expression remained solemn. "Yes, that's pretty much it."

A deep, hearty laugh escaped from his throat. "Good night, Jeydon," he said as he stood up to go into his house, but not without bending over to kiss the top of my head first.

Whenever he did that, it made me feel like I was eleven again, but I liked that feeling. Was that because of Adrienne?

I heard his footsteps as he walked away, and I suddenly didn't want him to leave.

"David?" I called before he could get too far away.

Usually, David was the last person I'd talk to about such a thing, but I felt like I needed to tell him, anyway. Actually, I didn't talk to anybody about it, because I'd never found a need to talk about it.

He turned around and stood next to me again. "Yes?"

Why was I nervous about telling him this? Maybe because I didn't know how he'd react. Usually, it was so easy to predict how he would react, but when it came down to this subject, I had no clue what he'd do.

I knew I had to tell him sometime, so I just spit out the words to get it over with. "I'm in love with her." But surprisingly, the words were as light as a feather on the tip of my tongue.

He didn't seem all that surprised, but I think I saw a glimpse of sympathy in his eyes. "Have you told her how you feel?"

It made me enraged to think that he thought I was incapable of winning Adrienne when he saw how she treated me like I walked on water. Of course, he probably wanted to think that I couldn't win over anybody at all. He probably thought I was incapable of loving or of being loved by anyone, much less this gorgeous girl who was on the cover of magazines.

I let my explosive temper get the best of me again, and I threw my knives where I knew it hurt him the most.

"Yes, after we kissed and she said she loved me. Just because the woman you love sees you as nothing more than a way to get rid of her kids doesn't mean I'm completely hexed in relationships too."

Though I knew I was speaking the harsh truth, when I saw the hurt look on his face, I hated myself. After a second, the hurt look on his face vanished, because he was used to me saying hateful things to mask my own pain. How could people like him and Adrienne still find hope in me after I showed them how much damage I could do? How'd they find any hope in me to begin with?

He sighed heavily with exasperation. "I'm sorry my question came out that way, but you know that's not what your mother thinks of you. She tried so hard—"

It made me just plain mad when he defended her when he knew the extent of what she'd done to the two of us. He should've been the one who hated her the most.

"To turn Anthony into a bloody pulp?" I finished, growling like the untamed, thrashing animal I was.

"No, to reconnect with you," he said as if she were a good person. This was the part of David that made me resent and hate him bitterly. "She felt so horrible about what she did, and you made her feel even worse, so naturally she went back on drugs."

I scoffed and was in the stage of anger where I didn't care if he was bleeding because of my words or not. "Yes, it was nature's intention for her to use drugs again and to break Anthony in the process. You're such a hypocrite. You say you love us like we're your sons, yet you are in love with the woman who destroyed our lives. You defend her when you know it's all her fault."

Just by the sound of his voice, I could tell that he was close to tears. It seemed impossible; I'd only seen David cry twice before. Maybe he was crying in an effort to extinguish my rage—and if so, it was working. I remembered how Adrienne had said that he loved us more because he'd helped us escape from that hellhole. For the first time, I considered those words.

"I'm sorry," I said with a weary sigh. "I guess we're not in that life anymore. It's a thing of the past now."

David didn't respond to this, but Adrienne did. "What do you mean, a thing of the past?"

She scared the crap out of me. "Nothing. It's just something about Keri." Was she even going to ask who I was talking to, or did she not care about that, either?

She rewrapped her arms around my shoulders, and I was looking into the most beautiful eyes I've ever seen. "Tell me about it. Let me remind you how much I've told you about my mother."

David looked truly concerned. "What about your mother?"

Her eyes became wide, and her cheeks became a deep shade of burgundy.

"What is he doing here?" she asked me in a hushed voice, as if he couldn't hear.

"We were talking," I explained. "You really didn't think I was talking to myself, did you?"

She looked both hurt and confused, but I couldn't tell which one she was feeling the most. "I thought you hate talking about her."

"I do. I'll tell you the rest of the story later, when he's not around."

David rarely got truly angry with me, but he did then. "So you can make me out to be the bad guy?"

"No, so you don't start defending her again!"

There was a brief wave of silence. David ended it by asking Adrienne about her mother again, and I shushed him for her.

"It's personal," she explained politely.

Instead of letting her be, he asked, "She's abusive, isn't she?"

Her already huge eyes became the size of the moon. "How did you—"

"You have the same body language Anthony had when I asked him about the boys' mom for the first time," he answered sympathetically.

He was one of the best people to know her secret, and I think she figured that out, because she didn't deny it or get the least bit teary eyed. Instead, she exhaled enough air to blow up a balloon. "Please don't tell anyone, especially not the authorities. She's a really rich fashion designer in Brooklyn. Nobody would believe you."

She didn't need to tell him that. If he didn't tell on Keri when he had actual evidence, then he definitely wasn't going to tattle on Adrienne's mother. Chances were that if he did, he'd in up falling in love with her mother too.

I was about to say that out loud, but David cut in by saying, "I won't tell anyone if you don't want me to, assuming that she's not hurting you anymore."

"She isn't," Adrienne said with a nod, "because I'm here with Jeydon now."

After saying that, she turned to me and pressed her lips against mine, and I instantly knew that I wouldn't be hurting or in pain anymore, either, not because I had managed to run away from Keri but because I was with Adrienne. I was determined to not let anything hurt her or even think of taking her away from me. Without her, life wasn't worth living, because the storm clouds would come rolling in even worse than before now that I knew what I'd be without.

I was true to my word. I would do anything for her. And I would never in a million years let that sadistic woman that I'd come to believe came straight from hell harm her in any way ever again.

CHAPTER 23

Ghosts

The next two weeks had more happiness in them than did the previous fifteen years of my life. Adrienne and I spent as much time together as we could, even if it meant bending the rules to do so. I didn't mind, considering that I'd done things far worse than that, but it was big on her part. We kissed often, and Mr. Fields got on to us because we were kissing in the hallway too much.

It was the talk of all the lunch tables. I was dating Adrienne Hudson.

Adrienne was a regular part of dinner on Friday nights now. Strangely enough, that was where I felt our relationship was tested the most, around friends and family instead of people who didn't know a thing about us—even more so since David knew about Adrienne's mother—but I didn't let that pressure affect my happiness any.

You know better than to waste something as precious as joy, especially when you've never experienced it before.

I spent hours staring at the ceiling thinking about how I wished she were with me at that moment. I felt so cold without her touch, just like I used to be. I might've not noticed it then because I was so used to it, but since I'd known the sensation of her soft, sweet, flaming-hot skin, I didn't want to ever go back. Just looking into her eyes was enough to keep me warm. I noticed that I'd picked up a little bit of color—not much, but just enough that I didn't look like a stone statue anymore. Maybe that was because of her too.

I was changing drastically because of that girl; everybody had already figured that out before I'd noticed it. But I knew it was for the better. I couldn't have stayed the same single-minded rebel that was burning in the hell of his rage forever. I would've probably killed myself at some point if I did. Hell can't be a whole lot worse than life on earth was for me.

The morning following my sleepless night, I told Adrienne that I'd spent the whole night wishing that she had been there with me, and she'd said that she had done the same thing more than once. So after curfew, we got Anthony and Laine to distract the dorm advisors, and as they did that, we snuck out into my car and left campus.

Since we were hungry because we hadn't eaten dinner, we stopped at a diner in Saint Petersburg that was open twenty-four hours a day. I told her how I'd stopped at places like it a lot when I was an insomniac.

Her eyes shifted down to my hand, which I'd extended out on the table. She smiled sweetly as she grabbed hold of it. "Jeydon, if you don't mind me asking, why did you leave Miami in the first place? You've never told me that."

I studied her, not sure why she was asking. "I already told you why. We needed to get out of there."

I knew I wasn't telling the full truth. Only Anthony knew the truth, and that was only because he was there too. I didn't want to tell anybody that. Not even her.

She closed her eyes and shook her head. "It's got to be more than just that. The other night, David told me—"

I felt a sudden wave of rage. "David doesn't know crap!" I objected as I banged my fists on the table. An elderly couple sitting a couple of tables behind us stared, but I didn't pay any attention.

The rage stopped when I saw the look of bewilderment on her face, and I realized that I was acting like a monster once again. It was bad enough that I looked like a monster, so I couldn't act like one too. After a second, her expression turned casual again, and she continued, "David might not know as much about you as he thinks he does, but I do. You know how from the very beginning you knew when I was lying to you? Now I know when you are lying to me."

"I'll tell you," I said with a heavy sigh.

* * *

It was May 17, which I'd later find out was Adrienne's birthday. Anthony was about three feet away from me, sleeping soundly for the first time in forever; his nightmares were almost as bad as mine. We weren't at home even though it was one in the morning, because we both hated being home.

The place reeked of tobacco, the one smell I couldn't stomach. Everything was stained or dusty, including the old sofa with springs sticking out, the air mattress with a leak that Anthony and I slept on the small handful of times we'd stayed home, and my favorite—the broken-down refrigerator that was useless for storing anything but bottles of booze.

It wasn't only the place we couldn't stand but the noises the bed made as Keri worked in the only way she knew how.

Most of the time, we crashed at David's apartment, because it was the only place where two basically homeless teenage boys were welcome, but some nights, we just found an empty lot and camped out for the night—and that night just happened to be one of those nights.

My desperate attempts to get some sleep were interrupted by the familiar sound of sirens.

"Crap," I muttered under my breath. I shook Anthony's shoulder violently. "Wake up, Anthony. The cops are coming!"

He didn't say anything but let out a hoarse groan. He then realized what was happening and swiftly got to his feet. We knew the drill. It wasn't the first time we'd been chased by the cops. We sprinted down the street as the sirens pounded in my eardrums.

As soon as I was sure we'd lost them, I slowed my pace, and somebody shone a blinding light into our faces. By the familiar sound of the cop's voice, I could tell that he'd personally arrested me more than once.

"These are definitely the boys she was looking for. That horrible scar on the blond one gives it away."

I dropped my jaw when he said *she.* No, that couldn't be. "Who's looking for us?" I demanded.

They looked at me like I'd been smoking crack. Maybe they thought I was on crack. Like mother, like son.

"Your mother," the cop said.

I demanded a further explanation, but they just told me to get in the car. I refused to, so they used their Taser on me and then forced me into the car after handcuffing both of us as a precaution. As they pulled up to my house, I saw Keri waiting out on the front porch with the light from the lantern she was holding shining off her sparkling halter dress with no back. It was one of the dresses she wore when she went to sing at a nightclub downtown, which was her second job. The only reason she had a second job was to buy more drugs and get child welfare off her case.

People said that maybe I'd look like the enchantingly beautiful Keri in another life. I did in a way resemble her with my pale hair, ivory skin, and delicately curved features. We both had eyes like gems, but while mine were like emeralds, hers were the same deep blue color of a sapphire. Before the accident, I'd asked her where I'd gotten my green eyes from, and she'd said that she had no idea. That meant that I must've gotten them from my dad, and I proved that theory right when I looked closely at the only picture Anthony and I had of him. Later, she burned that picture when she found it hidden in Anthony's sock drawer.

We got out of the car, and the two of us stood there on the porch awkwardly as she thanked the cops for the work they'd done. I exchanged a puzzled look with Anthony. For the past four years, Anthony and I came and went whenever we pleased, and she didn't give a crap, but now she'd reported us missing? As soon as the cops left, I confronted her. No matter how calm I tried to sound, whenever I talked to her, I couldn't help but growl and gnash my teeth at her. Literally, before I hit puberty when I'd fight her off, I'd bite and claw her until she left Anthony alone.

"What's the meaning of this?" I demanded through clenched teeth and fists aimed toward her almost nonexistent midsection.

She looked like she was going to cry. Of course she always looked like she was going to cry when she saw my face after the car accident. "Are you saying I shouldn't be concerned about where my sons have run off to?"

"Not when you've never given a crap about us our whole lives!" I looked over and saw that Anthony had gone into our room, probably trying to tune out our argument. He hated it when I screamed at or hit her, even when he knew she deserved it.

She closed her eyes, probably because the sight of my face was too horrid for her to handle. "You've never been more wrong. I know this won't make up for anything I've done, but I love you, and I swear I'm going to change."

I scoffed and rolled my eyes. As much as I liked throwing verbal knives at David, Jezebel herself was the one I let my rage out on the most. "Don't do this again! You're just setting yourself up for failure, because you're too weak to deal with pain! I've been in pain my whole life because of you, and you can't even look at what you've done to me! How do you think I feel about my face? How do you think Anthony felt when you used him as a punching bag?"

She bit her lip to fight off tears, but it was no use. Tears poured down her cheeks and messed up the excessive eyeliner she wore that screamed *prostitute*. I guess she had to look the part.

"Please don't—" she said.

I got so mad that I was about to have a seizure if I didn't punch her, but I somehow restrained—not because she was my mother or the woman that David foolishly believed was the love of his life but because I'd sworn to Anthony when we were eleven and thirteen that I would never hit her unless she hit me or him first. He failed to mention anything about words, though, so I continued, "This is exactly what I'm talking about! You never think or care about anyone else, because all you can see is your own pain! You never stop to think about anything; you just do it! And that's why you'll fail just like you always had, because you can't even look at me without getting high first! You can't see how you've drained the life out of Anthony because you're always drunk! You can't even think about—"

My knives were stopped by the weapon of her choice: a slap across my face so hard that blood started streaming heavily from my nose. She stared at me with the widest eyes I'd ever seen, started sobbing about ten times harder, and begged for my forgiveness.

Keri had never slapped me when she was sober before. Without thinking, I threw her down onto the ground with my hands wrapped tightly around her neck. The more she gagged, the more my hands constricted around her windpipe.

I barely heard Anthony's desperate pleas for me to let go of her over my own loud, hateful thoughts. I tried to tune him out, but I just couldn't. The woman I was choking might've been a monster, but so was I. Anthony's pleading only reminded me of that. Right as she turned a little blue, I couldn't stand the thought of me stooping down to her level, and I let go of her. She gasped for air as if she were a newborn taking her first breath, and then she passed out cold from lack of oxygen.

I darted into our room and gathered the few things I had.

Anthony ran after me in a confused panic. "What do you think you're doing?"

I grabbed a pillowcase and stuffed it with T-shirts, jeans, and sweatshirts for the both of us. "I can't take it anymore! We've got to get out of this hell!"

"We can't! There's nowhere for us to go!" He never yelled, but he was yelling then. He tried to pull my arms to my back, but I escaped from his grasp and accidentally elbowed him hard in the stomach doing so.

I turned around to look at him, and he looked at me with wide, pale bluish-gray eyes filled with shock. At least they were inflicted with another emotion besides fear for once.

I lowered my voice down an octave, and the tiny rational part of me came out. "Nowhere is better than here. Nobody knows that better than you."

A single tear escaped from his downcast eyes and trickled down his cheek. He didn't cry that much anymore. He used to, but then Keri knocked that sensitivity out of him. It made my heart ache to know that he used to be so full of life and a childish eagerness that I never knew, but now that life had been sucked out of him, and his happiness had been replaced with misery. He just looked down and nodded. He barely ever spoke anymore, and when he did, nobody heard him because he talked so quietly. When people asked what was wrong with him, I told them that he had social anxiety, and most people were stupid enough to believe that. The ones who didn't accused him of being mentally retarded. Whenever people said that, I wanted to slap them in the face, and I had a few times. They didn't know what he'd been through.

We both pulled on our jackets and put our hoods up. I made sure to pull the drawstring as tightly as I could so that nobody could see my scar. My scar was only useful for blowing my cover to the cops, because not that many kids had a huge bite taken out of their faces. It surprised me that Anthony was going with me this time; he had refused to run away and had been the only thing keeping me there.

Was he really going to go through with this? Would he chicken out like he had when we were little and tried to run away after she hit him for the first time? When he rolled up the pillowcase full of our things in a loose ball, placed it under his hoodie to make him look bigger, and nodded at me as if to ask, "Are you ready?" I knew the answer. I wasn't alone. Then again, I never was alone, because I had him. Though he was mostly mute, Anthony had been the best companion over the years that I could have ever asked for.

Right as we were about to leave for good, there was a loud crash, and then there was a powerful roar so familiar that I couldn't breathe—and not from the smoke that was so thick that I could have cut it with a knife. Besides something happening to Anthony, there was only one thing I was truly afraid of—fire. To me, fire had always been a very powerful deadly weapon of the dark force, used only to destroy, take, or cause agony. I could still very vividly remember the excruciating pain that made everything from inside of me scream for it to stop. When you've been in the fire once, you don't want to go back.

We both ran out of our room and to the front door, but the living room was almost completely engulfed in flames. I saw Keri curled up in the corner, screaming and crying. She wasn't burning, but I kind of wished she was. She had to be the one who set the house on fire. I couldn't understand why, but I knew that she deserved to be in pain. The smoke made my eyes water, and I felt more blood gushing out of my nose with every single rapid beat of my heart, but I didn't pay attention to that, because I was determined to find a way out. Then I saw a narrow passage to the front door where the floor wasn't on fire. We didn't think and just ran through it, getting singed along the way. Instead of using the doorknob, I used my shoulder as a battering ram to break it open, because I didn't want to risk burning my hand.

I gasped for fresh air and was about to run off, but out of the corner of my eye, I saw Anthony turn to go back into the orange glow of the fire. I grabbed hold of his arm before he could do so and pulled him back to safety. I had mixed emotions of anger that he was being so stupid and relief that he was okay. Did he want to end up like me?

"Anthony, what are you doing?" I yelled. "Come on! We've got to get out of this place before it burns to the ground!"

He looked in his right mind, but I still thought he'd completely lost it when he said, "I think she is still in there. We should go back." Besides his cowardice and lack of speech, he was still everything I wasn't—forgiving, compassionate, selfless, and extremely optimistic. His life might've been sucked out by Keri, but nobody could do the same to his golden heart.

I pushed the image of her curled up in the corner scared to death out of my mind, because I didn't want to think for a second that I was in the wrong. "You don't know that! If she's still in the house, it's too late, anyway. The doorknob has probably buckled in from the heat by now."

He reluctantly went with me, and we ran away from the house as fast as we could. It was going to be destroyed by the flames soon, just like my used-to-be-easy-to-look-at face. Maybe she'd die in the fire. Maybe she'd be a thing of the past too. Either way, I hoped I'd never see her again.

The metallic taste in my mouth reminded me that the harder I ran, the more blood gushed out my nose. I had no time to slow down, and I didn't want to, considering that, for all I knew, the cops could have been right behind us, so I used the sleeve of my hoodie as a Kleenex.

The two of us ran to the only place we knew we were truly safe from anything. When we finally got to the door, I pounded on it as hard as I could without breaking it down. When David opened the door, he gave me a look of shock that I'd never seen before. He should've been so used to this—Anthony coming to his door with a clobbered and tearstained face and me with my own various and sometimes gruesome injuries from fights. Whenever things got so rough at home that I couldn't handle them, his was the safe haven we'd fled to.

When he got over the shock, a sense of concern and fear replaced it. "Boys, what's going on? What happened to you this time, Jeydon?"

It was way harder than I'd thought it would be. "We have to leave now."

He was so baffled that I felt sorry for him. "What?"

"There's no time to explain it right now; we just need to get out of here," I said firmly with a deep breath, not trying to calm only him but myself, as well. I had to remain calm, and in all the situations that I'd been through that were similar to that, I had been, but something about this one made my heart beat so erratically that I felt it in my fingers.

I heard the creaking of loose floorboards and turned around. Laine was standing there in her pajamas. She sucked out all the air in the room when she saw my face.

"Jeydon, did you get in another fight? And what's stuffed under your shirt, Anthony?" she asked.

Honestly, Laine was the last person I wanted to see at that particular time. It was just too urgent. And besides, the only reason we were friends was because she was on the exclusive list of people that Anthony talked to without me around. She might've thought the three of us were a team, but without Anthony linking us together, we'd have had no relationship at all, which wouldn't really have hurt either of us that much.

I wouldn't have felt that guilty if I'd left her there, but Anthony was much kinder than I was.

"Jeydon and I have to leave right now. That's what the stuff is for," Anthony said.

She wrinkled her brow, and I answered her question even though she didn't ask anything. "We just have to leave."

I knew she understood. She knew just as much about how Keri had abused Anthony as I did, because he'd told her all about it, and she hated Keri almost as much as I did for it. She always backed me up when I told him that we should run away to live with David and begged him to report to the authorities about our home situation more than once. Sometimes all we could agree on was our mutual hatred toward her.

She turned to David and rubbed her temple as if she had a migraine. "And you're okay with them running off like this?"

By his expression, I figured out that he hadn't thought of it that way. If he were anybody else, he would have sent us on our way immediately, not caring what might happen to the two of us. Good thing he wasn't like everybody else, or I would be in jail, and Anthony would be either taking shelter in a dumpster or dead.

That made me shudder. I didn't even want to go over those possibilities.

After a moment of thinking it over, he shook his head and said, "Yes, because we're going with them."

Laine looked satisfied, but Anthony and I just stared at him in disbelief. We were unwanted, so I guess it was just a bad habit of ours to assume that we would stay that way. Of course, David had a bad habit of his own—loving the people that nobody else would ever dream of associating with—so I shouldn't have been too flattered.

Apparently, our doubt was comical, because David laughed. "After all I've done for you over the years, did you really think I'd just let you leave like this? You boys are basically my children; I've watched you grow up and held your hands along the way. I would never dream of sending you out on your own."

His words were drowned in the wave of my doubt, but at least they seemed to have an effect on Anthony, who gave him a big hug and thanked him for all he'd done.

I waited for their happy moment to be over before I asked, "So you're actually going to choose us over Keri?"

I expected him to get mad or possibly reconsider his decision since he knew what he'd have to leave behind, but he gave me a gentle smile and nodded.

When I asked why, he answered, "Because before I fell in love with your mother, I fell in love with the scrawny, explosive eleven-year-old who was in desperate need of some loving attention and discipline."

I shook my head, still not fully believing. I found it very hard to believe anything that was positive, because I was so used to crap happening. "I thought you only wanted me because of her."

He stared at me blankly. "If I wanted you because of her, I wouldn't have bailed you out of jail so much or let you live here for weeks at a time or taught you how to play guitar or all the other things I've done for you."

I took a deep breath, closed my eyes, and shook my head. I opened them and replied, "Okay, enough of the happy stuff. It's time to figure out how we're going to get out of here."

CHAPTER 24

New Beginnings

For the next couple of days, Anthony and I skipped school and hid in David's apartment until the cops cleared up from the area. Apparently, since the electricity was shut off, Keri had lit a candle on the coffee table, and while she struggled to stand after regaining consciousness, she stumbled and knocked it into the floor. That's what started the fire. The fire burned out on its own before the fire department arrived, and when the smoke cleared up, they found Keri curled up in the corner crying but otherwise completely unscathed. She told the cops all about how I'd tried to choke her, and that was why we had to hide.

The cops interrogated David, but he told them that he had no idea where I was. They believed him, and posters were put up all around town with a picture of my face on it along with my name—I went by the last name of Blackburn at the time—and a date of birth that also wasn't mine. Of course, there were no fliers whatsoever of Anthony posted, because nobody was out looking for him. He was kind of disappointed about that.

Finally, after four days, somebody found the hoodie with my dried blood on it that Anthony dropped out on a beach twenty miles away a couple of days before, and their search went there. The first thing Laine, Anthony, and I did was wait for night to fall, and then we put the hoods of our jackets up so that we wouldn't be identified right away. We snuck over to my friend Johnny's house, because I just had a feeling he could help us.

I rang the doorbell three times before I found out that it didn't work, and then I picked the lock. When I opened the door, the first and only thing I saw was Johnny and his girlfriend making out on the couch. I had lost track of which girl he was dating—Amy, Kat, or Lilly. I couldn't tell right away because they were all slender and blonde.

She—whoever she was—was the first to see me, and she screamed a note only dolphins could hear. "Somebody has broken in!"

Johnny was getting ready to clonk me on the head, but when he saw it was me, he started cracking up to the point where he fell on the floor. "Geez, Amy, it's just my boy Jeydon. Oh, man, am I so glad to see you! You must've really done it this time."

Amy stared at me with the color drawn from her face and china-blue eyes filled with disgust. "What happened to your face? It looks like you—"

I couldn't care less about comments, but like Adrienne, Johnny got flustered when it happened. "Babe, don't."

"You know I don't give a crap," I dismissed as I motioned for Laine and Anthony to come in.

They obeyed, creeping in cautiously as if there were shards of broken glass all over the floor.

Johnny gave Laine and Anthony a weird look. He respected Anthony because he knew how protective I was of him, but I could tell he thought of him as a spineless, retarded wuss. He liked Laine's sense of humor but was convinced that she and Anthony were secretly dating because almost every day they took walks on a route that went right past his house.

"What are your bro and his girl doing over here?" Johnny asked.

Anthony rolled his eyes. "We're not—"

As much as I hated to interrupt, Amy looked like she was about ready to whack me in the head with a baseball bat, and nobody ever listened to him talking, anyway. "You know how the cops are chasing after me?"

He nodded. "Yeah, everybody knows. That's all everybody at school's been talking about."

That wasn't a shock, considering the only thing anybody ever talked about at school was me even when I wasn't a person of interest. "Exactly. That's why we need to run away, and we need your help to do that."

The first thing we decided to do was cut my hair. I'd already cut it myself, so I didn't need any help with it even though I wasn't anything near a Hollywood stylist. I simply cut until all that remained was a bit of pale fuzz on my head. I knew this would be only a temporary change in my appearance because my hair grew back so fast, but at least it would buy me a couple months of a low profile—or at least the lowest profile I could possibly have with my scar, which was like a flashing sign pointing directly at me saying, "I'm guilty," or "Otherwise known as Jeydon Blackburn!" in dazzling neon letters.

To be safe, Anthony buzzed his mass of wavy, thick black hair, and I watched in shock as all of his hair—there was a lot more of it than I'd realized—fell onto the floor. The contrast in color between the two piles of hair on the floor made me wonder if we were actually full-blooded brothers or if Keri slept around a little after Anthony came along.

Laine pulled her hair back into a single braid going down her spine. At least she didn't have to disguise herself in any way, because now everybody knew that she was leaving. David had notified her cranky, child-despising guardian, Mr. Blake, about it, and as expected, he was more than happy for David to take her off his hands permanently. What he actually was concerned about was if I was being hidden somewhere in the apartment complex. He did a full inspection of his and Laine's apartments, during which I hid in the air duct.

She also knew where she was going. Mr. Blake's brother was the headmaster of some preppy rich-kid boarding school in Tampa Bay. Laine's mom agreed to send her there, and Laine sent an application for me as well without my consent.

She didn't really need my consent, though, because as soon as she clarified that she hadn't used my actual name and birth date on the application, I didn't care. The standards for that school were astronomical. With all my arrests, I wouldn't make the cut even if I wanted to. She even went as far as sending one in for Anthony too. Anthony had never gotten arrested, but his grades were deplorable, and 99 percent of all teachers thought he was just too retarded or traumatized to retain any new information. Needless to say, he had even less of a chance getting into that school than I did.

On the way out, Johnny and I said our permanent good-byes. I would never admit it to him, but I wasn't at all sorry that I was leaving him and the fellow delinquents I'd forged friendships with over the years. As I left, I saw that Laine and Anthony had gotten a head start. I watched as Laine ever so slowly wrapped her arm around Anthony's shoulder and actually found the will to smile a little at how crimson the tips of his ears got.

"Love," I whispered under my breath so nobody could hear me, "the simplest connection in the world."

The thing every human being was created to do—except for me. I was condemned long ago to a life without love, cursed with pink ribbon scars running down my limbs and a chunk of my face taken out so grotesque that little girls shrieked in terror when they saw only a glimpse of me. But maybe there was some hope for me.

As impossible as it was, maybe there was an open mind out there somewhere who could see past my hex. Maybe I just needed to be open-minded myself to find her ...

A loud, scratchy voice broke my peaceful thoughts. "Cute, ain't it? And he says they aren't dating when her hands are all over him like that."

Honestly, I wanted to beat the tar out of Johnny for interrupting the one positive thought I'd ever had. I just nodded, trying to hide the agitation.

I think he sensed the tension even though he was usually a borderline mentally disabled level of gullible, because he patted me on the back and said, "Come out to the back. There's something I want to give you."

I followed him to back of the house, the knife that I carried around for safety in hand just in case he was going to attempt to mug me. You never know when it's going to happen. I learned that the hard way.

Maybe I was just being paranoid, because I would have known the signs that he was going to jump me, and he wasn't showing them. Instead, he asked, "You know how a couple of weeks ago that lemon piece of junk my dad drove broke down?"

I nodded, thinking of the rusty red pickup truck that was older than I was. "Yeah, why?"

We reached the back, and I saw the truck. It still looked like it belonged in the dump, but at least it was more than pieces of scrap metal put together like Keri's car was.

"I fixed it up, but my dad thinks it's unsafe now just because I was the one who repaired it. I figured since you were leaving and didn't have a car that you'd want to take it off my hands," Johnny explained as I analyzed it.

Call me schizophrenic, but like the connection I saw between Laine and Anthony, I felt a connection with that car, but it was different with this one. We were two of a kind with scratches on the side that resembled the scar on my arm, the fact that we were rejected by everyone, and the names etched into the seat were similar to the labels the world had carved on me.

"Thanks," I said as I traced my finger across a particularly nasty word etched on the side of the car. "I'll take it."

The next thing I knew, Anthony and I were in the back of the truck with a big tarp covering us. David was driving, and Laine was in the passenger's seat. It was imperative for me to not show my face, because I was still at large to the police, and Anthony wanted to be with me, because it was taking an emotional toll on him. I don't know what got into me—maybe it was from finally getting away or how the stars were aligned that night—but for the first time in my life, I just closed my eyes and naturally drifted off to sleep.

I woke up lying on a bed in an unfamiliar, uncomfortably small bedroom. I panicked a little, because the last time this had happened was after the car crash in the hospital, but I calmed myself as Anthony walked into the room.

"I was starting to think you'd never wake up," he said. "I've never seen you sleep at all, much less two days."

I knew this couldn't be. How could I all of a sudden sleep for days when I couldn't sleep for an hour? "You've got to be kidding me."

He shook his head. "Kind of wish I were. You've missed out on a lot."

I raised my eyebrows at this. "Really?"

He actually smiled a little—something he did even less than I did—and nodded. "Okay, so get this: Keri turned herself in."

I just dropped my jaw in shock, for once being the speechless one. I'm sure he saw it as an opportunity to be the one who talked and explained everything out, so he gladly took it.

"The police suspected that you were hiding in the back of the truck and were about three miles behind us when she told them that she was high on crack trying to set the house on fire and that you were acting in self-defense. She'll be in jail for at least a year for lying and drug possession. Nobody can tell how long she'll be in for arson and child abuse."

I closed my eyes tightly, trying to take in the new information. I found it impossible to believe, but for once, everything was so uncertain instead of so painfully crystal clear like it always was. I couldn't help but ask, "Why do you think she did that?"

Without having to think about it, he replied, "She knew that you were going to jail for something she did, so she took your place. She might be a monster when she's on drugs, but she's not as selfish as you think."

"When you say stuff like that, it makes me wonder if the old Anthony is still in there," I mumbled as I rolled my eyes. When it came to that, I found the old Anthony extremely annoying and was glad his opinions about the nonexistent good in people were silenced.

He returned to his forever neutral state, hiding his pain behind a blank expression and a hushed voice that I could see straight through.

"Just because I'm not like how I was doesn't mean I'm a shadow," he said.

I couldn't stand to look at him whenever he tried to defend himself like that, so I turned away and closed my eyes like he was the one with a few grotesque intertwined arteries bulging out of his face. "You don't even believe in that bull crap."

He arched his brow and clenched his jaw in a way that was mine and not his. He couldn't be mad. Anthony never got mad. "So is that all I am to you? A soulless shadow of my former self instead of your brother?"

I stopped for a moment and wondered if that was what I really thought of him. Deep in my heart, I knew the answer, and I said it aloud. "No. You've just had the life sucked out by her. The same had been done to me way before, so I don't think of you as lesser person. But we're different in the fact that the pain you've experienced hasn't hardened your naturally golden heart any. I wish I could say the same for me."

He shook his head. "No, it hasn't. You're a better person than what you give yourself credit for."

I got mad, because he shouldn't lie. He was a horrible liar. "You're believing in more bull crap," I retorted hotly.

"I believe it, because it's true, and you can figure that out now that you're not going to be pulled into gang fights or drugs or Keri's crap every five seconds. This is a new beginning for both of us."

I tried to wrap my head around that. Up to that point, he'd always been something to protect and not to listen to. "Do you think things like this all the time?" I asked cautiously.

He nodded grimly, and I asked, "Why haven't you ever spoken them before?"

His cheeks became red. "Because when I do, it seems like nobody listens."

I studied his face and felt emotions of remorse and anger welling up inside of me. I was always too busy focusing on him remaining unscathed to give him a listening ear, but maybe now that she was gone, that could change.

"I will," I said.

At that, as if they had rehearsed it and she was right on cue, Laine walked into the room. She laughed and said, "I heard your voice for the other room and thought it was too good to be true. I was about to think you were put under a magic spell by a witch."

"That's an even better thing for you, Laine, because if he were, then you were the one who'd have to kiss him and break the spell," Anthony joshed.

She smiled sharply and told him to shut up between her giggles. I noticed she was holding a file, and she threw it toward me. I caught it and asked her what it was for. I felt like she was hiding something.

"Your Tampa Bay application, of course," she said.

I opened it, but before I read anything, I asked, "Why is this important?"

She smiled grandly. "Because you've been accepted on scholarship. Mr. Blake gave us a call yesterday while you were sleeping. Congrats."

I sat back for a second trying to think of a legitimate reason not to go to this preppy military school. Then I realized there was a huge one standing right there beside me. "You know I can't just leave Anthony."

"David figured that out even when you were unconscious. They wanted you so badly that I'm going there on a scholarship too just because it means they'll have you," Anthony explained with no hint of anything but gratitude.

I didn't like it. I didn't want to be that freaky kid genius anymore, considering how badly that ended up last time. I knew I had to, because where else would I go? I was completely positive that not all schools were as open-minded as this one was.

I looked at the slim file containing so little information and realized that they must've taken pity on me. Laine made sure not to give away any information that could land me in the slammer, and I guess she'd decided not to take her chances with anything. I noticed that the place where my last name was supposed to be was blank. "What's up with this?" I asked her as I showed her it.

"Using the last name Blackburn would've given away who you were at the time, so I used the name Brown. Now that Keri's come clean about what happened, the headmaster was informed and said that you can choose your own last name to go by."

Why was I given authority to choose this? Didn't they have a birth certificate? Of course they didn't; Keri probably lost or destroyed it. Did I even know what my own real last name was? My whole life as I went through different surroundings, I went by different last names, as well, so many that I had forgotten.

I doubted that Anthony would have a better memory than I did, but it was worth a try. "Anthony, what's my real last name?"

Without looking toward me, he said, "Green. You didn't know that?"

Jeydon Green. I shook my head, knowing that wasn't right. "No, that's *your* last name. Remember? After Dad left, Keri was so mad at him she made my last name her maiden name."

He scoffed, which was another thing that was mine and not his. "Good luck finding that out."

For once, I actually wished that Keri was there so I could ask her, but she was so drunk all the time that she'd probably forgotten it along with her dignity and children's respect. I didn't need her help, because I knew I knew it. It was common and started with an *S*. Was it Smith? No, that was too common, and it didn't sound even remotely right.

There was a celebrity with the same last name as mine. She was crazy and drug addicted too, just like her. Irony kills.

"Laine?" I asked in desperation.

"What?"

"You know that one girl who's famous? She's a pop singer, I think. She went crazy a couple of years ago and shaved her head."

Most people would've thought I'd gone insane, but not Laine. She wasn't the least bit judgmental no matter how weird I got with her.

"You mean Britney Spears?" she guessed with an arched eyebrow.

That was it. That was my name—my real one, not an alias. I put my two names together. Jeydon Spears.

It sounded right, because it was who I was, and I knew I didn't want to go by anything else—not Green, not Blackburn, and absolutely not Brown.

Those weren't who I am; this was. So I wrote my new name in the blank, and it gave me hope. The past was finally in the past now that Anthony was unharmed and Keri was in jail. It was truly over, like a vapor in the wind. Maybe I could pretend that it was just a bad dream. No, I couldn't do that. That would just be plain delusional.

But I could still change. I could be a new person with a new name at a new school. The slate was clean. Just like Anthony said, I could have a new beginning.

We all could.

CHAPTER 25

Clarity

The diner was vacant by the time he was done sharing his flashbacks with me. I'd moved from sitting across from him to sitting beside him about halfway through his story and rested my head on his shoulder. Like how his safe haven was David's house, mine was in his arms.

"You did the right thing by leaving."

He kissed the top of my head and said, "You're right. It's kind of funny now that I think about it. I was more than a little disappointed that I didn't get my new beginning when I got sent to the office on the first day, but it turns out I didn't really need a new beginning, because that day, I found something in that office that I'd never trade for the whole world—you."

I lifted my head up and kissed him on the lips. I whispered to him, "You have no idea how much what you just said means to me," and continued to kiss him until the waiter kicked us out because we'd been loitering for too long.

While outside in the parking lot, Jeydon grabbed a blanket with a logo of Tampa Bay from his truck and spread it out on the ground. He pulled me down a little too hard, and I fell on top of him and the blanket with a loud thud. I cracked up laughing, and we kissed each other over and over again.

Heaven was suddenly interrupted when he grunted a little like he was in pain. I stopped kissing him and brushed a long golden strip of hair away from his magnificent eyes so that I could marvel at them and wonder how anything as wonderful as him could ever be mine. "What's wrong?"

He closed his eyes, and I had a feeling that something bad was about to happen. "There's another thing I want to tell you that I've not told anybody else."

I was a little relieved but concerned at the same time. He seldom told me something he'd never told anyone else without me having to ask him first. But I was so glad that, out of all the people in the world he could open up to, he'd chosen me and not just because I'd opened up to him first.

"I'd like to hear it," I said.

I could feel his heart race. He barely ever got nervous about anything, so it must've been big. "I've secretly been on narcotics for about three years, but when we started dating a couple of weeks ago, I stopped using them, because it was just too hard for me to lie to you. The last several times I've tried to quit, the feeling of isolation I'd always felt when I was clean was just too much, but now—other than the fact that I can think clearly and am experiencing minor withdrawal symptoms—I can't tell a difference."

He looked at me as if he'd murdered somebody, and honestly, if he had been anybody else, there was a good chance that I would have treated him like he had. If Richard had told me that he'd secretly been using drugs throughout the years, then I would have gotten just as furious as I was when I found out that he'd cheated on me with Tori.

But this was different. I actually loved Jeydon. I couldn't look into his eyes and see anything but his pure heart and strong-willed, determined spirit. In other words, I couldn't see anything else but the boy I was unconditionally in love with. Instead of getting angry, I wanted to give him affection he never knew, the affection he rightfully deserved. It was pointless to get mad at him, anyway, because I never stayed that way for long even when he did infuriating things behind my back like this.

Then it dawned on me that he wasn't doing these things behind my back. He quit because he just couldn't lie to me again like he had about Keri. He was nothing like Richard, because in his eyes, my fragile heart was to be protected with his life instead of obliterated into little shards.

Instead of getting mad at him, I got mad at myself for being like the world, underestimating his goodness. I should've been the one who knew that the most, considering that I was the one who knew him better than anyone else. I had stolen his heart but had been as careless as to forget how large and pure it was. Anthony was right; Jeydon had no idea how precious he was. Without a shadow of doubt, he was the best person I had ever met.

I knew I had to say something, and I put it in a question form since I was curious about this secret door of his that he'd just given me the key to. Only God knows how many skeletons were lurking behind it. "So you don't feel isolated anymore?"

He smiled and moved in closer to me until his nose touched mine. "How could I now that I have you?"

My eyes were only about two inches away from his scar, but I ignored it. Now I didn't even think about it anymore. It was just a part of his face that if anything enhanced his features. "Why did you do drugs?"

His smile faded into a flat line. "Same reason I did it back when I was younger—to hide my intellect."

Now that I knew him so well, I could see into his eyes as if they were open doors. "Was it painful in any way?" I asked, wincing when I said the word *painful*.

I ached all over when my eyes that were a few centimeters away from his were inflicted with a spark of an old anguish. "It was painful in every way."

Pain shot into each one of my organs at the thought that he could've been suffering because of me. "Are you telling me the truth, or are you just saying you aren't hurting anymore so that I won't get worried? If you are, then please don't. I can't stand the thought of you being in any amount of pain and could never forgive myself if you're doing it for me."

He gave me a real smile that assured me that he wasn't. He might've been able to deceive people easily, but he could never fake a smile like that. "I'm not. Turns out that I don't need drugs anymore, because your touch dulls it down in a way a bucketful of narcotics can't. Besides, I kind of like having clarity."

"What do you mean by *clarity*? Didn't you have it before?"

He simply shook his head. "It's so hard to explain to you."

I laughed. I have no idea why I did. "At least try to. You can't just leave me here all confused like this."

A tiny chuckle escaped from his mouth, and he squeezed my hand. "You know how some people have really precise vision? Naturally, I'm like that, but instead of my eyesight, it's the world that's so crystal clear. Nothing's the least bit confusing. It seems like I have the answer to everything. My mind is basically a computer, absorbing the world around me in the blink of an eye."

I wrinkled my brow, wondering why he'd waste such a cool ability. "Why would you want to rid yourself of that?"

He used his free hand that wasn't held in mine to softly stroke my cheek, and he looked at me with eyes that couldn't possibly be those of a fifteen-year-old boy, but an angel that had experienced the tragedy of a broken wing.

"It's not as glamorous as it sounds," he said. "Along with a sense of clarity came a sharp pain of isolation. It hurt enough, but when I was little and people poked and prodded at me like I was a lab rat, I felt like I didn't belong inside my own mind. The attention from my scar didn't help, and my clarity was bringing me to the brink of insanity when I punched that kid. At the mental hospital, I was given some narcotics so that I might fall asleep and the mother lode of antipsychotics because they thought I had multiple major mental health disorders. And while that didn't work out, everything was instantly better. My drug-enhanced world was blurred and beyond miserable, but at least I wasn't losing my mind to clarity anymore. I knew what I stood for;

the normalcy of my violent path to self-destruction stood above the worse misery that came along with clarity. Then you came around and turned everything I stood for completely upside down. I didn't know what to think when the fog started to clear and a third road was revealed, but now that I can see things in a revolutionary way, I know exactly how I see you."

I sat there on his lap nose to nose with him. "How do you see me?"

"I was in a very dark place, Adrienne, and then you lit up my world so that it's clear. With you, I can have both clarity and my sanity coexisting, but there's something else coexisting that I never expected to have—happiness. I feel like I have everything, because I do. As much as I loved you on our first date when I was stoned, I love you a hundred times over for that very reason."

My jaw dropped in sync with my heart. "You were stoned our first date?"

I asked myself why was I making a big deal about it, but the answer was just as crystal clear as his mind. That night had so much meaning to it, and that little detail took that meaning away from me. Maybe all those words of love were the drugs talking, not him.

He looked unshaken. He obviously wasn't too worried about losing me, probably because he knew that even if I tried to run, I couldn't get far. "I hate to say so, but yes. I was pretty high on prescription painkillers and over-the-counter cough medicine. That's mostly what I took, because it was cheap and lowered my IQ exactly to the right level."

I was more than aware that I was still very much in love with him. "You didn't look or act like you were stoned. When Amelia was on drugs, I could tell from fifty yards away even if she'd just taken a gram."

He breathed in with a chuckle. "You're going to think I'm so odd."

I shook my head. "I've never thought you were odd before."

"Yeah, but your open-mindedness has got to end somewhere."

I leaned into him a little closer and said. "Try me."

He spit the words out like they were a bitter cough syrup. "Technically, I wasn't stoned. Because of all the narcotic overdoses over the years, it's impossible for the drugs to affect me in any way rationally. So, yes, I took enough medication that I should've been stoned, but in a sense, I wasn't."

I felt so happy that tears were welling in my eyes. "So you meant everything you said that night?"

He laughed. "It astounds me that you'd think for even a second that this love is nothing but a series of drug-induced delusions."

I relaxed my head on his shoulder and said, "If it is, then I never want to wake up." I squeezed his hand and took my head off his shoulder to look into his eyes. "So what's going to be different now that you're off drugs?"

"In some ways, everything," he replied in a clear, matter-of-fact tone that made him sound even more intelligent than he had back then. "In other ways, nothing."

"What's going to change?" I asked, a little bit uneasy of the unknown.

He ever so gently ran his fingers through my hair in a braiding fashion. "For one, I'm never going to hide anything from you ever again. Instead of depending on capsules in a little plastic bottle, I'm going to hold on to you and never let go. I'm going to try to be the best me that I can be for you so that I can truly say that I love you. And the fact that I love you is one of the things that will never change."

At first, I felt like I could fly. I kissed him on the neck and for no logical reason had a flashback from about five years earlier.

Leah was in love. If I listened carefully enough, I could hear her giggling as she told Amelia all about him—I say *him* because I never figured out what his name was. Mother soon found out about him, and as she started screaming and hitting Leah, I ran upstairs and waited with Angela for it to be over as we always did. Mother made sure that Leah never saw that boy again. Two years later, he was killed in a motorcycle accident, and I just lay there in bed listening to her sob into her pillow.

Maybe I had that same fate. If Mother wouldn't allow Leah to date a perfectly fine guy from what I understood, she wouldn't let me be involved in any way with Jeydon even if he was halfway decent in her eyes.

I was the heir. I was supposed to be with Richard, not Jeydon. I had a sickening feeling in my gut all along, but if it was wrong, it wouldn't feel so right. Yet I knew that it wouldn't still be right in Mother's perspective. I was to be with Richard, but my heart denied it and screamed for something that felt real. Jeydon had answered my call.

I felt tears trickling, and Jeydon was starting to get impatient. "But what if—" I began.

A spark ignited in his eyes. "No," he denied firmly. "I will never let that happen, Adrienne. Not in a million years."

I shook my head as tears blurred my vision. Maybe that's what his world was like when he was on drugs. Maybe that's why he'd found me unattractive.

"We don't have a million years, Jeydon. We have less than one," I whispered, my lip trembling along with my voice.

"No, we don't," he growled. "Not on my watch. I'm never going to let anything take you away from me. Not even Mommy Dearest herself."

I let out a few heavy sobs on his steady shoulder. "I wish it wasn't this way. I wish she wasn't how she is."

"There's no point in wishing," he replied bitterly but with great wisdom. "There's only point in doing something about it."

I lifted my head up from his shoulder and looked at him in bewilderment. My voice became that of a hissing rattlesnake. "What are you going to do exactly? There's nothing you can do, and you know it! She's not like Keri! She's so big that you can't hit her!"

He lowered his voice as soon as I raised mine. "You're wrong. The only reason I can't hit her is because she's thousands of miles away. It's not because of how big she is. You know I couldn't care less about that."

Now he was just being insane. Were the drugs what gave him a somewhat rational mind? "And what's going to happen after you hit her? She'll send you to prison or worse! She'll take extra precautions to make sure that we aren't together! Is that what you want?"

One of the tiny embers must've caught on to a gasoline-covered substance, because he exploded, "No, Adrienne, that's not what I want! Do you think I want any of this right now? Do you seriously think I want your mom to be the sadistic demon she is? News flash—I don't! I just want to enjoy here and now, because I can't even think about possibly losing you!"

At that, my tears were put to an abrupt end. I'd been too busy crying over how awful my life would be without him to think of how his life would be without me. I guess in that way, I was my mother's daughter. We both only thought of ourselves instead of anybody else.

I held him closer than before in my arms, inhaling his scent, which had become my favorite fragrance. "Oh, Jeydon, I never thought this might be hard on you too. I'm sorry I even brought it up."

He shook his head. "No, I'm actually kind of glad you brought it up."

I was about to let go of him, but instead I held on to him even tighter. I guess it was just a natural reflex. Still, it baffled me that in Mother's eyes, I was never to be associating with him. In her world, I was to be forced to love instead of loving naturally. What would she think if she knew I had actually developed a will that wasn't hers? As I did with the other occasional thoughts like this one that I'd experienced in the past few months, I pushed it into the back of my mind and focused on what was in front of me.

When I asked him why, he replied, "Now I'm even more determined to keep you right here in my arms, safe and sound and away from her. All those years I fought for all those pointless things or just to get through the day, but now I've actually got something that's worth fighting for."

"But how are you going to put up a fight?"

He inhaled, and I liked to imagine that he was breathing in my scent, as well. He said that he loved how I always smelled like roses. I didn't know I had a scent.

"One thing I've learned is that when there's love, there's always a way," he said.

I finally let go of him and beamed at the way his eyes shone in the moonlight. Though his expression was somber, his eyes still maintained the gloss that appeared after our first date. Just the thought of Mother trying to take this away from me was unbearable, and I could see his logic.

I wordlessly ran my fingers down his left cheek right where his scar was. Like I predicted, it had its own texture. Feeling a few swollen intertwined arteries that bulged in every place they weren't supposed to would've been too much to handle for any normal person, but as I gently grazed my lips on it, I knew that— like him—I'd found something worth fighting for too.

CHAPTER 26

The Key

It turned out that time flies by quicker than it should in paradise, and before anybody knew it, it was December. It wasn't until we passed our first month of dating when people finally got it through the thick cinderblock walls of their hollow skulls that we were an actual couple instead of a freak show and turned their spotlight over to the next big thing—honestly, I couldn't remember what the next hot topic of the lunch table discussion was.

But how could I remember, when all I could ever focus on was him? Whenever I was with him—which was as much as possible—everything else was deemed unimportant. It also turned out that as time moves along and I'm only focusing on one thing, everything else moves along with it without me.

Richard was soon a distant memory that was only recalled in an occasional nightmare. Before I knew it, it had been months since I'd called a single one of my sisters, and I sometimes wondered if they even cared that I wasn't a part of their lives anymore. Most of the time, I tried not to think about that, because even though Jeydon made me happy in a way none of my family members ever could, part of me still longed for them to care, though they hadn't even before I'd turned an icy shoulder on them.

However, the uneasiness I felt from everybody forgetting about me was a tiny prick on the finger compared to the terror I experienced whenever I thought of having to leave my angel to go back into a demon's arms, even if it was only for a week for Christmas break.

The cafeteria was full of commotion as I entered it with Jeydon's arm draped over my shoulder like a child's security blanket. As usual, Kody was giving us his most sinister death stare, and in his dark eyes, I could see Mother looking back at me—not only because their eyes were similar in color but because they were filled with just as much hatred as when Mother threw Amelia by the hair onto the stairs when she'd lost her virginity after a night of wild partying.

If she ever found out about me and Jeydon, she'd emit at least twenty times more hatred toward me. I'd be just like how I was to Kody now—a traitor. Of course, after what he'd tried to do to me, I didn't care what he thought, but I couldn't deny the fact that I cared deeply if Mother despised me. She already hated me enough that she sent me thousands of miles away so that she wouldn't have to look at me.

I laughed a little in remembrance of how I'd taken my punishment like it was a death sentence. Who would've known that a punishment as despicable as mine would be my key to salvation?

"What?" Jeydon asked. Obviously, I'd laughed loudly enough to be heard.

My cheeks grew hot. "I was just thinking about how awful I thought this year was going to be when I first came here."

He smiled a little. "Well, hasn't it? Now you're caught in my trap and will never be able to escape. That has to be really bad, hasn't it?"

I giggled and rolled my eyes. "Can't you learn to brag like a normal person?"

He chuckled. "But I'm not a normal person. You should know that by now."

I got on my tiptoes to peck him on the cheek. "Yes, and that's why I love you."

He smiled deviously—a telltale sign that the old manipulative side of him was emerging. "If you really love me, then you should try to convince Mommy Dearest to let you stay here for Christmas."

I sighed because I hated when he reminded me of my plane ticket with the marked destination of seven days in hell.

"You know that I would stay if I could. Maybe I'll get lucky again, like on Thanksgiving," I said. I was supposed to go home for a couple days then, but a canceled flight due to severe tropical storms meant that I got to stay in my safe haven uninterrupted.

We reached our table and sat down.

"Hopefully, but since pianos fall down on my head before raindrops do, I doubt that'll happen again," said Jeydon.

I shook my head as I took my regular seat next to him. We were the only ones there, but since he was the only thing I focused on, I didn't notice Laine's and Anthony's absence.

"You have the worst luck. You have a smoking-hot girlfriend and a loving father that both let you get away with murder. Your life must really suck."

He gave me a joshing smile. "Narcissist alert."

"So you don't think I'm hot?" I bruised too easily when it came to that matter.

He gave me a look that spoke for itself about how wrong I was. "So you'd rather me think you're smoking hot than value you as an actual person?"

I felt truly awful for what I'd said when I knew that was one of his triggers. "Sorry. I just sometimes forget that you're not like everybody else when it comes to that matter."

His flaming eyes became a little more docile. "You mean you forget for even a second that it's there?"

Honestly, I had no idea what he was talking about at first, but I guess he got my cluelessness and turned his head to the right a little to give me a visual hint.

"Oh, yeah. I forgot about that," I said, dumbfounded. I often went weeks at a time without noticing his scar.

He gave me the same look that I gave him a lot—a childish expression known as curiosity. "How could you possibly forget about it?"

I realized that it was the actual first time we'd talked about his scar in weeks, because I was forgetful, and he was elusive. "You don't?"

"When I'm around a bunch of strangers, I can't, because everybody acts weird, idiotic, or just plain cruel around me. When I'm with you or friends, I do, because you're over it by now."

"See, there you go. You forget about it too."

He let out an exasperated sigh. "Yes, but I don't have to look at myself all the time. You do, and even though you're used to it, you have to be a little grossed out by it. I am sometimes, so don't feel guilty. It's normal."

I became frustrated that even he was disgusted by his own appearance while I felt nothing but love and acceptance for him. "Apparently, I'm not normal, because I don't notice that it's there anymore. Does it really shock you that I see you as more than a scar? It's just a part of you that can't be taken away, and I love it."

There was pain on his face, but the corners of his mouth went up just enough to consider it a weak smile. "You never cease to amaze me, Adrienne. It concerns me, though."

I put my hand over his. "Why are you worried? Do you think I have a mental illness just because I love you no matter what your face looks like?"

He shook his head. "It has absolutely nothing to do with you. I was just thinking last night about how she did horrible things to your sisters because they weren't pretty enough for her. When I looked through the pictures of Mary, I noticed that she wasn't necessarily beautiful, but she wasn't particularly ugly, either. If she beat the crap out of her for her imperfections, imagine what she'll do to you if she ever finds out that you're dating me."

We hadn't talked about how Mother would react at all for a couple of weeks, because I'd figured that it wasn't worth frightening us about something that hadn't happened yet. It didn't really matter if I talked about it, because even if I wasn't being completely honest with myself, I knew that it scared the living daylights out of me that my two worst fears— my mother and losing Jeydon—could occur in a couple of weeks.

My lip quivered as I tried to think of what to say. Though I knew that he was a solid rock when I was afraid, I still didn't want to show any sign of cowardice in his sight.

Before I spoke, he did. "I'm sorry; I don't mean to frighten you. I'm just trying to be realistic. I might be your Prince Charming for some unknown reason, but I'm nothing like Richard."

It must've been serious to him, because that was the first time I'd heard him use Richard's actual name instead of *jerk*.

"Yes, you are nothing like Richard. You don't cheat on me with my best friend, you care about what I have to say, and you actually respect me. I never loved him, but I know without any doubt that I love you and would choose you over him no matter what."

He brushed a loose stand of hair out of my face and kissed my forehead. He whispered so softly that I'm sure the wind could have picked his words up and carried them away, "I just can't stand the thought of you getting hurt."

I stroked his mutilated left cheek, and he closed his eyes as a reflex. "Everybody hurts," I told him just as gently.

The whoosh of his warm, sweet breath calmed me, and when he spoke, I believed it was the same voice that belonged to the angels. "I would never forgive myself if she ever hurt you because of me. I know how it is to live in an abusive household."

"What's going on here?" a familiar and confused voice broke in. I turned my head and found myself staring straight into Laine's golden, troubled eyes.

While the blood rushed to my face and I wanted to disappear into a black hole, Jeydon gave her one of his infamous dirty looks that warned that the ice she stood on was paper thin.

I bit my lip to suppress my shame. It was about time for her to find out, really. I'd managed to fool her for this long. But there was a part of me that would rather have killed myself than tell her about the hell I called my home, even if she'd dealt with it before. Only God knew all of the awful crap that Anthony had gone through, and Laine was always the one who lent him a listening ear.

I watched the priceless look on her face as all of the pieces to my puzzle finally clicked together perfectly for her. Her voice also transformed into a softer tone.

"Oh, Adrienne, why didn't you tell me?"

For a moment, I said nothing, so Jeydon successfully got the vibe that I didn't want to talk and spoke for me. I expected him to get more than angry at her, but he explained things with a gentle, earnest tone that I'd thought he only used with me.

"She's not told anyone except for me and David, and he only knows because he overheard one of our conversations too. Don't be offended by it," he said.

She looked as if she didn't believe us, but I knew that she believed it all too well. "Why don't you tell anyone about it? If you actually told people, there's something somebody could do to stop it."

I felt as the muscles of my shoulders naturally tensed like they always did when I talked about it. "Nobody would believe me. There's nothing they could do, anyway."

Her face grew intense as she said, "There's always something we could do."

This angered me, because while I'd never told Laine that Mother was abusive, she knew all about how powerful she was. So I retorted, "Not when your mother has as much power and money as four regular people."

"It doesn't matter," she came back with a sour look of her own. "It's still not right or fair."

Something inside me just snapped like a nimble twig breaking in two. "Life isn't right or fair! You should know that by now after all the crap you went through with Keri, so get over it!"

She held her ground. She was so used to Jeydon snapping at her on numerous occasions over the past four years that it was an expected reaction now. "How could I get over things like this? You're hurting because of her, Adrienne; we love you and want the pain to stop. We'll do whatever it takes, just like we did with Anthony. You're part of us now."

I got as close to Jeydon as I could for a visual reference. "The thing is, I'm not hurting anymore. As long as I'm away from her, I won't be suffering."

"And what happens when the year's over and you have no choice but to be with her?" she asked with a skeptical brow raised.

I shrugged my shoulders and said, "Let's cross that bridge when we come to it." That was a good enough answer for her, wasn't it?

It must've been, or else she wouldn't have smiled and said, "Fair enough."

* * *

I knew Christmas was lurking around the corner, but I never thought that it would be there in basically the blink of an eye. There it was, though, gnashing its bitterly cold, icy teeth at me and slicing my skin with crimson ribbons that came wrapped on deceivingly pretty little packages. Yet somehow people called this the happiest time of the year. Did it ever occur to them that some people might hate their families?

A few days before actual Christmas, we gathered at David's house to celebrate it early before I left. The tree in the corner only reached up to my waist, and the few tiny packages were dwarfed by the overly expensive gifts at home. Still, I felt a lot more at home there with them than that manor a world away where the people that had my same blood lived.

The gifts we gave each other were small but meaningful. The four of us chipped in to buy David a gold watch that showed our gratitude for all he'd done for us that year. Anthony gave each of us thin, silver CDs that had our favorite songs on them. Laine's gift to me was a picture of us smiling straight into the camera, framed with seashells found right outside in our little strip of beach. Jeydon gave Anthony a new lava lamp, because a few months earlier, he'd punched the wall so hard that the vibrations knocked his old one over.

Every gift seemed to have its own story, none of which I would ever be a part of no matter how vivid Jeydon's descriptions of those times were. It made me feel like a foreigner, knowing just how much history they had together before I came along and completely knocked Jeydon's world right side up. What exactly was I to them? A nuisance? A damsel in distress? A face that would soon be a memory? With that thought, I felt a determination to prove to them that I would be sitting there with them again at that exact time the next year. There had to be a way out of the trap that clamped down hard on my throat. For once, I needed to try my hardest to be like the boy I admired so dearly and pry the snare off with an iron will. I at least owed him that.

David's gifts were the highlight of the night. He pretty much gave Laine and Anthony permission to destroy his SUV by giving them each a key to it. He also gave Jeydon a new guitar as a result of his remarkable progress over the year.

Jeydon wrapped his arms tightly around my waist and responded, "Don't reward *me* for it, because the person responsible is sitting right here beside me."

David's lips curled up into a smile. "Who did you think the next gift was for?"

I was handed a small silver package adorned with a white ribbon. As soon as I got my hands on it, I ripped it open with an anticipation I'd not felt in years, not even as a small child. Like back at home, I expected it to be a $500 genuine diamond piece of jewelry that I would stop wearing after two months—or at least something with as much worth as that.

But instead of a treasure chest awaiting me, there was just a small brass key on a thin, long chain.

"What's this?" I asked, making it more than obvious that it was a little bit of a letdown compared to everybody else's gifts. Then again, I knew that I shouldn't have been that disappointed, because I was the outsider of this group. The only thing that made me fit in was this wondrous boy whose lap I was sitting on.

David shrugged. "I seriously have no clue. It was Jeydon's idea."

For some odd reason, this fact made it about a thousand times more appealing, as much as a shining diamond in the rough as he was. I angled my face toward his. "What is it?"

With a small smile, he took the necklace from my fingers and put it up to his sternum. He then commanded me in a gentle tone to put my hand on top of the key. I obeyed, and he asked, "Do you feel that?"

"You mean the electricity?" I guessed. I thought it was actually pretty wise, considering electricity always jolted our bodies when we were together even without any aid from a metal object.

When a couple of chuckles escaped from his throat, I felt like an insignificant fool.

"No, I'm talking about my heart. I figured since you've already stolen it, you should have the key to it, as well. Take it with you, because they're both yours."

"Oh, Jeydon," I said in a hushed whisper. "I love it."

When our lips met in an instant, I felt no longer like an outsider barging in, because I realized that I fit perfectly into place with him. Laine was right. I was a part of them now, and I was determined to stay a part of them. Because like how I'd stolen his heart, Jeydon had a stolen a piece of me that was as vital to my body as oxygen was to any normal being.

I wouldn't be like how Aunt Margaret was to my biological family. I would never be a forgotten face to my new family, no matter how rough the skies ahead of me got.

* * *

Jeydon was the one who drove me up to the airport because I wanted to spend as much time with him as possible before our farewell. I asked myself why I was being so dramatic about it; it was only a week. But seven moons without him might as well have been seven years without rain. I had the red suitcase that united us together in the first place in one hand and his hand in the other as we walked into the airport. The building was chaotic with tons of people coming in for Christmas vacations and going out to reunite with their families.

Apparently, Jeydon wasn't as hexed as he thought of himself to be, because my flight was delayed two hours due to a snowstorm in New York. That meant two more hours that I got to spend with him. We spent the time with me cuddling up with him, flipping through magazines and talking about random things we'd never told anybody—or each other—before, like how I secretly admired Leonardo DiCaprio when I was younger or how Jeydon hadn't heard of three-fourths of the people mentioned in the magazines.

I guess when you're in jail or out on the streets or in hospitals for both mental and physical needs for most of your life, you lose your touch with the world of social media.

Then, as he flipped the next page, I saw the one thing I never wanted him to see. Me. Not as the me he loved so dearly, but in the form of me he first knew. The form of me he hated with a fiery passion.

In the picture, I was leaning against a wall at the same angle at which I was leaning against him. The slope of my neck was that of a swan's, and my eyes were the only thing that wasn't in a weird angle that everybody else found sexy but he found just plain ridiculous. The expression on my face was so unlike my gestures now with an open red mouth showing a bit of my overly bleached teeth. My eyes were like that of an animal's; the only reflection coming off of them was the flash of the camera. I might as well have been an animal, considering that the only clothing I had on was a Band-Aid for a skirt and a black lacy bra that showed an enormous amount of my cleavage.

I would like to say that was who I was, but I knew that was who I am. At least for a week, I had to pretend that I was that same girl in the hooker's attire. I had to hold my tongue like I used to. Hide my happiness by knocking the skip to my step before Mother did it for me.

I expected him be disgusted at the old me, but he just grazed his soft, porcelain-smooth lips against mine.

"I've got something else for you," he said as he looked at me with not a look of lust but of love even after seeing that image of me.

"You shouldn't have," I whispered with a shake of my head. "The key's enough of a gift for me."

He didn't listen to me and took another small silver package identical to the other one out from his jean jacket pocket and gave me a delicate smile as he handed it to me. "It's the least I can do to thank you. You have no idea just how much you've changed me."

I laced my fingers in his. "You've changed me from that girl in the magazine to who I am today, and I haven't gotten you anything."

This was true, because whenever I'd asked him what he wanted, he'd told me that he already had everything he'd ever wanted.

He grinned. "I don't need anything else, because you alone were the best gift I could ever receive."

"So are you, but you still got me things," I retorted with a scowl.

"Can't you just shut up and be happy that I'm doing this?" he asked without a hint of smile anywhere.

I must've really ticked him off with my questions. Seeing a glimpse of the old, angry Jeydon frightened me, and I obeyed by gently opening up the package.

Inside was a note labeled *Adrienne* in his handwriting and a jewelry box. "Don't read the note until you're boarded on the plane," he told me as I was about to grab it from the box and read it.

At first I was heavyhearted, but when I saw what was in the jewelry box, I no longer cared about what the note said. Inside was a pair of large, round emerald earrings that looked exactly like his eyes. I just looked back in forth from the earrings to his eyes, trying to find any difference, but there wasn't any. They were identical in every single way.

An excited yelp escaped from my mouth as I pressed my lips hard on to his. "This is perfect, Jeydon! They're just like your eyes!" I exclaimed, holding him so tightly that some would consider it strangling.

He sported the big, toothy grin that I still often found difficulty in triggering. "I remembered how the first day we actually talked, you said how you wished you had a pair of earrings that was like them, and now you do. I made sure to get ones with actual emeralds. I could only give the best to you."

That made my stomach twinge in guilt. "Were they expensive?"

He shook his head with an ever-dazzling smile. "No, because I found it at that pawn store in Petersburg on sale for fifty dollars. The look on your face right now makes it worth every cent I paid."

I wrinkled my brow. "Who would give away such a cunning pair of earrings?"

He shrugged his shoulders. "I don't have the slightest clue, but whoever the imbecile was, it was his or her loss and our gain."

I'd gotten used to his massive increase in vocabulary in response to freeing his mind of the narcotics. I said nothing back and just collapsed into his arms. He held me tightly as I sobbed on his shoulder, knowing that I'd have to let it out now before returning to my forced laughter that Mother was pleased with.

I remained that way until the unanticipated warning bell that my flight was about to depart rang. Jeydon dried my eyes and put my earrings on for me like I was too weak to do it myself. Maybe it was because I never had a mother who did these labors of love for me and that he was trying to fill her shoes. He could never fill her shoes, for she was a demon, and he was the angel sent to save me from becoming anything like her. As I gave him one last squeeze, he kissed me like it was the last time.

I thought I could keep my cool, but when I let go, I let out a sob from my throat that was a mixture between a newborn's first breath and a desperate scream for help. He consoled me once more, and I knew I had to be strong for once, considering that he was always the solid rock I clung desperately to. I'd rather be strong for him instead of Mother, anyway.

He held me close and whispered the words "I love you" tenderly in my ear.

With that, he kissed me and turned his face away from mine before he could talk himself out of letting me leave. With that, I turned to leave, but not without planting a kiss on his scar, which I had come to think was almost as enjoyable as kissing his lips. I smiled weakly as I finally walked away for good. It was too hard for me to even push the words *good-bye* out of my mouth.

As soon as I boarded the plane, I ran the key that was resting on my sternum through my fingers and traced the letters Jeydon loves Adrienne that he ever so carefully engraved on the back.

Though everything else was uncertain, I knew one thing. I was ready.

CHAPTER 27

Suspicions

The first thing I felt when I walked through the door of the Hudson manor was a fear that made my blood freeze solid until it clogged up my veins. The old but familiar feeling of the hairs standing on the back of my neck haunted me, and as I fumbled with my key necklace, I recalled Leah's silent screams as Mother told her that she was a reincarnation of Jezebel for being in love.

Like expected, instead of Mother, it was a maid who barely knew two phrases of English who greeted me and led me up to my room like I wasn't bred and raised in this household. Maybe since she'd never seen me around before, she thought I was an honored guest instead of their disappointment for a daughter.

The first thing I saw when I entered the room was the orange of Angela's hair right before she leaped up to give me a hug.

"Adrienne, you have no idea how awful it's been without you around!" she exclaimed as she squeezed like she was a human blood pressure cuff. "I was stressing out. I was starting to think you'd never show up!"

I gave her a fake but truly apologetic smile. I knew that things must've been rough for her being the only child living at home that year even without her saying so.

"Sorry I'm late; my flight got delayed because of the snowstorm," I said.

She released me from her grasp and studied me as if she could sense that something was different.

"You've gotten a nice tan. Of course, you've been in Florida, but I honestly thought you wouldn't tan. You never really have before," she finally stated.

I silently sighed in relief. If only Mother could as easily overlook things as Angela could.

"The weather in Florida has been very sunny all year, and I've been outside a lot. It just kind of came effortlessly," I said.

She gave me her famous half smile as she asked, "So how is it in Florida?"

I was about to tell her how it really was, but right before I said it, my filter reminded me that I had to convert back into my old ways and hold my tongue. Only with Jeydon I could speak my mind without getting thrown headfirst into the coffee table.

"It's hot," I answered instead with a shrug.

She giggled a little. "I figured out that much. Anything else besides that?"

I shook my head. "Not really. I've made a few friends, but nothing major."

Unknown to her, I had my fingers crossed behind my back, hoping that she wouldn't see through my lie. She didn't and instead offered to help me put up my bags. I declined her offer, and at that, she realized that I wanted to be alone and let me be.

When I opened my suitcase, the first thing I laid my eyes on was the box from Jeydon, and it occurred to me that I still hadn't read his note yet. I grabbed the note that I had discreetly hidden in my left jeans pocket, carefully opened it up, and read his scratchy script over and over again word for word. I could hear his lullaby for a voice playing in my mind, full of wisdom and sincerity just like he was there in person speaking it to me. I wished I could see his eyes again, but one touch of my earrings brought to me a calm and collected feeling I thought only looking into them could bring.

Dear Adrienne,

You might think this note is putting things over the top, but writing this is the least I can do after everything you've done for me. I can sit for hours at a time trying to find the words to describe what exactly you mean to me, but there are still no words to explain the exact depth of my love for you. No matter what happens, I will always love you in that way, because like I've said many times before, you are the girl who can see past my scarred face and love me for who I am. This may seem effortless on your part, but it isn't. Nobody else could ever show the love that you've shown me, no matter how hard they tried. Just like how it would be impossible to imagine loving anybody else.

Hopefully you're wearing the key to my heart and my earrings. I want you to remember me by these things this week, and take them everywhere you go. You've got my heart with you, so don't let Mommy Dearest break it. Whenever you want to look into my eyes, look at those earrings and see me inside of them. If she tries to hurt you at any time, remind yourself that you're the girl that has made me a better man and opened up my heart to love.

It may feel like forever right now, but remember that this is only a week. A week from now, I'll be waiting anxiously for you with my heart leaping out of my chest from anticipation. Actually, it already is just sitting here thinking about it.

I'm determined to find a way where you'll be in my arms safe and sound forever.

With all my love,

Jeydon

I read over it one last time and gently folded it back as it was in my pocket. With my index finger, I touched my left earring and heard him laughing hysterically over a joke that would make Richard groan in annoyance. The sound of his laughter running through my head made me laugh too, and for a second, I forgot all about how trapped I was there with the woman I feared more than death or spiders or anything else that a normal sixteen-year-old was supposed to be afraid of. I touched my key, and it reassured me that everything was truly going to be all right.

For the next few hours, Angela and I watched some of her all-time-favorite movies, which ranged from sappy love stories like *The Notebook* to adrenaline-raising thrillers like *The House Next Door.* My personal favorite, *The Breakfast Club,* was all of a sudden interrupted by a firm, repetitive knock on the door.

"Release the kraken," I muttered under my breath as Angela got up to answer the door.

Strangely enough, it wasn't Mother's voice I heard coming from the hallway but Amelia's. Though Amelia wasn't the sister I was closest to, I still preferred her over Mother any day.

I got up from the couch and met them out by the front door, where Angela was strangling her.

"I thought you were going to spend Christmas with your boyfriend. Did you guys break up?" Angela asked.

I raised an eyebrow. Amelia had a boyfriend now? If they were spending Christmas together, it must've been serious. What else had I missed while I was gone?

She shook her head. "No, I'm just dropping by to see if Adrienne's here yet."

Before Angela could, I answered, "I'm right here."

Amelia made a smile that looked a little bit forced. "Sorry for coming out of the blue, but I just need to talk to you about some things."

I was aware that the last time such a thing had happened was when Leah drove me home a few months earlier, but I was far too curious to reject her offer. We went out and sat down on an ice-cold, metal bench by the side of the pool. The pool that was a nice crystal-blue spring of cool water now had a tarp over it that now had a blanket of snow hiding it until next spring. The climate difference only reminded me that I was out of Jeydon's warm arms.

"Since when did you get a boyfriend?" I asked, trying to focus on somebody else's boyfriend besides mine before I threw another one of my pity parties.

A couple of snowflakes stood out in her jet-black hair as if she had a case of dandruff. "A couple of months after you left. We met at a party and hit it off."

Without saying anything, she got her phone out, and sure enough, there was a picture of her smiling ear to ear with a baby-faced guy sporting a Syracuse sweatshirt.

"His name's Steven," she said. "You can't even believe how charming he is."

She was right. Just by analyzing the picture, I couldn't believe for a second that this guy could be nearly as charming as Jeydon. I had to pop the big question.

"Have you told Mother?"

She laughed a little. "Why would you ask a retarded question like that? She doesn't care that I'm not staying for Christmas this year. All she would do is rant about how I'm a whore for dating a guy from Syracuse. There's no point in telling her other than to hurt me."

Yes, I truly agreed with her on that. "So why do we need to talk?" I asked, trying to focus my mind on something else besides him before I had the slightest chance of spilling out all my secrets.

She released a heavy breath and said, "I know Richard cheated on you," as if it hurt her almost as badly as it hurt me. But I could understand that, because Richard was more of a younger sibling to her than I was.

I had so many questions to ask, but all I could think of to say was, "How?"

Amelia told me about how, for the past month after Tori finally broke it off completely with Richard, he'd been asking all around about how to contact me without actually calling my number. He had a talk on the phone with Angela about how he loved me and was so sorry for what he'd done and that all he wanted was to win me back, but she was smart enough to not give him any information.

This is where I came in. Three weeks earlier, I'd noticed that Richard had been calling me. Instead of handling it myself, I'd informed Jeydon about it, and he left Richard a threatening voice mail swearing that if he ever called me again, there would be grotesque and unspeakable consequences. We completely forgot about the threat, but Richard tattled on me to Mother all about this mysterious, threatening boy and how he called me "his girl."

My stomach was twisting into knots, and apparently she could sense my discomfort.

"Are you his girl?" she asked in an uptight, snobbish matter so unlike the lighthearted, cordial Amelia I knew growing up.

My cheeks grew hot at two realizations—one being that Amelia shouldn't judge when she was dating a guy from Syracuse of all places, and that if Amelia acted like this was a sin, then only the devil himself knew what Mother had in store for me.

I assured her by saying, "He's just a crush." I crinkled my nose because I knew I was insulting my deep, undying passion for him as if it were only the result of a hormonal imbalance.

I had to give her credit that she was obviously trying very hard to believe me but was just able to see past my poorly concealed lie.

"I'd just watch my back if I were you," she said.

Since I'd already been caught red-handed, I knew there was no use in going into denial mode. Yet I didn't want to expose myself anymore, so just I nodded and promised, "I will."

* * *

Right after Amelia warned me, she fled as fast as she could. Two hours later, Leah came by to give me a similar visit, but she seemed to know nothing about Mother's suspicions. After Leah left, I asked Angela if she knew just to make sure, and she informed that as far as her knowledge went, only she knew about it.

Needless to say, she wasn't of much assistance. If anything, Angela was a nuisance trying to squeeze detail after detail out of me. Though she was the one I trusted the most out of all my sisters, I refused to confide anything in her. I knew very well that Angela would tell Mother anything to escape her evil hands.

When Mary called saying that she wasn't coming home for Christmas—honestly, nobody really could blame her—I asked her if she knew about the thing with Richard, and I could picture her staring blankly with a wrinkled brow as she asked, "What are you talking about?"

I counted out the math. Two of my sisters knew. Two of my sisters didn't. Tara had to be the almighty tiebreaker whether this was a huge stress factor or not. Who was I kidding? Even if she didn't know, it would still be a big stress factor, because it threatened to take away everything I loved and cared for tremendously.

Tara called and went as far as to make an excuse why she'd be a couple of days late to Christmas, but I didn't really have the heart to ask out of fear that she knew every detail about it.

It wasn't until ten o'clock that Mother finally arrived home, looking lovely in a classic little black dress with matching sky-high stilettos that I'd worn before Jeydon happened. It was so easy to be fooled by her appearance, but after noticing the hate in her eyes, I knew all too well what she really was.

Her all-too-familiar voice was a pain in my side. "Oh, Adrienne, you have no idea how long it's been!" she exclaimed as she embraced me instead of slapping me smartly like I feared she would do.

Honestly, I'd rather that she'd slapped me than hug me after Jeydon helped me open my eyes to the obvious truth about her inner demons.

"Mother," I said quietly, not knowing what else to say.

She stood back and analyzed me with a scowl. After her examination was over, she gave me a look of utter disgust. "There's something about you that's different, and whatever it is, I don't like it. And you're such a pretty girl. I thought you'd still embrace it after a little break from modeling."

I said nothing to this but just stood there trying to hide the redness of my cheeks. She had to know about him. I could see it in her eyes that her newfound purpose in life was to destroy me as she had destroyed my sisters. Or maybe I was being paranoid.

I knew I wasn't being paranoid when Mother asked, "Adrienne, where exactly did you get those earrings?" as she tugged on my earlobe hard enough for me to fear that she'd rip my entire ear off in one piece.

I gulped and gasped for air like a fish out of water as I managed to sputter out a faulty explanation, "My friend gave them to me."

She skeptically raised her eyebrow. "Who exactly is this friend of yours?"

Any name, I rhetorically told myself as my heart raced. *Just pick a random name.* "Rosie."

I guess that answer actually pleased her, because she just shrugged her shoulders and went on with bringing complete terror to my sisters' lives. But I reminded myself that for all I knew, she could be planning to bring terror to mine, as well.

For the next three days as Christmas passed, I played on the safe side so that I wouldn't get hurt. I spent most of the time up in my room listening to Anthony's CD or reading Jeydon's note over and over again until I had the whole thing completely memorized like it was biblical scripture. I slept for the majority of the time, knowing that the more I hibernated, the sooner it would be over.

But by the time day six rolled around, I was dying to hear his voice.

Unknown to Jeydon, I knew his home phone number by heart. I just couldn't fight that urge for one more second, and knew I had to talk to him even though I was going to see him in roughly twenty-four hours. As soon as I triple-checked to make sure that

Angela and Mother were sound asleep in their beds, I put some heavy winter clothes over my pajamas and snuck outside to the nearest pay phone. The fee I had to pay for the call to Florida was the least of my worries. I forked the money over and swiftly dialed his number, my hands trembling from the anticipation of actually hearing his voice in something else besides my dreams.

But I knew something wasn't right as soon as the imposter groggily answered the phone. "Hello? Is this Adrienne?"

It couldn't be him. His voice was one of his greatest beauties, and this boy's voice sounded like a bullfrog's. Wait a minute, who did I know whose voice was that of a frog's croak? "Is this Anthony?"

"Yeah, sorry," he began so quietly that I had to lean in really close to the speaker to hear.

"There's nothing to be sorry about," I retorted. "Just let me talk to Jeydon."

For the first time ever, he actually sounded a little cheerful. "I'll try, but nowadays, once he's out cold, it's almost impossible to wake him up."

I smiled a little, thinking about how Jeydon told me that once he got over the insomnia that plagued him, he could sleep for days at a time. "You do that."

But before I could hear Jeydon's voice, I heard a stereo booming in the distance. I reflexively turned around and saw a bright white light moving at a remarkable speed. As the vehicle approached closer, it became more familiar, and as I heard a drunken whoop over the stereo, I knew exactly who was driving the car.

Richard.

My first reaction was to put my hood up over to my face, but apparently after being my "best friend" for eight years, he'd learned to distinguish me from the average, everyday bums who are so out of touch with technology that they're using a pay phone.

I heard a maniacal cackle that I distinguished as one of my other "best friends" come from the car. "Is that *Adrienne?*"

I couldn't really make sense out of their murmuring besides a few curse words, but I still knew a few things very well. Number one: they were so sadly drunk that it brought me shame that I used to be one of them. Number two: as much as I disliked them then, I hated every single cell of them now that the joke was on me instead of somebody like Madison Huffington.

And number three: I needed to get out of there.

Just as one of them opened the car door enough to stick a foot out, I darted out of that phone booth. My home might've been a torture chamber, but after overhearing what they said they were going to do to me, it was as safe and warm as Jeydon's arms during that particular moment.

It was a close call, but I made it back into the house in one piece. I let out a sigh of relief, but this sense of comfort was short lived, for when I turned around, I was facing a far more sinister monster than a bunch of drunken preps.

She looked at me with the windows of hell, and practically every time she exhaled, she breathed out its flames, "Where do you think you're going?"

Coincidentally, my lungs acted as if they were filled with smoke. My breathing became increasingly rapid and painful. "I went out for a walk."

Without any hesitation, she shoved me onto the cold hard ground. "Do you honestly think I'm stupid enough to believe that? You'd better not think I am, because that would just make you even more of an idiotic whore than you already are. I should just shove you out into the snow where you rightfully belong for disobeying your own mother like this."

I just lay there on the floor, staring at her blankly as she delivered a swift kick to the side so hard the edges of my vision momentarily went black. I should've known from the day I walked in on Mother abusing Mary that I'd get my fair share one of these days. Yet somehow this was such a shock to me. A part of me expected her to treat me like royalty, even after Amelia warned me about Mother's suspicions.

I guess it served me right. Maybe I did need a little bit of enlightenment smacked into me. Maybe I needed more than Jeydon to see the ultimate truth. I wanted to punch myself for even thinking that.

Yet somehow I knew that I had a little bit of sense slapped into me, because while I was lying there on the floor, I discovered something. To get through this, I had to be brave and strong. Even though I wasn't either of those things, I had to show Mother my true colors, like how she'd shown me hers long ago. I had to be like Jeydon and fight through it.

I couldn't be like how I was now forever.

CHAPTER 28

The Lucky One

I had begun to develop a theory that Mother had an undiagnosed case of bipolar disorder, because after a long sleepless night, she hugged me good-bye as I left for the airport. Now I knew how Laine must've felt whenever Rosie acted like this with her. Honestly, I'd rather have Mother abuse me 24-7 like she did with everybody else than pretend she hadn't bruised my rib cage.

Since it did hurt a little when she hugged me, I let out a forced groan in an effort to remind her that I was no longer on her good side in case she'd forgotten. However, she paid no attention to it and just sent me on my way out, probably because the fact that she was causing me pain didn't interest her.

I was on the edge of my seat trembling with excitement as the plane came to a landing. Even before the passengers were instructed to exit the plane, I jumped up and ran out. People all around were looking at me like I'd gone insane, but I couldn't have cared less. They didn't understand my love for him.

He sat in the crowded lobby alone, waiting patiently as I called out his name. When he looked over my way with his ghost of a smile that haunted me when he wasn't around, I couldn't help but sprint over as fast as I could, leaving my stuff unattended and leaping into his arms like it had been six months instead of a week. For a moment, he just held me there, and I wanted to start crying. I reminded myself that I needed to be more like him, and Jeydon never cried.

I kissed him hard on the lips before I spoke. "You have no idea how much I missed you."

He gave me a tiny chuckle, a sign that his happiness was returning now that I was there. "Yeah, whatever. This entire week, all I could think about was you no matter how much Anthony and Laine tried to get my mind on other things. I couldn't help but be worried."

Heat rushed to my cheeks as I grazed my fingers along my rib cage. "Yeah, about that ..."

His face immediately turned into a fiery furnace, but I knew I didn't need to fear this time, because this fire was fighting for me instead of against me. His tone was that of a beast's roar. "What did she do to you?"

I felt a sudden sensation of shame and looked down at the linoleum floor so shiny that I could see my reflection in it. "She didn't do that much."

A nuclear bomb could've detonated and there would be no difference. "It doesn't matter what exactly she did to you! She still hurt you—that's the important thing!"

He let out a deep, rumbling thunder of a roar in frustration and smacked his hand on his forehead so hard that it left a red mark. "It was because of me, wasn't it? Why do I have to screw everything up?"

"You don't screw anything up!" I replied as I felt tears forming out of the corners of my eyes. So much for trying to be like him.

"Yes, I do," he hissed through gritted teeth. "I swear sometimes that the flame has stuck with me even after all of these years! I bring misery and destruction to everybody I come in contact with, Adrienne! I've screwed up everything that matters to me, just as I feared I would. I've ruined your life for you!"

Branding irons for years streamed down my cheeks as I bellowed out, "How dare you say that when you're the best thing that ever happened to me? You didn't screw up anything. You've taken my screwed-up life and turned it right side up."

He scowled bitterly. "We both know that I'm not the kind that turns things right side up but the kind that turns things upside down."

I grabbed hold of his hand so hard that I wondered for a second if I was cutting off his circulation. "It doesn't matter which way you've turned it, because you've saved me from becoming like her. You haven't screwed me up but instead have turned my life into something worth living."

He scoffed in the smart-alecky way he used while having discussions with anybody else besides me. "So in your mind, a life where you're constantly tormented by your mother is worth living?"

I nodded. "As long as you're in it."

His face lightened up, and I could tell that he was turning back into the Jeydon I was the most comfortable with. I say most comfortable because I was still madly in love with him even when his temper got the best of him.

"You're out of your mind," he said.

"You haven't figured that out already?"

He chuckled. "Yes, I have, but only when it comes to me. I thought I was just crazy in general, but this week, I've found out that I'm only truly insane without you. I should've figured that already, since you are my clarity."

His smile transformed into an upside-down parenthesis. "You have no idea how hard it was for me to stay clean this week, but I managed to, because I could never be able to live with myself if I let you down like that."

I leaned in to his chest with my ear against his heart. "Why do you have to be so perfect?"

"I'm far from perfect, Adrienne. You should know that by now," he retorted, obviously believing the lie that the world had told him.

"I do know you, Jeydon," I said, smiling at the fact that I could actually say that and be correct this time around—at least I really hoped I could. It would devastate me even more if he were hiding even more things from me than if he went back on drugs.

This was verified when he answered with a nod, "You do know me, better than anybody else in the world. Even God himself." He managed to form a small, delicate smile. "It kind of blows my mind sometimes that you actually found a way to open me up. My philosophy has always been that it's bad enough that I have physical scars, so I never wanted to show anybody my emotional ones. I began to think that I was incapable of telling anybody my whole story, because the words couldn't fall into place."

"What do you think made you tell me?"

"Because my gut told me that you'd still love me even after I told you what happened," he explained lightheartedly. "Besides, it was about time for me to come out of my shell. I just never had anybody I trusted enough to tell besides you."

I looked at him in disbelief, though I shouldn't have been shocked that he wasn't exactly somebody who trusted easily. In fact, earning his complete trust was one of the highest honors I could ever receive.

"Not even David?" I asked.

He gave me a grim look. "I was going to tell David on that fishing trip, but before I could say anything, he confessed his love for the woman who was responsible for 80 percent of the crap I went through."

I sucked in more air than I should have. "Is that why you—"

"Pierced his lip with a fishhook?" he finished in his smart-alecky manner. "Yes, both that and my temper."

With that, he looked down at the ground with shame, and I responded by stroking his cheek.

"Don't be ashamed by it," I said. "I would've let my temper get the best of me too."

He gave me a look that was the combination of disbelief and humiliation. "I seriously doubt you'd shove a fishhook through his lip. I can't picture you doing that to anybody, not even Mommy Dearest or that jerk."

My face grew flushed with the realization that he was yet again right. "Yes, but you aren't the only one who'd get mad."

He glared at me with a look of death. "Nobody gets mad like I do."

I grimaced back at him with a look only half as unpleasant. "We all have our issues, Jeydon."

He began to laugh but then lowered his voice so that I wouldn't get the wrong vibe that this was a laughing matter. "Really, Adrienne? You've seen me at my absolute worst. I've confessed to doing every bad thing in the book, and yet somehow you're still here. I have more issues than you, Laine, and Anthony combined! You have no idea how much time I've spent wondering what you see in me."

I shook my head. He didn't say that often, but I hated it when he did. "I wonder the same things."

The loudest, nastiest, most annoyed sigh escaped from the back of his throat. "You're perfect compared to me, Adrienne, so shut up! I hate it when you think you're so screwed up just because your mother beats you! Trust me; I know exactly what it's like. While it leaves bruises that don't fade away, it doesn't turn you into a monster."

I narrowed my eyes at him, wondering if I knew him as well as I thought I had a brief moment earlier. "What do you mean you know exactly what it's like?"

He bit his lower lip to suppress the pain from his long-healed scars. "Is it really that much of a shock that I got my fair share of beatings from Keri back before the car crash?"

I was not surprised, but I was a little hurt that he'd never told me in those exact words. I shook my head, and we left the airport.

As I was sitting in the car thinking about the boy sitting next to me, he said out of nowhere, "I know this might be too much for you, but there's one last thing I want to get off my chest."

I exhaled a shaky, agitated breath, but when I looked at the sincerity of his eyes, I couldn't resist. "What more do you have to tell?" I asked.

In retrospect, I shouldn't have been so agitated, because if he hadn't told me, then it must've been a dire secret that had been weighing down his chest for several years.

His eyes were like daggers that pierced deep into my soul. "You know how a few months ago when we were sitting in this very car, I told you that Keri died in the car crash?"

I nodded, feeling a twinge of pain in my chest from the memory of him hurting me just so I wouldn't know the awful truth. "Yeah, why?"

His eyes became wider than usual, almost like those of a child's. Honestly, I couldn't have imagined him showing any childlike qualities. But that wasn't the thing that made my heart split in two for him. His eyes were those of a suffering child, a common sight in my household growing up. His voice trembled, but no tears came out as he said, "I wasn't lying when I said somebody had died."

The small compassionate part of me surfaced, and I tentatively held his hand in mine.

"I had a sister," he continued. "She was only two when she burned to death in the same fire that burned me."

His lack of tears caused a surplus in mine.

"I'm so sorry," I whispered.

"Don't be sorry for me," he retorted, his voice a low rumble. "I was the one who just lied there in my own excruciating pain and watched her die in the worst way possible."

I clung to him as I tasted my own bitter tears. "Don't beat yourself up like this, Jeydon. There was nothing you could've done."

I asked myself why I was crying over this, but it was simple. I was merely crying enough tears for the both of us, as I always was. Or at least that's what I liked to think, because deep down, I knew the truth was that I was just as weak as he was strong.

He exhaled a breath and mumbled words that sounded a bit labored—as if his diaphragm had stopped working properly. "When we were little and Keri used to beat us, I always tried my best to make sure that I was the one to take the punches instead of her. As young as I was, I took all the responsibilities that Keri was too stoned to do. All the awful things that happened to me at hospitals, out on the streets, living with Keri, and in jail combined aren't even close to competing with the pain I felt when I woke up in the hospital only to discover that the child I shielded as well as I could from Keri's hands had slipped into her fingers, fallen six feet under."

I ran my fingers through his cotton-soft golden hair. "Have you ever told anybody this?" I asked cautiously, having no idea what else to say.

As I'd expected, he gave a grim shake of his head. I tried to look away from his anguish-inflicted eyes, but no matter how long I tried to look around, my line of vision stayed forever locked onto them.

He spoke in gentle, quiet whisper that wasn't his own as he looked straight ahead with the newfound color of his cheeks faded. "I wasn't lying, either, when I said that everybody was saying she was the lucky one. I didn't understand, but after it got through to me that I'd be stuck with this mutilated thing on my face for life, I realized what they were saying. When things got even worse, I began to wonder why I was spared."

He became more animated as the old flame stirred within him. "I thought I knew the answer. I thought the only reason I was spared was to be crushed from the inside out every single day of my life. You have no idea how much I desired to lie cold in the ground like her. I thought I was way better off dead than

I was on earth, where the odds were against me everywhere I turned."

He squeezed my hand and gave me a look that possessed the luminosity of stars in the sky. "But now I know exactly why I was spared. I was spared to find you. Now I know that she's not the lucky one, but I am. I got to know you, not to mention fall in complete love with you and for you to actually share the same feelings."

I shook my head. "I don't have the same feelings as you. I love you so much more than you could ever imagine."

He scoffed in a lighthearted, teasing manner. "Obviously, you don't listen to 90 percent of the things I say."

I laughed. "No, it's just impossible for anybody to love anything as much as I love you."

He didn't laugh with me, but stayed solemn. "Love comes easily for you, Adrienne—or at least when it comes to me. For some unknown reason, you loved me from the start. I, on the other hand, tried my best to reject the idea of love, because it rejected me a long time ago. A couple of years ago when I was talking to David, he told me that whenever I did love, I loved too hard. I had no idea what it really meant until you came around, and my passion for you outweighed all of my other emotions. It was devastating enough when a cynical woman took her away from me, so I'm not going let that happen again."

I marveled at this wonderful boy and pondered if he'd possibly fallen straight from the sky. And how could this beautiful creature that resembled a man but had a heart of solid gold ever come to be mine?

I asked him what his sister's name was, and in a quiet. monotone mumble. he replied, "Grace."

CHAPTER 29

Impressions

After that short setback, my paradise resumed exactly the way it was before except for the fact that our bond was even stronger because I now knew even the deepest, darkest skeletons in his closet that he'd managed to keep hidden remarkably well. Whenever we were conversing with Anthony and Laine, I couldn't help but notice that he was starting to open up about how he really felt about things too. Of course, it was nothing compared to some of the things he'd confided in me, but it was a start.

Just a week and a half after my return, I received an invitation to an event I'd honestly forgotten all about—Tara's wedding. I remembered vaguely at Christmas how she'd gone on and on to Angela and me about her wedding plans, but while Angela was giving her undivided attention, my mind was drifting off to more comforting settings like right outside David's little beach house property with my head on Jeydon's chest.

I still felt a little ignorant, though, that an event I was once so excited for had completely slipped my mind, but it wasn't that shocking, because I was more than aware that all I ever thought about was Jeydon.

"And get this," I informed Jeydon, Anthony, and Laine at breakfast, "I'm her maid of honor!"

Laine chuckled. "How could you possibly forget that?"

"It's kind of hard to remember that after all of this happened," I explained as I rubbed my temples with my middle and index fingers.

Jeydon grinned mischievously. "And when you say 'all of this,' you really mean that I happened, don't you?"

I couldn't help but giggle as I playfully nudged him with my elbow. "Yeah, pretty much. Don't rub it in."

"So when's the wedding?" Laine asked, obviously trying to change the subject.

"Valentine's Day," I answered flatly.

"That's such a cheesy tradition," Jeydon muttered. "Their marriage will only last about two years, tops."

I let out a fake agitated sigh. I had the same microscopic expectations, but I didn't really want Laine and Anthony to know about them. "How do you know that? You've never even met Tara."

Of course, I should've known that arguing with him was only a waste of time.

"Yes, but I've heard so much about her from you that I have a pretty good idea what she's like, so unless you don't really know her, I'm going to stay true to my abysmal expectations."

Laine, who was truly annoyed by Jeydon's pessimistic yet usually valid view of the world, rolled her eyes for real. "So what does your mom think about this, Adrienne?"

Jeydon shot her a dirty look even though I didn't really mind that question being brought up anymore. The only person in our group that I hadn't told was Anthony, but both Laine and Jeydon had told me that he'd caught on not very long after David had. He was just really good when it came to keeping his mouth shut.

I shrugged. "I've learned not to pay attention to her opinions anymore."

Laine snickered. "Good, because if she ever found out you that are dating Jeydon, well, that would cause some conflict."

Everybody, even the usually doe-eyed Anthony, glared at her with disbelief. "I'd watch my mouth if I were you, Laine," Anthony suggested just loudly enough to convince me that he did in fact know my not-so-much of a secret anymore and wasn't nearly as stupid as I'd thought.

She mumbled her apology, but it was more than obvious that Jeydon didn't accept it. Instead, he announced with shaking, clenched fists that he needed some fresh air, so the two of us walked out of the cafeteria hand in hand.

As soon as we exited the crowded area, he murmured angrily to me, "You have no idea how badly I wanted to pound that insensitive little imbecile that we call our friend's face in."

I stared at him blankly, because it seemed like not showing any emotion helped calm him down. "I don't think she meant it."

"It doesn't matter if she did or not!" he said through clenched teeth. "She knows all about how I can't even bear the thought of losing you or anybody hurting you, and she went ahead and crossed that line though she knew she was already past her limit by bringing the thing up in the first place!"

I placed my hand gently on his shoulder. "Listen, Jeydon, what she said was wrong, but you just need to calm down. You're acting like your old self again."

He shook his head. "If I were my old self, I'd be doing worse things right now. I'd probably be shoving hundreds of leeches in her pillowcase."

Honestly, I kind of liked that thought, for what she'd said had kind of offended me too, but of course I didn't tell him that. "It's good to hear that you aren't like that anymore."

He gave me his gentlest, most grateful smile. "You should know that the reason I'm not like that anymore is standing right here in front of me."

I couldn't help but lean in to kiss him, but before his lips met mine, my phone vibrated wildly out of nowhere, and I grimaced as I read who was calling me. "Speaking of the devil," I mumbled to him unexcitedly.

I switched gears as I answered with my most polite, "Hello?"

Without even bothering to acknowledge me—probably because I wasn't worth a simple how-do-you-do in her eyes—Mother asked, "Have you gotten the wedding invitation yet—and if you did, how many did you receive?"

I wrinkled my brow. I was more than used to her being queer and random like this. "Yeah, just one for me. Why?"

I could picture a cruel, demonic smirk darkening her countenance as she deviously sang out, "You'll see."

And with that, she hung up, leaving the both of us to wonder aimlessly what exact form of torture she had in store for me. Another week passed before we had our answer. A second ticket, one that failed to make it to Tampa Bay for whatever reason, was addressed to none other than Jeydon Spears.

He crushed the invitation in his fist. "Does that woman who should be locked up in the loony bin at this exact moment really think I'm going to show up?"

"You have to," I muttered quietly, obviously not too thrilled about the idea of them meeting. "This is my mother we're talking about."

"Yes, but this is also *me* we're talking about, and you should know better than anybody else that I don't give a crap whatever that demon worshipper does."

"Not even when it has something to do with her hurting me?" I asked reluctantly as a black-and-white rerun of the incident over Christmas break flashed into my mind.

"She'll never hurt you, Adrienne," he assured me sternly. "At least not on my watch."

"But what about when it isn't on your watch? What about this summer?" I interrogated tensely.

He closed his eyes and appeared to have a difficult time breathing, possibly because I'd sent him into one of his old rages. I wrapped my arms around his rock-hard body and kissed him tenderly.

"I don't want this, either," I whispered to him softly.

He took one last deep breath in order to successfully get hold of himself. "Why me? Why can't it be one of those preppy witches that you used to hang out with? I'm sure Mommy Dearest would identify with them very well."

I shook my head. "She doesn't want to see them. She wants to see you."

I received a sour look. "I'll go, but only because I want to confront this beast."

* * *

Though I was the maid of honor, I was mostly excluded from all the planning and other aspects involving the wedding except for a tuxedo size for Jeydon. Apparently, one of Malcolm's brothers couldn't make it for some unknown reason, so they were short on groomsmen. They were getting desperate to fill the slot, so as soon as they discovered that I had a friend whom they'd never met coming to the wedding, they automatically filled him in that position. He was a little bit less than eager about it, to say in the least.

The day before the wedding, we boarded our flight to New York, during which Jeydon slept because he hadn't gotten any sleep the night before. I felt sick to my stomach, knowing that this beautiful boy sleeping soundly on my shoulder could possibly be called anything less than perfect by my cruel, judgmental family members. He might not have cared, but I did tremendously. I didn't like to listen to things that weren't the truth—and by *truth*, I meant *my opinion*—because that was the only one that mattered to me.

I turned my head toward his face. I didn't have that much of an idea what he looked like while he slept, because I always fell asleep long before he did when we slept together. The few accounts I had of his unconscious facial expressions were grim ones, a couple of times which they were inflicted with the most tragic horror from the awful nightmares he had almost every night.

But now he slept there with a smile that stretched across his face, as if all the pain of those horrible nightmares were gone forever. Maybe they would as long as I was there, for I knew now that he truly needed me almost as much as I needed him. The question was who needed me more—Jeydon or Mother?

Luckily, instead of Mother, Angela was the one waiting patiently at the airport for us. Her mixed expression of shock and disgust toward the both of us turned my stomach inward, knowing that it would likely be the most accepting reaction that any of my family members would give us.

In the car driving to the church where Tara's wedding would be held, there was little talking but mostly me showing her with my actions just how much I was in love with him.

I reminded myself and him that we had to pretend that we weren't a couple, so we walked into the church just far enough apart that we weren't touching, but also close enough to keep the electric urges between the two of us satisfied.

I held my breath as I walked through the doors. I was truly frightened even though he was standing there right next to me—which was a first I never wanted to experience. Nobody could imagine how much I wanted to hold his hand as we walked through the vacant hallways, but we couldn't—not with an already suspicious Mother basically attached to our hip.

At the end of the hallway stood Leah, who basically suffocated me as soon as she first sensed my presence. When she finally eased her grip on me, her smile faded into a look of horror as her eyes met his face.

"You must be Jeydon. I'm Adrienne's sister Leah," she replied as she held out her hand, truly trying her best to remain cordial.

He took her hand in his for a friendly handshake, obviously not minding that she was holding her stares way too long. "Yeah, Adrienne's told me a lot about you."

She responded with nothing but a nod, because she was just as pathetically speechless as Angela was.

As we were going to get our clothes, she pulled me aside and whispered in my ear, "You'd better not be trying to make a fool out of that poor boy, Adrienne. I'm just warning you now."

I tried not to get all fired up, but it was no use. Leah had grown up with me, so she should've known that I would never do something that heartless. Okay, maybe the old me would have, but it still made me mad that she'd automatically assume that about me.

"I'm not making a fool out of anyone!" I denied hotly. "Don't pity him, because that's his biggest pet peeve! He hates it when people judge who he is by his face, which is exactly what you're doing right now!"

Her eyes grew two sizes too big as she took a step back. "Do you really think Mother would ever approve of him? Also, I'm assuming that this is the boy who sent that horrible message to Richard. His voice is familiar."

I clasped my hands as I shrieked, "You *knew* about that?"

She shook her head. "Not until a couple of weeks ago. Besides, it's not hard to tell that he doesn't have the cleanest record, if you know what I mean."

I held my glare as I said, "Amelia and I don't, either, but you still love us."

She looked down at the ground. "I'm so sorry, Adrienne, but I don't believe you. Even if what you say is true, I couldn't. Not with Mother around."

I scoffed bitterly as Jeydon would do if he were listening, and I felt a sense of poignancy that there was a little piece of him inside of me. "I've never noticed how much of a coward you are until now."

With that, I reunited with him, not caring anymore that I was linking my arm with his even when it was forbidden, but actually feeling a sickening sense of pleasure in knowing that

Leah was watching us walk off into the hallway united as one odd yet proud to be so couple.

* * *

As the maid of honor of a Hudson wedding, my job was to sit there pretty and not say a word other than to praise the happy couple. I guess I sort of did that as I was getting myself and the blushing bride ready, except that I was informing my sisters about how special Jeydon really was.

Of course, they didn't believe me, and behind closed doors, I heard Leah—who was really bad at whispering—tell Amelia about what she thought he was. Angela, who now reminded me of a female Anthony in some aspects, said nothing, but I could tell that she was silently wondering with all my other sisters what happened to the old, silent Adrienne.

Tara's favorite flower and color was violet, so all of us wore light silk lavender dresses with almost no back and elegant buns that were tied back by a perfect periwinkle flower. My earrings, which I hadn't taken off since the moment I got them, matched the outfit nicely even with the plain diamond necklace Mother had given me a few years before.

After Tara was ready, Mother was let into the room and laughed aloud when she laid eyes on the gorgeous daughter that still wasn't good enough in her eyes.

"You'd think the bride would be the most shining one in the room, but I guess Adrienne will outshine you all every day," she said.

This comment outraged me almost as much as it devastated Tara, but I still didn't find the strength to speak up. I found out that telling her off wasn't nearly as easy as speaking my mind to my sisters. I guess that made me almost as big of a coward as Leah was.

Apparently, though, the largest coward of them all was Tara's fiancé, Malcolm, who—after only taking a quick look at

Jeydon—deemed him unworthy of being anywhere up onstage.
Jeydon couldn't have cared less and was actually glad, because
he'd never wanted to be at the wedding, much less a part of it.
I, on the other hand, wanted him up there with me so that I
wouldn't feel like I didn't belong there. Of course, he would've felt
that way, and I needed to put his emotions over my own.

The ceremony dragged on forever as Tara and her new
husband uttered traditional words of love that I was almost 100
percent certain they didn't mean. Since I didn't like listening to
words that were most likely lies, I searched the rows of people,
frantically trying to find him, but he was nowhere to be found.
Why were he and all the other people that I loved not there and
the people that I loathed, like Mother and Richard, sitting in the
audience, elated by this event? Maybe I was the abnormal one
not to be happy for them. Either way, the absence of Jeydon was
troubling me.

Finally, the ceremony ended, and as the people poured out
into the reception hall, I saw one lone, dashing figure with
glowing skin and styled golden hair that sat on his head like a
regal crown at the top of the staircase that led up to the dressing
rooms. As he came down the stairs, I waited at the bottom of the
staircase with a heart beating more rapidly with every step he
took.

Finally, he came to the bottom and grazed my forehead with
his lips. I made sure to tell him, "You look so handsome that it
almost makes up for the fact you weren't in there."

He smiled deviously. "I wanted to plan a surprise attack on
Mommy Dearest. Besides, even if I'd wanted to go to that waste
of violets and silk, I wouldn't have been allowed to, because I'm
not presentable enough."

I examined him carefully, not finding a flaw in his appearance.
"I honestly don't get that," I told him. "You look absolutely perfect."

He chuckled. "You should take a look at yourself. You're
even more radiant than the bride tonight, Adrienne. Of course, I

shouldn't be shocked, because you're always the most beautiful girl in the room."

My head spun around at those words, because that was the first time he'd ever told me that I was beautiful. I guess he did that all the time in his own way, but he used the traditional way I was so familiar with. Then again, the way I was used to was the way of the world, and everything in his nature commanded him to rebel against it.

I took him by the arm, and I told him about all the things I'd said about him in the bride's dressing room as we walked straight across the dance floor. He was appalled about my mother's comment to Tara and swore that his confrontation would be even larger as a result. We lost our way and crashed into someone else Jeydon would've planned on confronting if he'd known he was there.

I was the one who stumbled into Richard at first, and when he realized who I was, he completely acted like nothing had ever happened. "Oh, Adrienne, I swear to God this is the hands of fate working. I just want you to know ..."

After he rambled on that far, Jeydon figured out who exactly he was, and without hesitation, he grabbed the drink from Richard's hand and threw the contents in his face. While his eyes were still squeezed tightly, I grabbed a nearby vase and shoved it over his head, and Jeydon pushed him onto the ground—from which I felt the sickest sense of delight—and then we ran off before he realized what we'd done. We were laughing so hard that I grew parched and had a sip of what I thought was water, but when I discovered that it was vodka, I spit it out, and Jeydon laughed ten times harder.

As we had a good laugh, I felt a strange sensation that I was being watched, and I turned around only to find Leah and Amelia up against a wall staring at us intently. Amelia motioned for me to come over toward her, and without thinking, I grabbed onto Jeydon's hand and dragged him behind me.

As we got closer, I found Mother was gathered there too, her face the same crimson as a fire truck.

"You," she addressed Jeydon as she pointed at him, every little part of her dry-heaving with disgust, "are the ugliest thing I've ever seen! Adrienne, what on earth do you think you're doing associating with this vulgar beast of a boy? What filthy little crevice did he crawl out of exactly?"

Nothing in him flinched from the sticks and stones she was so deviously throwing as he replied, "It doesn't matter where I came from, because I didn't come straight from hell like you."

The way her upper lip snarled made her look more like a ravenous wolf than a human being. "Those are big words coming from a boy that looks like one of hell's fiercest monsters."

By the way he scoffed, I could tell that what he planned to say was so much more than anybody else ever could. "Listen here, Jezebel. Adrienne's told me exactly all of the suffering you've caused over the years, so before you try to throw another pathetic insult at me, think about this. If people saw you as you truly were, you'd look far worse than I do. And if that doesn't blow your demon-possessed mind, maybe this will: Adrienne hates you. She always has from the moment she saw you beating her sister when she was really little. Remember that day, the day you scarred your child for life? Do you even care that you did so? You don't have to answer, because I can already tell that you don't give a crap about the own beings you've created. You've caused so much horror the sight of you makes me far sicker than my face will ever make you."

She laughed deviously. "The thing you need to understand is that you are the sickening one. You're absolutely pathetic if you think for a second that this gorgeous girl could ever hate her own mother or love a disfigured wretch such as you! You're pathetic if you think anybody could ever love you, for that matter! I mean, your own mother probably rejected you because of that face!"

I couldn't stand to hear these lies, so I shrieked as loudly as I could, "I *do* love him, Mother! And he's also right about me hating you! And don't say he's ugly, because he's the most beautiful thing that ever lived!"

She became tranquil for a second as if she had one moment when the demons ceased and she gained lucidity, but then the wild look in her eyes returned as she got all up in my face, growling, "You don't love him! You've only chosen this inhumanly hideous beast of burden to punish me! Yes, you're telling a really sick, pointless joke. Nobody could be able to tolerate that thing, much less think it's beautiful."

With all my brute force, I shoved her repulsiveness away from me, and I yelled, "Don't you dare say that when he's the best thing that's ever happened to me!" I wrapped my arms around Jeydon's neck on impulse and kissed him hard on his scar to further declare my love for him.

My sisters quietly muttered such words as "Does she really mean this?" and "I think she's actually being serious." A large crash interrupted the touching moment I had created, and I turned around only to find Mother with animalistic eyes as she threw another pot at me with accurate aim this time around. Luckily, Jeydon pulled me by the arm to safety, and before she could even think about attacking me again, he quickly led me through the crowd and up the staircase. On the way out, he swiftly grabbed his duffel bag, which was positioned right by the door as if he'd planned for it, and we ran out.

"Now that you've shown me exactly how monstrous she really is," he said as we were leaning against a wall trying to catch our breath, "it's going to be my treat to show you exactly what I did before I met you."

"You mean there's a chance that we'll end up in jail by the end of the night?" I asked, not knowing what to think of this enticing invitation.

The last time a guy asked me to do illegal stuff with him, I ended up getting arrested. Of course, I wouldn't have met Jeydon if it weren't for that, but if it happened again, I probably wouldn't have that same fate.

He wore a mischievous grin as he said, "Without breaking too many laws, of course. We wouldn't want that pretty dress to be traded in for a jumpsuit, now would we?"

I giggled but tried to hide my amusement by saying, "Not funny. You know that's happened before."

He put his arm around my waist. "And it's happened to me seven times. What's your point?"

I smiled, but a question popped into my head that I had to ask. "Do you honestly not care what she said about you back there? She was even more cruel and heartless than usual."

His smile faded. "It's not like I haven't heard it before. I only care if you think that's true, so unless you're using me to punish her ..."

I shook my head rapidly. "I'd never think that about you in a million years. All she ever tells is lies, Jeydon. I can't believe you'd ever fall for one of them."

"I'm not falling for her lies, Adrienne. I'm just checking to make sure that you aren't using me. That would just be my luck." He squeezed my side as he lowered his voice. "I've never opened up to anybody about my past or loved anything that didn't come from a prescription bottle or pipe. I'd be so devastated if I were to find out that was the case. I'm sure you would be too."

I nodded. "You're right, but you really need to learn how to trust me."

He placed his index and middle fingers on my chin to draw my face as close as possible to his. "I already do trust you, Adrienne, more than everybody else in the world combined. You're actually the one who taught me how to trust."

With that, he kissed me in what felt like the first real kiss for a couple of weeks since we'd first found out about the wedding and began stressing about all the pains that would go along with him meeting Mother. "Now let's get out of here before Mommy Dearest catches onto our night of fun."

CHAPTER 30

Magic

"Are you sure we should do this?" I asked him with obvious reluctance, though I knew exactly how he'd respond.

Just like I'd expected, he nodded and said, "Yes, I've done this like a thousand times before and never got caught once. When it comes to vandalism, this is as easy as it gets."

A moment before, I'd pointed out Richard's shining silver Mustang he was always so proud of, and now Jeydon was standing in front of it with the pocketknife he always carried for safety in hand.

"Come on," he told me as he motioned for me to grab the handle of the knife. "It's been a while since I've done anything of this sort, so we'll do it together."

He suggested that we deliver our fatal blow on the count of three, and I liked that idea, so on three, we both plunged the knife deep into the first tire, and I felt a whole sense of relief for my rage toward Richard that was all so new to me. Without any more aid from him, I slashed the rest of the tires and went as far as to key the sides. For a final finishing touch, Jeydon found an old, rusty crowbar just obscurely lying in the middle of the sidewalk and used it to shatter both headlights. Just like the Carrie Underwood song, maybe next time, Richard would think before he cheated.

But he'd never cheat on me ever again, because I had a new man in my life that was so much better than what he'd ever be even if he actually ever cared about me at one point or another over the years.

Angela had left her keys in the ignition, so it wasn't that hard to find a way to finally leave that forsaken place once and for all. At the nearest gas station bathroom, Jeydon changed from his suit into blue jeans with more than one rip in them and the old gray T-shirt that he'd worn the first time I'd ever hugged him.

"So where exactly are we going?" I asked him as he pulled out of the gas station.

"Somewhere with no monster for moms or bratty, moronic, and cowardly siblings," he answered, smirking in a way that made the left side of his cheek wrinkle up to where it looked sort of like a distorted dimple. I'd noticed it before, but it didn't matter to me, because I'd always been a sucker for dimples no matter what shape or form they came in. Richard didn't have any dimples, but I guess he just couldn't heighten my hormones like Jeydon could no matter how hard he tried, if he even tried at all. It didn't really matter how hard Richard's miniscule effort to keep me was, because he still would never get the amount of affection from me that Jeydon rightfully deserved even if he had treated me like the fairy-tale princess I once foolishly believed was the case.

I touched his left dimple with my index finger and told him how adorable it was, but he just stared at me with a blank expression. "Adrienne, sometimes even I wonder if you were hit on the head at some point."

I looked at him, confused. "Why would you say that?"

"Because people aren't supposed to look the way I do!" he snapped like a twig under a three-hundred-pound weight. "You'd think that having to look at me 24-7 and what Mommy Dearest and every other human being with eyes say about my appearance would get that through your head!"

After a moment of me staring at him with nothing to say and him getting through his most recent tsunami of rage, he spoke with a tone so low that it could compete with Anthony's croaks.

"What you just pointed out wasn't anything near close to a dimple. It's a small spot where there's absolutely no tissue whatsoever underneath the skin, so it caves in all the way to the bone. It's one of the most grotesque features of my deformity. It just got me fired up that you could possibly say it's anything near adorable," said Jeydon.

I shook my head as I lowered my voice enough to match his. "It's not a deformity, Jeydon. It's your face."

He rolled his eyes and scoffed. "A *deformed* face! How could you possibly ever see past it, Adrienne? I need to know that much."

I wrapped my hands around his balled-up fist and held it up to my heart, knowing exactly what I was going to say next. "Because behind the scars is the most incredible man I've ever gotten to know. I'll be honest—while I think your face is alluring, it isn't what I'm in love with. I love you for *you*. I hope you feel the same way about me."

He pulled my hands back toward him close enough to kiss my fingers. "I do. That's why I've never said that you were beautiful until tonight, because I didn't want to mislead you into thinking I was any other boy, because you know better than anybody else that I'm not like that. But I guess what I'm trying to say is that I've always thought that you were so beyond beautiful that I never could picture us together even if my face were normal."

I leaned over to place my head on his shoulder. "But we are."

He looked toward me with the big, toothy grin that always made my day. "We are," he whispered in agreement as he kissed my neck. "And I thought for so long that I'd be alone my whole life."

I smiled at the sight of his face shining like the sun and confessed something I hadn't even noticed about me up until then. "So did I."

He gave me a weird look. "How could you feel that way when you're a gorgeous supermodel with swarms of boys crowding up all around hoping to get a simple acknowledgment from you?"

I knew he was going to ask something like that, and I knew just how I was going to answer it. "It doesn't matter how many admirers I have, because all my mother destined me to have was Richard—a lying jerk that somehow met the standards as my best friend although he didn't have a clue about the horrors my family kept concealed. He had no idea who I was as a person instead of a face. I didn't even know who I really was besides a face until you came along. I was so afraid that I'd be stuck with him for the rest of my life, because that was supposed to be my destiny. But now I know my true destiny, and it's you."

He kept his huge smile that was turning my heart into a furnace. "You're the most beautiful girl I've ever met, both inside and out."

I rubbed my nose against his. "Same thing for you."

He abruptly stopped the car in a jerky fashion that startled me. He sensed my sudden fear and explained that we were at the secret destination.

As we went through the doorway, I saw mobs of rampant teenagers that gave me a sickening feeling in the pit of my stomach. I did the math in my head. At a gathering of this multitude is where I'd gotten arrested the last time.

The stench of alcohol and possibly other drugs lingered in the air, so without thinking, I turned to leave. He must've expected this, because he already had a firm grasp on my arm.

"I used to go to a ton of parties like this, invited or not, with Anthony and Laine or members of my gang like Johnny," he said. "I never did have somebody to dance with, though, so all I ask is you to let me have the experience. I've never recalled dancing at all."

I stared at him in disbelief. "You've never danced before?"

He nodded. "Does that really shock you? I was always too busy guarding Anthony from getting his face smashed in by Keri to bust a move, and when Anthony was safe, I was always too high to think about having any other type of normal fun. When I was little before all the drugs and arrests happened, I was just glad that I could walk without needing leg braces or crutches like the doctors thought I would."

"Wow, Jeydon, that's kind of sad."

He shrugged his shoulders with a grim expression. "Well, my childhood was kind of sad, if you didn't already know."

I felt an enormous wave of compassion for him as I took his hand and recalled to him my last dancing experience with Richard that was coincidentally at the wild party I attended that I thought would be my last. I told him about how he told me he loved me that night and how I foolishly believed that lie.

"It will be so nice having someone who actually loves me to dance with me for once," I concluded.

He chuckled. "It's so nice to just have someone that'll dance with me."

A chuckle escaped from my throat, and I kissed him on his scar to declare him mine. "As strange as it is, you're my Prince Charming, and I'm your princess. I'd always dance with you, even if you didn't have any legs."

And indeed, dancing with my prince was just like how it was in a fairy tale, if not better. Somehow, he was remarkably good at dancing, and he surprisingly was more than tolerant of my flawed coordination skills. I actually wasn't that horrible with him, though, because he maneuvered me along with every graceful move he made, basically sweeping me off my feet in the process. As he twirled me around, I felt as if we were soaring through the sky together, and it was further proof that where I belonged in the universe was right there on the dance floor with my Prince Charming.

Dancing might've been a ruined experience for me before not only because of my drunken dance with Richard at the party but also because of my two left feet, but Jeydon fixed it into something as wonderful and enchanting as he was. I made sure to tell him that, but strangely enough, he just smiled and held me as close to him as he could instead of trying to take advantage of me like Richard would've. I guess it was just a new feeling for me, a guy willing to take a bullet for me instead of lustfully staring at the curves of my body.

At one point during a particularly romantic song, we just kissed each other again and again passionately, which was a billion times better than at the last party when Richard and I got drunk and made out on that forsaken pool table.

Yet I still kept having flashbacks not only of the party like somebody in their rational mind but of that fateful day when I walked in on Mother beating Mary—not of all the painful blows, hurtful unnecessary hits, bloodcurdling shrieks of terror, and sobs of desperation washing away the fresh blood on her face but of afterward as Mother was stroking my hair and telling me how it would always be our dirty little secret. I guess it always was—until I found Jeydon, that is.

Out of nowhere, my forehead was dribbled in sweat, and I began to breathe really hard. Jeydon's eyes grew wide with concern. "What's wrong?"

I blinked, and Mother was there before me, asking me why I resented her. Looking back on it, I should've replied by screaming, "What do you think is wrong, you hypocrite? You just want to pretend that I don't know exactly the woman you are, if you're even a woman at all! Yes, it's as clear as the summer sky now! I figured out that you're a demon on my own long ago!"

But I said nothing. I always said nothing. Suddenly, I couldn't breathe.

"I need," I yelled as I took a huge gulp of air, "for us to get out of here!"

Before he was able to ask why, I caught a glimpse of a police officer with Angela accessing the crowd from all the way across the dance floor.

Apparently, Jeydon caught on to the unwanted attention, because without thinking, he darted off like an arrow leaving its bow to slice through the wind in the most aerodynamic way. I use that analogy because I felt as if the two of us were still basically flying through the halls and up the staircases with interlocking fingers that might as well have been superglued to each other.

For some unknown but borderline psychotic reason, I couldn't help but burst out laughing the entire way, and in retrospect, I wondered if I might have had a drink or two even though I didn't recall drinking a single drop.

We eventually found a way out of the loft and rudely pushed baffled bystanders aside as we made our way to the elevator. I pressed the very top button with my index finger, and soon enough, we were on the roof of the building, looking down on the earth below us. From up so high, I could make out very clearly the flashing red and blue lights that were familiar to both of us.

As exhilarating as the view was, the lights gave me more important things to focus on.

"Do you really think we've lost them?" I asked him, fully trusting his expertise because he was the guru of hiding techniques.

"They probably think we left the building. That's why I made sure we didn't."

His words calmed me, and I went back to thinking about my sister and mother. "I can't believe her."

"Who?" he asked. "Angela or Mommy Dearest?"

"Both of them," I replied grudgingly. I closed my eyes and took a deep breath. "When we were dancing and I had that episode, it was because I had flashbacks to some of the things that I saw her do when I was little."

He formed an understanding smile as his ivory skin glistened in the moonlight. "I figured. When I was younger, I used to get that way too when I had flashbacks, except I had full-fledged panic attacks. They were just so real that it was like I was living them all over again, you know? I could still feel the excruciating pain that was tearing my flesh apart little by little. I could still hear Grace's shrieks as I watched her burn."

I winced at the thought of somebody that I loved so dearly experiencing both burning alive and the trauma that came afterward. "Even though half of my sisters are horrible to me, I still couldn't imagine having to watch them suffer like that. It was bad enough that I had to watch them suffer like they did."

He nodded as he leaned his back against the railing that was keeping both of us from plummeting to our deaths. "I know. Back when I was really little, I used to make sure that I was the one to take all of Keri's punches so she wouldn't experience that."

Admiring his bravery at such a young age, I replied, "I should've done the same. I hate the fact that I'm so self-centered."

He shook his head and scoffed. "Please. Compared to Keri or your mother, even back before me, you were a Mother Teresa times ten. All Keri ever did was indulge in mind-numbing doses of drugs and dirty men who only wanted to get in her pants so she'd forget her misery and remorse."

"At least she has some remorse," I noted, thinking that she was at least worthy of that though I cursed her with every bone in my body for hurting him so much. "My mother has no guilt about anything that she does and thinks everybody else is in the wrong. She hasn't once apologized for anything that I can remember of."

"So?" he asked as he threw an almost microscopic pebble over the edge. "Just because she has guilt doesn't make her any less of a monster."

I drew myself in closer to him. "I think it does."

A strong gust of wind messed my formally firm bun up, so on my request, Jeydon took it completely down for me. As he refastened the vibrant, delicate violet in my hair, I felt the oddest case of déjà vu coming on.

Honestly, I'd felt it a little dancing with him too, because I'd never actually danced with him until that night but felt like I'd experienced that particular sort of magic before. I wondered if maybe it was because we were making out during one song as we were slow dancing, and I'd felt the familiar but still riveting electricity I'd felt a hundred times before. Maybe that was where it came from. But yet I knew that couldn't be it.

The spark was something I'd always felt and was therefore used to, ever since I had that first dream … Wait a minute …

"The dream!" I exclaimed. Of course, Jeydon looked at me weird and asked what I was talking about, and I replied, "I had a dream exactly like this except that there were no cops in it. I had it so long ago, right after I found out you were a real person instead of something from my imagination."

His eyes widened, and I feared that he thought I'd gone insane. "Has it happened before?"

I contemplated this for a moment, because honestly I'd never thought of my dreams as signs, fate, or predictions like people who needed some aspect of hope to cling on to. "They predicted us being together, and that happened, so I guess it has."

He laughed, and when I asked why he was laughing, he replied, "I envy you. You know on the plane ride over here? That was the first time in my life where I just peacefully drifted off without any of the demons from my past disturbing me, and I had dreams about us. You don't know how much I'd enjoy having dreams about you where you aren't suffering all the time."

"You mean you've dreamed of me before?"

He chuckled. "How could I have not?"

I shrugged. "I guess I just thought you were incapable of dreaming anything besides a nightmare."

"So did I. Of course, I have had dreams about you and your mother. You don't have to have a brain to predict that those didn't go well. This dream was different."

"So what were we doing?"

He smiled a little timidly though he had never showed the least bit of shyness before. That was what Anthony was placed on the face of the earth for.

"Lie on the ground with me, and I'll demonstrate," he said.

I had no idea what to think, but of course I went along with it. I lay down flat on my back and scooted up close to him, and he wrapped his arms around me.

"We were doing exactly this," he said. "We were looking up at the stars with my arms wrapped around you. That's how it should be, Adrienne—just you and me without any crappy moms or judgmental kids or jerk ex-boyfriends or unorthodox, baffling love affairs or shadows from the past. There was none of that in my dream, so I hated waking up to the cruel reality that I was about to be judged yet again for my face by a heartless, sadistic sociopath who threatened to take my very reason for still walking on the forsaken face of this cruel world away from me."

I shook my head. "I'll never let her take me from you."

He grinned enough to light up the dark, almost completely starless sky. "Would you like for me to show you where the Big Dipper and Little Dipper are?"

I nodded eagerly, and for the rest of the night, I just stayed there in his arms without any care in the world. He explained where every single constellation known to man was and told stories of how he and Anthony would climb up on the roof and lie under the stars like this when they were very little before the car crash. It was how they would escape from the hell they were forced to call home sweet home where they were constantly battered and could actually let their guards down and be actual children instead of punching bags. He said how he hoped I shared the same tranquil, at-peace feeling in my gut during this state of relaxation—and I was glad to say that I did.

We both eventually drifted off to sleep in each other's arms, and long before the night ended, I knew that I too wished it could be like this all the time. I was the first one to arise in the morning, and when I did, the first thing I saw was the silver lining of it all: a peaceful smile that once again ever so pleasantly stretched across his face.

CHAPTER 31

Confrontation

The next day came, and since I didn't have a change of clothes with me, Jeydon and I went to a small thrift shop with no alarm system, and he snuck a pair of jeans and graphic T-shirt of my size into his duffel bag when nobody was looking. For somebody who stood out in the crowd, he concealed himself very well. I had to give him credit for that, because I could only imagine how difficult it would be to get away with stealing something if everybody was constantly staring at you.

In a public restroom nearby, I changed from my dress into the stolen merchandise, and as we walked back to the place where we'd parked Angela's car, our bad karma came back to bite us in the butt, for the car was gone. We weren't all that shocked since the cops and Angela were probably at the party the night before to investigate where her car thieves had wandered off to. We heard from whispers on the street that the cops busted the party along with finding the car, and we'd escaped just in time. I was grateful for that, but I still wished we had a car so that we wouldn't have to ride the bus to the airport.

I started to walk to the bus stop, but Jeydon grabbed on to my arm. "Where do you think you're going?"

I was confused. "If we want to make it to the airport on time, we have to ride the bus."

"Why would we ride the bus when we could ride in a taxi?" he asked slyly.

"We don't have any money for a taxi!" I replied hotly as if I were explaining it to Anthony and not him.

I could sense the rebel without a cause in him coming to the surface. "Who says we need money?"

"The government," I replied, which I thought was pretty smart. "And we can't just go out and rob a bank."

He shook his head with an amused smirk. "You're right; that would be too classic. I was talking about that taxi over there."

I looked in the direction he was pointing and found a highlighter-yellow taxicab left unattended. I felt a loss of color in my cheeks. "You're not saying ..."

He solemnly nodded. "Yes, I am." I continued to stare at him in disbelief, and he explained, "There's nobody attending it, so why not?"

I wanted to be the bigger person and deny ourselves of this temptation, and I should've, but I couldn't say no to him, and experiencing the joy of creating havoc when all I'd ever done my whole life was behave was overpowering.

We lucked out, because hot-wiring was going to be the hardest act in committing the crime; Angela's keys were left in the ignition. You'd think people wouldn't be as trusting of others when they lived in Brooklyn. I giggled as he fearlessly started the car, and to my shock, nobody even noticed that we'd committed grand theft auto until we drove off victoriously into the sunset.

The drive was spent with the stereo blaring our shared love of classic rock and anything alternative. We laughed as people came running at us pleading for us to stop and Jeydon would stomp hard on the gas pedal.

We parked the taxi up against the sidewalk about five blocks from the airport and took a walk that seemed to last forever, during which we continued to chatter on about which bands were hot and which ones were not and whose albums just belonged in the garbage.

After we finally made it to the airport and through airport security, which was almost as time consuming as the walk, we were about to drop everything and wait for our flight when we spotted somebody whose very figure made me turn up my nose in disgust. Why did it have to be Richard, of all people?

As we inched up just close enough that we could see the whites of his eyes, I could also pick out an alarmingly protruding lower lip that had recently been stitched back into place. I winced in the sight of it, for it wasn't the prettiest of pictures to begin with, but since it was on Richard, it made things twenty times worse. Still, he looked at Jeydon with an utter disgust. How could his scar even compete with Richard's wound?

Richard's mouth was even more distorted as the corners twisted up in to a smile. "It's kind of funny. I get hit directly in the face with a fifteen-pound vase, and I still look better than your new choice of man."

Jeydon gave him an unforgiving glare. "You should be thankful that I didn't make your face look worse than mine after how you hurt her."

There was a presence of guilt on his expression, but not nearly enough that I would ever consider letting him into my life again. "I have to admit what I did was stupid and awful, but it's not that hard to tell just by that voice mail that you've done things way worse than I have."

"That might be true," Jeydon replied, "but the only person I was hurting when I did those things was me. You hurt her way more than you hurt yourself."

Flustered, Richard spat out the hasty comeback, "You *do* hurt others, because your face hurts everything that has eyes!"

Jeydon was about to make one of his quick remarks, but before he could, I kneed Richard where it hurt him the most as hard as I could. "Don't you dare say that, you jerk! I'm sick of everybody calling him ugly, because he's not!"

He fell to his knees grunting in pain, and the sound of his groans was music almost as sweet as Jeydon's voice. Jeydon must've taken pity on the pathetic thing that I called my ex, because he went to get him some ice, leaving us alone sitting on complete opposite sides of the couch.

His voice was hoarse when he called my name. I looked over at him, and he asked, "What are you doing with a guy like that? I mean, you're so much better than he is. You deserve a guy like me, not a guy who looks like a deadly, inhuman creature from one of those gory horror movies that I remember giving you nightmares for weeks."

I gave him an even dirtier look than usual. "Yes, I deserve a jerk who cheated on me with the one girl I couldn't stand, and if that wasn't bad enough, you've lied to me from the time we were little kids! I thought our friendship was special, Richard, and that's what crushed me. I can't honestly say that I ever loved you, but I love him more than you could ever imagine."

His cheeks grew the shade of a fire truck. "You have everything any girl could ever ask for—me being one of those things—and you're just going to throw all of it away for a disgustingly hideous criminal?"

I gladly said, "You'll always be way more disgusting than he is." He gave me the classic hurt look, and this only made me turn into a female Jeydon. "Did you honestly expect that you'd win me back after what you did to me? Who do you think you are exactly, thinking that you're so much better than he is when you slept around with Cruella de Vil just because she wasn't me?"

I might as well have knocked him down onto the ground, but after a few moments when he recollected himself and sternly began to say my name, I was more than ready to snap.

"Are you really that pathetic?" I said. "Shut your trap, because no matter what, you're never going to win me back—even if the whole universe depended on it!"

"The whole universe may not depend on it," he replied, "but your family's universe does. You should know that."

That reminder only made the blood rush to my face even more. "Do you honestly think I care what she thinks anymore?

All my life, she's controlled me, and I let her! This is my life, and Jeydon has helped me realize that! That boy's the best thing that ever happened to me, and you've been the worst, so you'd better shut that big, ugly mouth of yours!"

He lay back and let out an exasperated groan. "You have no idea what a big mistake you're making."

Without hesitation, I proposed, "Give me one reason to believe that bull crap."

I was reluctant to listen as he told me his side of the story. Apparently, he was loyal to me while we were dating, but after I left for Tampa Bay and totally ditched him for my fantasies about Jeydon, he couldn't help but feel abandoned.

Days turned into weeks, and I still hadn't bothered to call him once, and after many failed attempts, he gave up and started looking around for ways to get back at me. Then it happened. Tori went over to Richard's house one night asking why he hadn't come to another wild party she'd thrown. He explained he just didn't feel like coming after what happened with me, and she, for the first time in her life, was actually concerned about anything but herself. Richard explained the whole situation to her, and she concluded that I was obviously seeing somebody else because I was such a whore even when I was loyal to him and that he needed to totally forget about me. She said he needed a real girl that was actually there in his life, and he couldn't see past her logic. They had sex that night, in the middle of which I randomly called and found out about his act of betrayal.

"It was wrong," he concluded, "but it felt so right, you know? Please believe me, Adrienne, when I say that I'm truly sorry about what I did, and even though you abandoned me, I still loved you unconditionally."

Though I felt a twinge of guilt for deserting my former boyfriend, the majority of my feelings toward him hadn't changed. "You never have loved me unconditionally, and even if you did, I never loved you that way. I never loved you at all, because every time you kissed me, it felt like you were trying to shove your tongue down my throat!"

This made him explode. "Well, half of the time, you acted like you were pretending you were somewhere else with someone else instead of with me, but I still want you back!"

His anger brought me back to my senses a little, and I realized that I could never let myself get to his stage of anger.

I replied calmly, "Yes, Richard, I did try to pretend I was somewhere else with somebody else, and that place was on a beach in Tampa Bay with Jeydon. I might not have imagined him exactly as I did back before everything happened, but as soon as I saw him, I immediately knew that he was the one. So it doesn't matter how much you plea or even if in another life you hadn't done crap to me in the past, because I'll always choose him over you."

He shook his head with vengeance. "I'm going to see to that you're going to regret your choice."

I could already predict the future without any doubt. "I won't."

He took a hasty breath, and to my surprise, he got up to leave, but to my dismay, before he left, he turned around and said to me, "Oh, and I'm not stupid. You're going to pay for trashing my car."

He then turned back around and walked out of sight and out of mind—out of mind, that is, until I turned around and saw cops slapping handcuffs on Jeydon's wrists.

I darted toward the small cluster of cops surrounding my perfect angel, but when I tried to penetrate the circle, a particularly macho man effortlessly shoved me to the ground with one arm. As I knocked my head hard due to the fall, I bit my tongue and tasted the bitter blood. I saw stars that spun around rapidly, but still I struggled to get up. That was when I felt a sharp pain of a Taser in my chest and screeched at the top of my lungs. As soon as my senses came back to me, I realized that there was an all-too-familiar silver restraint on my wrists.

CHAPTER 32

Wishes

It took a little more than twenty hours for David to drive up to New York and bail us out from the separate detention centers in which we were being held. He bailed me out first since where I was held was closer to the airport, and when we arrived at the male detention center and David walked out with a shaggy-haired, fatigued boy that I missed so dearly, I couldn't help but leap out of the car and go over to embrace him.

As soon as we got in the car, David, who clearly was even more exhausted both physically and mentally than the two of us combined, asked in a disappointed tone, "So now that my wallet has been cleared out, do you have a halfway decent explanation for trashing a poor boy's car and stealing your sister's?"

I felt more than a little bit guilty for putting him through so much trouble, but I was also furious at Richard and Angela for ratting us out. "He wasn't a poor boy. He's my lying, cheating ex-boyfriend who after all he did deserved to have his car destroyed. It was my idea, so don't get mad at him."

That wasn't 100 percent true of course, but I didn't want David to think that Jeydon had become a bad kid again.

Jeydon objected, saying, "I am the one to blame, not her. I thought it would be fun to show her what I used to do. I was being an idiot."

David breathed heavily with utter exasperation. "Jeydon, do you realize what your little night of fun has done? You've not only ruined yourself even more, but Adrienne, as well."

I shook my head, preparing to defend him against his own family like how he defended me against mine. "I was already ruined. It's not like I haven't been arrested before."

He looked at me astonished, and I realized that I'd forgotten to ever mention that to him. My cheeks flushed, and I stared down at the floorboards of the car awkwardly as I explained how I'd gotten drunk at a party, and that was the real reason behind Mother shipping me out to Tampa Bay and suspending my modeling contract.

David was shocked. "I'm sorry that I'm surprised by this. I really shouldn't be, because the things Jeydon has done are by far worse than what you have done will ever be."

Jeydon didn't say anything to this, so I looked over only to find him resting against my shoulder in a deep sleep that only spending a long sleepless night in jail could bring him. I put my arm around him and kissed the top of his head. I was more than a little bit agitated that somebody who was supposed to love him unconditionally was criticizing him, which was supposed to be our judgmental classmates' job.

"If you see him like that, then why'd you take him in?" I asked.

"Because, like his mother, the boy's got something incredible about him that somehow makes up for all the trouble he's caused in the past. I expect that you'd agree with that."

I nodded. "Yes, about him, I agree, but not about Keri. He talks about her sometimes, but not a whole lot because he hates her so much, and I have come to hate her too after all the things she's done to him that he hasn't told you before."

I heard a chuckle escape his throat that confused me. "He thinks I'm so clueless about him, doesn't he? What he doesn't understand is that even though he hasn't told me anything verbally, I can see straight through his walls in the same way he can see through everybody else's so easily. I've always been able to see through him ever since the first day I met him. Behind his scar and temper lie a shadowed past I don't exactly have the full story to, and even though I don't know that necessarily doesn't mean I don't know him. I'd always known that he was in a constant pain that made my heart split in two for him. He only said hurtful things in an attempt to mask his own pain, and because of that, most people saw him as a brat. But I've known from the beginning that he just needed to be loved and guided in the way Keri tried to do but couldn't because he wouldn't let her be his mother. Also, when he was little, it was kind of freaky but fascinating how he understood everything in a way most adults couldn't and just in general how bright the kid was."

Since I knew that—like with Richard—my opinion about her probably wasn't going to change, I asked, "So is the only reason you took him in was because he was fascinating and in need?"

He shook his head. "Not exactly. You understand better than anybody else that he's a one in a billion. I've never come across any boy more incredible in my life, and I'm not going to. That was the main reason for me taking him in."

I looked over at Jeydon with a warm smile and stroked his hair as he breathed his warm, steady breath on my neck. I was surprised to hear David break into my pleasure by asking, "So since you asked me why I chose him, I think it's fair for me to ask you the same thing. I love him dearly, but I honestly never expected him to ever win a girl's affection, much less a girl as beautiful as you. I apologize for asking that, because I know it makes you mad, but I'm just curious."

Heat rushed to my cheeks as I shot back, "Why do you love Keri?"

He must've expected for me to get angry, because he said, "I'll tell you that after you tell me how you could see past it. I mean, I'm ashamed to say that I was almost fooled by the poor boy's appearance."

I grew flustered. "Is he really that hideous? Because I just don't see it. I think his face is in a weird way one of the most attractive things ever, and I love his scar, because I love every part of him like how God loves every single little star in the sky. I have since the first time I ever saw him. While everybody thinks I'm insane for doing so, I don't get why it's that big of a deal. I guess no one, not even a man as good as you, can see what I see."

"It doesn't matter if nobody else can see it," he said, "because your love alone has made him happier than a million loving caresses from me or friendly hugs from Laine and Anthony ever could. Your open-mindedness has been awarded not by the approval of others but his transformation from a juvenile delinquent who was enraged at the world because he believed nobody could ever love him into a boy that walks around with a skip to his step because he's so happy. He's so lucky to have you."

I couldn't help but smile at the thought of me changing him like that, but I shook my head and replied, "No, I'm lucky to have him."

We talked some more about him, but I didn't ask any more about Keri, and he didn't tell—probably because he knew very well that Keri was a forbidden discussion topic for Laine, Anthony, and Jeydon and figured that the same rule applied to me. Also, some things were best left unsaid, because I could tell that he saw her as a diamond in the rough or at least somewhere similar to my view of Jeydon. I agreed that with him that David was a fool to think so, though, because after she'd caused him and Anthony all that pain and the death of Grace, it should've been a red flag that she wasn't a good woman to fall in love with. Then again, Jeydon gave me tons of red flags as well in the very beginning, but I ignored them and never looked back on those early warning signs until later. Maybe it was the same thing. I wanted to ask him those questions badly, but before I could do so, I got caught up with my thoughts and feelings about the incredible boy sleeping next to me, and I fell asleep, as well.

* * *

Time resumed to its usual warp-speed pace, and as a couple of more weeks went by, I began to hear whispers on the street about somebody in the group's birthday coming up. I knew that it couldn't be Laine, because she'd already had hers at the beginning of September, and I knew for a fact that Anthony's was in July. I didn't exactly know when David's birthday was, but since they were always pretty big on making his special day remembered, I knew that it couldn't be anytime soon.

That meant it had to be none other than Jeydon.

It made sense. He hid everything else, so why not his birthday, as well? The real question was why he'd hidden it from me, for I was the person in whom he'd chosen to confine even his deepest, darkest secrets that had never seen light until I unearthed them. I reversed back in my head to a couple of weeks before we kissed for the first time when he said that he saw his birthday as a marking instead of a reason to celebrate. I knew that he'd only had one actual birthday party before, but that was about it.

Otherwise, he'd never gotten the chance to celebrate or be a real kid for once, but that didn't seem to bother him, so why did it bother me? Because I was so used to colossal clusters of pink balloons, birthday princess tiaras, and birthday cakes taller than I was that the idea of never having a party was unheard of.

I learned from Anthony that his birthday was indeed coming up, and as the date of his birth—March 3—approached, I grew more eager about making sure that his birthday didn't go without any recognition. Of course, he didn't like talking about it when I brought it up and like with Christmas told me that I was all he ever needed to make him happy, but to me, that didn't matter; I had to give him something. So about a week before his birthday, with the credit card Mother had given me in hand, I went out and bought him something worthwhile.

* * *

February went by just as fast as I expected it to, and as March came, he still didn't say a word about his birthday. I bit my lip often to suppress the surprise gift I was so anxious to give him, and since Laine knew, I suppose she had a hard time keeping her mouth shut, as well. Anthony knew too, but of course, keeping his mouth shut was like second nature for him. Soon enough, it was March 3, and Jeydon and I were taking a walk with our fingers interlocked.

"So how does it feel to be sixteen?" I asked him as I bit my tongue again so that my secret surprise I was saving for that evening wouldn't slip out like all my other secrets had done so easily.

He shrugged his shoulders, for the first time not showing aggravation that I mentioned his birthday. "It's the same difference."

I looked at him in disbelief. "Aren't you excited about tonight?"

"Of course I am," he replied. "It's just that nothing has changed. But I don't want things to change since they're perfect right now."

"Well, hopefully tonight will make things even more perfect for you," I hinted, which I thought was pretty clever on my part.

The day passed uneventfully, and by the end of it, we were more than ready to sneak out of the campus. I hid Jeydon's car keys, and as he fumbled around looking for them, I announced, "There's a reason why your car key is missing."

His face lit up with irritability. "It must be a pretty good reason, Adrienne! You were the one who wanted to celebrate my birthday, and you've lost the keys to my car?"

I honestly didn't think he'd get that mad about it, and I knew I should've thought it through a little better. "I know exactly where they are."

"Well, don't just stand there!" he growled. "Tell me!"

I grinned. For some strange reason, I found his temper adorable now. "Promise to close your eyes?"

Instead of closing his eyes, he rolled them, mumbling with exasperation, "Promise not to be ridiculous?"

He hesitated to close his eyes, and when he finally did, I led him by hand out to the parking lot where his present was. My heart palpitated in anticipation of his reaction as I told him to open his eyes, and as he did so, I watched the transformation of a completely blank slate for a face into a lighted Christmas tree. Before us was a motorcycle the exact color—which was jet black—that he'd always dreamed about riding when he was a little kid. I remembered him saying one day that owning a motorcycle of his own was the only dream he ever had, so I wanted to make it come true for him.

In my fist, I held the keys, and before I could hand them over to him, he swallowed me up in a huge embrace that mimicked the ones I gave him after we were severed from any amount of time. It was a rarity to see him mimic me in any way, much more in this way. He kissed me full on the lips after he was done squeezing me, and he smiled wide enough for his dimples to dance along with his eyes.

He said under his breath with gratitude, "You really shouldn't have gotten me anything, especially after I got us both arrested."

I rolled my eyes, for he brought that up often. "Stop beating yourself up about that, Jeydon. I love you and just wanted to make your dream come true."

He wordlessly walked over and put one hand on top of the bike. "I don't deserve this," he declared. "I've already got my dream girl, but now I've gotten my dream bike too. Sometimes I think it's just too good to be true."

I approached him and put my hand on top of this. "You *do* deserve all of this, Jeydon. Don't tell yourself that you don't deserve love."

He shrugged his shoulders. "I guess it's a force of habit, because that's all the world ever did."

I used my other hand to run my fingers through his hair, which was my way of showing him my deepest sympathies and the affection the world failed to give him. "I know it was rough, but you're out of that life now."

He closed his eyes as he exhaled, but it was one of pleasure by the smile that lit the night. "I know I am, and if I went back to a year ago today when I was stoned and bloodied up from fights and told myself that I'd be completely clean with the world's most beautiful girl to call mine ... well, I'd probably slap myself in the face for saying such a horrible lie—or crack up laughing."

I kissed him on the cheek, because I just couldn't help but do so. "More importantly, you have a girl who loves you so much that she just can't help but smother him with hugs and kisses. She doesn't care at all what he looks like, because she knows he's the most incredible man that she'll ever know—and she knows him well—and she can actually claim him as hers."

He laughed. "Yes, and you might as well get the shackles out, because I'm your slave now."

I giggled nasally and shook my head. "No, I am forever yours."

He wrapped his arms around my waist and held me there. "We can argue about this for hours, but I really think we should be heading off on our date."

He hopped onto the motorcycle like he'd been driving it for years, and I just stood there. "Well, aren't you going to get on?" he asked with a light chuckle escaping from his throat.

I told him how Leah had a boyfriend that died in a motorcycle accident and that was why I was being a coward, but he just motioned for me to come on and said, "Just hold on tight to me. I won't let anything happen to you."

I cautiously obeyed and wrapped my arms around his waist as securely as I could, and I gritted my teeth as I heard a roar from the engine as we took off. A small scream escaped from my throat as the wind gusted in my eyes so much that they burned, so after more reassurance from Jeydon, I squeezed them shut and told myself to be as fearless as he was. I opened my eyes again and realized how fast we were flying. I told myself that we were traveling at the speed of sound even farther away from Mother than we already were, because the farther away we were from her, the less I felt that odd but familiar pain in my chest known as fear. This imagery made me love the sensation, and I pretended that we were two birds of a feather flying far away from the cruel, harsh world instead of on a motorcycle driving to a destination a mere seven miles away.

When we got to the restaurant, the first thing Jeydon said as soon as we were on our own two feet was how much he loved his new motorcycle, and I actually agreed with him. We went in and had a good time despite the all-too-expected stares of people, where we drank some whiskey with Jeydon's fake ID and toasted my special boy's special day. We came out laughing at something I can't remember, and I couldn't help but be satisfied by how well the evening had gone. Of course, every evening with him always went well.

Then the most lustful desire hit me, and I whispered in his ear my request. I led him by hand to his motorcycle, where we flew out to the beach house that was the closest thing to a home for me.

"What do you want to do now that we're out here?" he asked as we walked along hand in hand along our strip of beach.

I wrapped my arms around his neck and ever so passionately kissed the rough, scratchy skin that might as well have been a kissing sweet spot. "I just want to show how much I love you."

"Haven't you already done that?" he asked in a puzzled tone, obviously not knowing what to think.

I shook my head as I kissed him again. "I don't think I could ever be able to show you how much I love you, but I can at least try."

To my dismay, he didn't kiss me back but instead retorted, "You already have shown how much you love me by giving me a perfect night as always." He then leaned in close toward me and stroked my cheek gently. "Every night we've spent together is a reassurance that you actually love me. I can't thank you enough for everything you've done."

He leaned in to kiss me, and I couldn't help but kiss every single little part of his body. He let me roll up his jeans and kiss and stroke his mutilated legs that always pained me because it reminded me of how he had suffered, so with a pounding heart that broke so easily and overwhelming desire, I began to unbutton his flannel shirt, but he pushed my arm away before I could do so much as remove a single button.

"Please, Adrienne," he grimaced, "not tonight."

I felt as if the world crashed down on me. "Why not?"

His eyes were inflicted with a pain I was so familiar with that I could feel his same hurt along with disappointment. "It's not you; it's me. I'm just not ready for you to see my scars yet."

The rejection—it didn't matter what way, shape, or form it came in—made my eyes well up in tears. "I saw your legs already. They can't be worse."

He pressed his lips together in a thin line as he said, "They are."

With compassion and an outstretched arm, I laid my head on his shoulder. "I still will love you," I promised him, hoping that maybe my words would change his mind, "no matter what's underneath your shirt."

To my further disappointment, he didn't do anything but nod and say, "I know you will." He paused and looked at me with a small smile as if he had a desire he just couldn't relieve although he knew I'd do anything for him. "I kind of want to see something, though," he finally said.

I knew what he was talking about, and I was more than happy to do that for him, so without hesitation, I took my shirt and jeans off, revealing my lacy undergarments.

He gave me a look that made me so excited that I wanted to bang my head against a wall, and with a large smile, he replied in a soft, hushed voice, "You're so beautiful."

We embraced, and as he lowered his hands onto my butt, I forgot all about my earlier rejection and my mother and all other negative thoughts because I was back in euphoria with him so close to me, kissing me over and over again whispering sweet nothings in a breathy, melodious voice that reminded me of a childhood lullaby. Of course, how would I know, because my mother never sang lullabies to me? Maybe Mary did a couple of times, but if she did, I had no recollection of them. I guess it didn't matter, because his voice was the most beautiful music my ears had ever heard, and it was saying such beautiful things to me. It always said such beautiful eloquent things.

Then there was a blinding white light that shone on us. At first, I thought maybe it was heaven's light, but when handcuffs came out and a gruff voice replied, "Yes, these have to be the kids Mr. Blake was looking for. That scar is definitely something you don't see two of," I knew our perfect night had now turned into a nightmare.

CHAPTER 33

Courage

The next thing we knew, we were sitting in the headmaster's office in two chairs that were too far apart from each other. Mr. Blake gave us a long, fiery-worded lecture, but it didn't really catch my attention until the end when he said he was going to suspend Jeydon.

I jumped out of my seat in objection. "No, you can't do that! And why will you suspend him and not me?"

He scoffed and said like Jeydon wasn't in the room, "Because the boy's arrest record has more dirt on it than the bathroom floors!"

"Mine's not that clean, either," I replied, more than willing to be a sacrificial lamb for him like how he had been for me the day he fought Kody.

He scoffed again like I had an IQ of a three-year-old. "We all know it's nothing compared to Mr. Spears. Do you understand that, Miss Hudson?"

I shook my head, but I don't think he cared. The phone rang, and he answered it, and while he was doing, that I received a note from Jeydon that read, "It's okay. I've been suspended before, and I can be suspended again."

I quickly jotted down, "No, you can't."

He wrote down, "Look at me." When I obeyed him, he mouthed the words "It's fine," and a strange sense overcame me that everything was going to be okay even with him gone for a while.

That was short lived, though, because when Mr. Blake got off the phone, he addressed me and said, "I just spoke to Mrs. Hudson-Chase. She's in Washington, DC, right now for something, so she's going to fly all the way down here and have a word with you."

That sense of relief vanished, because I learned a very long time ago that fear of the unknown was a powerful thing.

* * *

The first sign of her presence was the clonking of her sky-high heels on the linoleum floor. I could feel my already racing heart leap out of my chest, and as a result, my fingertips were throbbing. Of course, Jeydon showed no fear as the clatter got louder but instead an intense determination of keeping me safe. I again wished that I could be like him, for he was so brave, while I, on the other hand, was afraid of my own shadow.

Mother walked in the room wearing a much skimpier outfit than most professionals wore, but she somehow pulled off the plunging neckline and hem that met her upper thigh beautifully. Her charismatic body language transformed into something disgusting in my eyes, just as somehow Jeydon was something disgusting in hers.

She greeted Mr. Blake with a polite, complacent smile I could see directly through. How could I have ever been anything remotely like her?

Her voice was a dagger as she said, "If you don't mind, can I please talk to Adrienne alone for a few moments?"

As soon as Mr. Blake okayed that, Jeydon jumped out of his seat. "No, you can't do that! This woman's abusive, and she'll hurt her even more than she already has!"

Mother scoffed with body language that revealed just how badly she wanted to destroy him. "Are you seriously going to believe this mere juvenile delinquent over a respected woman of business?"

I jumped out of my seat, more than ready to defend him and for once speak against the true monster. "Not when he has somebody who lived with her for her entire childhood to back him up."

Apparently, Mother wasn't expecting me to fight back for a change, and she didn't like that one bit. "Silence! I've heard enough of your lies! It's bad enough that you say you love this criminal just to punish me when I have done nothing!"

"Really," I retorted, "I don't think throwing Angela's head by her hair into the coffee table just because she isn't good enough for you is doing nothing."

Her face grew as crimson as her lipstick as she growled, "I've had enough of your pathetically awful lies!"

Unknown to me at the time, Mr. Blake had also grown flustered at all our arguing. "I've had enough! Jeydon, can't you please obey orders for once and step outside so these two can settle this alone?"

Jeydon didn't budge. "There's nothing that needs to be settled! I'm not going to let this girl that I love be tortured by her awful demon for a mother! And you should know that I'm never going to let you push me around!"

His face grew as red as the rest of ours already had. "I've had enough of your lies, you delinquent! You need to learn to obey your betters! Do I need to get the police officers standing outside in here to carry you out?"

"I'm not leaving here. and you can't make me!"

As Mr. Blake motioned for the officers to come in, I spoke up. "This is unbelievable! Are you seriously just going to dismiss this? I'm telling you we're right, and I've got emotional scars to prove it!"

"Shut up, Miss Hudson, unless you have better proof why should I believe two juvenile delinquents over a respected member of society."

Though the security officers were tall and strapping with muscles bulging in all the right places, it was an obvious challenge to restrain an enraged Jeydon. He slapped one of the officers, and while another one tried to hold him in line, he kicked and bit and clawed just like he had when he was little and fighting his crack-crazed mom.

It took a while, but to my dismay, they finally overpowered my sweet angel from above and carried him out, leaving me alone with the person I wanted to be with the least.

"So let me get this straight," she said as soon as everybody else had left. "When they found you and that awful boy, you were half-naked! You take just after Amelia, I'm afraid. Like her, you're such an idiot and a whore. Yes, ever since you, for some stupid reason, broke up with the perfectly fine guy I set aside for you."

It occurred to me that I'd spent all my life fearing this woman, but now I had no idea why. "He cheated on me, you demon! And I never loved him, so it doesn't matter! I love Jeydon now, and we were just doing what people who are in love do!"

In a simple snap of her bloodthirsty, cruel fingers, she slapped me so hard that I was seeing stars, and blood fell in a steady stream from my nostrils. "I guess if you're going to act like Amelia, I'm going to have to treat you like her. Except since you've chosen him, you're even worse, so that means you get treated even worse. Of course, you can just admit that you don't love him, and all this pain and humiliation that you rightfully deserve would be over."

As I hacked up some blood, I declared, "I'll never say I don't love him, because then I'd be a horrible liar like you!"

She smiled deviously. "Well, then, welcome to hell on earth." She punched me hard in the gut.

I in return slapped her hard enough that my hand smarted. Enraged that I'd actually fought back, she came back by pulling my hair hard enough that it came out in a bloody clump, punching me in the face multiple times. She took her high heel off and started beating me with it, and it occurred to me that maybe that was the only reason she wore those things. It was apparent that I wouldn't win the fight, so I only screamed, hoping that somebody would hear me.

With one hard kick to my back, the corners of my vision went pitch black, so I could only hear the voice of an angel as he growled, "Get off of her!"

With that, he kneed her hard in the gut so hard that she fell down limp on the ground like a rag doll in a tsunami, coughing up only God knows what. I'd never seen her hurt before, but strangely enough, it was nice to see her suffer for once after all the suffering she caused.

I leaped into his arms, and he stroked my hair and squeezed back hard, apparently never wanting to let go of me again. "I heard you screaming," he said. "I just couldn't take the thought of her laying a hand on you and me not being there to stop her."

"And you did stop her," I concluded.

He shook his head. "Not without her hurting you first."

"It doesn't matter," I told him, honestly not caring that I gotten a little roughed up, because maybe my sisters wouldn't hate me anymore because I'd finally gotten my fair share. "You still stopped her."

"But she still hurt you," he retorted firmly. "So it does matter."

I shook my head, trying once again to be as brave as he was instead of collapsing like a small child into his arms and crying. "I don't mind that I got a little hurt."

He growled, "What kind of boyfriend would I be if I didn't mind that you got hurt? I'd be like Richard! And you didn't get just a little hurt, Adrienne! You're bleeding through all the openings in your face! And you're saying I shouldn't care?"

I just stood there speechless, tears welling in my eyes and having no idea what to say. Since I didn't say anything, he did. "You can cry. You don't have to be completely emotionless like me."

"You're not emotionless, and I can't cry, because then I'd be just as cowardly as all the others. I'd be stupid little Adrienne who's always such a coward and cries in every situation."

He placed his hands on my arms. "You're not a coward in the least. You stood up to her, and I saw the mark where you slapped her. None of the others ever did that, so you're way braver than what you give yourself credit for."

"I'll never be as brave as you," I retorted.

He shook his head. "You don't want to be as brave as I am. I haven't cried since I was a little seven-year-old and saw my face in the mirror after that awful experimental surgery. Since then, I've not shed a single tear because that sensitivity and life was knocked out of me. My heart will permanently be hardened because of some of the sights I've seen and the things I've done, and trust me when I say you don't want that. And you are braver than you know, because last night, you didn't run away screaming when you saw my legs but stroked and kissed them like they were how they're supposed to look. Only somebody who's really brave could ever bring themselves to do that."

"I'm not brave," I retorted again. "I just love you."

"And that takes bravery," he concluded.

When Mr. Blake came in and saw the condition of my face—apparently, I was bleeding from every opening, as Jeydon had said—he contacted the authorities. They took it to court, and I stood as a witness. Jeydon couldn't, for his arrest record made him ineligible of earning the trust of the jury. I believe because of that reason, as much as I hate to say it, once again, Mother and her overly expensive lawyer won the case, though my broken nose still hadn't healed and every single one of my sisters also testified against her. I guess I'd always lose to her, because despite what Jeydon had said, I wasn't brave.

After the failure of the trial in March, I found myself growing more and more paranoid, fearing that Mother's terror could be lurking around any corner. I didn't tell anybody else about these fears, for Jeydon would just say he'd never let her hurt me any more than she already had, and Laine would simply advise me to not worry so much. But after witnessing all the damage she could do, I couldn't help but wonder what her next move in the lethal chess game would be.

But March turned into April, and still nothing had happened, and since Mother was never one to delay punishments, I wondered if she was waiting for the right moment or if I was being stupid, because there was no payback whatsoever. Yes, I was being stupid, but then again, what if she just was waiting for the right moment? What would happen then? I remembered her words: "Well, then, welcome to hell on earth."

But this felt nothing like hell on earth, at least not with the boy whom I had come to love so dearly constantly caressing my hands and wrapping his arms around me, displaying his affection as a prince would do to his princess in every fairy tale. Though a year earlier, everybody thought I was living the dream, that was a nightmare, and I was living a true fantasy now with the thief who had managed to steal my heart.

Every time he wrapped his arms around me, I could feel that it was easier for him to let me go, but once I said that, it only made him more determined to show me that he'd never let go no matter how rough things got.

Honestly, it was easier for him to let me go, especially with my mother constantly trying to split our inseparable bond and my paranoia of that fear growing worse with every passing minute.

Almost every night, he'd sneak over into my dorm room and lie in my bed with me until I fell asleep, except he usually fell asleep way before I did. For hours, I'd just lie there with my head on his chest and think about how awful this demon was for trying to take away this angel that had rescued me from the hell I had called my home for so long. With every heartbeat, I fell more in love with him, and a couple of nights while he was sleeping, I stroked and kissed the scars on his legs even though it pained me to look at them—not because they grossed me out like they did everybody else but because the scars looked so painful that they inflicted me with poignancy.

But like he had told me whenever I brought it up, now all that pain was worth it, because he'd found me. Whenever he said something like that, I was reassured that I never truly loved anything before him. I thought it through multiple times, and I didn't know what I'd do if we ever were to be apart. I'd probably shoot a bullet into my own temple or would let Mother beat me to death, because life would have no meaning if he wasn't in it.

Eventually, though, I'd get to a point of sleep deprivation where I'd forget all about my lunatic for a mother and fall asleep in his arms, only to then experience the worst night terrors of my life. In one dream, I was bound in chains and forced to watch young Jeydon and his deceased sister that I never got to know be burned in the car wreck, forced to take in all the shrieks of innocent children who didn't deserve their twisted fates. In another, I watched in my own little corner just as I had when Mother beat Mary in front of me all those years ago.

In both, I did something that I didn't do back then that I should've; I screamed as loudly as I could for it to stop, but it was clear that nobody could hear me. Mother wouldn't even try to hear me, because she was too long gone, and the elusive Keri was nowhere to be seen, and I cursed both of them for scarring their own children just to follow their own selfish desires. So with nobody hearing me out, I had to watch as the people I loved were tortured, and the most awful truth about these visions were that they really happened, and there was nothing I could do about it.

One dreary night in late April was the first time I ever went to sleep before he did, but the terror I had was the worst yet.

I was being restrained back by a little devil who was choking me to death, but that was the least of my problems. Right before me stood Richard, his brother Eddy, and a man with an abundance of curly black hair and narrow gray eyes that looked sort of like Anthony's except that they looked like all the color had been sucked out of them. These three men all had looks that struck terror in my heart, and they all surrounded Jeydon, and I watched as they tore him apart limb by bloody limb.

I woke up to Jeydon holding me close and reassuring me that everything was all right, and as I sobbed, I told him about the awful dream with the little devil choking me and the men tearing him apart.

"It was like you were made of paper," I concluded as I let out another heavy sob, "and there was nothing I could do about it."

In a hushed whisper, he replied, "It's all going to be okay. I'm not made of paper, and I'm never going to let Richard of all people tear me apart."

I finally, with Jeydon's assistance, got hold of myself. "It was all just so real, you know?"

He gave me a grim yet understanding look and replied, "Yes, I do know. Possibly more than anybody else."

He held on to me and promised to never let go, but I still believed it was much easier for him to let me go. "You know you don't have to deal with all of this. Sometimes I think you'd be better off without me."

His face went completely blank. "How can you say that, Adrienne, when I love you so much? I couldn't live without you, and do I need to remind you that you're the best thing that has ever happened to me? It breaks my heart that you'd possibly think I'm better off without you, because that is so far from the truth."

"What is the truth?"

He said the words so easily in such a carefree fashion that I could believe them to be true. "That you're the love of my life, and after the love you've shown me that I've never received my whole life, I can't bear the thought of losing you to her. I also can't bear the sight of you being tortured like this by her when she isn't even doing anything to you."

My eyes grew wide as it occurred to me what he was saying. Of course, I thought of him as the love of my life. I couldn't picture loving anyone else; because even if it ever were to happen, it would never be in the way I loved him, and honestly, the thought of loving someone else sounded like a jail sentence, just as my relationship with Richard was. The thing that shocked me so much was the fact that he saw me in that way, for he'd said he loved me several times, but he'd never declared I was the love of his life. And now he had.

I honestly couldn't think about marriage, though, not because I couldn't stomach it like with Richard—I knew I would love waking up every day for the rest of my life with my angel beside me—but Mother was what scared the living hell out of me. But I knew that I needed to stop being so afraid, because that's what pained him. I didn't want him to be in any type of pain, and I was being stupid and selfish for causing him any type of pain.

I told him that I was being stupid and selfish, and he replied, "If you're being stupid and selfish, then I'm being a coward."

This, of course, I thought of as ridiculous. "You're never a coward. How could you possibly be a coward?"

Raw emotions from deep within him came to the surface as his eyes pierced me like daggers. "Because I'm afraid too, Adrienne."

"I thought you were never afraid."

"Like I've said before, everybody hurts, and everybody fears. I'm no exception. I'm not a hero, either."

In denial, I shook my head back and forth. "You're both a hero and an exception, Jeydon. That's why you're so special and different from all the others."

He smiled a little as he said, "I'm not special; I'm just in love."

I pecked him on his left cheek. "Yes, you are special. You are a hero, and above all, you are an exception."

I leaned back in his arms, still pondering if he was indeed better off without me despite his words.

CHAPTER 34

Tragedy

April passed before we knew it, and I was all of a sudden realizing that I had less than a month before school was over, and I had to go back to Richard's tongue being shoved down my throat. I asked Laine what she thought, and she said that love would find a way, but with my mother interfering, I doubted that would happen. So like always, I just pushed it into the back of my head even though it was coming so soon, and I focused on what was in front of me.

Before I knew it, was my birthday. The day started out so typical at first that it struck me as any other day when I woke up in the morning with him lying next to me asleep. His eyes opened into narrow slits, and it sounded like he was humming the tune "Safe and Sound" by Taylor Swift, a song he used to sing to Anthony when they were little. I'd never heard Jeydon sing, but Anthony had told me that, like Keri, he had an amazing voice. It was very easy for me to believe that.

At breakfast, Anthony and Laine gave me a scrapbook full of pictures of us that were adorned with seashells. Laine told me to go to the bathroom with her, and while we were in there, she gave me another scrapbook.

"What's this for?" I asked, feeling a little ambushed for no particular reason.

I flipped though it as Laine explained to me that these were all the pictures of Jeydon that David had of him as a little boy. Apparently, Keri had given him couple of pictures of him before the accident, and even though she knew they all couldn't bear to look at what was called his once normal face, she thought it might interest me, and she was right.

Jeydon at age three was unrecognizable from Jeydon at sixteen, and not because of the age difference. I couldn't stop staring at the adorable little boy with huge green eyes that even back then had a spark of intelligence and a cute little grin even whiter than his skin. His face was angelic with a heart-shaped face he didn't possess now, and he had some definition to the left side of his chin, which was the only thing I actually noticed that was obscure about his face. He had two little dimples that were in the right places that made me find this little boy irresistible. How could anybody possibly mistreat this innocent, beautiful little child? If I were lucky enough to have been this little boy's mother, I would've drowned him with my affection and would've made him know that he was loved.

"Who in their right mind would want to hurt such an adorable little boy?" I asked her.

"Now you see why we all hate her so much, because she introduced such an innocent little child into such a world of cruelty that he never deserved, and to make matters worse, she completely ruined his face."

This angered me. "I'll agree he's been through a lot, but I don't agree that his face is completely ruined forever."

She squinted at me like I was stupid. "You realize that he'll never look like that again, right? He won't just wake up with a normal face. I mean, the poor kid can't even look at these pictures without shuddering at what could've been if it wasn't for the accident."

I rolled my eyes. "Please don't go back to this when you know that I think he's the most beautiful thing in the world."

She sighed. "Adrienne, sometimes you say the most outrageous things."

I shrugged, not caring at all at the moment what she thought of my apparently outrageous devotion for him. "It's how I feel, so I'm going to say it."

Instead of replying like a coward, she flipped to the next page and showed an even more painful image.

It was Jeydon moments after waking up from the hospital, as she explained. There were tubes connecting to him in all directions, and his eyes showed just how much pain he had to have been in. He was skin and bone, as he was in many of the other pictures, and the left side of his face was puffy and discolored. I just wanted to run out of the bathroom and into his arms after seeing for myself his suffering, but I continued flipping through picture after picture of him in a wheelchair hooked up to a catheter machine with legs that looked like burned pieces of meat, him taking step after painful step as he learned how to walk again, him with a half-bandaged face right after his operation, and most tragically, when it was taken off and the look of complete disgust as his new face was revealed.

Then she went into later photos of him when he was around eleven when he'd first met them, and they were photos that David had taken. Though it was supposed to have been a happier time, his expression still hadn't changed much even though he had two freckled, smiling faces as his biological and hypothetical siblings and a loving father figure who took him out fishing and taught him how to play the guitar.

I had totally forgotten about my earlier annoyance toward Laine when I reached the end of the book, where on the last page was a picture of me kissing Jeydon on his scar with hearts around us. I'd never really noticed the completely baffled but joyful look on his face every time I did this, but the look completely transformed him into somebody else who actually felt loved.

"In this picture alone, you can tell how much you've changed him," she said with gratitude that I really hadn't seen from her in a while, because even though I said some things that might've been stupid and on the brink of insanity to her, I was the only thing that made one of her best friends truly happy.

I guess I'd never really stopped to think in detail for the longest time how I had changed him, because I was so caught up in being paranoid about the school year ending and meeting my mother again. For the first time in a while, I truly thought that love could find a way for the two of us, and I didn't have to panic like I had been for weeks. I felt stupid for losing all my trust in him. Wasn't he the one who'd stopped Mother from beating me to a bloody pulp in the office that day? I needed to take his word for once, since he was always true to it.

Still, I didn't know what I would've done if I were there to experience all of those painful moments with him. Of course I didn't know what would happen later that night.

As soon as I walked out of the bathroom and regained my seat next to him, he announced that he was going to take me out to the beach house for my birthday. It felt like forever since it had been just him and me without worrying about Mother, so I was thrilled.

That night when he took me out to the beach house on his motorcycle, my heart was leaping out of my chest in excitement, and I felt like I had been dead the past few weeks. Those photos, as painful to look at as they were, had brought me back to life. I felt alive, young, and in love, like how I was intended to feel as long as he was at my side.

Apparently, he noticed how upbeat I was when we got to the beach house, because he chuckled and asked me as we took a seat on the rickety boardwalk with our thighs touching, "What happened to you today that got you so happy?"

I interlocked my fingers with him and debated whether I should tell him about the photos. Of course, I couldn't keep a secret from him, even if it might enrage him.

"In the bathroom this morning," I began, "as a birthday present. Laine gave me a scrapbook full of pictures of you."

He stopped me there with a low rumble. "What? She asked me if she could do that, and I told her exactly not to! Please tell me that you didn't look at them. I couldn't bear the thought of anybody, much less you, seeing me like that."

"Well, of course I looked at them, but only because I was curious." I thought that was a really big confession on my part.

He sighed long and heavily. "Why are you so curious when you know everything there is to know about me?"

I shrugged. "Because you never cease to fascinate me, Jeydon. You're without a doubt the most incredible man I've ever met. The fact that you survived all of that amazes me, and I'm more than happy to call you mine."

He smiled a little bit and asked, "You might be remarkably open-minded when it comes to me and my appearances, but you've got to admit that I looked pretty bad."

Honestly, the word *bad* had never come into my mind when I looked at those pictures. The words *horrible* and *tragic* were more like it. "You looked like you were in pain."

He bit his lower lip down to where it was visibly hard. "I sensed it would only bring pain to you, and that's why I was so big on not letting you see the photos that Laine, David, and Anthony all can't stand to look at. I thought you might burst into tears at it not because you are weak but because those sights were just that horrible. But you didn't shed a single tear, and that means you're actually braver than I originally thought."

I blushed a little, which made me feel like an insignificant little girl. "I know what I am and know what I'm not, and I am not brave."

He stood up on the dock and started to unbutton his shirt. I asked him what he was doing, and he replied, "It's time for me to put your bravery to a test. It's time to reveal my scars."

One by one, the buttons of his plain white button-up shirt came undone, and as he took off his shirt, I was astonished at what I saw. The burn scars were without a doubt the worst. They were pink in some places, but in others, they were a purplish tone and puffy. Like his legs, there were ripples and ripples of rough skin almost the texture of leather. He turned around, and on his back was a large trench for a scar right in the middle. It was from the skin graft, he explained. He had two others a bit smaller but like it, one on his arm—which I had seen before—and one on his butt that he didn't show me.

I closed my eyes, opened them, and absorbed all the new information, and it occurred to me after a moment that I didn't think of him any differently. I still loved him much more than anybody could ever possibly have imagined and saw him as the irresistible angel sent from heaven to protect me from the demons that threatened to kill my newfound light.

I said nothing but placed both hands right on his torso and kissed him harder than I ever had before. I felt delight as he lowered his hands down to my waistline. I kissed every single little part of his body, making sure every single little scar and imperfection he had was loved, when I heard a gunfire.

I screamed in terror as Jeydon let out a groan of agony. He looked at me in bewilderment and pain, wondering what exactly had hit him. I gave him my blouse in a mad dash to cover the wound, and in a split second, it was covered in his blood. Then another bullet fired. The sound hurt my ears almost as badly as it hurt to see the gaping hole in his chest. I let out a few sobs, and he embraced me, promising that he would never let go no matter what was happening.

Suddenly, we heard voices—three, to be exact—all whispering like little devils that I was sure only someone suffering from schizophrenia would have to endure.

"Man, is he ugly!" one particularly strange voice whispered. "I don't feel half as bad now taking this job."

"I don't understand why she was so insistent for us to kill him; she's obviously just choosing him to punish her," another voice said a bit louder.

And finally, the painfully familiar one said, "I can't believe she thinks she can fool us that she loves that hideously deformed boy."

I turned around, my body covering Jeydon's, and with a hasty breath, I shrieked at the top of my lungs the name who I knew the voice belonged to.

Richard.

All three guys came out of the shrubbery with guns pointing directly toward me. The guy in the middle, who had an abundance of curly black hair and narrow gray eyes that looked like all the color had been sucked out of them, was about to pull the trigger when the other—which I recognized as Richard's older brother, Eddy—stopped him.

"We're only supposed to kill the boy, remember?" Eddy reminded them with such a sense of clarity like this was a noble task in his eyes.

"No!" I shrieked. "You'll have to kill me before you kill him!"

In a split second, he fired the gun, but before it hit me, I was pushed into the frigid water and swallowed a mouthful of the salty, gritty fluid. I stood up and gasped for air, for the wind had truly been knocked out of me, but I ran toward the screaming of agony that was coming from the dock above. When I sprinted back up, I expected for the worst. I saw a man down and screamed at the top of my lungs, but I noticed it wasn't Jeydon. It was the man with the curly black hair that almost pulled the trigger at me.

He was holding his throat in his hand as he coughed up blood that seemed to just ooze out of his mouth. I screamed once again at such a horrible sight, and all eyes turned on me. I noticed that Jeydon's lips were coated in so much blood that they were as slick as cherries.

I also noticed how he was bending over in pain that must've been excruciating, blood from his stomach and leg trickling down like a fountain.

Something occurred to me. Seeing a horrible sight in pictures and in real life were two different things.

The oddest sense of rage came over me as I screamed without my brain connecting to my mouth and my feet moving to their own incredibly fast rhythm, as well. I directed all of this rage toward Richard, the one I despised the most. I tackled him head-on and punched him in the face a couple of times, but he still overpowered me, and I found myself biting, clawing, and screaming for him to get off, but he kept holding me there.

The gun fired again, but there weren't any groans this time. I prayed to God that he just had missed and that it wasn't what I thought it was. I looked all around to find them, and when I saw that Jeydon was on top of Eddy punching him, I cheered. Jeydon went straight for his jugular, but Eddy anticipated this move and moved his head just enough that he couldn't dislodge it.

He chuckled maniacally, so unlike from the Eddy I thought I knew. Then again, I'd thought I knew Richard too.

"I underestimated you, kid! You're a good fighter. Such a shame we'll have to kill you. Of course, with that face, you were probably beyond miserable," said Eddy.

Jeydon gasped for breath before speaking. "I'll only ever be truly miserable if you take her away from me."

While Jeydon was speaking, he was caught a little off guard, and Eddy saw this as an opportunity to grab his neck and choke him. So that's what he did. Richard covered my mouth because I was screaming so loudly, and in response, I bit his hand so hard that it bled. He slapped me in return, and in between breaths and shrieks, I cursed him with all my heart for doing everything.

Meanwhile, Eddy was winning. And as I heard the gunfire and the most agonizing groan of all, tears started pouring down my face. Who would've thought the one second I was off guard he would be taken away from me? And who were they to do such a thing? I cursed them with all my heart as gallons of tears poured like waterfalls. But these tears were nothing like the tears I cried when he first confessed his love to me. These tears tasted bitter and felt like branding irons.

I found myself stating every fact I knew about him. "His eyes are the color of emeralds. His smile is as dazzling as diamonds. His hair falls down in golden waves. His laughter is my favorite music, and his voice is my favorite lullaby. His skin is as pale as an angel's. He's my angel. He has a broken wing that everybody else thinks is repulsive, but I don't see it. I saw him in a dream before I met him, and then I knew he was the one. He's shared with me things he'd never shared anybody before, and I in return told him things I've never told anybody else, either. The first thing he ever asked me was why I was staring at him. The last thing he said was how he didn't believe how I could see past it all, but I knew exactly how I could. I love him with all my heart. I've never opened up or truly loved until him."

I honestly didn't think anybody was listening, but apparently Richard was, because he interrupted, "Shoot me. Don't ask why. Just do it." He released his hands from my neck and handed me the gun.

I looked at him with wide eyes and without hesitation shot him right in the gut. Richard collapsed on the ground crying in pain, and Eddy—who was just about to shoot Jeydon in the temple to finish him off once and for all—dropped his gun right into Jeydon's hand.

At the same time, Jeydon and I both shot him. Since Jeydon had summoned enough strength to stand up behind Eddy, he shot Eddy right in the temple. He collapsed, and I'd later find out he died right then and there.

I bolted into Jeydon's arms, as bloody and weak as they were, and sobbed into him. "Oh, Jeydon, look what they've done to you!"

"I'm all right," he said as he gasped for air and coughed up blood. "Everything's going to be all right."

I didn't believe him. "I'm going to get some help."

I gave him my blouse, which was already covered in his blood. and ran in to the beach house and called 9-1-1. When I came out, to my horror, Jeydon had collapsed right next to Eddy's lifeless corpse.

CHAPTER 35

Questions

Before I knew it, I was in the waiting room of the hospital waiting for David, Laine, and Anthony to arrive. In my head, I reviewed the facts that I knew that the doctors would tell me. For starters, both Jeydon and Richard were in critical condition. Jeydon got shot three times, and the last shot punctured his right lung, and it had collapsed. Richard had only been shot once by me, but that one shot was lethal even though I didn't know exactly where I'd shot him.

Why did I feel guilt at shooting him when he had tried to kill Jeydon? I tried to keep telling myself all the awful things he had done, but it was no use. I still felt an overwhelming guilt for what I had done.

Not too long after they were contacted, Laine met up with me in the waiting room, and like that night after I found out that Richard was cheating on me, I sobbed on her shoulder.

"They let David and Anthony in to see Jeydon," she explained. "David said that he was his father, and since Anthony's his brother, they let them in the ICU."

"Will it be a while before we get to see him?" I asked desperately. The separation from him at such a dire time made it unbearable.

She nodded. "I'm guessing, unfortunately. I think the doctors wanted to talk to you, though."

She gestured over to a classic TV doctor, a man in a white lab coat and a balding head. I went over and asked him what he needed.

The doctor looked at me grimly, and I expected the worst. "He wants to see you."

I lightened up a little as I wiped one red teary eye. "Jeydon's awake?"

He crinkled his nose, and it sickened my stomach to know that there was yet another person who couldn't picture us as a couple. "If that's the kid with the scar, then no; he's not going to be conscious for a while. Your boyfriend was the one who wanted to talk to you."

I looked at him, baffled. "Jeydon is my boyfriend."

He looked at me like I'd been hit on the head. "No, Richard is. That's what he said."

This angered me, and a grunt escaped from my throat. "No, he's my ex-boyfriend. He tried to kill Jeydon."

"I am aware of that," the doctor said, "but he is awake, and he says he has something important to tell you."

I shook my head. "I don't want to see him."

The doctor sighed, and I felt guilt at the fact that I refused to see the damage my act of pulling the trigger had done.

"Richard might be conscious," the doctor said, "but he is in a very critical state in many ways. The police are charging him with attempted first-degree murder, and the bullet entered his gut and went right through his spinal cord, which will paralyze him for life. And I might not know the situation well, but I do know it would make him happy to see you."

I gulped in air and exhaled it before speaking, trying to contemplate the situation. I might not have thought clearly, because I said, "Okay."

The doctor led me to Richard's room, and the sight of his parents with tears in their eyes and Richard hooked up to so many machines almost made me cry again. How could I have done such a thing? I disregarded everything he'd done to me in that moment as his parents turned around and gave me a look of mixed emotion, probably contemplating which one of our deeds was worse.

Yes, Richard may have tried to kill the love of my life, but somehow, my deed was way worse, probably because it was done without a single thought or feeling of remorse going through my head. That would have to come later, and now was later.

Richard asked for his parents to leave in a hushed, hoarse voice I only heard really sick people dying from cancer on TV soap operas use, and I knew just by the sound of things that he wasn't doing well. I sat down in a chair right next to him with no words to say, so I just stared at him with tears welling in my eyes. I noticed that his hand was cuffed to the bed.

I could tell when he looked at me with red-rimmed eyes that he'd been crying too. He smiled a little bit at me, but it was a sad little ghost of a smile that was nothing like Richard's.

"You came," he stated.

I nodded and for whatever odd reason chuckled. "I had to after what the doctors told me about you being paralyzed at all. I don't know what got into me. I just wasn't thinking straight. I'm so—"

"You're not the one who needs to apologize," he interrupted.

"Why shouldn't I?" I questioned bitterly. "I shot you without even thinking about what I was doing."

His voice grew a bit irritated. "I didn't want you to think, Adrienne! I wanted you to shoot me!"

"Why?" I asked. "Are you suicidal or crazy?"

His once magnificent blue eyes were now gray. "Because I'm in love with you. I always was in love with you. I just never bothered to show it—and that obviously didn't make either of us happy—but *he* does. I was just so stupid and jealous and stubborn that I kept telling myself that you couldn't have possibly loved him, but deep down inside, I could see it in your eyes that you did. That made me so jealous that I went crazy, so when your mom said something about wanting him dead, I was all for it. I never thought about anything else that went along with that, and as I was watching you being tortured watching him suffer, it occurred to me that you really did mean everything you said. It was like a moment of lucidity for me, and I knew that for once I had to show that I loved you enough to let you go."

I inched up closer to him, and our hands joined in the same friendship that had united us forever ago. "Thanks, Richard. That means a lot."

"Well, you love him, don't you?"

I nodded, and the words were as light as a feather off the tip of my tongue. "Yes, with all my heart."

All of a sudden, his smiled faded, and there was a loud beeping coming from his machines. I asked if he was okay multiple times, but he didn't seem to hear me, clenching his chest and moaning in pain. Then when blood started trickling out of his mouth in sync to the tears pouring out of my eyes, I rushed to get help in a heartbeat, but there was a crash cart already waiting at the door. They pushed me out of the room and wouldn't let me back in no matter how much I screamed and cried for them to let me in.

Then came along the infamous flat line I only thought I'd hear in those sad movies nobody ever wants to see, because they are tragedies that will just bring you down.

Time went by like molasses as I sat curled up against a wall, wishing Jeydon were there to comfort me. I went through all the memories of Richard and I as kids in my head, replaying all the times he'd made me smile and the bubbly feeling I felt whenever he made me laugh after I was about to cry. We might've been through a lot of bad things, but we went through a lot more good times. But that was now dead and gone, and a nurse wearing bloody scrubs verified that.

"He had a pulmonary embolism from the gunshot," she explained. "There is nothing anybody could've done to prevent it."

Except I could've done something to prevent it by not shooting him, I thought to myself bitterly. I told the nurse bluntly to leave me alone, but not without receiving a pamphlet on grief first that

I tore in half as soon as she left. I just sat curled up in my little ball against the wall crying for the longest time. After a while, I wasn't mourning the death of Richard but the fact that he'd said to me that Mother was the one who'd organized the shooting. Why was I not surprised? It was just another thing that was my fault.

Mother always said what she meant. I've learned the hard way, and when she says something like "Welcome to hell on earth," she finds a way to make that possible. I tried to remind myself that it could be much worse. Jeydon could be dead. But who was I kidding? This really did feel like hell on earth no matter if he was dead or alive, because he was suffering again, and much worse, he was suffering because of me.

After collecting myself as much as I could, I went back to tell Laine the awful news, but she was gone, and Anthony was sitting on the bench with tears in his eyes. He wasn't sobbing or anything of that sort; he was just stone cold with tears slipping down his speckled cheeks. I again feared for the worst.

I approached him gingerly and sat down beside him. I don't think he even noticed me until I asked, "What's wrong?"

His eyes stayed on the floor as he spoke at his regular tone, which would be considered a soft whisper if you asked most people. "Nothing, really. Seeing him in the hospital again just brings back some horrible memories from when we were little. So what's wrong with you?"

I honestly didn't want to tell him, but whatever reason I did. "Richard, one of the boys who tried to kill Jeydon, just died."

He looked so puzzled that I felt bad for telling him. "And you find that sad?"

I shook my head. "He was my boyfriend before Jeydon came along and my childhood best friend, so his death just brought up a lot of memories of us when we were little."

"Same here," he replied, a little bit more clear now. Anthony always had a way of making his few words mean something, and I could see now why he was such a great companion for Jeydon.

"It must've been hard," I agreed. "Laine showed me some pictures of him right after the accident this morning."

"I can't stand to look at those pictures, so I don't get why she wanted to show them to you so badly."

Honestly, I didn't really understand it, either, but I wouldn't admit that to him. "She thought I'd think they were interesting, and I did find them interesting even though it was really painful to think that he went through all that suffering."

His eyes were inflicted with pain for his brother's misfortunate past. "It's even harder when you have to see it, and I never thought I'd see it again. But I did get to see it again, and it brought me to tears."

"And it's all my fault," I whispered to myself bitterly.

He gave me another truly puzzled look. "How is it your fault?"

I told him as much as I knew about the situation—about how my mother would do anything to destroy Jeydon and assembled three men to do her dirty work. I went in to detail about all Jeydon and I had been through together with my mother, including when he beat her so badly that she vomited up blood. I shared with him my theory that since Jeydon was too strong for her to handle alone, she tried to defeat him using a team. We both agreed that it hadn't worked.

His deep-set icy eyes had a mixture of empathy and pity in them. "I knew your mom was abusive, and even though I didn't know it was that bad, it still doesn't make it any less wrong. It isn't your fault at all; I know that for a fact. She'll always try to make you feel like it's all your fault. Trust me, I've been there before, but that's far from the truth. The truth is that you're nothing like they say you are. You're your own person, and you don't have to be defined by her. I let it define me for so long, but I'm not going to let it define me anymore. I guess I'm trying to figure out who I am. Anyway, that's what I have to say. It isn't your fault, and don't let her control you like how it controlled me."

I gave him the first real smile I'd given anybody for what seemed like years. "Thanks, Anthony. You're really smart and brave, you know that?"

He chuckled a little, and I realized that it was the first time I'd ever made him laugh. "Thanks, but I think you're confusing me for my brother. Speaking of which, if you want to see him now, you can. They're letting people in."

"I'm always ready to see him," I said with a smile.

I foolishly thought I could just leap into Jeydon's arms, but tragically, that wasn't the case. It brought tears into my eyes just to look at the boy I loved lying there with violet bruises from head to toe. He was on a ventilator since his lung had collapsed, and he couldn't breathe on his own. He was hooked up to so many machines, just like in the photographs, and I had to remind myself that even though the scene was awful, he was the boy I loved. I had to stay for him.

I walked over to him as he lay there and squeezed his hand. He squeezed back to my surprise, and it made a smile warm my cheeks. I told him that I loved him. No response came from him, but the doctors looked at me in fascination. I couldn't help but be pleased that for once they found my love as intriguing instead of crazy.

I stayed with him day and night, just sitting there and holding his hand waiting for him to come back to life. And finally it happened with an opening of those emerald-green eyes that never ceased to take my breath away.

CHAPTER 36

Safe

Told from Jeydon's perspective

When I woke up, I blinked a few times, and the first thing I saw clearly was her face smiling. I was relieved that she was unharmed in any way that I could see. I tried speaking to her, but before I could, a doctor explained that there was a tube down my throat from where my lung collapsed. It was then that I realized exactly my state and where I was. I was in the hospital in critical condition again. But somehow, I knew that it was going to be different this time, because I had this angelic figure that was perfect in every single way holding my hand in hers. Since I had no other way of communicating, I just stared straight at her, but she didn't seem to mind. She leaned over and kissed me on the forehead.

In the next fifteen minutes, I had no other option but to give her a listening ear as she told me how she'd shot Richard and witnessed his death and that her mother was behind the shooting. It was the worst time for me being unable to do anything but stare and squeeze her hand as she cried. How I loathed myself for being as incompetent as I was. Were it not for her bravery, my paradise would've been short lived. Now I owed this girl my life and couldn't even say thank you.

And I boiled in my own rage sitting here thinking about what exactly her mother had tried to do. There were no words to describe the bitterness and resentment I felt toward that demon.

Adrienne, on the other hand, was just happy that I was alive. She always stayed as long as she could—not that she enjoyed me lying in a bed all day with a tube down my throat but because I was alive, and that was what mattered ... or at least that's what she said. Without her touch, I felt completely devoid of life, so whenever she left, I found myself asleep.

After the third day I was awake, my tube was taken out, and the first thing I requested was for Adrienne to go back to the beach house and bring me my guitar. She might've not understood why I wanted this so badly, but I smiled knowing that she would very soon.

When she came back, I sat her down, and she asked why I wanted this. I replied, "I wanted to give you your birthday present. I didn't get to the other night."

Before she could ask another question, I started strumming a few simple chords that I had put together. Even though my throat was scratchy from the tube, I began to sing. Only Anthony had heard me sing before because I sang to him a lot when we were little to calm him down, and he'd always rant about what a good voice I had. I'd always thought of it as mediocre, but Adrienne went on once about how she really wanted to hear me sing because even when I talked it sounded musical.

Okay, here goes nothing, I thought to myself as I began to sing:

> Sometimes life feels like it's worth not living
> When you feel alone, but you're not alone
> Things get tiring, so uninspiring
> When you have no hope, but there's always hope

I breathed deeply and looked at her face, which reminded me exactly what I was singing about and inspired me to continue with the chorus:

H. R. Brock

I know it's hard, oh so hard
I've been there before
I've been through pain, been through scars
But with you, there are no drops of rain anymore
You are my home
Shadows and fears come and pass
Right outside my door, outside our door
I have learned they'll never last
But love will, though; yes, it will stay strong
I know it's hard; oh, it's hard
I've been there before
I've been through pain, been through scars
But there are no drops of rain anymore
Because you are my home
I know that you're struggling now
Because I will be gone, I wish I wasn't gone
But you just remember someday soon
You get to run back into my arms
I know it's hard; oh, it's so hard
When you feel like you don't have a home
But please hang on, please hang on
I've learned that wherever you are
Love will always find a way into your heart
And into my arms
Yes, baby, in my arms
And a thousand years from now
When our world is gone, yes, when the time has come
Don't you think luck has run out
'Cause you still have my arms, you'll always have my arms
Because they are your home.

I looked over at her, and she was crying.

"What's wrong?" I asked her in bewilderment.

She sat on the side of my bed. "You're such an angel!" she exclaimed as she threw her arms around me.

I smiled a little, knowing that she'd liked my present, but I knew what she thought of me was far from the truth. Of course, there was nothing I could say that would change her opinion of me, and it wasn't something that would hurt us if it didn't change, so I asked, "So what did you think?"

"I thought it was the most beautiful thing in the world," she said as I dried her eyes for her. "It's without a doubt the best thing anybody's ever done for me."

"It was no problem," I said, and I meant it.

She kissed my cheek, and I smiled a lot as I always did whenever she did that. I swore that I would go my whole life without feeling another person's warmth, much less this beautiful supermodel's. I knew it was ancient history, but it still blew my mind that she loved me with my scars and all.

"You know I've never shown anybody them before, right?" I asked.

She nodded, not shocked in the slightest. "Figured."

"I never thought I would show anybody them," I told her, my mind completely blown by her open-mindedness.

She took my hand. "I promised you that I'd love you no matter what was underneath your shirt, and I did do that. In fact, I think I love you more now not only because of that but because I almost lost you."

"You'll never lose me," I replied, determined to remain true to my word. "I'm not going anywhere."

"If you're not going anywhere, then I'm not going anywhere, either," she declared as she put her head on my chest.

I smiled and held on to her tightly, not wanting to ever have to let go, but soon enough, a doctor came in the room and told us that we had a visitor. A strapping, business suit–wearing man walked into the room. He had a few gray hairs in his chestnut-brown hair similar in color to Adrienne's and minimal crow's feet. He held a large bouquet of flowers in one hand.

Adrienne looked truly astonished. "Dad, what are you doing here?"

So this was the man who let his wife do unspeakable things to their innocent children? Not somebody I really wanted to see. I observed him and noticed that there wasn't a glimmer of disgust in his eyes. Instead, there was pity. Great. This egotistical, foolish man who showed no pity to anyone but himself somehow pitied me even though I was nothing to be sorry for even if I did get shot three times and had a severe facial deformity that made little girls cry.

He went over and hugged his daughter before speaking. "I came because I just signed the divorce papers."

Both of our eyes grew wide. Of course, I knew their marriage was loveless, but it was nevertheless shocking.

"Seriously? Why?" she asked with her jaw dropped open.

"I just couldn't take it anymore. Her trying to murder a poor, innocent boy was the last straw," he explained like I wasn't in the room.

I was about to raise my voice when Adrienne said, "He's not poor, Dad, and he's not just some boy, either. He's my boyfriend, and I love him very much, so much more than I ever loved Richard."

He took a quick glance at my face and then back to hers. "Really? Because that's nothing like what your mother said."

I finally found a place where I could butt in to the conversation. "Do you really believe your nightmarish ex-wife who you don't even love over your daughter?"

"Of course not," he retorted as he blinked a few times. "This is just kind of a hard concept to wrap my mind around."

Great, I thought to myself with irritation. *Just another critic who can't believe that she's in love with me.* I guess I could see where he was coming from, but he didn't have to be so much like everybody else and so vocal about my mutilated appearance. How did somebody so accepting come from two such shallow, superficial people?

I wasn't the only one who got irritated. "You're stepping on really thin ice right now by acting like it's so impossible for anybody to love his face when I love him so much for who he is."

He appeared shocked and didn't speak for a few seconds. "If you don't mind, can I talk to Jeydon for a second?"

"So now all of a sudden you're starting to show courage?" I asked skeptically as soon as she left the room.

He arched his eyebrow at me. "Diana warned me that you had a mouth on you, but you do treat my daughter well from what I've heard, and she really does seem to love you, so I guess you have my blessing."

I had so many questions to ask him, but since, for the first time, somebody related to her actually approved of us dating, I was flattered and said simply, "Thank you."

He pulled up a chair and sat next to me. "I just love my daughter and want what's best for her, so I want what's best for you too. So I'll pay whatever it takes to have that thing ..."

A sickening feeling entered my stomach as I explained how my scar couldn't be removed. His face was inflicted with disappointment for bringing up such a delicate subject for nothing.

"That's a shame. You'd be a nice-looking boy otherwise," he said. "How'd it happen?"

"Car crash. The engine burst into flames," I explained, getting a little bit tired of it. Nobody ever had really told me I'd be nice looking if it weren't for the scar, but still I felt like I needed to be cautious and not get too comfortable, because this was the man who'd watched and done nothing as his daughters were tortured.

His sky-blue eyes were inflicted with a pity that made me want to tell him that I hated it when people pitied me when they barely knew me.

"So you were ... burned?" he asked in horror.

I nodded. "Yes, I have burns all over my body, but I'm lucky to be alive, so I don't dwell on what could've been. There's no use in pitying me, either, so if that's what you're doing, then you're being even more foolish than you were when you let your wife do all those awful things."

His face grew a little red, so I was shocked to hear him say, "You must really care about her."

The words came straight from my heart. "Is it really that big of a shock that I'm a caring boyfriend? She's everything I've ever wanted. She's a dream made reality, and out of all the guys, for whatever reason, she chose me. That alone is a reason to care tremendously about that girl."

He actually smiled a little bit at me. "I had my doubts, but you're actually a much better suitor for Adrienne than Richard ever was. When I get custody of Adrienne, I'll make sure that she attends Tampa Bay so she can be with you."

"And what if you don't get custody?" I asked with an eyebrow arched.

"They'll let her choose, I'm pretty sure."

"Hopefully, because I don't know what would happen if we ever were to be apart," I said truthfully.

He got up from his chair. "Well, this was a good talk. I'm going to go out into the hallway and tell Adrienne what I told you about the custody situation. I'm sure she'll be thrilled."

As he turned to leave, he stopped and looked back at me. "Oh, and Jeydon? I'd watch my back if I were you."

I dismissed what he said, and the next day, Adrienne didn't come at her usual time. I asked David where she was, and he said that she coming soon, but I didn't believe him. The night before, I'd had a dream in which she was once again terrorized by her mother, and I couldn't help but fear that dream had become a reality because of her absence. Earlier, a pair of crutches was placed by my bed, and with them, I took step after excruciating step. I kept going, though, because the thought of her suffering hurt was worse.

That is when I heard someone running behind me. I turn around to see Jezebel herself with a scalpel in hand. How she got to it, I don't know, but I did know one thing. I should've listened to Adrienne's dad when he'd said that I should watch my back. I swiftly tripped her with my crutch, and she dropped the scalpel. We both scrambled to get it, and even though I was injured, she still couldn't overpower me. She gnashed her evil teeth at me.

"How dare you make my husband divorce me!" she screamed.

I scoffed, wondering if some kind of mental illness was responsible for this monster. Then again, no mental illness could ever be responsible for the demons that clouded over her vision.

"I didn't make your husband do anything. You're the one who tried to kill me and hurt the girl I love, so shut your trap!" I told her firmly.

She snarled like the wild, untamed animal that she was. "I was doing the world a favor by attempting to remove you from the face of this earth so nobody will have to look at you anymore!"

She could throw all the verbal knives she wanted. I didn't care. I'd heard it all before. What I was angry about was that she was trying to hurt Adrienne, so in a fury, I got a tight grip on the scalpel and placed it against her neck.

"If you ever hurt her again, this will happen," I said.

A devious thought entered my head, and I grinned wickedly as I drew the blade in vertical line on her right cheek just hard enough that it would scar.

That is when the police officers came and pulled me off of her. She kept screaming with blood mixed with tears running down her cheeks that I had caused everything. Of course, the police had to believe her, but as soon as the handcuffs were put on me, Adrienne's father stepped in and told the police that she was in no mental state with Richard's death to be pressing any charges.

To my shock, I was released on the spot, and when Adrienne later came by and was informed that her mother had tried to kill me again, she jumped into my arms, and I held her there for

H. R. Brock

what seemed like forever. She was safe and sound here with me. If only it could stay that way until the end of time. I hummed our song in her ear, and she smiled sweetly.

I kissed her neck, to which she responded by saying, "For the first time in months, I feel truly safe here with you."

CHAPTER 37

The Unknown

-Adrienne-

At the hearing for custody, I chose to stay with Dad, of course. He requested full custody, and so did Mother with a horrid gash in her once perfectly plump cheek and a new voracious desire to destroy me. In the end, the courts came down to the decision that I would spend summers in the care of Mother and the school year in the care of Dad. Most people would've considered it fair, but tears came to my eyes, as I thought the world was crashing down on me.

One summer without him would be like a thousand years without rain. Why didn't anybody understand that? Because no matter how hard I tried, nobody could possibly understand how much I loved him.

The remaining two weeks of the school year passed remarkably fast as Jeydon's leg healed from the gunshot and he was able to walk again without using crutches. Before I knew it, it was the last day of school, and the thing I'd feared so much for so long had become a reality; I was losing him. Even if it were temporary, I was still losing him—and facing Mother.

We had a farewell party for me in which I received hugs from Anthony and Laine and a kiss on the top of the head from David as he said that I was his daughter now. I smiled as I saw Anthony

- 367 -

and Laine walking down the beach holding hands and wondered what sweet romance the summer might bring them.

I felt my fingers interlock with Jeydon's, and immediately, all my attention was focused on one thing.

"I have something I want to give to you," he said as he handed me a note. "It's to help get you through the summer."

I started to open it up, but he stopped me as a chuckle escaped from his throat. "Don't open it up just yet. Wait until tomorrow after you leave."

I groaned, but I kept my promise. The next day, Jeydon drove me to the airport. It was an old-fashioned farewell. He said just how much he loved me one last time for a while, and I in return squeezed his hand enough that hopefully the feeling would last a whole summer. Then, last but not least, I kissed him hard before I went on the plane destined to my own summertime misery.

As soon as I got on the plane, I carefully unfolded the note and began to read it, my eyes picking up every little detail written on the lines of the cheap piece of notebook paper.

> Adrienne,
>
> I hope you've learned by now that I love you more than you could ever imagine, and I hope you also know that you're without a doubt the best thing that's ever happened to me. I tried my best to never let you in to see the truth, but you somehow managed to open up the wounds that would never seem to heal and stitched them closed. I have written the words to my song on the back of this piece of paper, and I hope you hear the song in your head and learn the lyrics by heart just as I have. Hopefully, this song will help get you through the summer. That and the hope that I am about to give you.
>
> It doesn't have to be this way. I was discussing it with Laine, and she jokingly asked, "Well, why doesn't she just run away like you did?"

At first I scoffed and dismissed it, but I've thought about it, and the idea keeps sounding better and better. Of course, we'll have to wait until next summer if you're going to actually agree with me, and I'm sorry to say we'll still have to endure this one long, hot, painful summer that lies ahead of us. But it's worth a thought. You may think of me as insane, but I think it's completely logical. We could run off with Anthony, Laine, and David to San Francisco or someplace like that, get married, and live the life two lovers were intended to live, never to be separated like we are this one summer.

There are three sole things I'm completely sure about.

1) I love you, Adrienne Destiny Hudson, with every single aching bone of my body, and I was more than happy to take that bullet for you. Yes, I was the one who pushed you out of the way just in the nick of time.

2) The hardest task I will ever have in my life because I'm so hopelessly lovesick is to stay completely clean and sober for you. You've made me the best me I can be, and I don't want to change that just because you're gone.

3) I never wanted to leave you that one day up in your room before I kicked Kody's butt. I was just such a coward of the unknown and thought that it was indeed easier for you to let me go than to hold on to you. I thought if I was alone, I couldn't have made you bleed, but it turns out I was needed. I actually thanked Kody today, because if he hadn't shown me that I was needed, I would've drowned in my own misery. But instead, you caught me.

I apologize that I haven't ever mentioned these three things before, but I figured it would make a nice note for you. I'm so grateful that you're able to see right through the walls that I thought were solid rock. I was always so afraid to ever let a love get so close, but now whenever you wrap your arms around me, I know I'm home.

With all my love, heart, and soul,

Jeydon

I read through the note three times before I truly knew three things of my own.

Number one: I've never met anyone that lived and breathed as incredibly as Jeydon Spears.

Number two: I'd always secretly known that he'd taken that bullet for me, because out of the corner of my eye, I'd seen him push me out of the way into that murky water. He was my guardian angel now.

Number three: Even though I knew the skies ahead of us would be rough and stormy, I knew I loved him more than anything and couldn't wait until the day I'd get to run into his arms again—because like what he'd written and in his song, his arms were my home.

And the last thing I knew was that I was ready, but when I got to the house, I made a discovery I that wasn't prepared for.

Mother was running for governor.

About the Author

H. R. Brock was thirteen when she began writing her first novel. She is currently a sophomore in high school and is working on a sequel to Only In My Wildest Dreams.